By the same author:

OUR MOTHER'S HOUSE

A novel by

JULIAN GLOAG

A SENTENCE OF LIFE

SIMON AND SCHUSTER

NEW YORK

Second Printing

Library of Congress Catalog Card Number: 66-13844
Manufactured in the United States of America
by H. Wolff Book Mfg. Co., Inc., N. Y.

TO MY FATHER

CONTENTS

THE PRISONER

I

It wasn't even in the stop press. He dropped the evening papers onto the seat beside him and looked out of the window. It was already dark. He had been forced to take the later train and, although it was emptier, its slowness vexed him. Not that he was in a hurry to get home, but this stopping at each station destroyed the comfortable rhythm of the usual trip when he knew where he was at every moment of the journey.

Just a habit, like always ploughing through the ineffable dullness of the evening papers, for instance, or like the mid-morning cup of tea which he didn't really care for and only took because June would have been upset if he hadn't.

And June was dead.

June is dead—he considered it, waiting for some stronger feeling than the sense of mild surprise which had been his reaction when the superintendent told him this afternoon. "There's no doubt it was murder, sir." His scalp ought to have crawled or his palms sweated or something. He looked at his hands, slightly dirty from newsprint but dry as paper. "Thank God you haven't got clammy hands," Willy had once said to him in a moment of intimacy before they were married. He smiled.

He glanced up and the window reflected his smile back to him. Beyond it were the funereal shapes of the pine trees, blacker against the black, and vaguely annoying. Conifers weren't indigenous to Surrey, and he thought of them as dark trespassers on the deciduous forests of Southern England—oak, ash, beech, elm. He liked places where you could stand and say, "It must have looked just the same in William the Conqueror's day or when Julius Caesar came." That was

11

something Willy could never appreciate. She'd give him a quick look and, if he went on too long about it, tell him not to be dotty. If Willy considered history at all, it was as an infinite backward extension of their own life in the stockbroker belt, except that in "the old days" there had been rather more lapses from good taste than are permissible today.

He wondered how she'd take the news of June's death. If June had been "people like us," the judgment would be simple and devastating. But June clearly wasn't, hadn't been, like us.

He tried out an opening sentence: "The police came to see me this afternoon."

It sounded ridiculous. But then the whole thing sounded ridiculous.

"I'm Chief Superintendent George and this is Detective Inspector Symington."

Jordan had not expected this when Miss Lawley had told him there were two policemen to see him. "We're investigating the death of June Emily Singer who, I believe, was in your employ. We'd like to ask you one or two questions." And he had told them the little he knew. Yes, she had been there six years. No, no trouble. Yes, an excellent worker. It was as though he were giving her a reference—to a pair of heavenly inquisitors. But they weren't angelic; they were unbelievably ordinary.

Well, he'd tell Willy as soon as he got home. Thank God she wasn't the hysterical type.

It was a tragedy—that was all there was to it. One couldn't *do* anything.

The train slowed gently into Woodley station.

Jordan Maddox picked up the papers and his attaché case from the seat beside him and stood up.

She had her coat on when he entered the hall.

"Hello, where are you off to?"

"It's the Wednesday Meeting. You're late. I thought I was going to have to get Mrs. Hillman to come in and baby-sit. Was there a delay on the line?" She put on her hat in front of the mirror.

"No. That ghastly hat."

"Isn't it?" With a decisive thrust of the hatpin she secured it to her head. "Dinner's ready. Cold. All you've got to do is carve the beef. I've had mine."

"Couldn't you put it off? I rather wanted to talk to you."

Willy glanced at him quickly. "You look tired. It'll only be a couple of hours—old Ma Windbag is ill, laryngitis believe it or not, so that ought to speed things up." She put her hands on his lapels and kissed his cheek. "I'd like a talk."

"Oh well," he said.

"Run up and say good night to Georgia, there's a dear. She's been a perfect pest all day."

"How?"

"Oh, silly questions." She went to the door.

"I hope you gave her appropriately silly answers."

"Bye-bye."

"So long," he called.

"Common," he heard her say as she shut the door. He grinned momentarily.

He pulled off his coat and went upstairs slowly. He was tired. Perhaps June's death had affected him after all.

"Hello, my Georgia peach."

"Hello, Daddy." She was sitting cross-legged in the centre of the bed and leapt up to kiss him. "Why'd you call me peach?"

He laughed and held her closely. "Because a peach is fuzzy just like you and has smooth soft skin just like yours and because a peach is the most beautiful fruit of all, just like you."

"Just like me!"

"Just like you." He laid her down in the bed.

"What animal will we do tonight?"

"Let's see. . . ." He usually worked out the evening animal story on the train home, but tonight . . . "What about the lamb?"

"Oh, not lambs—they're wet."

"Not wet—innocent."

"Chris says they're wet. And besides they're always getting killed."

Jordan smiled. Chris was the kindergarten dogmatist. "Well, the goat?"

Georgia considered for a moment. "That'll do," she said.

This was the hard part. The story had to rhyme.

"The goat.

The goat loves to climb to mountain tops
With a bell round his neck to chime;
However steep, he never stops
Where all others fear to climb.
The best of goats wear beards and horns
And—"

"Daddy, let me!" Georgia bounced with excitement. "And even if they climb for days and days they never get any corns!"

Jordan laughed.

Georgia frowned anxiously. "Isn't it any good?"

"It's wonderful. They ought to get corns, oughtn't they—with all that running around?"

"Like Mrs. Hillman. Mrs. Hillman has corns something terrible. She showed me—through her stockings."

"She did, did she?"

"They were very ugly. You don't have corns, do you, Daddy?"

"No. I spend my day sitting down, you see. Most of it."

"Mummy has corns, I 'spect. She never sits down."

"No, she doesn't have corns. She has a lot to do, but she does sit down and rest. When you're asleep."

"She isn't sitting down tonight, is she?"

He leaned forward and rubbed his hand in her hair. "Let's go back to the goat."

"But we've done the goat. Let's have another animal. Let's have the elephant. I like the elephant."

He smiled at her. A week or two ago she'd still have been saying ephelant. "Alright." He liked the elephant too.

"I'd adore a whiskey."

"Soda?" he asked, although she never took it any other way.

"Mmmm."

"What was the meeting like?" She had though—once. The week they'd spent at Sibley just after they were married. They'd hidden a bottle in the suitcase under the bed. Uncle Trevor and Aunt Mary disapproved of a woman's drinking whiskey—sherry was alright—so he and Willy used to take a nip out of a tooth glass in the bedroom before dinner. Neat or with a bit of water. The damp religious smell of the rectory bedroom had strengthened the vague but pleasurable midnight-feast guilt of their tippling.

14

". . . fifty-three minutes. A record. But then Mrs. Twining caught me . . ."

He handed the drink to her. He took his neat. The room was chilly. Too warm for a fire, too cold for comfort. Another in-between day.

"Sorry—what?" He hadn't been listening.

Willy nodded at the manuscript on the table. "Have you been working?"

"Not really. Just skipping through it again."

"What is it?"

"It's called 'The Incidence of Mental Deficiency in Selected Villages of East Anglia, 1840-1937.' "

"It sounds a bit obscure. Why 1937?"

"God knows. Yes, it is a bit. The reader says it's a 'serious contribution.' " He laughed.

"Are you going to do it?"

"If I can get the author to change the title to 'Sex Life of the Village Idiot.' "

Willy frowned. "Is that what it's about?"

"In parts."

"Aunt Mary's maid—Annie Brierly—doesn't she have an m.d. sister or something?"

"Yes." Only she wasn't a maid.

"She has an odd name. Sapphire?"

"Emerald. She's a mongoloid."

"Oh, yes."

They were silent. He stared into the empty fireplace. The andirons were early Georgian, pewter; rather rare, because of the oriental dragons' heads.

Willy had closed her eyes and was resting her head against the back of the chair. Her hair was thin and lank, like the Pardoner's—she ought to wash it more often.

"The police came to see me this afternoon."

"Don't say you've bashed in the car again?" Her eyes remained shut.

"No. It was about June."

"June?"

"June Singer."

"What has she done? Got herself into trouble, I suppose?"

"No, no. Well, yes—in a way . . ."

15

Willy opened her eyes. "I thought you told me she was on holiday."

"She is. I mean, she was. She's dead."

"Dead? How on earth could she be dead? Was she run over?"

Suddenly Jordan felt as though he were making it all up. "The police think she was murdered."

"I can't believe it." She sat up. "Give me a cigarette, Jordan. What a frightful tragedy."

"Yes." He offered her the silver cigarette box.

"How? Why?"

"Well, I don't know."

"When did it happen? Where? I bet it was at Brighton."

"Willy, I really don't know. They just said they were investigating her death."

"But didn't you ask?"

"They were doing all the asking. They insisted on seeing everyone —even old Timothy in production. I must say I was impressed with their thoroughness. Of course it all took time. That's why I was late."

"What did Uncle Colin say?"

"He wasn't there. I told you, he's at the Textbook Fair. He'll be back tomorrow. I dare say he'll manage to take it in his stride." Willy tended to think of Colin as an ogre.

"You don't know much. I suppose it was a bit of a shock. It'll all be in the papers tomorrow, I suppose."

"They just weren't very forthcoming, you know."

"Were they from Scotland Yard?"

"I imagine . . . No, wait a minute, I don't think they were."

"Poor little Miss Singer. I'm not surprised."

"Good God—what do you mean, you're not surprised?"

"It was probably a *crime passionnel*. It's always the plain ones that get killed for love."

"I can't see June Singer involved in a crime of passion." But then he could not see June at all in his mind's eye, except as something habitually there; like a book in the shelf among a hundred other books, you would notice it only when it was gone.

"Darling, you couldn't see anyone involved in a *crime passionnel*. That's why I love you. I'm glad you're being sensible about it. I wonder if you shouldn't call Tom Short."

"What on earth for?"

"He *is* a solicitor. He knows about these things. Besides there's sure to be an inquest and you'll probably be called as a witness. You are her—were her employer. You'll need a solicitor. And then there's the trial too."

"What trial?"

"Of Miss Singer's murderer. There's bound to be—"

"Willy, don't be ridiculous." He stood up.

She stared at him for a moment. "I wonder where she went for her holidays."

"Not Brighton. No one goes to Brighton in March. Somewhere in the country." Now how did he know that? He remembered her telling him, because she'd intended to go to Switzerland, then changed her mind. It must have been on Monday when . . . He heard the superintendent's voice: "When did you last see Miss Singer, sir?" And he'd said on Friday, Friday evening when she'd gone off on her holidays. But of course he'd seen her on Monday morning, the day before yesterday—he'd have to rectify that.

"I wonder whether it *was* a *crime passionnel*," said Willy lingeringly. "Well, I'm for bed."

He was tired too. Perhaps it was the whiskey.

He said, "I'll lock up then."

He went round the ground floor, snapping the window locks and bolting the doors. At the back of his mind he realised how ludicrous such precautions were—as though a pack of thieves were waiting nightly to pounce on Woodley. Sometimes he would forget a window and, when Willy accused him in the morning, would murmur "I'm sorry." But he wasn't really. One window unlocked, one appointment unkept, one letter unwritten—there was an obscure satisfaction in those.

At Sibley Rectory, when he was a boy, there had been the same iron ritual of locking up—against the unknown threat of the peaceful villagers.

He opened the french windows and stepped out onto the narrow stone terrace. There was a small moon flicking behind high, quick clouds, like morse. *Crime passionnel.* Willy's easy gallicisms were the badge of two years spent in France—governess to a rich family in Bordeaux—about which he knew nothing and of which there was no other mark upon her. She was quite unable to distinguish a good claret from an indifferent one.

17

A crime of passion. If there was a murder, there must be a murderer. It had not even occurred to him.

He moved back into the dining room and shut the french windows and shot the bolts.

Willy was already in bed, reading.

He undressed in front of the electric fire and stood in his pyjamas, watching her.

"Did you look in on Georgia?" he asked.

"Yes." She smiled and started to go back to her book.

"Willy." He sat down on the edge of her bed. He reached up and took off her glasses and kissed her.

After a moment she found his hand and squeezed it. "Not tonight, Jordan—it's curse time."

2

"Bit of a university press project, isn't it?" Colin Sutlif looked at the huge manuscript on his desk.

"Yes, we're rather lucky to get Ballard away from London."

Colin smiled; like a kindly headmaster, he was pleased to be contradicted or wilfully misunderstood by a bright pupil. "All these tables and statistics—there'll be a devil of a comp charge."

"Ballard's agreed to cut several of the tables."

Colin examined the title page. "Ummm. Mental Deficiency. Formidable. I hope he's not going to be an expensive author." He lifted his head to stare hard at Jordan.

Jordan found it an unusual effort to play his godfather's game today. The rules were simple: Jordan could generally win his way so long as he made a show of firm, even arrogant, enthusiasm. But the performance often exhausted him, opening him to the boredom and doubt against which his decision had always battled. This morning he was already tired. But all the same he said, "No, he won't be an expensive author. I lunch him at Blain's."

Colin made an old-maidenly moue, which indicated pleasure. There were Blain authors and club authors. Important authors were always lunched at the club. It was possible for a Blain author to be stepped up to the club or, if a book had not at all lived up to expectations, for a club author to be demoted to Blain's. It was an absurd convention really; Blain's food was much better than the club's.

"You really want to do it then?"

"Yes, I think so. It ought to pay for itself in the long run certainly and . . ." He tried to think of some decisive reason why this incredibly dull book should be published.

Colin supplied the reason. "And it's all part of your 'campaign'?"

When he had first come to Sutlif & Maddox, Jordan had been eager to break the claustrophobic concentration on, mainly medical, textbooks and do some general publishing—no fiction, nothing wild, nothing unsound. History, perhaps. After fifteen years the closest he'd got to history was "The Incidence of Mental Deficiency in East Anglia." He switched his burgeoning sigh to a chuckle.

Colin took it for assent. "That's settled then. Minimum terms, naturally." With the palm of his hand he hit the old-fashioned bell on his desk. He leaned back. "I suppose you're a bit short-handed?"

"Yes, but—"

He was interrupted by the entrance of Colin's secretary.

"Miss Lawley, put this away, will you?" Colin tapped the manuscript. "And draw up the usual contract for Ballard."

"Yes, Mr. Sutlif. Minimum terms?"

"Yes. And, oh, Miss Lawley, I'm afraid you'll have to look after Mr. Jordan for a bit in view of what's happened."

"She already is," Jordan said. "June was on her holidays, you know."

Miss Lawley nodded slightly, like a head housemaid acknowledging a tradesboy. Dusty yet regal, she wore a brown stole that might well have been a counterpane she'd whipped off the bed and slung round her shoulders before leaving home. She didn't like Jordan. She was supposed to have a kind heart.

She went out, but returned almost immediately with a cup of coffee for Colin and tea for Jordan.

Jordan took the cup. "Miss Lawley," he said casually, "I think I'd like coffee in future, if I may."

"Coffee, Mr. Jordan? But you always take tea."

"Yes, but I think I'd prefer coffee."

19

Miss Lawley seemed to be waiting for an explanation of this extraordinary request. None came, and at last she said, "Very well," and left the room with sweepingly dismissive speed.

Colin Sutlif lit a cigar, first dipping the end of it gently into his coffee. Immediately the fragrance filled the room and reminded Jordan, as it always did, of the time when the annual Christmas visitor at Sibley had inexplicably changed—Father had been replaced by Uncle Colin—and the smell of festivity had switched from whiskey to cigars. Father had reappeared only once, to lie exposed in his coffin for a day and a night in the small rectory chapel. When Jordan had obediently kissed the white, drained face, he had been puzzled by the absence of the old familiar odour. For a long while after, he had secretly thought they'd buried a waxwork by mistake and that his real father lived on somewhere, red-faced and rich-smelling as ever.

"Seen the *Telegraph* this morning?" Colin asked.

"No—I'm a *Guardian* man."

"That faded liberal rag. Have a look at this." He threw the *Telegraph* across his desk. "At the bottom there."

Jordan found the short paragraph headed "Kensington Murder."

The body of a twenty-four-year-old woman was discovered yesterday at 27 Panton Place by Mrs. M. Ardley, landlady. Death was due to strangulation. The police, headed by Chief Superintendent S. George of the C.I.D., are vigourously investigating the murder. The victim has been identified as June Sanger, a secretary at the firm of Sutcliff & Maddox, well-known London publishers.

It had been the same in the *Guardian*, almost word for word. So she had not gone away after all. Jordan felt an uneasy flutter at the thought he'd seen her on Monday, a couple of days at most before the murder. He'd give Superintendent George a ring as soon as he was finished with Colin.

"Well-known publishers, my foot," said Colin. "Not well-known enough to get the name right."

He meant, Jordan knew, *Sutcliff*, not *Sanger*. Colin had a mania about the misspelling of his name: S-U-T-L-I-F, he'd shout in rage. Jordan had once heard him yelling down the telephone, "Not s—f! F—f—f—f! F for fart!"

"They're not giving much away," Jordan said.

"They probably know who did it alright. Don't like to show their

20

hands until they've got a watertight case. Poor kid. A bloody business." He clenched the cigar in his teeth. "I hope they catch the bugger quick."

"They haven't talked to you, have they?"

"The police? Yes. They were on the phone first thing I got in this morning. Want permission to look through our files."

"What in heaven's name for?"

"Just 'routine.' I suppose they're hoping to find a compromising letter or two. God knows how the police mind works. I wish them joy of it. I'm just wondering how to break the news to Miss Lawley—she'll scream bloody murder at the . . . Damn. How wildly out of proportion one's language gets. Well, if she doesn't like it, she'll just have to put up with it."

"It seems rather unlikely that June would have filed compromising letters."

"Yes, old chap, but it seems rather unlikely that she should have been murdered. I suppose you had a word with her people?"

Jordan sipped his cooling tea. "Don't think she had any. Her mother died a few months ago. Her father had been dead for years. I don't know that she had anyone else."

"Well—perhaps it's just as well." Colin turned and stared out of the window. "Poor child."

Whenever Colin dropped his gruff and caustic manner, Jordan felt inexplicably ill at ease, as though he'd accidentally stepped into a prayer meeting. It didn't happen very often. Jordan shook his head to disperse the memory of those other occasions.

He was glad to be rescued by Miss Lawley.

"The police are on the telephone, asking for you, Mr. Jordan." She paused. "I thought," she said meaningfully, as though the police had been called in to investigate his strange preference for coffee over tea, "that you'd prefer to take the call in your own office."

He grinned at her. "Right you are. We're all settled, aren't we, Colin?"

Colin grunted.

Jordan was glad they'd phoned. Saved him the trouble of ringing them up himself. In his own office, he picked up the phone.

"Superintendent George, I was just going to ring you. There's—"

"Inspector Symington here. You were going to phone us? Yes, what about, Mr. Maddox?"

"Well—" he instinctively disliked Symington, the official tone without any pretence of humanity—"I was just going to say it's quite alright for you to have a look through our files."

"Mr. Sutlif has already granted us permission to do that, sir. Was that all?"

"Yes, that's all," he said sharply.

"Well, Mr. Maddox, we'd rather like to have a word with you."

"Fire away."

"Not on the telephone. We'd like to see you."

"See me? But you've already seen me once."

"There are one or two small matters we'd like to clear up."

"Alright then. If you must. When do you want to come up? The afternoon would be—"

"We'd like you to come to the station, Mr. Maddox, if that's alright."

"It certainly is not alright. I've got a very great deal to do—"

"To assist us in our enquiries," Symington said flatly.

"Look, Inspector, I'm perfectly willing to assist you in your enquiries, although I'm blowed if I can see what more I can tell you, but I really can't go gallivanting round to Scotland Yard or wherever it is—"

"Sarah Street. Sarah Street police station. Chelsea. Quite easy by bus, you just—"

"I've no doubt you are a busy man, Inspector, but I too am busy."

"We're investigating a case of murder. Surely it is not too much to ask a citizen to do his duty by assisting the police in their enquiries? I'm quite sure we won't need to keep you long, Mr. Maddox, if that's what you're worried about."

"Oh . . . blast! Alright. I'll come down this afternoon. Where did you say it was?"

"Sarah Street, Chelsea. We'd like you to come now."

"Now? I can't possibly . . ." He looked at his watch. Ten-thirty. What difference did it really make anyway? The day was clearly going to be ruined. "Very well then. I'll be with you in half an hour."

"Sarah Street police station. It's easy enough to find. Take a number—"

"Yes, yes. I'll find my way." He put the phone down. Bloody nuisance.

He'd been holding his cup of tea all this while. He put it down on the desk. At least he wouldn't have to drink any more of that. Suddenly he laughed. It was ridiculous—he was behaving as badly as Colin. And after all, he did have a kind of responsibility towards June.

The sun was out, and it mollified him. He walked a bit, then took a cab. He was at the police station in twenty minutes.

He was asked to wait. "Won't be a minute, sir," said the uniformed sergeant.

It was much more than a minute. Ten, then fifteen, then twenty-five. "Sergeant, I really can't wait all day."

"I'm sure Mr. George won't be five minutes, sir. You just sit tight."

Forty minutes. He had long ago ceased to be interested in the sergeant's telephone calls. "Look," he said, "I'll wait another five minutes, then I shall simply have to go."

The sergeant said he would go and have a look, and went. He came back to say that Mr. George would be out right away.

But it was another twenty-five minutes before the superintendent appeared. "Sorry to keep you waiting, Mr. Maddox."

"So am I," Jordan said, and immediately felt ungracious.

"Come this way, will you?" said George with impassive kindliness.

They went to a tiny room, where the superintendent sat behind a desk. Jordan sat in front of it. In the corner, slightly behind him and to his right, was a third chair. Apart from a three-tier file, that was all the furniture.

"Let's go on with it, Superintendent, shall we?"

"Just one more minute till Mr. Symington gets here, I'm afraid."

"Mr. George, do you realise that I've been waiting here over an hour? If this is an example of police efficiency, I—"

"I appreciate it's inconvenient, Mr. Maddox. I appreciate it all the more that you were able to come here this morning. It's one of the drawbacks in police work, unfortunately—a policeman's time isn't his own."

"I was practically ordered to come here!" He sounded, he knew, not so much indignant as feeble.

"Ordered? Oh, no, Mr. Maddox. Not ordered. I do hope you didn't form that impression. Ah, here's Mr. Symington."

The inspector came in, nodded, and sat down in the third chair with an air of hostile efficiency. He opened his notebook with a snap. When Jordan looked at George, Symington was just out of his line of vision.

"Now we can begin," said Superintendent George, but he didn't

23

seem in any particular hurry. He was a maddeningly slow man—Jordan wondered how he could ever have risen to be a chief superintendent. For the policeman was now leisurely turning the pages of his notebook.

"Ah," he said. "Well, now. How long was June Singer in your employ?"

"Six years."

"Six years. I see. When did she first come to you? Do you recall the date?"

"June the twenty-sixth. It happened to be my birthday."

"Did it now? June the twenty-sixth. Well, then, it wouldn't be quite six years, would it? More like five and a half?"

"Five and a half. Superintendent, you asked me both those questions yesterday and I answered them. Can't we—"

"Just making sure, Mr. Maddox. Now, perhaps you could tell us what you thought of Singer?"

"What I thought of her? What's that got to do with anything?"

"We want to form a picture of the sort of girl she was. Anything you can tell us will be of great assistance, I'm sure. You did know her for nearly six years. What sort of an impression did you have of her?"

"Well . . ." He stopped. That was just the trouble—he really hardly had any impression of her at all, as a person. "Well, she was efficient."

"Efficient. Is that all?"

"You don't get to know someone in an office very well." He was apologizing—where June had been there was now just a vacuum in his mind.

"Would you have said she was quiet, for example?"

"Oh, yes. She was quiet. I mean she talked—but she wasn't a chatterbox or anything like that. Quiet and efficient. Got on with her work. Responsible—one didn't have to look over her shoulder or tell her what to do all the time."

"Now we're getting somewhere, aren't we?" The superintendent smiled, and Jordan noticed for the first time a thin veil of close-cropped hair on his upper lip. "What else? Was she attractive?"

"I suppose she was attractive enough, yes. I never thought about it." He could hear the pencil scratching away in Symington's notebook. He was unpleasantly aware of the inspector, not three feet from his shoulder.

24

There was silence. The water in the hot pipes gurgled. It was stuffy and very hot in the room. The window didn't look as though it had ever been opened.

"Well?" Jordan said at last.

"I thought you were going to tell us a bit more about Singer."

"It really is a waste of your time—and mine. I know—knew—very little about the girl."

"Did she ever confide in you?"

"Confide in me?"

"Confide," George repeated the word firmly.

"Well, she told me about her mother dying and that sort of thing, if that's what you mean?"

"When Singer first came to you she was living with her mother?"

"In Putney, yes. She only moved quite recently—when her mother died."

"And when was that?"

"Er—which?" Jordan gave a quick grin.

"When did Singer move to Panton Place?"

"I don't recall precisely. Some time in December—before Christmas, I think. Mrs. Ardley could give you the exact date."

"Mrs. Ardley?"

"June's landlady." Jordan was puzzled. "Did you know Mrs. Ardley?"

"Good lord, no. June, you know, used to talk about her a good deal. She was something of a joke—rather a character, I understood."

"Did you ever meet Mrs. Ardley?"

"No. I said that."

"Just tell us anything you can remember Singer telling you, Mr. Maddox—doesn't matter how trivial it sounds."

"Well, she told me about her mother dying. And she talked about her new flat—room, rather. And about Mrs. Ardley, what—"

"Room?"

"Room, yes."

"She had a room, not a flat?"

"I believe so. But you must be aware of that, Superintendent."

"Don't you worry what I'm aware of, Mr. Maddox. You just tell us what you know."

"Well, I . . ." He was ashamed suddenly. Surely he should have known more of June's life. Or was there any more to know?

25

"Did she ever tell you about a boy friend, for instance?"

"No."

"She never hinted she might have a boy friend?"

"That wasn't the sort of thing she'd tell me about. I wouldn't expect it." He shook his head in irritation. It was unfair somehow—this prying. When she was alive, no one would have asked such questions —no one cared. Her private life was her own. But now that she was dead and all should be done with, the most personal things could be raked over. It was sordid. "She wasn't the kind of girl to go tattling about her private affairs."

"But she did confide in you?"

"Well, if telling me about her mother's death is confiding, yes—she confided in me. But really . . ."

"But she didn't tell you about any boy friend?"

"I've answered that, Superintendent. Surely there's not much point in going over the same ground again and again."

"We want to get it absolutely clear. You never can tell when some small detail won't be very important, Mr. Maddox. Now, you say she didn't have a boy friend—but, well now, did she receive any private correspondence at the office?"

"I simply do not know." He almost laughed at the stupidity of it.

"Well, then, personal telephone calls?"

"Again, I haven't the faintest idea."

"Ummm." Superintendent George leafed slowly through his notebook once again. He looked up. "After five years—nearly six, wasn't it?—you were fond of her?"

"Fond of her? No, I don't—"

"You *liked* her?"

"I liked her? If that's what you mean, oh yes, I suppose I was fond of her."

"She was an attractive girl, wasn't she?"

He was suddenly blazingly angry. "I was not fond of her in that way! I don't know what the devil you're trying—"

"*What* way?"

"In a—in a sexual way, if that's what you're driving at. This is quite preposterous. I—"

"You never took her out?"

"I certainly did not!"

26

"Not even for a friendly drink? Lots of people take their secretaries out for a friendly drink. There's no harm in that."

"Well, I . . . I may have done . . ."

"Did you?"

"Yes, I think I did, once."

"When?"

"I can't remember. Look—"

"Last year? This year?"

"I really can't remember. And I most strongly resent this question."

"Why is that? We're only trying to get at the truth. Why should you object to that?"

"I don't object to . . . That isn't the point." The point was that he felt, absurdly, in some kind of unknown danger.

"Very well. You can't remember whether you took Singer out this year or last year. Can you remember where you went to have that drink?"

"No."

"It wouldn't have been Panton Place, would it?"

"Good God, no. What on earth do you think I am?"

"Have you ever been in Number Twenty-seven Panton Place?"

"No—I . . ."

"Have you ever visited Number Twenty-seven Panton Place?"

"Well, I . . ." He'd only got to say it now—yes—but it would sound all wrong. It would sound as if . . .

"Come on, Maddox," Symington's sharp voice. "Have you or haven't you ever been to Twenty-seven Panton Place?"

"No!" Damn it! He half turned to look at Symington, the little bastard.

"You're quite sure of that now, Mr. Maddox, aren't you?" said George.

"What? Yes. Yes, quite sure."

"And when did you last see June Singer alive?"

"I told you yesterday. On Friday."

"Friday, March the sixth, that would be, would it?"

"Yes."

"And you did not see her after that?"

"No. I . . . did not." They'd trapped him into lying. But why, why did he let this oafish policeman trap him into lying? Not that it

27

mattered—no one could possibly know. But all the same, it was elementary to tell the truth to the police unless—precisely, *unless*.

"What?" he said.

"I said, do you happen to own a dark-brown cashmere scarf?"

Jordan put his hand to his throat and looked down. It was his dark-blue scarf. No wonder he was hot.

"Well, do you own such a scarf?"

"Well, yes, I do have one, I think. Brown cashmere." It was Willy's last Christmas present—she always gave him scarves and gloves—and he'd lost it. He didn't know when.

Superintendent George leaned over and opened a drawer in the desk. He pulled out a brown scarf, shook it unfolded and laid it on the desk top.

"That it?"

"I'm not sure. I imagine there are lots of brown scarves in London."

"Examine it."

"Well—" But already he had spotted the white marker tag which Willy sewed on all his clothes, and the red initials, *J.J.M.* "Yes," he said, "that's mine."

"Would you explain how it came to be found in June Singer's room at Number Twenty-seven Panton Place?"

"I . . . I really have no idea." He knew that he was smiling. He might have guessed. Everywhere he went he left something behind. Galoshes usually. He went through a dozen pairs of galoshes a year. And gloves—he had hundreds of mismatching lefts and rights. Just because you left a scarf behind didn't mean—well, it didn't mean anything. Why, come to that, it wasn't even certain he'd left it behind. "I haven't the faintest idea, Superintendent. I can only suppose Miss Singer took it in mistake for her own and forgot to return it."

"That's your explanation?"

"What other explanation could there be?"

George frowned. Slowly he took the scarf and folded it into an immaculate oblong. He put it back into the drawer. "Mr. Maddox, there's usually a reasonable explanation for anything—however silly it might sound. We policemen are simple men; we don't try to trick people. We just want the truth. That's all, Mr. Maddox. Now why don't you just tell me the truth, ummm?" He looked away, as if to spare Jordan embarrassment. "It really can't do you any harm, can it?"

"I . . ." He could hardly swallow. His palms were sticky with sweat. He thought ironically how proud he'd been of their dryness last night. But they didn't know anything—for the very simple reason that there was absolutely nothing to know. With great care he found himself saying, "I have told you the truth, Mr. George."

George looked at him and sighed; he nodded to Symington, and Jordan heard the inspector get up and leave the room.

"Alright, Mr. Maddox. We'll leave it at that."

"Can I go?"

"I'd be much obliged if you could wait for five or ten minutes. Have a smoke?" He took out a worn leather case and a box of matches and put them on the desk top. "Help yourself. Woodbines, I'm afraid."

"Thanks, I will." He reached over and took a cigarette. He never thought he would actually need a cigarette.

"Nasty scratch you got there," said George, looking at Jordan's wrist, which was exposed as he reached for the cigarette.

Jordan said nothing—this time he had sense enough.

"How did you get it?"

"Cat or something, I suppose," he said noncommittally.

"You have a cat, do you? My missus loves cats. Got a pair of Siamese. Seal points. What kind of cat's yours?"

"Haven't got one, actually. The neighbours, they . . ."

"Neighbours have a cat, eh? Oh, well, once they take a fancy to you, can't get rid of 'em, can you? I know just what you mean. . . ." He went on talking, evenly, calmly—as though he'd seen it all, and perhaps, thought Jordan, he had. And yet not been soured by it.

"Like a cup of tea, would you?"

Jordan glanced at his watch. Christ—it was quarter to three. He'd been here for three hours, four. "Yes, but . . ."

"It won't be long now. Just wait here and I'll see if I can't rustle up a cup for you." He got up and went to the door. "Sugar?"

"Yes."

Left alone, Jordan took out his handkerchief and wiped his face and his hands and his wrists. What an awful little hole it was. He stood up; he ached all over.

The sergeant brought his tea, and Jordan drank it, not caring that the heat of it numbed the roof of his mouth.

Inspector Symington came in quickly, shut the door behind him and went round to the other side of the desk. He was holding a sheet of typewritten paper in one hand.

"Where's Mr. George?" Jordan asked.

"Busy." Symington stared aggressively at Jordan, who noted that the inspector's jacket was sharply, spivishly waisted. Just what you'd expect, he thought.

"Sign this, then you can skedaddle," said Symington.

"Sign what?"

"This." Symington handed him the piece of paper.

"What's this?"

"Your statement."

"Statement? What are you talking about? I never made a statement." Jordan glanced at the sheet; it was headed "Statement made by J. J. Maddox to Chief Superintendent George and Detective-Inspector Symington at Sarah Street police station, March 11."

"It's exactly what you said. Read it. Alter it, if you want to."

"I never understood I was making a statement."

"What did you think you were doing, playing grandmother's footsteps?"

Jordan stared at Symington. "You're insufferably offensive aren't you?"

The inspector smiled. "Well, that sounds like the truth at any rate."

Jordan dropped the paper. "I'm not signing this."

"What are you afraid of? Isn't it true?"

"If it's what I said, then it's true."

"Well, read it and see if it's not what you said."

Jordan hesitated. Then he picked up the sheet of paper and began to read.

NAME: Jordan John Maddox
ADDRESS: Woodley Road, Woodley, Surrey
OCCUPATION: Publisher

June Singer was in my employ for five and a half years. She came to work for me on June 26th, which I remember because it was my birthday. I thought she was efficient. But I did not get to know her very well in the office. She was quiet and efficient and got on with

30

her work. I did not have to tell her what to do all the time. She was responsible. She was not a chatterbox. She was attractive, but I never thought about that. She confided to me about her mother dying and about her room at Panton Place where she moved before Christmas. She talked a good deal about Mrs. Ardley, who was something of a joke, although I never met her. She did not tell me about any boy friend. She was not the sort to go tattling about her private affairs. I do not know if she received any personal correspondence at the office. I have not the faintest idea if she received any personal phone calls at the office. I was fond of her, but not in a sexual way. I took her out for a drink once, but I cannot remember when. I did not go to Panton Place. I have never visited No. 27 Panton Place. I recognise the brown cashmere scarf as belonging to me, but I cannot explain how it came to be in June Singer's room. I can only suppose she took it in mistake for her own and forgot to return it.

I last saw June Singer alive on Friday, March 6.

I have read over this statement and it is in all respects a true one.

He looked up at Symington and smiled. "You think you're going to get me to sign this?"

"We're not trying to get you to do anything, Maddox. But I would like to know why you refuse to sign that statement."

"Because it's an utter farce."

"Oh, no. It's not a farce, Maddox. It's a very serious matter. Very serious indeed. We're investigating a murder."

"I don't mean the murder. I mean this statement, so-called. Here, look at this: 'I was fond of her, but not in a sexual way'! I never said that."

"I can assure you you did. I took down your words just as you spoke them. I'll be glad to show you my notebook."

"I may have *said* them, but not like that. My God, you make it sound the exact opposite of what I said. The whole thing—the way it's put—is loaded with false implications. What you need, Inspector, is an elementary lesson in the use of the English language."

It was Symington now who smiled. "I'd be glad of that. But if the statement isn't the truth, it's only you that can correct it, isn't it? We don't have to bother about literary criticism, do we? All we want is the simple facts."

Superintendent George came in just as Jordan was about to reply.

"Hello. Still here, are we?"

"Mr. George, have you seen this ridiculous piece of paper?"

George held out his hand and took the statement. He read it through, now and again mouthing a word. "What's wrong with it exactly, Mr. Maddox?" he said when he had finished reading.

"The whole thing's wrong!"

George brightened. "Oh, I see. You want to make a new statement, is that it?"

"I don't mean what I said was wrong. What I'm saying is, this is a completely false representation of what I did say."

Frowning, George turned to Symington. "Didn't you copy this from your notebook, Inspector?"

"Yes, sir."

"Well," said George, puzzled, "I must say, Mr. Maddox, I thought I heard you using these words. But we can easily check up on it. I wouldn't want you to sign anything that you don't feel to be completely true. Let's just go over—"

Jordan made up his mind. "I'm not going over anything, Superintendent. It seems to me I've been kept here long enough and—"

"Kept here? No one's keeping you, Mr. Maddox. Dear, dear, what ever gave you that idea?"

"In that case, I'm going." He moved to the door.

"There is just one thing, Mr. Maddox," the superintendent said mildly, "and I tell you this for your own good. You don't have to say a word to the police, if you don't want to. No one does. That's fair enough, isn't it? Of course, if you don't tell us anything—tell us the truth—then it makes our work all the harder. And then, of course, another thing—it looks bad, if you know what I mean. After all, why shouldn't a man, a citizen, help the police, tell them the truth, sign a statement—why shouldn't he? Unless he's got something to fear. Well, think it over, and if you have any second thoughts, just let us know, eh?" He paused. "Well, Mr. Symington will show you out. Good afternoon, Mr. Maddox."

Out in the street, the fading sunlight and the shoppers beginning to hurry home, Jordan could hardly believe what had happened in there. He'd told them a small lie, for almost no reason—except that in that little stifling room it had seemed vital to prevent their finding out he'd seen June on Monday morning. He stopped on the pavement and half turned. He could go back, as easy as winking. And yet it was unimportant. Trivial. Whichever way he told it, it would sound guilty now. And she quite easily could have taken the scarf home with her by mistake. What *did* it matter? Damn all!

He might, perhaps, give Tom Short a ring, to be on the safe side. But he could do that in the morning. He hailed a taxi and told the driver "Waterloo." He'd catch the early train today.

3

"Manzanilla, Mr. Maddox?" enquired William dutifully.

"Yes, thank you, William. Er—no. Make it a whiskey. A large one."

"Right you are, sir."

"And give me twenty cigarettes, would you?"

"Any particular kind, sir?"

Jordan shook his head. He took the whiskey and the cigarettes and a box of matches and gave William the exact change.

He went over to the tall Georgian window and turned his back on the club bar. It would be at least fifteen minutes before Tom arrived, and by that time the place would be full of smoke and brash chatter. Now it was empty as a private drawing room and silent except for the faint rattle of ice and chink of glass as William marshalled bottles and tumblers for the lunchtime rush.

Perhaps he should have waited in the parlour upstairs, away from the Friday crowd. But he wanted people. He didn't want to mix with them, but he wanted them to be there, as usual, as normal. He wanted to forget that in his pocket was a scrap of paper that Archie, the porter, had given him as he came in. A scrap of paper asking him to ring a Chelsea number. He wondered whether it would be Symington or George this time—but whoever it was, they could wait.

He half closed his eyes and the pale sunshine misted and glimmered. The same pale light had filled his room that Easter at Sibley more than twenty years ago, when chicken pox had released him into a lazy world half out of life. Most of the time he had been left alone in his room with the Holman Hunt on the wall, "The Light of the World" tiptoeing sadly in his long nightgown. And Jordan could

33

hear, unusually loud, the pleasing sounds of the house, doors and footsteps and the gong for meals and the strike of the fat, squat clock in the hall (for some unknown reason, Aunt Mary disliked the really good long-case clock, which therefore remained perpetually silent, its weights hanging exhausted at the end of their wire tethers), and the passing of Uncle John, clearing his throat as if to give some stentorian military command, and Annie humming away on the landing as she dusted the willow pattern china displayed on top of the linen cupboard. He remembered the invalid peace of it all.

He would be quite content to sit this one out too.

"Hello, Jordan."

The whiskey swirled in his glass as he turned. "Hello, Frank. How's advertising?"

"Oh, pretty bloody." Frank Wade grinned.

"How's Ellen?"

"Alright, I suppose. I wouldn't know." Frank put a cigarette in his mouth and began patting hopelessly at his pockets for matches.

"Here." Jordan handed him the box.

"Well, as best man, you should be told, really. Ellen and I have separated." Frank lit the cigarette and shoved the matches into his pocket.

"Oh," Jordan said, "I'm sorry."

"Not legally, of course. Nothing like that. Not yet." He took a deep breath of cigarette smoke and coughed. "We've not seen eye to eye for some time. You know how Ellen is. No warmth. Not that she says anything—but it comes across all the same. Worse."

Jordan sipped his whiskey. He could think of nothing to say. He remembered Ellen on her wedding day, standing beside him as he read the telegrams—she had been pretty then and happy. He had seen her since, but she hadn't made much impression.

"I'm a sexual man, Jordan," said Frank with a little laugh.

Jordan smiled automatically. "Don't let's start that again."

Frank said, "I've got a little flat off Sloane Street." He looked at Jordan. "With Sheila."

"Sheila?"

"Sheila Steggins. My secretary. You met her."

"Oh, yes—in your office." He made an effort—"She'd been in America or something."

34

Frank smiled. "That's right." He stared out of the window. "You know," he said quietly, "it may sound silly but I feel I've got someone now who understands me. Who *wants* to understand me."

"I see," said Jordan.

"Oh, God!" He gulped his drink. "I might have expected that from you."

"I'm sorry."

"Forget it." Frank looked down at his empty glass. "I need a drink. Get you one?"

"No, thanks."

"Well, keep it under your hat." He turned away to the bar.

Jordan took out a cigarette and discovered Frank had gone off with his matches. He slipped the cigarette back into the packet.

Tom Short came across the room briskly, his arm upraised to brush away impeding elbows and shoulders.

"I'm late," he said. "What's this important business? Do you want to talk about it at lunch or shall we go up to the parlour?"

"Let's go to the parlour. Look, I'm sorry to drag you away from your conference."

"Think nothing of it. Lot of rich old bastards trying to cook up a tax fiddle. I was only there to make it look good." But all the same, his air was hurried. "Let's get out of here," he said loudly, looking round. "Full of queers these days. I don't know why I bother to belong."

The parlour was empty.

"Do you want a drink?" Jordan asked.

"Not in the middle of the day, old boy. The pot."

Jordan was uneasy. Perhaps he was really making a fuss about nothing. "Have you got a match, Tom?"

"Yes, right. Here." Tom snapped open his lighter. "It's about Willy, isn't it?" he said abruptly.

"About Willy?" Jordan was puzzled. "No—why should it be?"

Tom laughed. "I didn't think you'd be looking so worried about anything else."

"Oh. No, it's about my secretary—June Singer."

"The one that was murdered?"

"How did you know?"

"Plastered all over the papers. Besides, Willy told me."

35

"You've seen Willy?"

"She gave Norah a ring and I picked up the phone. Couldn't wait to spill the beans." He laughed again.

Jordan was annoyed; it wasn't like Willy to go tattling about his private affairs. "Well, I . . ." This was going to be difficult. "I saw the police yesterday afternoon. Yesterday morning and afternoon. I was there—at the police station—for nearly five hours. And . . . I feel they badgered me, rather."

Tom merely grunted.

"They asked me a great many questions. All rather pointless, I thought. And I can't say I liked their attitude. And then they wanted me to sign a statement. . . ." He felt as if he were back in that hot little room. "Well, I didn't sign it because it seemed to me that they'd got what I said hopelessly garbled. And besides that I . . . it sounds so bloody ridiculous—but I told them a lie. It's not important but . . . You see, they asked me when I'd last seen the girl, and I told them on Friday, when she left the office as usual. But in fact, and I only remembered this yesterday morning—or perhaps it was Wednesday night—in fact I'd seen her on Monday morning. And I also told them I'd never been to Panton Place—well, that's where I saw June on Monday. And then there's this business of my scarf."

"Wait a minute," Tom said. "Let me just get one thing straight. When was the girl murdered?"

"On Wednesday, that's when the police found her—or rather Mrs. Ardley."

"They *found* her on Wednesday, but when did she die? Did they tell you?"

"No, I just assumed . . ."

"In other words, she could have been murdered on Tuesday? Or on Monday?"

"I suppose so. I hadn't thought of that."

"Hadn't you?"

"Well, maybe it had been in the back of my mind. Perhaps that's why I . . ."

"Very likely," said Tom without expression. "Alright now, just tell me the whole thing—what happened on Monday and what happened yesterday at the station."

Lamely Jordan told him. When he had finished, Tom sat silent.

"Well?" said Jordan.

"Well what? Do you want me to advise you?"

"Yes—I think I do."

"Right. Go straight round to Sarah Street. See this Superintendent George and make a statement. Tell him exactly what you've told me."

"But I feel such a bloody fool—"

"With the greatest deference, you are a bloody fool. What on earth possessed you to lie to the police?"

"I imagine—perhaps I didn't want to be involved."

"Involved? You are involved. What you mean is that you didn't want to be suspected of murdering the girl, isn't it?"

"I don't know that I'd go as far as that, but . . ."

"When it comes to a layman and the law! Let that pass. But let me just ask you two questions. One, have you told me everything that happened on Monday morning?"

He was hot again, terribly hot. "Yes."

"As extension of that—the reason you saw the girl, to pick up a manuscript she'd been typing for you over the weekend—you can prove it, can't you? You have the manuscript?"

"I've got the carbon, yes. Yes, I can prove that."

"Second question: Were you having an affair with the girl?"

"Of course I was not."

"Or anything like it?"

"Absolutely not. God, Tom—"

"Look, Jordan, I know you're not the man to go running after a piece of skirt. But the police don't. No, please let me finish." He held up his hand. "On what you have told me, there is not the slightest chance of the police arresting you. Even if—if the girl was murdered on the Monday morning. Even if the police think or suspect you might have murdered her. There still is simply not enough evidence to give them a hope in hell of bringing a successful prosecution against you. This is not my field at all, as you know, but any lawyer will tell you the same."

"I see. Then you think there's nothing to . . . worry about?"

"So long as you tell them the truth, absolutely nothing." He grinned suddenly. "May I break my rule and have a drink?"

"By all means." Jordan got up quickly and pressed the bell. He felt both elated and depressed—as if something had been taken away from him, and he wasn't quite certain whether he was bereft or freed.

The waiter came and they ordered.

"You must excuse me," Tom said when the drinks had arrived and the glass was in his hand, "if I was a bit brusque. We lawyers often get pulled out of bed for the most ridiculous things. That's half the time. The other half, of course, we get called in when it's far too late. Cheers."

"Tom—if it should turn out that I do need a lawyer after all, will you act for me?"

"Still not convinced, eh? Yes, of course I'll act for you. Although it's not my field, really. But if it'll make you happy—okay."

"Thanks."

"So long as you don't neglect to trot off to Sarah Street. Now," he said, finishing his drink, "what about the main business?"

"The main business?"

"Lunch." Tom laughed.

As they went to the door, he said, "Would you like me to give Willy a ring and put her in the picture?"

Jordan said, "No, I'll do that. I think perhaps I'll skip the office this afternoon. An unproductive week altogether."

"If you say so," said Tom. He ate a large lunch.

4

He decided on a short walk to clear his head of the three brandies he'd had after lunch. He'd rung the Chelsea number and told them he'd be down. So there was no need to hurry.

He wandered into Trafalgar Square. He had a look at St. Martin's in the Fields and Edith Cavell. Then, as he was already at the door, he went into the National Portrait Gallery—which he could seldom resist.

It was almost four when he reached Sarah Street.

The sergeant took him directly to the same room and asked him to wait. Jordan sat down behind the desk. Although the room was bakingly hot, he was quite cold. He was sleepy, too, and when he closed his eyes, his whole body slipped sideways and came to rest in the queasy but comforting motion of a ship at sea. He shook his head and sat up straight. The inside of his mouth was marred and dry. He ought to have asked for paper and pencil—he could be getting on with his statement while he waited.

He tried the desk drawers, but they were all locked with the exception of the bottom right-hand drawer. He pulled it out and looked down at his brown cashmere scarf. That was careless of them, to leave it there. He touched it with the tips of his fingers. He could easily put it in his pocket and slip away. Carelessness or design. He shut the drawer with a snap. Tampering with evidence. But the scarf wasn't evidence of anything, or at least not good enough evidence. He tried to recall what Tom had said. They haven't got a hope in hell, something like that.

He was saved from sleep by the sergeant.

"Excuse me, sir. Would you mind taking part in an identification parade?"

Jordan glanced at his watch. "I don't think I can do that. I'm waiting for Mr. George."

"I'm afraid he won't be along for another five minutes, sir. The parade won't take but a moment."

Well, it would be better than fighting off the doze. "If you're quite sure, then." His limbs were stiff as he stood up.

"Just follow me, sir, would you?"

He was taken down a long corridor and shown into a large room set up like an auditorium, with a small dais and a blackboard at one end and folding wooden chairs, which had been pushed to one side, for the audience. It smelled like a school gymnasium.

In front of the dais were a police constable and eight men, all wearing overcoats. Jordan was taken to join them.

"Alright," said the sergeant, "just line up, would you, facing this way. Take your hat off if you don't mind, sir. Right, won't be a moment." He took his place at the other end of the line from the constable. "Now please don't speak or draw attention to yourself in any way."

The door opened and Jordan heard the words ". . . want you to be quite certain . . ."

She was a woman in her late fifties, Jordan judged; a strong, righteous face, grey hair, dark overcoat, dark scarf, and a beige felt hat which contained the only colour she wore—a small flourish of orange feathers in the band. Inspector Symington was behind her, and he lightly guided her to the end of the line away from Jordan. Jordan was

39

irritated to see the inspector; all the world had to wait upon the convenience of the police, it appeared.

The woman stood in front of the first man in the line and stared. Then she did a right turn, walked two paces, a left turn, and stared at number two. Probably a hospital matron, Jordan thought, whom a patient had attempted to rape.

As she stared at him, Jordan was surprised by her rather melancholy brown eyes. They didn't fit with the rest of her face. She moved on to the man at his left, the last one. She turned slowly down the line again, not stopping this time, then back again.

"This is the man," she said clearly.

Jordan wanted to laugh—she was standing directly in front of him.

"This is the man you saw leaving your rooming house at Number Twenty-seven Panton Place on the morning of March the ninth?"

"My boarding house," she said. "Yes, I am quite sure. At quarter to ten. This is the man."

"Thank you very much, Mrs. Ardley. Right." The two of them turned and walked quickly from the room.

"Okay," the sergeant said. "Thank you very much. That's all." He came to Jordan and touched him on the arm. "You come with me."

The afternoon's alcohol came together and abruptly drenched his brain. "But . . ." he murmured, aware of nothing but the curious looks of the other men as he was taken away.

Taken away. As they came to the door of the little room—the interrogation room—he realised the sergeant still had hold of his arm. He shook himself. "Do you mind?"

Superintendent George was seated behind the desk. He was smoking a pipe. "Sit down, Maddox."

The smell of the tobacco was horrible.

"I most violently object. I refuse to sit down."

"What do you object to?"

"That identity thing. It seems to me you're pretty damn high-handed, Superintendent."

"Didn't you give your consent to appear in the identification parade?"

"Yes, but I didn't know it had got anything to do with me!"

"Oh, I see. And if you had known, you would have refused, would you?"

40

"I most certainly would." The anger hurt his head.

"Why?"

"Why?" Why? He'd come to tell them he'd been there anyway, so why object? He remembered Tom saying that there was nothing to be worried about—but he knew they'd cheated him somehow. He reached back for the confident normality that had been his only a couple of hours ago. "Superintendent, you're trying to confuse me," he laughed, but was unable to reproduce the phlegmy assurance of Tom's chuckle. "Of course I would not have refused if I had been properly informed. It's these underhand methods I don't care for. In fact, I could have told you—if you'd thought to ask—that the whole thing was unnecessary. As it happens, that's exactly why I've come here."

Symington entered and sat down in the third chair. Again that smart rattle-slap as he opened his notebook.

Jordan refused to allow himself to become annoyed. He sat down. "I want to make a statement—not that thing you gave me to sign yesterday. But this morning I remembered—"

"Just one moment, Maddox." George took the pipe out of his mouth and laid it on the desk. "Before you begin, it is my duty to tell you that you are not obliged to say anything unless you wish to do so, but whatever you do say will be taken down in writing and may be given in evidence."

"What does that mean? Are you . . . ?"

"I'm not doing anything. I'm just warning you, as is my duty. It means no more no less'n what it says."

It was the "Warning," of course; he wished Tom had told him about this. He made a great effort to clear his head. He would have to be careful.

"Well, I want to say that what I told you yesterday was not—does not exactly conform to the facts, which I have now remembered. The fact is that I did see June Singer on Monday. March the ninth. I went to Panton Place to pick up a manuscript which she had been typing for me over the weekend. This was about nine-thirty, I suppose. I saw June, collected the manuscript and the portable office typewriter which I'd lent her to do the typing and then went to my office. I must have taken off my scarf and accidently left it there. This just completely went out of my mind until yesterday evening when . . . I

41

suddenly remembered." Well, that was it. He felt a swell of relief as his body relaxed. "If you have that typed up, I'll sign it."

Symington continued writing for a few moments; then there was quiet. A tiny bubbling from the superintendent's pipe. Nobody said a word.

"I said, if you have that typed, I'll sign it."

Nothing. Neither policeman moved. George looked steadily at the wall and puffed gently, as though remembering old times.

"Mr. George!" The irritability of his exhaustion overcame him. The superintendent moved in his chair and regarded Jordan.

"I've made my statement, Mr. George."

"Oh. *That* was your statement, was it?" His tone was one of genuine surprise.

"Yes. I mean . . . Why . . . Yes, it was. Is."

"Quite sure that's all you want to say?"

He'd covered it, hadn't he? He had a sense of inadequacy before George's kindly puzzlement. "What more is there to say?"

George smiled. "That's for you to tell us, isn't it, Maddox?"

"I don't understand what you want."

"The only thing we want is the true facts. Now let's start with Monday morning. Why not tell us everything you remember about that morning in your own words? Begin at the beginning. For instance, what did you have for breakfast that day?"

"How could that be remotely relevant?"

"It might help you to remember. Just tell us about that morning as it happened. Don't bother about anything else; we can deal with that later."

"Anything else? Mr. George, really, I hardly know what you're talking about. Anyway, this is ridiculous. I don't want to say any more."

George was looking at the wall again now. "That's up to you, Maddox. But I think, in all fairness to yourself, there are one or two things you might like to explain."

"Such as what?"

The superintendent sighed and his pipe bubbled quickly. "You said you arrived at Panton Place about nine-thirty. How long did you stay there?"

"Five minutes perhaps."

"So you would have left Panton Place at about nine thirty-five."

42

"Roundabout, yes."

"Well now, Mrs. Ardley says she saw you leaving Number Twenty-seven at nine forty-five. How do you account for that?"

"I said *about* nine-thirty. It could easily have been nine-forty. Mrs. Ardley may be right; on the other hand she might be mistaken. I don't see what the difficulty is."

"Alright then. Let's say you arrived at nine-thirty, maybe nine-forty. Let's try to pin it down as near as we can though. Might it have been nine-fifty?"

"I shouldn't think so, no. Too late. No, I should say between nine-thirty and nine-forty."

"Nine-twenty, perhaps?"

"I think not. Not as early as that."

"And you stayed five minutes?"

"Yes."

"That morning, how did you come up to town, Maddox?"

"By train as usual."

"That would be the train from Woodley to Waterloo?"

"Yes, the eight twenty-four."

"From Waterloo, how did you get to Panton Place?"

"By tube."

"Didn't stop on the way to have a cup of coffee or anything?"

"No. I went straight there."

"Now tell me how long all that took you—from Woodley Station to Panton Place."

"Woodley to Waterloo is forty-five minutes exactly. Fifteen minutes in the tube, I suppose. Two or three minutes to walk at either end. A bit over an hour, I'd say. Sixty-five, seventy minutes at most."

"So, on that basis, you would have arrived at Panton Place at between nine twenty-nine and nine thirty-four."

Jordan smiled now. "Yes. Which is what I said at the beginning."

"So you did, yes. But all this is based on your having taken the eight twenty-four train from Woodley. Now I want to be fair with you, Maddox, so I'm not going to ask you whether or not you took the eight twenty-four that morning because I know you didn't. However—"

"But I did take it. I always take it. How can you know—"

"Please, Maddox. I'm not trying to trip you up. It just shows you

43

how faulty memory can be. I can prove you took the seven fifty-nine from Woodley that morning. I've got two independent witnesses. I see no harm in telling you that the parking attendant and the porter J. Whitaker have already made statements to that effect. Well, as you know, the seven fifty-nine arrives at Waterloo at eight forty-eight. Fifteen minutes in the tube, two- or three-minute walk either end—that means you must have arrived at Panton Place just before nine-fifteen. You say you stayed five minutes, which would mean you left about nine-twenty. Mrs. Ardley is positive you left at nine forty-five. That's a discrepancy, isn't it? A rather large discrepancy. I'm sure you can explain it—and I think you ought to."

Jordan was shocked. It wasn't so much that he'd made a mistake about the train times—and if old Whitaker said he'd taken the seven fifty-nine, he probably had—as the knowledge that they had been investigating him. He felt ensnared and soiled and—not frightened, no, but worried. And Tom had said there was nothing to worry about. In that case . . . "I'm not contradicting you, Superintendent. Come to think of it, I rather imagine I could have taken the earlier train—I know I didn't want to lose much time before getting to the office. I had a ten o'clock appointment with an American publisher. I may have stayed ten minutes at June's—perhaps fifteen, though it seems unlikely to me. Perhaps I did stop to have a cup of coffee at Waterloo. As you say, my memory is far from perfect. I'm not trying to be unreasonable—but I do think all this is rather footling."

George took a ring of keys from his pocket and examined them. He inserted one into the lock of the centre drawer of the desk. He picked out several sheets of paper stapled together. He turned the pages slowly, mumbling to himself here and there. "Ah, yes," he said at last. "Here we are: 'Time of Death . . .' let's see . . . 'can be placed with some accuracy as having occurred between the hours of seven A.M. and eleven A.M. on the morning of March ninth!" He glanced up at Jordan. "That's the Monday, Maddox. I'm reading from the pathologist's report." He dropped the papers back in the drawer and locked it methodically and put the keys in his pocket. "Between seven and eleven. You were there fair and square in the middle of that period in which Singer was murdered. So you see there's nothing footling about it. The time element—what happened that morning and exactly when it happened—all that's extremely important. I'll be honest with you, Maddox—you're the only person who can tell us what

44

happened, because we don't know of anyone else who visited June Singer that morning."

"I didn't realise that. I see it's important."

"Very well then. You just tell us in your own words the events of the Monday morning, eh? Everything. Doesn't matter how silly it might seem to you."

"Alright, I'll try." Labouriously he attempted to collect his memories. "I got up a bit earlier than usual . . ." He had begun. As he spoke, the dead triviality of it all embarrassed him, like the sight of an old man exposing his flaccid penis on the street.

". . . I arrived at Number Twenty-seven and went up the steps—I think there were steps. June answered the door and—"

"Half a moment. How did she know you were there?"

"Oh. I rang the bell."

"I see. Then she answered the door?"

"Yes. We went up one flight of stairs—June led the way—and then we went into her room. . . ."

It was very simple—he'd just had a look at a couple of obscure spots in the manuscript, which June had discovered. Then he'd left. But Superintendent George would not have it so simple.

"Did she offer you anything to eat or drink?"

"Oh, yes—now you mention it. She gave me a cup of coffee."

"Did she have one herself?"

"Yes."

"Anything to eat?"

"She offered me some cake, I think. I didn't have any, but I rather fancy she had a piece."

"What sort of cake would that have been?"

"Oh—why, I think it was Swiss roll, chocolate Swiss roll. A rather inappropriate breakfast."

At last he finished. He was tired and weak. He took a cigarette from the packet he'd bought at lunch. The superintendent lit it for him. Oddly enough he felt better now—a couple of hours' nap and he'd be as right as rain.

George lit his own pipe. He said something, but his words were obscured by the mouthpiece. Jordan asked him to repeat it.

"I said, let's just run through that again, shall we? There are one or two things I'm not quite clear about still. For instance, what was Singer wearing? What did you say to her and she to you? You must

45

have conversed? It'd be useful if you could describe her room. Oh, yes
—and did you touch her?"

"I certainly didn't touch her."

"Did she touch you then?"

"No. She did not. Why should she?" His sense of purgation
vanished—they didn't believe him, after all this. They weren't playing
fair. All those soothing words meant nothing. He was filled with resentment. "Look, George, I've just about had enough of this."

"Well, it does seem a pity, now that you're here, not to straighten
out one or two last things. You've made a very clear statement," good
boy, full marks, "and there are only really a few minor loose ends to
tie up. Why don't we just dot the *i*'s and cross the *t*'s, as it were—and
have done with it?"

"Oh, al*right*." Such a reasonable bloody bastard.

Slowly, grindingly, he was taken through it all again, until he nearly
cried out in agonized boredom. What did she wear? What did she say?
What did you say? What did she say? Was there a cloth on the table?
Milk in the coffee? Sugar? Was the bed made or unmade? Was this,
was that . . . ?

And then, unexpectedly, while they were still apparently in the
middle of it, George said suddenly, "Well, I think that's quite satisfactory. I don't think there's anything else we need to go into now.
You've been very helpful, Mr. Maddox. I wonder if I could ask you to
wait just a few more minutes while Mr. Symington types your statement." Symington had already gone. George rose now and smiled.
"These things are always a bit trying, I'm afraid. You just make yourself comfortable now." And then he, too, departed.

Jordan smoked the last cigarette in the packet. He was a bit bewildered. One expected people, even the police, to behave in a reasonable fashion most of the time, and when they didn't—just gave up or
walked out on you—well, it was vaguely as though one had been let
down. And that is what he felt—let down. He was too tired to be glad
it was over. He was too tired to bother with the absurdity of it, although in the back of his mind there was a touch of worry that it had
all been too easy (*too easy!* he smiled wearily). He was too tired even
to look at his watch; he knew it was late. Willy would be worried. Let
her worry.

He dozed. He was wakened by the cigarette burning his fingers. He

46

sat on, thinking of nothing, forgetting almost where he was. It was quite a shock when Symington returned and handed him the statement.

Jordan had to force his mind to focus. It seemed fair enough—not like the other one yesterday. He took the pen Symington handed him and he signed it.

"Just put the date and time at the bottom," the inspector said. "It's seven thirty-two."

So early. He was surprised. He wrote it down.

"Well, there you are." He handed pen and signed statement to Symington. He sat back. It was going to be a hell of an effort to get up.

Symington stared at him critically. "Alright now, Maddox," he snapped, "we'll forget about the load of shit you been giving us, shall we?" He shook the statement. "What I want to know is why you killed her. Why'd you do it, Maddox? Why'd you have to knock off your little bit of fluff? WHY?"

Unconsciously, he knew, he'd been expecting this assault. But the very expectation, admitted now, drained him of his defensive powers. God, how he loathed rows! The source of revivifying anger was buried so deep within him he could not draw upon it. Instead he would have to splash valiantly in the thin saucer of exasperation.

"Now look here, Inspector. I've had just about enough of this . . . this bullying. I've half a mind to report you to the commissioner—or whoever it is."

"Threats now, Maddox. Threats, is it? Just like you threatened little June Singer, eh?"

"I did not threaten June Singer! I had nothing to do with June Singer. I—"

"I had nothing to do with June Singer," Symington mimicked. And then savagely, "What about the scarf you strangled her with? What about the front doorkey you left on her table? What about those *lovely* flowers you brought her? What about the tussle you had? And the clock you knocked down? I s'pose you've forgotten all that too, Master Maddox!"

"I don't know what you're talking about."

"He doesn't know *what* I'm talking about! How your mother must have loved you, you lovely innocent little thing you. You're—"

47

"I've had enough of this, Symington. You're not fit to—"

"Don't pull the old chicko on me, Maddox! You're in real trouble, you are. You'll have to forget about the officers' mess now, laddie."

"I wasn't ever in the army," he said, hearing the feeble idiocy of it.

"Nor were you now! Unfit, weren't you? I keep forgetting you're a sick man. Sick men should be in bed, Maddox—and I don't mean in bed with their willing little secretaries."

"Symington!" Jordan stood up; his legs shook.

"What bad luck she went and got herself pregnant, wasn't it?"

"Pregnant? June was pregnant?" He gripped the edge of the desk.

"If you shoot your lot, you've got to expect the consequences, haven't you? You're not one to bother with precautions, are you? We know that."

"June pregnant. She couldn't have been pregnant. I—"

"Oh, very convincing, Maddox. All that time you were urging her to get rid of it. All that stuff she was taking. All fixed up nice to have an abortion—and then at the last minute she changes her mind? And you couldn't stand that, could you, Maddox? You couldn't have that. It would all come out then, wouldn't it? That wouldn't be officerlike conduct. That would be letting the side down." Suddenly he was soothing. "Alright, Maddox. So you had to knock her off, didn't you? We understand that. You didn't have any choice. Now why don't you just make a clean breast of it, eh? Save everyone a lot of trouble."

Jordan shivered. "You're round the bend, Inspector. God knows what your motives are. I had nothing to do with June Singer's death. I've signed my statement. Now I'm going." But he did not move.

"Now, Maddox. Why don't you be reasonable? We know you did it. We can prove you did it. Listen, the pathologist says she died ten minutes to half an hour after ingesting a piece of chocolate cake. At most, half an hour, Maddox. Now that makes it you, doesn't it? Come off it, Maddox. Sit down and get it off your chest—why not? I'll get Mr. George in and you just make your statement and it'll all be over. And then you can get a bit of shut-eye—you look as though you could do with it."

God, how he wanted to sit down, lie down. "I won't," he said. "I won't sit down. You're . . . I'm going to go." He took his hand from the desk and went to the door, trying fiercely to stop the trembling in

48

his legs. "I think—I think your behaviour is reprehensible." As he left the room he saw Symington smile and pick up the phone.

Jordan steadied himself against the wall and then began to walk down the corridor.

A door opened and Chief Superintendent George came out so fast he almost knocked Jordan over.

"I'm sorry. Nearly had a nasty accident there, didn't we? So you're off, are you, Mr. Maddox?"

"I've only got one thing to say to you, George. That man of yours—Symington, he ought to be thrown out of the force. Thrown out of the human race."

"Symington? Oh dear oh dear. He's a very good officer, he is. He's just a bit keen. I shouldn't let that worry you, Mr. Maddox."

"It doesn't. Nothing worries me." He moved, but George was blocking his path.

"There's just one thing, Mr. Maddox. I wonder if you'd oblige me. Only take a moment, I promise you."

"I'm not saying anything more."

"You don't have to say a word. Just a little test. Won't take five seconds. In here." He'd taken Jordan's arm and was leading him into the room he'd appeared from. "Nothing to it."

"Test? What do you mean? What for?"

There was another man in the room; he smiled as Jordan entered. "This is Dr. Larraby."

The doctor kept smiling. "Ah. Now we'll just roll up your sleeve, shall we, and . . . won't take a moment."

"I demand to know what this is all about!"

George said, "Just a skin test, Mr. Maddox. Quite simple."

The doctor was already swabbing his exposed arm.

"What for? I don't think . . ."

"You don't want to do it?" said George.

The doctor paused, a metal instrument in his hand.

"I didn't say that," Jordan said. "I just want to know—"

"Ah," said the doctor, "we just take a little nick out of your arm, very neat, very quick. Won't even feel it. And there we are."

"But what for?"

"For purposes of comparison," said George.

"Dammit, comparison with what?"

49

"With other tissue, Mr. Maddox. Tissue found under the nails of June Singer's right hand."

"No." Jordan jerked his arm away.

"You are refusing? Now why?"

"I didn't say I was refusing. I want to know more about it."

"Oh, well, it's very scientific. The doctor will tell you that. It's rather like those blood tests they take in paternity suits. You must have heard of them?"

"I don't see the relevance," Jordan said. There was something here which should be quite clear to him. But at that particular moment he didn't feel that anything would ever be clear to him again.

"It's like a negative test," George said. "I'm not much of an authority on this sort of thing, I'm afraid. A bit above my head. But roughly, if your tissue and the tissue under the girl's nails don't match, well, then you're in the clear."

"But if they do match?"

"Well, they're not going to, are they? Or are they?"

"I . . ."

"Are they? She inflicted a wound on some one in her death struggle. That person wasn't you, Maddox, was it?"

"No. No, of course not. I've told you that."

"Well then?" George smiled.

Slowly Jordan raised his arm. The doctor's hand moved down. There was no more than a pinprick. "I said you'd hardly feel it, didn't I?" The doctor beamed.

"Yes." Something had gone wrong. He had made some ghastly mistake. He felt it. He knew it. But, for the life of him, he couldn't sort it out in the stale brandied muddle of his brain.

5

"Sorry I'm late." He paused with his overcoat half off his shoulders. "Is anything the matter?"

She stood in the kitchen doorway, looking at him, silent.

"Is it Georgia? There's nothing wrong with—"

She shook her head quickly. "Where have you been, Jordan?"

He had prepared himself for this with two stiff drinks at the White Hart on the way home.

"I had some catching up to do at the office. It's been a bad week for work, particularly with June not . . ."

"Tom rang me."

"Oh, did he?" He wasn't surprised. People seemed to be making a habit of going back on their words lately.

"I've been ringing the office all afternoon."

"Oh, yes. Well, I spent a bit of time in the National Portrait Gallery." He laughed. "Wanted to think." Actually the Portrait Gallery was the blessed place for not thinking; the faces of the past were as alive as ever, but their troubles were all comfortably disarmed of any power for present damage.

"Why didn't you phone me? You always phone me when you're going to be late." She hadn't moved from the doorway.

"Always, always." He smiled to mask the irritation. "I just got completely immersed—you know, that manuscript on the village idiot's sex life."

She stepped towards him. "Did you go to the police?"

"What? Oh, yes. I did pop round to see them."

"What did they say?"

"I did the talking. Not them."

"Tom said . . ."

"Yes, yes. I gave them a statement, as Tom said I should."

"Jordan, I'm worried."

"There's absolutely nothing to be worried about, old girl. Didn't Tom tell you that? Absolutely nothing."

Her face was tight so that her cheekbones stood out and the hollows of her cheeks were deeper than ever.

He was suddenly touched. "Don't cry," he said.

"Of course not." She jerked her head. In all their years of marriage he had never once seen her cry.

He came close to her and she put up her cheek for him to kiss.

"Did you have anything to eat?" she asked.

"No. Forgot all about it."

She frowned. "You poor lamb, you must be starving."

"Not a bit. Couldn't eat a thing."

"You must have something. I'll get you some tea—and toast."

"That would be nice." He watched her go back into the kitchen. "I'll just go up and look in on Georgia," he called.

In the dim light from the open door he looked down on his daughter, awry with sleep. She was beautiful. Even if she had been somebody else's child, he thought, she would be beautiful. He hadn't really wanted Georgia when Willy had first told him. It had not been Georgia then, of course; just an object, just another thing which would have to be attended to. That's what he must have thought, because he could not fully remember now. He had been totally unprepared for Georgia's sensual softness and for the effortless answer that it evoked in him.

Nothing else in the world really mattered but Georgia. If he were arrested, they would keep it from Georgia. She could not read, thank God, and they would take her out of kindergarten for a while so that the other children, the knowing ones, would have no opportunity to tell her. She would be protected against knowledge of that meaningless, cruel accident. And it would make the severance more bearable for him too. She must be undisturbed by any rumour of war.

He bent and kissed her lightly.

Downstairs in the living room, Willy was waiting. She gave him a fleeting bird smile and bent her head to pour the tea. She performed the ritual movements abruptly, as if to admit a soothing quality would be a weakness.

She handed him the cup. All she did was like this: quick, abrupt. Even love, the hard jerky movements, like a dog shaking off drops of water after an unwanted bath.

He took a piece of toast. "You mustn't be upset," he said.

"I'm alright." She glanced at him. "It's you I'm worried about."

He slopped a little tea into his saucer. "What did Tom tell you?"

"Everything."

"That's not much, is it?" He smiled. He could almost hear her thoughts clicking: *Don't be frivolous, Jordan.* He walked around a little and set his cup and half-eaten piece of toast on the mantelpiece. "He told you about my visit to June's flat, then?"

"Yes."

He hesitated. She made it hard work. "And why I went there?"

"Of course."

"Idiotic of me to have gone, as it turns out."

52

"It was rather silly."

"Silly?"

"You know how people talk."

"Oh, really! Who was there to talk?"

"Miss Singer. And there must have been other people in the house."

"Don't be ridiculous. You'll be talking about no smoke without fire in a minute."

Willy's face grew tighter. She said nothing.

"You don't believe it, do you?" he said.

"You are a silly goose. Of course you couldn't do a thing like that." Her tea was untouched, her hands folded in her lap.

"That's comforting." He opened the cigarette box on the table.

"Oh, Jordan!"

"What?"

"Just look at your hand."

His fingers were brown with nicotine stains. The scars of battle with the police, he thought.

"You don't need another, Jordan. You know what Dr. Wilcox says about smoking."

"Oh damn Wilcox." He lit a cigarette.

"May I have one?"

"Sorry." He gave her one and lit it. She smoked just like her mother, with an awkward nineteen-twentyish nonchalance. It was about the only thing she and her mother had in common.

"Tom says," Willy began.

"Tom isn't God almighty."

There was a pause. "That's not very fair," she said.

"No, I suppose not. I'm sorry." He was irritable, but—why couldn't they leave him in peace? "Well, what did Tom say?"

She shook her head. "It doesn't matter."

"Your mother will be upset."

"It'll do Mummy good to have something worthwhile to be upset about for a change."

He couldn't help laughing.

"Is that funny?"

He nodded, smiling. His irritation melted. "I'm going to have a drink. Want one?"

"No thanks."

He didn't expect her to drink, not now. He remembered his headmaster saying once, "Never take a drink before you make a speech." Willy thought like that. Life's hurdles had to be crossed stone-cold sober. If you really needed it, you shouldn't have it. Aunt Mary had a rule that no fires were to be lit before November the first or after the end of March. To break the rule would . . . He stopped pouring. The ghost of Uncle John rose before he could prevent it—jolly and dotty and uncomplaining and broken dead at last against Aunt Mary's iron rule. With an almost physical effort, he pushed the thought away.

He poured a larger whiskey than he'd intended and drank half of it at once. Insulation. He turned and looked at Willy. He smiled at her and she smiled back with the cold edges of her mouth.

"I wish you got on better with your mother," he said, surprising himself.

"She's impossible."

"Yes." But in a charming way. "At any rate," he said, "It's a good thing you get on well with Mary—and Trevor."

"I admire Aunt Mary tremendously."

"And she thinks the world of you. And expects the worst of me. This won't come as much of a surprise to her."

"What do you mean? You said there was nothing to worry about!"

"No, no. There isn't. Absolutely nothing." Why did he do it to her?

"Tom says it's all circumstantial," she said, earnestly. "There's nothing concrete. Unless they've got something up their sleeves. And what could they have up their sleeves?"

A piece of me, he thought. Just a tiny nick from my flesh. She went on talking, but he didn't listen. He thought of his arrest now as a foregone conclusion. But only, he told himself, because it was a habit of thought always to expect the worst, so that when it turned out that way—and on the whole it did—one wasn't too surprised. It was only a common safety precaution, and of course it was quite useless against the worst disasters.

Willy stopped speaking.

"Well," he said, "it's no good getting worked up. All we can do is wait and see." He poured himself another drink. "It's a bit nerve-wracking, isn't it?"

She was still for a moment, and then she nodded.

He felt he had won a small victory. And with the weekend to get through, every little bonus helped.

54

6

He held the daffodils awkwardly. Willy never appreciated the problems of carrying flowers on a crowded Monday-morning bus from Waterloo to the office. It was easy enough in the train—just put them in the rack and forget about them. And he often did forget about them, leaving them for some lucky porter.

He struggled out of the bus, holding the daffodils high, like a talisman. He felt slightly sick—he could hardly remember a morning lately when he hadn't been a bit hung. He made himself walk fast; get the alcohol circulating. He was almost at the door of the office when he heard the familiar voice.

"Excuse me."

He stopped. "Well, what is it now, Mr. George?" He was aware of a tingling excitement in his legs. Perhaps this was it.

"We'd like you to accompany us to the station, if you don't mind."

He didn't mind. He was past caring. He saw Symington standing behind the superintendent. "Why?" he said.

"For further questioning."

They even had a car waiting for him. He got in the back beside George. Symington sat in the front.

"Bad day for traffic," said Jordan after a little while.

Neither policeman answered, or even appeared to have heard him. Jordan felt a flush of annoyance. Still, the police weren't paid to be courteous. Nor were they paid to sit sulking while they might be using this travelling time for a good purpose.

"I suppose you want to ask me about the flowers," he said. It had been on his mind all weekend long. "Not these." He touched the daffodils resting ridiculously on his knees as though he were an undertaker's assistant. "I mean the flowers I took—left with June, rather. You found them, didn't you?"

Again they said no word; didn't even look at him.

"Well, you see—" he wasn't going to be put off like this—"Willy— that's my wife—always gives me flowers from the garden, you know.

Every Monday. To brighten up the office. Tell you the truth, I don't much care for flowers—but there you are. Well last week it was tulips. Yellow tulips, weren't they? Yes, yellow I think. June always seemed rather keen on flowers, you know. In fact, I very often used to let her take them home with her. I mean, there was hardly any point in chucking them away. Not that I would have, of course, but . . . Well, anyway, there I was—home, or, rather, at June's home, so I thought I'd just leave them with her. She was very grateful. I suppose you want to know all about that. Well, they were wrapped in green—"

"Save your remarks for the station, Maddox," said George tonelessly.

"I was only trying to help." Bloody rude they were. If they wanted to ignore him, he'd ignore them. Then why the blazes were they taking him to Sarah Street, if they were just going to ignore him? Further questioning. But he had every right to supply the answers before they asked the questions, if he wanted to. And he did want to. After all— and he saw this quite clearly now—it was important for them to understand exactly what happened last Monday morning. He wasn't making any bones about that any more. He cleared his throat.

"You're probably wondering how I came to forget about the tulips. You must think I have a rather exceptionally faulty memory." He laughed and, as he did so, Chief Superintendent George turned and stared at him. "I have for some things—not for others of course. Flowers—well, as I said, I'm not awfully keen on flowers. I said that, yes. That makes them rather easy to forget. Eminently forgettable, in fact. What I'm getting at . . . is that . . ." He turned his head away quickly and looked out of the window. One couldn't go on talking to wax dummies. It was bloody humiliating. If they didn't want to hear what he had to say, why didn't they say so? They *had* said so. In that case . . .

He tried to concentrate on the people hurrying to work along the pavements. But all he was aware of was the rising nausea in his stomach. He clenched his teeth. But there was no effective way of fighting off car sickness except to stop and get out, and, although to vomit over the black leather seats would be the ultimate degradation, he could not ask that. He just had to hang on, battling every yard of their progress in the creeping traffic; not thinking beyond, of their time of arrival, of their destination. He tried to mark each street, craning to read the names. He concentrated on the advertisements on the buses and hoardings—every one seemed to be for whiskey or gin or beer or, in bright characters that leapt out at him, for milk.

They passed the bottom of Panton Place, but he could hardly connect it with anything in his mind except the ingestion of chocolate Swiss roll. He swallowed desperately and gripped the daffodils on his knees, crushing their bright yellow trumpets.

Even when the car finally stopped and they got out and went up the steps of the police station and along the familiar green corridor, Jordan hardly dared relax his inner concentration to ask for the lavatory. He asked, and as he did so he knew it was only a matter of seconds.

With the impatient paternal tolerance of a father left in charge of a child at the seaside, Symington escorted him to the place and waited as Jordan staggered into one of the open cubicles and knelt tremblingly on the damp stone floor. The stained bowl, a cigarette end shredding gently in the yellowish water, was a vision of surcease. But he only managed to bring up a trickle of brown watery matter—remnant of uneaten meals. The agony of his empty retching gradually dwindled and at length he was able to stand up, the bitter taste filling his mouth and his eyelashes wet with tears.

The water in the tap was cold and there was no towel. He dried his hands and face on his handkerchief. As he followed Symington, he felt as though he were being led to an operation where the surgeons would slice open his stomach and read his guts for portents. He would accept it gladly, in return for a dose of anaesthesia and long drugged weeks straight in a hospital bed.

It was a different room this time. Larger, with two desks at right angles. George was sitting at one, and Symington took his place at the other. Jordan sat down uncertainly, not knowing who was going to ask the questions or whom he should face.

In front of each officer was a cup of tea. Jordan longed for one; but he determined to maintain his silence—to say nothing until he was asked.

But he wasn't asked. George sipped his tea and said carefully, "I must warn you, Maddox, that anything you say will be taken down in writing and may be given in evidence." Then he went on drinking.

The telephone rang and George picked it up. He listened for a minute, then hung up without having said a word.

57

Jordan looked at Symington, who seemed to be absorbed in something he was writing.

"Shall I—?" He cut himself off. And then, closing his eyes for a second, he accepted as inevitable that any promise he made to himself now would almost immediately be broken. "Shall I tell you about the flowers?"

"You would be well advised to tell us everything, Maddox," said George.

"Well, I will." He paused because he sensed the policeman knew something he did not know; there was something that George was grimly withholding from him. Perhaps if he could find it out and—tell *them*. Perhaps it would be alright. "It's only the flowers that I forgot to tell you about," he said.

But the superintendent didn't respond.

"I'll tell you about the flowers then." He tried to order his thoughts, but it was hard to do in the face of George's impassive hostility. "I told you, really, in the car, but . . ." He began again the vapid tale of how he had brought tulips to June.

As he talked, he found he didn't care what he said. If it sounded as though he had carried an offering of love to his mistress, very well. Not to worry—it was almost a physical relief.

"Again," George said dryly.

"What?" Jordan was dragged from his pleasing mist of incoherence.

"Let's go over that again."

He started to protest; but protestation would use up more energy than compliance. But this time it was not so easy. George kept harshly interrupting him.

"How many flowers, Maddox?"

"I don't know. Quite a few. I didn't look at them."

"Six, eight, ten?"

"Eight. I don't know. I really don't—"

"Seven?"

"It might have been seven."

"There were seven tulips, weren't there, Maddox?"

"Alright. There were seven. Seven tulips and some leaves."

"Leaves? That's new. Tell me about the leaves."

He couldn't really remember about the leaves. He'd just thrown them in for good measure. There must, of course, have been leaves.

58

There always were. He didn't know what kind—but eventually they settled on rhododendron leaves.

"And what did Singer do with them when you gave them to her?"

"I told you. I didn't give them to her. I just left them there for her. I probably said she'd have more use for them than I would or something like that."

"In other words, you gave them to her."

"If you want it that way. Alright—I gave her the flowers."

"What did she do with them?"

"I don't know what she did with them."

"Did she put them in water?"

"I don't remember. I don't think she did anything with them."

"Think, Maddox."

He tried. All he wanted to do was shut his eyes and go whirling off to a place of private peace. But he had to concentrate. He found himself concentrating only on the possible right answer. "I suppose she put them in water. It would have been the logical thing to do." He tried to detect from George's countenance whether or not he had given the correct reply. If only he could get a hint of what it was the superintendent was hiding, what he was holding up his sleeve.

And then he had it—up his sleeve. He'd had it all the time. He even managed to smile at his own obtuseness. Up his sleeve—the short deep scratch the cat next door had given him. There was no cat next door. They'd probably checked that already. They had certainly got the results of the skin test. So they knew that too.

And suddenly Jordan didn't mind any more. He knew what they wanted, and he would tell them, tell them the truth, and then it would be all over and they would be happy and he would be happy. But wouldn't tell them at once. He'd save it up a little—as they had saved up their knowledge—and there was something oddly exciting about that thought.

As George pushed and pried, Jordan answered gently. The superintendent's hard anger didn't worry him—he'd make the old man smile again soon. The only discomfort he felt now was the dryness of his mouth—and hunger. He was actually hungry. They brought him a sandwich at one point. He was surprised to see that it was lunchtime. A cheese sandwich—stale, butterless bread. But he ate it. He didn't mention his great thirst. The slaking of it he held out to himself as a kind of reward.

59

The superintendent leaned back in his chair and lit a cigarette; there was something particularly ridiculous about the tiny Woodbine in that huge hand.

"You're in very serious trouble, Maddox. You're a well-educated man—do you really think it's amusing to be flippant in your situation? Or wise, Maddox? Is that what they teach you at Oxford?"

"Cambridge."

"I don't care a bugger where it was!" said George loudly. There was a momentary tremor in Jordan's good humour—but he clung to the comfort of the simple explanation he would give, when the cobwebs would be swept away. "I think," he said, "you're making a fuss about nothing."

George grunted. "It might interest you to hear we've got the results of the skin test." His voice was quiet now. "It's no use beating about the bush."

"Oh, I know that." In fact, it was rather funny. Quite a joke.

"What exactly do you know?"

"I know the results are positive. That's obvious." He smiled at the alert expression on George's face—poor chap, he was on pins and needles. "It's quite simple."

"Then it won't be any trouble to tell, will it?"

"Quite." He savoured the moment. "That memory of mine again, I'm afraid." He gave a little laugh. He lifted up his wrist and pulled his sleeve back to show the thin thread of scab. "June scratched me, you see. It was an accident, of course. I remember when we went up the stairs to her room, she warned me about the carpet at the top— the runner had come away and it was loose. Well, when I left, she didn't come all the way to the door with me. She came to the top of the stairs. And as I turned to say goodbye, my foot—right foot, if you want to know—skidded. I was holding the typewriter in my left hand, with the manuscript under the same arm, so that I couldn't steady myself on the banister. I must have instinctively put out my right hand, and June tried to grab it. But all she managed to do was give me a rather nasty scratch on the back of my wrist. I stumbled down a couple of steps but didn't hurt myself. She was very upset about it. Wanted to put iodine on it, et cetera. And, well—" he smiled—"that's about it. She went back to her room, and I went off to the office."

He waited, but the policeman just stared at him. Perhaps it wasn't a huge joke, but at least, Jordan thought irritably, it was worth some reaction.

Then George turned to Symington. "Did you note that down, Bill?"

"Yes, sir."

"Well, tear it up. We won't be needing that page."

Jordan was puzzled. Was it a jest? "Surely . . ." he began.

"When did you think that one up?" asked George mildly.

"Think . . . I didn't . . . Don't be absurd. It's absolutely true. That's what happened." He felt a frightful lurching in his stomach.

"Wouldn't convince a child of two."

"But, good lord . . ." His voice trembled. He tried to get control of it. "Can I have a drink of water?"

"Help yourself." George indicated a jug and a glass on top of the filing cabinet.

Jordan got up. He clutched the jug tightly, but even so spilled water as he filled the glass. He drank one glass, two, three. It was warm and heavily chlorinated, and went from his lips to his throat without moistening his leather-dry mouth.

As he sat down, he felt the water flushing last night's whiskey into his bloodstream. He was beginning to feel sick again.

"Now!" said George sharply.

Jordan jerked as though he had been hit.

"The truth, Maddox." He picked up his pipe and tapped the bowl rhythmically on the desk. "No more mucking about. What happened?"

"But I've told you. You really must accept it."

The tapping ceased. "Did you strangle her from in front or behind?" Immediately he'd asked the question, he started rapping again.

"I didn't strangle her. I didn't touch her." This was unfair.

"From behind, wasn't it?" Tap-tap, tap-tap.

"No," Jordan raised his voice above the noise of the pipe against the desk. "I tell you, I didn't even touch her!"

"You had quite a tussle, didn't you?"

"No!" They should be typing up his statement now; they should be letting him alone.

"Did you knock the clock down?"

61

"No, I didn't even—"

"June knocked it down, did she?"

"No—I . . . How do I know wh—"

"What'd you hit her with?"

"I didn't hit her."

The staccato became more rapid, ceasing only when George asked a question. Asked? Thrust it, propelled it at Jordan.

"You got in a panic, Maddox, didn't you?"

"No. I don't know—"

"You left your scarf in a panic, Maddox?"

"No—"

"You dropped the key because you were panicked, Maddox?"

"What key? I don't know what you're—"

"Where did you get the key? Where?"

"I don't—"

"We *know* where you got the key, Maddox! Where?"

He couldn't think. Wildly his mind ran over car keys, garage keys, typewriter keys.

"Where, Maddox? Where?"

The bowl of the pipe was hammering at his head now. Perhaps he did have a key. What key? Which key?

"Where, Maddox?" That was Symington. Jordan turned to look at the inspector, and, as he did so, George cut in harshly, "Forget about the key. What did you hit her with? Your fist?"

"The clock?" Symington.

George: "Did she scream?"

"How long did it take?" Symington.

"You just dropped everything and ran, didn't you?" George.

"Panicked, Maddox!"

"Frightened, Maddox?"

As he twisted from one to the other, the pipe blows rapping at his skull, he heard his own voice, high and plaintive, calling again and again: "I didn't do it! I didn't do it!"

He knew that it was a form of madness, he even cried to them, "You're mad!" but he no longer knew who was mad. If he was mad, then sanity lay with them.

"Let me alone, let me alone!"

Abruptly the questions ceased, the hammering stopped.

He heard a voice say, "Don't be too hard on him, Mr. George."

And in the sudden peace, he looked up to see the shimmering figure of Symington standing beside the superintendent. It was then he realised he had been crying. If he had wept in panic, now he was overcome with gratitude. Symington was on his side; he'd misjudged Symington. He glanced at George. If only he would relax his grimness too.

Slowly the lines in the superintendent's face softened. "Well, perhaps you're right, Bill." Bill—George—Jordan; it was going to be okay now.

"If . . ." said George. "If." He leaned forward. "Why don't you tell us, son, uh?"

"It's not so hard, is it?" Symington murmured.

He felt the sweet weakness of sex in his thighs.

"Think of yourself, lad," said George quietly, almost sadly. "Think of your wife—and your little girl, Maddox. Now wouldn't it be better for everybody just to have done with it, just to get it over with?"

Yes, God, yes. He didn't think of Willy or Georgia. He wasn't even thinking of himself. Smiling, he felt himself touched by the ineffable grace of surrender. They were his friends. He opened his mouth to speak.

There was a bang behind him, steps. He half turned. A voice said, "Sorry, sir, didn't know you were using number five." The door slammed shut.

Jordan looked back to the policemen. They had not altered their positions—they bent gently towards him like priests.

Like priests. Jordan took out his handkerchief and wiped his face.

Like vultures!

He put away his handkerchief and met George's stare. "Go to hell!" he said.

7

And then it all began again.

Perhaps if he had realised the hard arrogant retribution which George would exact, he would have stayed silent.

But he had regained a partial ability to think, at least, and he was struck with the obvious thought that if they had all the proof they needed to arrest him, then surely they'd arrest him. If they arrested him, well and good. But if not—he would not give in to browbeating.

Although Symington wasn't browbeating. He disappeared for a time and came back and gave Jordan a statement, which he signed. He read it—but as he read each sentence, he promptly forgot it. He was left with the vague impression that he had said a lot of silly, damaging things. But these were of no importance.

He was worn down, worn to the bone, but he didn't break. He resisted the rage and the blandishments, the wooing and the shouting. But he saw it now as a kind of bargain—they must give him something for what he gave them. But it was up to them to make the first move, to make the offer. So long as they kept asking him, a non-swimmer, to dive into a deep pool without hope of a lifebelt, he would refuse.

"If you're so sure, arrest me," he said over and over again. It became a taunt, his only weapon. He was sorry to have to use it, but it was only fair that if his soul was being demanded of him, he should at least be promised a bed and a cell in return.

And then suddenly, without explanation, they both departed and left him alone. He was sorry to see them go. But he knew they'd be back.

He stretched a little and stood up. He wandered about the room, sat for a bit behind George's desk. He tried all the drawers. They were locked. Symington's desk and the file cabinet, too. Sensible fellows. He felt quite at home. Everything was locked up at home too.

He looked at his watch. Twenty minutes past four. They'd been gone nearly half an hour. It was early. He began to get a little bored and started to repeat aloud all the limericks he could remember. A feeble lot. Clerihews. He could only think of three.

Half past four. He'd give them another ten minutes.

Where the hell were they? Probably eating their dinner—or high tea or whatever they called it. He was annoyed; he was hungry himself. There wasn't even any water left in the jug.

At quarter to five he looked out into the deserted green corridor. He went back inside. But he could not sit still.

At five he left the room and went a little way along the corridor. He stopped outside room number four—his old room. He tapped at the door. No answer. He went in. Nobody there.

64

Perhaps the police had gone on strike.

He went to the end of the corridor and the entrance hall.

The sergeant at the desk looked up. "Good evening, sir."

"Good evening." Jordan was nonplussed. There were only the double doors between him and the street.

He made up his mind. If they wanted him that much, they'd have to come looking for him. He went to the door.

"Excuse me, sir."

Jordan turned eagerly.

"Are these yours, sir?" The sergeant held up the bunch of this morning's daffodils.

"Oh." Jordan went slowly to the desk. "Yes," he said.

"Here you are then. I had the stems in water all day, so you'll find them fresh."

Reluctantly Jordan accepted the flowers. He stood, holding the wet stems.

"Anything else, was there, sir?"

"No," he answered. Then angrily, "Nothing at all."

He turned and left the station, down the steps and into the street. He walked slowly. At the corner, he glanced back at the Bristol-blue lamp. He felt let down.

So what he needed was a pick-me-up.

He began to move quickly. Soon he was in the King's Road. He went into a pub and ordered a double gin and orange. It was a large, anonymous and practically empty pub. He liked it.

He had five gins—doubles—a sausage roll, a Cornish pasty, a pickled onion and a hunk of Wensleydale. He left because the place was getting full and because there was a man in the corner who looked like a policeman. He wanted to see if the man would follow him. But when he got outside he forgot about it.

He still had the daffodils in his hand when he entered the train for Woodley. Between Waterloo and Vauxhall, he let down the window and flung the flowers into the dark. Then he went to sleep.

He woke up three stations down the line from Woodley. It was half past eight when he finally got into his car and drove home. As the car zigzagged over the white line and back again—always back again—he tried to sing. But his gentle euphoria was vanishing.

As he turned into the drive, he scraped the wing against the gatepost. Somehow that made him feel better.

Willy was waiting for him in the living room.

He looked at her, sitting, her hands folded in her lap.

"I've—" she started to say.

"Alright, alright. I know. You've been ringing me all afternoon."

She stood up. "Jordan, I rang Tom."

He crossed the room. "Haven't we got any gin?"

"Jordan, I know where you've been. I rang Tom and he rang Sarah Street. They said you were there. They said you refused to speak to him."

Jordan slopped whiskey into a glass. "Maybe I did. Talking to Tom isn't my idea of a cosy chat." The whiskey tasted vile, but he drank it.

"Jordan," she stood, hands together—like a maiden in prayer, he thought. "Jordan, what is wrong?"

"Nothing's wrong."

"Why don't you tell me?"

"Tell you what? There's nothing to tell." Cold, miserable, forlorn —she might at least have lit a fire. She could learn a lesson from the police about heating.

"Please, Jordan. You never tell me anything. Please."

"Blast and damnation. I haven't got anything to tell you. Why do you always accuse me of not telling you things?"

"I'm not accusing you, Jordan."

He laughed. "About the only one who isn't."

"I'm your wife. You must tell me what happened today."

Cold as any icicle, he thought. Hard to rhyme *icicle*. Bicycle—then what? He'd forgotten Georgia's verse for tonight. "How's Georgia?"

"Jordan, I won't be put off. Don't you realise you have a responsibility? Surely—"

Something curdled inside him. "Oh . . ." He hesitated. He saw the tiny movement at her temples. "Oh, alright," he said. What was the use?

He didn't tell her much. Just that he'd made another statement. Grudgingly he mentioned the scratch and explained the significance of it to her. He felt miserly.

"We must ring Tom at once."

"No."

"Jordan, of course we must!"

"I forbid you to telephone Short."

Her cheekbones reddened. "Why? But why?"

Because he wasn't going to have anyone else interfering. Because he'd just about had enough of it. Because . . . there were five thousand reasons. He was absolutely determined.

They stood and stared at each other in silence.

The bell was a relief.

"If that's Tom, tell—"

"It's the doorbell, Jordan, not the phone."

He smiled—he must be really very tight.

As she went to the door, he stood in the living room, wondering if it could possibly be anyone but the police. In Woodley nobody called after six. He switched on the lamps at either side of the fireplace, but the light only made the room more gloomy.

They came in behind Willy, expressionless in their raincoats.

"Hello, Superintendent," he said. "Had a nice trip down? Darling, this is Superintendent—sorry, Chief Superintendent George and Inspector . . . I'm awfully sorry, I've forgotten your name."

"Jordan John Maddox—"

"Symington! That's it." They had spoken simultaneously.

The superintendent paused and then started again.

"Jordan John Maddox, I'm going to arrest you for the murder of June Emily Singer."

He was embarrassed. How ridiculous to feel embarrassed, he thought. He smiled at Willy. "Well," he said and coughed a little.

"You are not obliged to say anything at this time, but if you do so it will be taken down in writing and may be given in evidence."

There was the familiar snap of Symington's notebook.

"Yes," he said. And then again, "Well."

"You'll have to come with us."

"I see."

"We must ring Tom," said Willy.

"Is that alright?" Jordan asked. It didn't matter now—let her have her way. "He's my solicitor."

George nodded, and Willy went quickly to the telephone in the hall.

"Like a drink, Mr. George?"

"No."

"Okay for me to have one?"

"We don't have much time."

"I'll make it a quick one, then." He felt a rush of affability. "One for the road." He'd like to make them feel at home. It would be fascinating to sit down and have a long chat with the superintendent—what an interesting life he must have had. Symington, too, of course.

Inspector Symington moved his stance a little so that he could watch Jordan pour the drink. "It's alright, Inspector, I'm not going to do a Himmler."

Symington looked at his watch.

"I suppose I'll be allowed to pack an overnight bag?"

"I expect your wife can do that."

"What a good idea." He took a sip of the drink. "It was quick work, Mr. George, wasn't it?" The superintendent said nothing. "Barely had time to get back here before you turned up. I've still got my coat on, see?" He didn't object to their silence—all part of the job. He knew now they were not waxworks. "Extraordinary, really, isn't it? A week ago I bet you didn't even know I existed. Even last week I was still only—what?—a potential witness. And now here I am—a prisoner. It's a bit of a joke. The sort of thing you dream about. Then you wake up and the laugh's on you. Not that I mind. And it's not nightmarish or anything. Just a rather interesting dream. Of course I know it's real. My Aunt Mary would say I was frivolous," he laughed. "Did you ever read *The Diary of a Nobody*, Superintendent?"

George shook his head.

"What a pity. You wouldn't remember then."

Willy came into the room. "He's coming over at once."

"I'm afraid we can't wait, ma'am," said George. "If you would be good enough to pack some things for your husband, we'll be off."

"Oh, but Mr. Short is only two minutes away in the car," Willy said protestingly. And Jordan felt sorry for her. She caught the smile he'd meant for her reassurance and she opened her lips as if to snap back at him. But instead she turned away and said to the superintendent, "I'll go and pack. I won't be long."

They heard her going up the stairs.

Jordan coughed. Whiskey always made him cough. "As I was saying. Pooter—he's the nobody, the hero—"

"If you take my advice, Maddox, you'll remember you do not have

68

to say anything at this juncture," George said evenly. "You may make a further statement at the station, if you wish to do so."

Jordan was a bit dashed. He'd noticed Symington jotting down everything he'd said. But he supposed his remarks were not the kind of thing one "gave in evidence."

They waited in silence.

Tom Short arrived before Willy came downstairs. Symington let him in.

"Hello, Tom, sorry to get you out of bed."

Tom Short was startled. "Bed?"

"From your dinner then."

Tom examined Jordan closely for a second, then said to the superintendent, "You have a warrant for the arrest? I'm Mr. Maddox's lawyer."

"Yes, sir." George reached into his pocket.

"That's alright." Tom waved his hand. "You taking him to Sarah Street?"

"Yes, sir."

"He'll be coming up tomorrow, I suppose?"

"No, sir. Wednesday, at Sarah Street."

"Why the delay?"

"Couldn't say, sir."

"Hum. Wednesday." He took out his diary and made a note. "I'll want to see Mr. Maddox tomorrow then."

"Very good, sir."

"Like a drink, Tom?" said Jordan.

"No thanks."

"Worried about the pot?"

Tom ignored that one. "Where's Willy?"

"Upstairs, packing a toothbrush for me."

Tom nodded. "Did you make a statement today?"

"I suppose you'd call it that."

"Well, don't make another. You haven't said anything now, have you?"

"No—oh, well, I was just talking to Mr. George here about Pooter, that's all."

Tom opened his eyes wide. "Sometimes I think you publishers ought to be locked up."

Jordan laughed.

"Sorry," said Tom. "We'll have to start thinking about getting someone briefed. We might get Bartlett with luck."

"Who's Bartlett?"

"Geoffrey Bartlett. Good man. Well, that's my worry. Oh, and about Willy, don't you worry about her. I'll look after her. She and Georgia might come and stay with Norah until—"

"It all blows over?" Jordan felt that he could quite easily fall into a deep pool of warm laughter if he didn't watch out.

"It may take a little time," said Tom heartily, "but don't you worry."

Jordan looked round to see Willy and realised that Tom's heartiness had been for her benefit.

"Hello, Tom."

"Hello, Willy. I was just telling Jordan—"

"Yes, I heard."

"Is that the bag, Mrs. Maddox?" asked the superintendent.

"Yes."

"Well," said Tom, automatically rubbing his hands, "all set, then?" As if he were about to lead a team onto a rugger field, thought Jordan.

They trooped out into the hall.

"Goodbye, Jordan." Willy touched his cheek swiftly with hers.

"Goodbye. Georgia—is she asleep?"

"Yes, I just looked in."

"Well, take care of her. And of yourself, Willy."

"And you too," she said. In the badly lit hall her face seemed softer. Jordan smiled. "They'll take care of me alright."

And then he was outside and Superintendent George was holding open the door of the police car.

As he moved to get in, Jordan remembered something. "Oh, Willy. By the way, I scraped the wing coming in this evening. You might take it into the garage tomorrow and have it fixed." The last nagging duty done.

"Half a minute, Jordan." Tom laid a hand on his shoulder. He leaned forward. "Pull yourself together, man, and don't say a word," in a whispered hiss. And then, stepping back, cheerfully, "Chin up. See you tomorrow."

And then they were away, out of the gate and onto the Woodley road.

Jordan sat in the warmth of the back seat, beside Superintendent George. He was exhausted—and potted. But he didn't feel sick at all.

The car rushed on through the darkness. He smiled. Soon he was asleep.

A DREAM OF SUMMER

8

He lay in a kind of dream.

It was so warm in his small, private ward that he was perpetually drowsy. The prison authorities couldn't be faulted on their heating arrangements, at least not in the hospital wing.

Unbound by any necessity, his mind wandered languidly among great subjects. He moved slowly in a large garden, noting here and there a summerhouse, a pool with swans, a treed alcove or a path of immaculate stone slabs ending at an iron gate in the wall. He was happy that all these things were there, waiting for him, and the knowledge that one day he would investigate them was a pleasure—a promised treat enriched by postponement. He was not in the mood, now, for exploration.

It was the small things to which he gave his attention: the way a dandelion grew among the grass, the dusty-textured branch of an apple tree, the marks of a rake upon the gravel.

He was exhausted easily.

Outside he thought of it as being summer. A summer afternoon. Only his visitors brought the winter with them, and he was glad to see them go. He would come eagerly back to his private prison and lie down again on the bed or do a little more work on Uncle John's puzzles.

The afternoon was always the best time, for it was largely his own. The business of the prison took place in the morning: the sudden flash of lights, the rising and shaving and dressing, the vast breakfasts brought over from Ben's Café, the orderly to make his bed and straighten and dust, the scheduled trip to the lavatory, the daily visit of the medical officer, sometimes a pallid chat with the prison psychiatrist, and half an hour of private circular exercise in the prison yard. And always the effort of banter with Prison Officer Denver or Orderly Samson or whoever else was on duty. He was under constant observation, of course, and perhaps they sought to ease the coldness of that by talking, or perhaps they simply thought he needed human company. He hadn't the heart to tell them he would prefer to be silently observed. But at least the garrulity was a thousand times better then the first night's horrible proximity of bodies in the large ward. He had not slept, then, at all, but had listened all night to the snufflings and snores and the dreamt obscenities until the glare of lights and the almost immediate jolly pounding of the Light Programme.

They were all murderers, or mad or psychopathic, but it was not this which had—well, yes—frightened him. It was the awful alacrity of their companionship. It was as if they had been looking forward to his arrival. " 'ere, can see you never had to make your own bed," one of them had said. "Want to get the corners squared off, like this"; and he had shown Jordan how to do it. And another had fingered his suit. "Nice bit of cloth there, Maddie. You want to save that, mucker. You want to ask for a prison-issue suit, like mine, see, and put that away." They had happily shared the breakfast he couldn't eat. They had been eager for him to play dominoes.

When the governor had told him he could have a private ward if he paid for it—and service, and meals sent in—Jordan felt as though he had been granted his life. "You are entitled to anything you may want, Maddox. Within reason, of course." Major Forster smiled, and his silken smooth lips were at once cut with a thousand tiny vertical wrinkles. "Write and receive all the letters you want. Newspapers, provided you pay for them . . ."

Not newspapers, no. He hadn't read a paper since he'd been in. Nor had he once turned on the ancient wireless in his room. He wanted silence and privacy, and, except for the prison ritual which had already become second nature, he got it. They treated him kindly, as an invalid, and he was quite contented.

The termination of all this would be the first, the day his trial began. Occasionally he would get out his engagement diary and turn the pages, day after blank day interrupted only by some royal birthday or a full moon, until the first of May, where he had marked in capitals, *TRIAL BEGINS*. It was still several days away—but the distance was not to be measured in days, any more than the entry that used to

76

appear in his diary three times a year, *TERM BEGINS,* had indicated an actuality. For time—the waiting time of holidays or, now, of prison—had no urgency and thus, no measure. It was like God, the God of the Church of England, who was, maybe, bright up there in his heaven but whose reflection in the world was dim and gentle, like the long complex sermons that Uncle Trevor preached on Abana and Pharpar, rivers of Damascus. One did not count days.

He put the diary away and lit a cigarette. He was careful to let the ash fall into the cracked white ashtray. Like the brown Bakelite hood of the wireless, it could only have been produced in hideous and inconceivable mass which could not ask, let alone demand, any variety of affection or effort of eye. There was nothing in the small room with its white-washed walls to suggest that any particular person had ever lived there, or would in the future, or, except for the lazily flaunting smoke, lived there now.

He smoked twenty or thirty cigarettes a day, against the ponderous advice of Wilcox and, now, the sprightly admonitions of Dr. Hogben, the M.O. He had read somewhere recently that cigarette smoking was no longer considered harmful in a case of inactive tuberculosis. He'd tell that to Wilcox one day, who would of course grow red and mutter about professional competence. Yet it also pleased Jordan to think that maybe smoking was harmful. It would be a sin of commission at last.

He smiled to himself, as he often did nowadays. He had miraculously recovered the amusement of trivial thoughts, which only now did he realise that he had so long lost. His mind was garrulous, like a child or an old man laughing and nodding as he talked. Perhaps by some circuitous route he had inherited the dottiness of Uncle John.

I have not done the things I ought to have done, and I have done the things I ought not to have done. For him it had always been the first—the meal he could not quite finish, the hair not brushed, the bed not made.

He lit a new cigarette from the stub of the old.

He would have no visitors today.

9

"Can I come in, Uncle John?"

John turned his head quickly to look at Jordan in the doorway of the little attic workroom built under the eaves. John's worktable faced the high dormer window, immediately below which was a narrow shelf arrayed with a long row of small glass jars of tempera, blue and purple and crimson and orange and scarlet and yellow. On the right, easy to John's hand, were fretsaws and knives and chisels and planes, each in its bracket on the pine plank partition wall in perfect size order. Above them were bookshelves heavy with the faded splendour of military and regimental histories.

"Yes, yes," said John. "But not a sound out of you. No sound." He always said this, and the rule would be strictly enforced for five minutes or so.

Jordan sat down with his back to the window, on the chair to the left of the worktable.

Uncle John dipped his paintbrush into the tin of clear liquid and applied it to the rectangle of wood before him with clean, even strokes. There was something almost ferocious about his face as he worked. This was the only time his square military shoulders ever unbent.

The room smelled of wood. Wooden floor, wooden roof, wooden walls, stored wood ranged against one wall and carefully marked for size in Uncle John's minute handwriting, wooden worktable, wooden chairs. Jordan moved his head slowly (so as not to disturb his uncle's concentration), enumerating all the wooden objects in his mind. Then he would go to metal, then cloth, and finally human beings. He would not be ready to talk until he had reached this happy climax. He regarded the classification of animal, vegetable and mineral as silly. Wood was supposed to be vegetable—he could just see Aunt Mary serving up a plate of wood with the Irish stew. "Eat up your wood, my dear, like a good boy." He let out a little giggle. John paused and glanced sideways at him, and then continued his brushwork.

And animal—was Uncle John an animal?

Irish stew was revolting—what awful people the Irish must be. Or perhaps he should feel sorry for them: "We must be charitable to our Irish friends." Jordan tried a purse-lipped Uncle Trevor face. But the point was, he didn't *have* any Irish friends. And what's more, he didn't care.

It was a day for not caring, he decided, guiltily defiant of the chilling plate of half-eaten stew that would wait all afternoon for him on the dining-room table. "Go up to your room, my dear, and don't come down until you are prepared to be sensible and finish what you have begun."

The afternoon sun shone straight in, glimmering the few white hairs in Uncle John's tobacco-brown moustache.

"What are you doing?" said Jordan.

"Varnish, Jordan, varnish."

Uncle John always called him Jordan. With Aunt Mary it was *my dear*, and Uncle Trevor *my boy*, and Uncle Colin *old chap* or, contradictorily, *young-feller-me-lad*, in about equal proportions. The maids called him *Master Jordan* and the postman *son* or *sonny*, which was worst of all. But for Uncle John it was always Jordan, except once (when Jordan had almost been run over by a van) when it had been *man*—"Look out, man!"

Sitting in the attic, he felt mannish.

"Is it a puzzle?"

"Will be. Not yet. Have to cut it yet."

"Are you going to cut it now?"

"Let the varnish dry first. The third coat. Must be absolutely hard. Hard as a French girl's heart—ha!—as we used to say." He drew the brush over the surface of the painted wood in one last smooth stroke.

Jordan was familiar with every step in the making of a puzzle. First the infinitely careful tracings from a plate in one of the books or from an old etching, of which John had hundreds filed in an old chest of drawers. The tiny additions and alterations and, with the aid of different sizes of graph paper, the enlargement or diminution of scenes or even individual figures; the master tracing and the transfer of the whole to the perfectly sanded surface of the plywood. And then the painting—the tiny delicate touches of the brush from saucer to wood, sometimes with the aid of a magnifying glass, and all the time the

79

unyielding ferocity of John's blue-eyed glare. The painting alone often took as long as three months. The varnishing and the intricate fretsaw work that followed were comparatively simple.

But although Jordan knew all this, he still liked to ask. And Uncle John answered invariably as though he'd heard the question for the first time. Only the subject of the puzzle was taboo until, if it were not to be given to Jordan, the very last stages.

"Can I have a look, Uncle John?"

"No. Mustn't spoil the fun."

"Is it for me then? Is it for my birthday?"

"No. This one is for your Uncle Colin. It's his turn this year." He squinted up into the sun.

"For Christmas? But that's miles away. Besides Uncle Colin isn't my proper uncle."

"Ah, well, but he's been seconded, so to speak. To the family. Hasn't he?"

"But he's *always* been sconded."

"Seconded. That makes him one of us. He messes with us, eh?—when he's here."

"Only at Christmas."

"I'll tell you what. I'll let you do the trial run on this one."

"Really? Do you really mean it?"

"Of course I do." For a moment Uncle John was huffy. "I said it." He put the brush in a small pot of turpentine. "Got to see it all fits properly, haven't we?"

"Aren't I getting a puzzle for my birthday?"

"Yes."

"What'll it be—what'll it be of?"

"Ha—that's a surprise. Military secret. But it's a good one, I'll tell you that. One of the best."

Jordan was satisfied. He didn't really want to spoil the surprise. "What's this one then?" he said.

"Colin's? Minden. A great battle, Minden. A great infantry victory. Minden day. The Unsurpassable Six . . ." He stared out of the dormer, and his hands, busily tapping the lid into place on the tin of varnish, paused.

"Tell me a battle, Uncle John."

"Eh—what's that you say, Jordan?" He blinked down at the little boy. "A battle *now*? That's for lights out. Can't tell you a battle now."

80

"That's alright then," said Jordan, knowing that his irregular request had somehow upset his uncle.

"You should be out on the terrain."

"I can't. I'm supposed to be in my room. I didn't finish my lunch and Aunt Mary sent me up to my room."

"You shouldn't be here then?" Uncle John said doubtfully. And then, straightening his shoulders, "Must obey orders, you know, Jordan. First rule. Don't want to be court-martialled."

Jordan shook his head.

"Well then. Better nip down to your room, hadn't you?"

"Yes." Jordan slipped slowly off the chair and went to the door.

"Jordan."

"Yes, Uncle?"

"Your birthday. It's not far away now, is it?"

"June the twenty-sixth."

"How'd you like to go to Istoke Park and hear the band, eh?"

"Istoke Park!"

"A birthday treat. A good band that day, first-rate—"

"Uncle John—but would Aunt Mary . . . ?"

"Have to clear it with Mary, of course. Don't see why not, though. It's your birthday. First-rate. Band of the First Battalion Scots Guards. Doing a tour, I believe. The Kiddies."

"The kiddies?"

"Nickname. Formed after the Grenadiers—First Regiment of Food Guards then, of course—and the Coldstream. 1662. They were the junior regiment of foot guards until the formation of the Irish Guards. The youngsters, you know. The Kiddies."

"The Kiddies." Jordan and his uncle smiled at each other. "Thank you very much, Uncle John. I'd love to go."

He went down the bare wooden stairs from the attic, humming to himself a tune into which easily fitted the words, "I'm going to see the Kiddies, the Kiddies, the Kiddies. I'm going to see the Kiddies at Istoke Park."

I O

He pressed gently into place the gold chevrons of the serjeant of the Lancashire Fusiliers. It was the last piece. The Dettingen puzzle was complete. Dettingen, Blenheim, Salamanca—he had done each several times. He had remembered, even at his first try, the masses, the colours, the stiff-legged stance of Uncle John's soldiers. The puzzles were child's play for him.

He was probably the only person ever to have done any of John's puzzles. He could not imagine Colin or Uncle Trevor or Aunt Mary, each of whom in turn had received one every third Christmas for so many years, sitting down to sort out a puzzle. The infinite care of John's painting—the detail of dress and equipment, of colour and cannon and position—was an unconsidered trifle. But in Jordan's mind each battle flourished, each drum beat, each bugle blew, each army marched.

Even today, military music—a band playing magnificently on a bandstand—made him want to weep.

He lifted the puzzle on a sheet of paper and slid it into the flat wooden box. He shut the lid and latched it. For the first week he'd had to make do with the prison puzzles—scenes of merry England, garish and ghastly, on poor, thin cardboard. Until at last the governor, bewildered but benign, had permitted Jordan to import his own.

Willy had brought all she could find. Everyone seemed to approve. The puzzles would, as Tom said, "take your mind off things."

Tom thought it his duty to come at least every other day and "bring the news," "keep you up to date" with manufactured details of hope. He was due today.

Jordan got up restlessly from the chair. Hope—what did he care? Before these conferences Jordan would be possessed with an irritated impatience to get the performance over with. Afterwards, and sometimes even during the interview, he would be amused at the ponderous sympathy for the man he was supposed to be. How could he tell them that he was quite happy and undisturbed in this place? Here, by himself, he was young, but each visitor made an old man of him.

But he couldn't let them down.

He had always disliked interviews—the cold, anxiously Christian sessions in the study with Uncle Trevor on "Your new School," "Why God made us the way we are," "The University," "The Sanctity of Love," "The Responsibility of Marriage"; or those rare moments with Colin when the gruff, kindly tone and the caustic twinkle were dropped to reveal an awkward, sidelong sincerity.

Yet there had been one which had been a pleasure—the most dreaded, perhaps, of all. The scholarship interview. That array of serious faces that could not but be wasting their time on J. J. Maddox, a somewhat doubtful candidate, until that unexpected question on military tactics. He'd lectured them for ten minutes with no interruption.

And he had won his scholarship—exhibition, rather.

Annie, whose mother was Sibley's postmistress, had brought the telegram with her up to work at the rectory one morning just after Christmas.

And Annie had been the first to know—the only person it mattered should know.

"Jordan, I'm so pleased." She had touched his arm.

He had not been able to stop smiling, from Annie to the telegram and back to Annie.

"Wouldn't Colonel John have been proud!" she had said.

"I'd never have got it if it hadn't been for Uncle John." And he had told her in a sudden expansive flurry about the interview. And then he knew that for some reason she wanted to cry.

She had said quickly, "I must get on with my work. And you'll want to be telling Miss Freeman and the Rector."

"No. No—I don't want to tell them yet." He could already imagine Trevor's damply fervid congratulations and Mary's praise, barbed with some moralistic axiom. "No, they can wait." It was not their satisfaction, but his own. "I'd like to—I'll tell you what. Let's ride over to Istoke Park this afternoon. We could go to the flicks later on and have dinner at the Grange."

"I couldn't, Jordan. Really. You know I've got to study in the afternoons."

"Oh, come on, Annie. Forget the books. Let's have a bit of fun. . . ."

"Come on, Maddox. Solicitors' room for you," said Prison Officer Denver from the doorway.

The door of his room was left unlocked nearly all the time now. Presumably they had decided he was harmless, although he was quite often observed from the barred trap, which was shut at night to leave only a small peephole.

"Okay," he said, "I'm ready."

"Quite a popular demand for you, Maddox," said Denver, handing him over to another prison officer, who escorted him on his journey to the solicitors' room.

Tom was waiting. "Thank you, thank you," he said to the officer, who might have been a porter delivering a piece of baggage. "How are you, old man?"

"Alright." Jordan sat down. He looked up at the square of grey morning light high in the wall. The room was lit by a single bulb, its flex hanging lankly from the ceiling.

"Getting enough exercise and all that?"

Jordan was used by now to Tom's probing of his sexual deprivation. Others in the prison did it too—particularly the psychiatrist—but not with Tom's salacity. "Like to tell me a bit about your sex life?" the psychiatrist had said at their first meeting. When Jordan had refused, the psychiatrist had smiled, his thin, rather sharp face twisting with sincerity. "I'm not a policeman, you know. All this is absolutely confidential. Prostitutes?"

"No," Jordan had said flatly, for he realised the man was more interested in the way he spoke than in what he actually said.

"Marital sexual adjustment quite satisfactory then?"

When Jordan answered that it was normal, the psychiatrist's steady stare had flickered momentarily, as though he had found the key to a dark mystery.

"What?"

"I say, you're quite comfortable then?" repeated Tom.

"No complaints, sir."

"Ha-ha!" The mildest crack got a good deal of laughter from Tom now. Jordan wondered vaguely whether he had been a good choice of solicitor. Beneath his abrupt jollity, Tom not very effectively concealed a hard, unillusioned mind which sometimes moved close to contempt for people who did not press logic to its bitter, or profitable, end. But now Tom, with all the earnestness of a newly commissioned

84

subaltern with his first platoon, was forcing a companionate humanity that Jordan found tiring.

"Bartlett's coming to see you this afternoon."

"Oh—why?"

"You should at least be acquainted with your defence counsel. He's a very good man, Jordan, very good. I don't think we could have done better. We've had several briefing conferences—he's got a really first-rate mind." He hesitated and then went on. "He's a mite worried about one or two things."

"Such as what?"

"Well, that second statement—the one you made on March the sixteenth. It's not that it doesn't chime with the first one, but . . . well, there's so much more to it. So much more detail. If only you'd told them the whole thing before that damned skin test. Of course the beak admitted it at the preliminary examination, but Bartlett thinks there might be a good chance of excluding it."

"But why, Tom? Surely we don't have to go over this again. The statement was true. And even if it is excluded, the same ground will have to be covered."

"Ah yes, but it will be different when you're in the witness box. I mean there will be no question of duress then, or—"

"Oh Tom!" Jordan closed his eyes.

"Alright, old man. I won't press. By the way, Bartlett thinks it's a very important point in our favour that there were no fingerprints on that key."

Jordan opened his eyes. "Why?" He felt he should pacify Tom, whose irritation could almost be heard bubbling beneath the surface of his words.

"If there are no fingerprints, they must have been wiped off. Correct? But that doesn't fit the picture the police want to build up of you as a murderer. After all, for a murderer, you were pretty careless—left clues littered all over the place. The scarf she was done in with, the broken clock, the flowers, fingerprints on the coffee cup. You were very careless, of course, in the heat of passion. Just turned and ran. That will be the prosecution's line, naturally." Tom laughed. "But then the question is, why did you go to all the trouble to wipe the key clean? It doesn't fit the pattern of sudden violence and then panic."

"But I didn't touch the key—never saw it."

"No no, old boy, of course not." Tom was pleased to have to ex-

85

plain patiently. The more silly questions I ask, Jordan thought, the happier it makes him. "But the prosecution will certainly suggest that you had the key—that you let yourself in with it."

"But, Tom, if I never handled the key, how on earth could there have been fingerprints on it?"

"That's not quite the point. You're confusing what actually happened with the case that is going to be made against you. You have to find the weak points in the prosecution's case and slam into them hard. The weak point here is that the only way the prosecution can explain the absence of the fingerprints is by suggesting that you wiped the key clean, and that doesn't—"

"Wait a minute," said Jordan slowly, knowing as he spoke that it would be better left unsaid. "That's not the only explanation."

"Precisely—but the alternative explanation, that you never had or touched the key, opens a serious breach in—"

"No, there's a third possibility. I might have been wearing gloves."

"Gloves? In the house?" Tom was suddenly alert, a fat lizard.

"Yes. Until I was in the room. I always wear gloves—keep myself well wrapped up, you know."

"I see." Tom took out a tin of Benson and Hedges. He tapped the tin against the edge of the table. "I see."

"And if I'm asked in the witness box," Jordan said remorselessly, "I shall have to tell them, won't I?"

Tom opened the lid and regarded the neat white sleeves of the cigarettes. "I don't think you need me to advise you on that." He picked out a cigarette.

"Why not?"

Tom gave a lizard-quick smile. "We lawyers are a pretty stuffy bunch when it comes to ethics. Have one?"

"No, thanks."

"Drink?"

"What?"

"Would you like a drink?" Tom pulled out a hip flask and grinned, back in command.

Jordan glanced hurriedly over his shoulder at the door. "You can't —my God, you'll be in trouble if—"

"Don't worry, old man, no one's watching. You and I are guaranteed privacy." He reached for the glass that stood beside a carafe of stale water in the centre of the table.

86

"But . . ." He longed for that drink, but "There'll be hell to pay if you're caught."

Tom chuckled. "Not a chance—I never take chances." He unscrewed the cap and poured a stiff measure into the glass. "Norah gave me this thing when we were married. Never knew what to do with it. Always thought a hip flask was for racing touts. Now I wouldn't be without it. All these damn businessmen's meetings I have to go to—some of them never think to offer you a drink. But no one minds if one pops out now and again to the directors' lavatory. I've got quite a reputation for a weak bladder." He handed the glass to Jordan. "Brandy."

Jordan swallowed half of it and immediately it soothed the weariness of his bones. "You're a genius, Tom."

"Just don't breathe it all over the screws, that's all."

He smiled and drank the rest. "How is Norah?" he asked, pushing the glass over to Tom.

"Better than she's been in years. Think I'll have a nip myself. It's having Willy and Georgia in the house, you know." He poured a small tot. "It gives her something to do—particularly with Willy away these last couple of days." He drank and rinsed out the glass with water. "I suppose I sound a bit callous."

Jordan shook his head. He knew exactly the mechanical confession that was coming, but it didn't bother him now.

"It would have been different if we'd had children. Norah needed children. Not me—I can look after myself." He paused. "You're a lucky man, Jordan. I mean . . ."

Jordan smiled. "I know what you mean."

"Willy—a marvellous woman. Bearing up wonderfully. Norah says she wouldn't believe it. I came up in the train with her the other day. Willy, that is. I must say she's got guts. You know she tries to cheer me up." He laughed. "Would you believe it?"

"You two sound as though you're getting as thick as thieves."

Tom said, "I've always been fond of Willy."

They were silent for a time. "Well," said Tom eventually, "is there anything I can get for you? No? I'll leave you to your—your puzzles. Still doing those puzzles Willy tells me about?"

Jordan nodded.

"You know," said Tom, standing up, "I've been considering a rather curious possibility. June Singer—I wonder, I just wonder if she

87

wasn't in love with you without your knowing it. Have you thought of that?"

"No." Jordan shut his eyes for a moment. When he opened them, the well-being instilled by the brandy had vanished. "Would it make any difference if she had been?"

Tom rubbed his chin. "I'm not sure. I don't imagine it would, perhaps. On the other hand . . . But it's an interesting supposition, isn't it?"

Jordan was terribly tired. He got up. "Yes, very," he said.

"I thought you might think so. Never can tell where the light may dawn."

"I heard it always dawned in the east."

Tom laughed jovially. "It's a damned good thing you haven't lost your sense of humour, Jordan, old man." He suddenly became serious. "Bartlett's a bit short on humour by the way, but don't let that worry you. His mind's as keen as a razor. With his intellect and old Gladding's tenacity, we won't go far wrong."

"Gladding—oh, that's your clerk. Hasn't he given up yet?"

"Given up? By God, no! I never see him any more—he's always out interviewing somebody. We're trying to see everyone who had anything to do with June Singer, you know. School, secretarial place she was at. The lot. It's a big job. By the way, if Gladding needs assistance —and he may—would you object to my getting a couple of detectives onto it too?"

"If you like. I don't mind."

"I only mention it because it might be rather expensive."

"I don't care."

"Good. Thought you'd see it my way. Don't you worry, we'll get a line on the bastard, bound to."

Jordan smiled stiffly. Encouraging the encourager was the hardest part of it all.

"Well then," said Tom, "I'll see you on Wednesday. Willy will be in tomorrow—I talked to her on the phone last night. She sends you her love."

"Thank you," said Jordan.

II

The first winter of their marriage at Woodley was dissolving into a bright calm spring. As Jordan stood on the porch, wrapped for the office and watching Willy cutting flowers in the garden, he felt uncomfortable. Galoshes and scarf and coat and gloves and hat (he'd never worn hats) were alright for the winter—but now the mildness had come, they changed him from a cautious man of sense back into a patient. He smiled slightly—a conspicuous consumptive.

"Wives are the best nurses in the world," Dr. Wilcox was fond of saying. "You get far better care at home than any sanatorium could give you. Far better." But all the same, the doctor'd had several fatherly chats with Willy about Jordan.

"A normal life," was another of Wilcox's favourite phrases. "Just because you're missing half a lung doesn't mean you can't lead a normal life, a perfectly normal life. Got to take care, of course. Wrap up well. Don't overdo it, that's all. Don't overdo it—you know what I mean?"

The first time, Jordan had said, "No. What do you mean?"

"Well, I mean, newlyweds and—er—everything."

Newlyweds—well, they were. Yet, muffled and coated, he did not feel particularly like a newlywed. He might have been married to Willy for ten years instead of just under one. Their marriage had been established as a comfortable converse almost from the first day, and there had been no interruption.

He breathed in deeply and looked up and down. The trees were still leafless and skeletal, but their bark had the dark, wet look of spring rain. He would plant a few trees one of these days—at the back, to screen the raw new house that was already going up. But not poplars or anything brash. Chestnut. Oak. An oak could last for a thousand years. At Istoke Park there still stood an oak mentioned as a boundary marker in *Domesday Book*.

Willy was coming towards him briskly. She wore heavy gardening gloves, monstrous clumsy hands at the end of her spindly arms.

"For the office, darling." She smiled.

"Lovely." He held out his hand.

"I'll just put some paper round them."

"You'll catch cold in only a cardigan."

"I'm alright. I get my one cold a year in Feb. and that's all over now. Shan't be a sec."

He looked at his watch. "I'd better be off," he called back into the house.

"Here we are. Have you got a vase?"

"Er, no."

"Well, I'm sure Miss Lawley can find one for you."

She probably would if he asked her. But already he had made a policy of asking no favours from Miss Lawley.

Willy put up her cheek for a kiss. "It's really about time Uncle Colin let you have a secretary of your own," she said.

"I haven't been there a year yet, you know."

"But you're a partner. Knowing Uncle Colin, he'll probably get some pretty little poppet and give Miss Lawley to you."

"I'd prefer the poppet."

"Darling, you wouldn't know what to do with a poppet." She smiled.

"Well, I have my poppet."

A faint, pleased flush touched Willy's angular cheekbones for a second. "You're a lamb."

"Bye-bye," he said. He had fallen quite easily into the nursery language of marriage.

Willy stood on the porch, clutching each elbow tightly. It was not that she was cold, he knew, but because the position slightly raised her breasts, of which she was obscurely ashamed. Once, in her teens, they had been startlingly plump, as he had seen in an old photo, but now they drooped. "You don't mind," she had whispered to him on their honeymoon, "about my breasts?"

He put the flowers on the seat and started the car.

As soon as he was out of the gate and on the Woodley Road, he took off his hat. He smiled to himself at Willy's idea of Colin as a skirt chaser. It had been Jordan's error—also on their honeymoon—to tell Willy of the week he'd spent at Colin's house when he was sixteen or so. The first evening Colin had come round heavily to the subject of women of the street. "I've nothing against them. Nothing. They're there for a purpose." Then, staring fixedly at the ashy tip of his cigar, Colin had said, "As soon as you decently can after the act—I can't impress this upon you too strongly—go to the bathroom and, er, wash the instrument with carbolic soap."

Although Willy had not disapproved of the advice, she had most certainly disapproved of its source. She knew men were like that, but did not appreciate elderly bachelors of the family bringing it so close to home. She had thereafter treated Colin warily, expecting perhaps at any moment a dirty old man to spring out.

Jordan drove slowly, amused at the byways of intolerance. They were infinitely less dangerous than main roads and were, moreover, so unalterably English.

12

He felt drugged and uneasy. It had been raining hard, so that he'd missed his exercise period. The quick march with Denver along the corridors and down the steps to the solicitors' room was no substitute. He resented being torn away from his slow, dreaming afternoon.

"Mr. Bartlett you're going to see, is it? He's a good bloke. Remember the Greenwood case? Wouldn't have given much for his chances when he was in 'ere. Greenie we called him—he was an odd one. Wouldn't never talk to you; all he liked to do was build towers out of dominoes. He'd sit there watching his towers and then, when no one was looking, smash-bang, he'd knock 'em down. You never could catch him at it. He liked to make people jump, I reckon. Mr. Bartlett got him off. Mind you, I always had my doubts if Greenie had done it. But Mr. Bartlett did a beautiful job—just beautiful. He's not flashy or anything like that. Quiet he is—like all the best ones are these days."

"Oh?" said Jordan. They turned a corner. Denver wasn't bad. He'd go rattling on with the aid of only an occasional interjection. He was entirely without malice and never tried to draw Jordan into conversation—monologue or dialogue, he was happy with either. It was the tall, thin hospital orderly, Samson, that Jordan disliked. He was always wishing to be congratulated upon his banalities: "What's your opinion, Maddox?" or "Don't you agree, Maddox?"

"Oh, yes," said Denver. "It used to be different in the old days. When I was a lad I saw Sir Patrick Hastings in number one court. And Marshall Hall once, too. They were the dramatic school. Always give you a run for your money, they did. It's changed now—all that's gone out of style. I wouldn't have it different though. I've seen too much ranting and raving in my lifetime."

Bartlett was small, neat and round, a well-groomed bird in a morning suit. "I'm Geoffrey Bartlett."

"How do you do." Jordan gripped the lawyer's hand; it was smooth and freshly soaped.

They sat down.

Jordan suddenly felt that he was going to have to make the running. "I'm very glad Tom Short was able to get you," he forced himself to say.

"Umm." Bartlett did not look at him directly, but Jordan had the feeling that he was under very close examination. "Short tells me that you have no strong ideas about the way the case should be conducted. Is that so?"

"Yes, I think so. I'm in your hands."

Bartlett smiled without revealing his teeth. "You want, of course, to be acquitted?"

"Of course," he answered, but the question made him feel foolish. It recalled the ponderous choices posed to him in the past—"You do want to get a scholarship, don't you?"; "I'm assuming, of course, you want to come into the business?"; "Do you take this woman to be your lawful wedded wife?"—the answers to which did not grow from any preference within himself but were totally, and obviously, dictated by outside circumstances.

"I'll begin then by giving you a brief outline of what I think should be our general strategy. You just interrupt me as you will. First—"

"There is one thing. Tom suggested that you might try to exclude the second statement I made to the police."

"Ah—what are your views on that?"

"I'm against it. It would only mean rehashing the whole thing in court."

"I'm inclined to agree with you. It had crossed my mind to try for an exclusion, but mainly because I am not too happy about the manner in which the statement was obtained." He looked at Jordan. "I

92

understand the police brought a good deal of pressure to bear upon you."

"Not really." What was done was done. "They behaved quite correctly on the whole."

"I see. But on March the sixteenth you were at Sarah Street for six or seven hours. That seems a rather excessive time to produce a fairly simple statement. I don't wish to put any words into your mouth, but are you entirely happy with the way in which the—shall I say—interrogation was conducted?"

"I don't see there's anything to be gained in fighting it."

"The value of attacking police evidence is certainly dubious—you're quite correct—unless one has excellent grounds for doing so and unless there are very definite advantages to be had. We would have to examine the grounds with very great care. As to the advantages, they tend, I believe, to be somewhat negative. The chief point is that the police patently made up their minds at a very early stage that you were the culprit, and therefore they did not make a fully adequate investigation in any other direction. This point—which I intend to bring out in any event—would be considerably reinforced if it could be shown that the police employed browbeating tactics so far as you are concerned. You understand?"

"Yes." It was almost a sigh. It had been a matter of give and take, and he was not going to repudiate his gift—it would be a repudiation of part of himself. George was a figure in the past now, but Jordan remembered him without rancour. The superintendent had believed in what he was doing, and Jordan was not inclined to dispute that belief. "Let's give it the go-by."

"Right. Well now, the general strategy. At the moment—and I say at the moment because there is the possibility that Short and his clerk will turn up evidence that might cast doubt upon the Crown's version of the case—at the moment, I do not think it would be desirable for us to call any witnesses. We will stand solely on your statements and on the evidence you give on your own behalf. In the prosecution's case there are two particular points which I shall attack strongly. First, the evidence of the Home Office pathologist. I want to get it quite firmly fixed in the mind of the jury that the time element—the span of time in which June Singer was murdered—was not as narrow as suggested in the preliminary examination. Secondly, Mrs. Ardley's evidence, which is at the moment quite damaging, will have to be shown as open to doubt."

"I don't think you'll find that easy," said Jordan.

"Why?"

"She struck me as a strong-minded woman."

"Ah, but we know that she is lying, don't we? She says that she would undoubtedly have seen you entering the house if you had rung the bell. You did ring the bell. She did not see you. The stair carpet was loose, yet she asserts that it was not. She is positive that no one else entered the house after you left that morning. But we know that someone did enter—and leave—with or without Mrs. Ardley's knowledge."

"I'm afraid I don't follow that."

"The murderer. The murderer must have entered the house not too long after you left it."

"Oh, yes."

"It's difficult," said Bartlett, "for a witness to lie convincingly when he knows that counsel knows he is lying. It's easier for a woman, of course."

Jordan laughed. "Women are congenitally less truthful?"

"Congenitally? I don't know," said Bartlett, unsmiling. "Probably more a matter of social training. But the fact is that a high proportion of miscarriages of justice are due to perjury on the part of women. Perhaps women forgive less easily than men."

"I've not harmed Mrs. Ardley."

"But she may well think you have—her reputation, the honour of her house, that sort of thing. By the way, when you left Panton Place, how did you proceed to your office?"

"Underground, I think. No, wait a minute, I might have taken a bus."

"Not a cab?"

"No."

Bartlett grunted. In disappointment perhaps? A taxi would be traceable and the driver might recall the time. But it was impossible to tell anything from Bartlett's plump, expressionless face. Jordan wondered if he was always like this—perfect in his morning suit. Did he go to the club and play bridge, or pop round to Pimm's for lunch or a whiskey and soda between verdicts? Did he mow the lawn on a summer's day? Jordan tried unsuccessfully to picture the barrister red-faced and sweating. Was he married? Did he ever get into trouble with the . . . no, that was ridiculous, inconceivable.

Bartlett seemed to be meditating. He brought out a silver cigarette case and offered it to Jordan. He lit Jordan's cigarette and his own in silence and shut the case with a small silver click. "There's one thing I feel a little wary of," he said. "And that's the matter of the girl's being pregnant. I have the impression the Crown attaches a good deal of weight to that fact."

"I find it very hard to believe."

"Why?"

"It's so unlikely—so unlike June." It was so outrageous and—vicious that he had dismissed it from his mind.

"Unlike her? Nevertheless, it might provide an excellent motive, and not an uncommon one. If the prosecution could show you were responsible—or were even privy to the fact—it would fill a gap in motive. A married man, with children—"

"I've only got one child."

"Married with a child. In order to protect that, a man driven to desperate foolishness. It's happened before."

"But it's absurd."

"Yes, quite—unless the Crown can adduce some evidence to suggest there was or might have been a liaison between yourself and the girl. It would immeasurably strengthen their case."

"You mean the case against me is not very strong now?"

Bartlett tapped the table with one fingernail. "It's strong, yes. It's always strong, superficially at least, in a murder case, or no charge would be brought." The barrister blew a plume of smoke and watched an eddy of draft touch it and draw it higher. "Were you in love with June Singer?"

"No. I don't think so."

Bartlett faced him directly across the table. "Doubtful?"

"No." It was just that June had been, was still being, treated so callously. And he felt himself to be a part of that callousness. "Not doubtful. No."

"There isn't anything, is there, which, if they found, might look incriminating? You did not, for instance, write her any letters or anything like that?"

"No."

"What about that drink you had with the girl? Do you remember anything about it—when, or where, or what was said?"

"I'm really afraid not." It sounded lame and, to his own ears, oddly false.

"Umm." Bartlett rolled the cigarette gently between his fingers, then carefully stubbed it out. "Now," he said briskly, "this business of the scratch on your wrist. It's the lynchpin of the case against you, of course. I want to be absolutely clear in my mind how it happened. Perhaps you could demonstrate?" He got up and stood on his chair. "I'll be the girl. Above you, right? Good, now—show me exactly what happened."

Jordan stood up. "I turned, you see, like this. In my left arm were the typewriter and the manuscript. I slipped and put out my right hand—" he flung it wide— "and June tried to grab me."

"Like this?" Bartlett shot out his right hand and gripped Jordan's wrist firmly.

"She wasn't as quick as you."

"Ah. Again then."

This time Bartlett's fingers slipped over the skin below Jordan's hand.

"That's it," Jordan said.

Bartlett dismounted. He was frowning. "I didn't succeed in grazing you, though."

"But June had long nails."

"A typist with long nails?"

"Yes. She was very proud of them. She typed with the balls of her fingers." He had quite forgotten. But he recalled now the familiar click-click as June's nails hit the keys in the row above.

Bartlett had his head on one side—his momentary ruffle of feathers had passed. "Did she paint her nails, by any chance?"

"Yes."

"Red?"

"No, a kind of silvery colour, I think."

Bartlett nodded as though he had secured a valuable tip. "I don't think I need take up any more of your time." The close-lipped smile. "I think probably I should like to see you again before the trial. And if you remember anything that might be of help, of course, let me know at once. I am particularly concerned with Singer—I don't have a clear impression of her at the moment. But Short's researches may throw a little light on that, if they do nothing else."

They shook hands. Jordan was very conscious of the lawyer's clean, impersonal touch.

Back in his room, he realised that the ordeal had not been as bad as he'd envisaged. He was grateful for Bartlett's abstract, matter-of-fact inquisitiveness. It was less wearing than Tom's fussy and sometimes brutal heartiness or Willy's relentless patience.

13

Most of the prisoners whispered. And their visitors too.

But Willy was undaunted by the churchlike atmosphere of the large visitors' room with its long row of open-backed cubicles. Her clean, silvery elocution carried to every ear with all the insouciance of a drunk in the hush of a public lavatory.

"How are you, darling? You're looking a bit peaky," she said.

"Am I? I can't think why. I'm really very fit. I get more exercise than I've had for years." Jordan kept his voice low and tried to make his answers long. "I'm really extremely comfortable. My room is very nice and warm. Washbasin in the corner. All mod cons. For all one knows, it might be a nursing home. Except, of course, they don't allow flowers."

"You sure it's not damp? You know how bad the damp is for you. It feels rather damp in here."

"No no. It's very warm where I am. Hot, even. Sometimes I have to take my jacket off, it gets so hot. I feel almost embarrassed at the treatment I get."

"Is the food alright? I expect it's terrible, you poor—"

"It's all sent in, you know. From a place called Ben's. First-rate cooking." He could hardly tell her how superior it was to her own dry shepherd's pies and overdone roasts and thin stews.

"I brought some apples for you from Sibley. I'm sure you don't get enough fruit."

"Apples?"

"A dozen James Grieve. Aunt Mary sent them with her love. I had to leave them outside, of course."

Jordan smiled. He leaned forward so that his face was close to the grille. "That reminds me of the time I had chicken pox in the Easter holidays once. Colin sent me a box of—Cox's Orange Pippins, I think. Aunt Mary brought them up and watched me open them. You know what she said? 'Rather sending coals to Newcastle, isn't it?' Typical Aunt Mary."

Willy smiled very faintly. Neither of them ever mentioned the wire separation between them—it was taboo, like the details of the murder and the prospects of the trial and . . . so many things.

"I remember the smell of them even now. Woody—from the box —and a bit damp. The cool appley fragrance. And the crisp flesh that was suddenly moist when you bit into it." He was foolishly voluble in the memory—perhaps it was a reaction to Willy's controlled patience. He pulled himself up. "Did you manage any cigarettes?"

"Yes. I brought you a hundred Players."

"That should keep me going for the next couple days." He watched her say nothing. "What Wilcox doesn't know won't hurt him. There isn't much to do in here. I regard smoking as a form of exercise."

Willy said stiffly, "I brought you some more puzzles."

"From Sibley? Which ones?"

"I didn't look, I'm afraid. Does it matter? Oh, one was much bigger than the others."

"That'll be Waterloo!"

"Is it a good one?"

"I think it was probably Uncle John's finest. It was one of the last he did before . . ."

"Before he died?"

"No, before . . ." He shook his head. "Waterloo is almost twice the usual size. And the technique is quite different. It's really a series of smaller pictures. John usually tried a panorama or else took just one point in the battle. But here he tried to get everything in: Hougomont, La Haye Sainte, Picton's charge, Blücher coming up on the left, even the Duke. He used the smoke and darkness to divide up each scene. It took him over a year to do it." He glanced at Willy. "It's quite a story. Quite a puzzle." He might just as well have been talking about the economic situation in Cambodia. "Did you have much trouble digging them up?"

"Well—you didn't tell me that little attic room was locked."

"Oh?" The long iron key was on his ring, where it had been for twenty years, and now, with all his other personal possessions, was impounded. "I'd forgotten. How did you get in then?"

"I had to force the lock."

Jordan felt a sudden pang at this violation.

"It was absolutely filthy. No one can have been in there for simply ages. What it needed was a thorough spring cleaning."

"Yes. How were they at Sibley?" He'd been putting off the question, which would, he knew, loose a flood of chatter. Sibley irked him —small and mean and hung with a thousand unseen cobwebs, not as he chose to remember it—but it revivified Willy.

". . . now old Graham has gone, Aunt Mary is secretly finding the garden a bit much for her. She won't say anything, of course. Annie Brierly—you remember Annie—still comes up to give her a hand whenever she can get away from the post office, which is very nice of her. Trevor is upset about his new curate. He has a little red MG, you know, only secondhand, but Trevor thinks it's most unsuitable. Of course it is. When he mentioned it, the curate was frightfully rude. He said he thought it was about time clergymen stopped behaving like a bunch of dowdy virgins. That's what he *said*—'a bunch of dowdy virgins.' Poor old Uncle Trevor. Aunt Mary is dying to take a hand, but Trevor has put his foot down. He thinks it's up to him. He wrote a letter to the archdeacon about it and got a very brusque reply. So he's going to the bishop. They're not on speaking terms now, which makes it very difficult. The curate and Uncle Trevor, I mean. They send each other little notes. Ever since Mansard left they've had nothing but trouble with curates, poor things."

"Mansard always had egg on his bib," said Jordan.

"He was a bit grubby. But he seems like a treasure now, particularly when . . ." She went on talking. When she was wound up like this, each sentence became a sharp, breathless burst. As if she had been running a long distance with important news—a fire or an earthquake—and could only get it out between heartbeats. The first time he had met her he had been amused by it. Frank Wade had called her a babel of clichés, and Jordan had half humorously taken her part. In an odd way he had felt sorry for her—to see so much desperate earnestness lavished upon trivialities. And that had been the beginning—although nothing could have seemed more unlikely at the time.

99

". . . trouble with the lilies of the valley. It's a continual battle to keep them in control, and Aunt Mary—"

"Yes, I remember. She thinks they're a weed." He paused for a moment as the prison officer passed behind him. "Has Trevor planted a new fig tree yet?"

Willy shook her head. "I don't think he ever will."

"I suppose not." Ever since the destruction of the fig tree, it had been understood that one day a new one would be planted. But that was twenty years ago. And by now those bricks, so rawly uncovered on the side of the rectory, had weathered with the rest. There was nothing for a new tree to conceal any more. It was probably better, on the whole, just to pretend these things had not happened.

"Uncle Trevor says to tell you that he is praying for you."

Jordan imagined Trevor kneeling in the little chapel off the vast hall of the rectory. It was a miserable room, smelling of unpolished parquet and stale air. The frosted window was not designed to be opened. And next door was the lavatory, so that Trevor's meditations would sometimes be interrupted by the gurgle and sigh of flushing water.

"Are they coming up for the trial?" he asked.

"Yes. They're very set on it. I tried . . ."

"I saw Geoffrey Bartlett yesterday."

"I know. Tom—Tom told me." Her voice was low. The murmur from the other visitors' boxes hung over them.

Jordan looked at the thin face of his wife. Time, he thought, must hang heavy on her hands without him to take care of. There was nothing in the world he wanted of her. Except— He nerved himself to the question which he so hated having to ask.

"How's Georgia?" His voice quivered.

"Oh, she's blooming. I've never seen her so well."

"I'm glad. She doesn't miss . . . ?"

Willy leaned forward and her voice rose high again. "Of course she misses you terribly, Jordan. She misses your stories. I'm absolutely rotten at them. It seems you've done every animal I try—and a hundred times better."

"She doesn't miss kindergarten?"

"Not yet. She's very busy exploring the Shorts' house at the moment. Norah takes her round the garden every morning, and she's learning the names of the flowers. She'd never do that with me. But she's very good at it. She can't understand why flowers don't walk. She kept asking that, and Tom made the mistake of telling her that there were some, oh, South American varieties, I think, that *did* walk, and—"

"Tom said that?"

"Oh, yes. He's a mine of odd information. So Georgia got it into her head that . . ."

He listened to her, trying to see or sense Georgia in her words, her face. But there was nothing. Suddenly he could stand it no longer. "Willy!"

"Yes, darling?"

"I've got to go now. I've got—to see the M.O."

"Is there anything wrong, Jordan?"

"No no. I see him every day. It's time now."

"Very well." She smiled hesitantly. "I'll come at about the same time tomorrow, shall I?"

Already he had stood up. "If you want to. I mean, yes. Yes, that would be nice."

"Goodbye then, and do take care of yourself."

He nodded. He was unspeakably grateful for the wire mesh that prevented their touching or kissing. "Goodbye, Willy."

He turned away and a prison officer was waiting for him.

14

"Well, my dear," Aunt Mary said when the doctor diagnosed the "growing pains" as chicken pox, "that means you'll miss the Easter service."

Jordan spoke the penitential words, "I am sorry, Aunt Mary."

"No hot cross buns for him, I think, doctor?"

"Oh, I don't fancy a hot cross bun would do him any harm," the doctor murmured. Opposition to Aunt Mary was generally murmured.

"Well, we'll see," Aunt Mary said, examining the doctor with her protuberant eyes. "I'll show you out."

When they left, Jordan lay very still, propped up on two pillows.

He looked around the room without moving his head, which might tire him. Anyone who's ill tires easily. And he was ill, with a real illness. Chicken pox—he wondered if it was the same pox they used to have in the old days. "I've got the pox," he said aloud.

But now that he really was ill, he didn't feel in the least ill. Perhaps it would come later. His headache was gone. He just felt light and hot. Very hot. When he rubbed his feet together, they slid stickily, foot on foot. He was in a sweat.

In Harrison Ainsworth they were always getting the "sweating sickness." Perhaps he had that.

Sweating sickness would be even better than the pox. He always admired boys at school who sweated. Jordan could run about all afternoon on the field or, on wet afternoons, sprint up and down the eighty-nine steps of Old School twenty times—twenty up and twenty down—without raising a bead of sweat.

He stared at "The Light of the World" and wondered whether Christ had ever had sweating sickness—or the pox. He called him "Christ" in his own mind, although at Sibley it had to be "Jesus" in conversation. But Christian names were embarrassing. Initials were alright; indeed they could be prized possessions. J. J. Maddox was rather feeble. The one Jordan envied most was A. H. T. de St. G. Simple-Carfax. It had everything, including a de and a St. J. Christ was pretty feeble too.

Jordan slipped easily into his favourite pastime of inventing heroes illustrious with honours. He had got as far as Admiral of the Fleet Sir Lionel Leslie Anthony George Patrick Bassington-Bassington-de Lancey, K.G., Bart., G.C.B., G.C.S.I., K.C.M.G., K.B.E., C.V.O., D.S.C., and was trying to decide whether or not to slip in a D.S.O.—or a C.H. perhaps?—when there was a knock on his bedroom door.

"Come in," he said. The knock was so small and shy he was sure it would be Mr. Mansard.

But it was the new maid.

"Hello," said Annie.

"Hello."

She held a duster in her hand. "What have you got?"

"Pox," Jordan said. "And you'd better go away or you'll get it too."

"What sort of pox?"

"Hen pox," said Jordan, reluctantly relinquishing a fraction of his superiority. Although she was almost a year older than he, she would never go away to school, despite the fact that she was supposed to be "clever." She wasn't a proper maid, really; she was only to come in the holidays, when Istoke Grammar School was closed.

"You mean chicken pox. I've had it."

"You can always get it again."

She looked at him consideringly. "Well, I don't mind."

He thought of various witty replies to this unexpected remark, but rejected them all. Although she was a girl, he guessed she was not likely to be a complete bore. She actually looked more like a boy— small, with a small face and ears like a pixy—except that she already had breasts. He blushed and was immediately annoyed with himself— after all, *breasts* was used in the Bible.

"You can come in if you like," he said.

She closed the door and came closer to the bed. "You look white," she said, "except for the spots."

"I'm getting more all the time."

"In the end you'll be just one big spot."

He laughed. "Out, damned spot!"

"That's *Macbeth*." She smiled at him. "We did it last term."

"So did we."

"What's your school like?"

"Alright. What's yours like?"

"It's too far to walk."

"Well, haven't you got a bike?"

"No. Besides, Istoke's too far to cycle every day. I have to take the bus."

"Not cycle—bike."

"Bike then."

"Why don't you ask for one for your birthday?"

"Dad couldn't afford it."

"Oh," Jordan said, "that's hard luck." But he felt it was inadequate. "Wouldn't you like to sit down?"

"Where?"

"On my bed, of course."

"I should be dusting, really. Would you like me to dust?"

"I don't mind."

"Miss Freeman'll be up here any minute."

"Oh, Aunt Mary will be gardening by now."

Annie looked round for dust. "She likes to know what I'm doing."

"Same here," said Jordan.

"Well, I better be off."

But she didn't move. Jordan rather liked her being there. He wondered if she would be bringing up his lunch.

"You really are ill, aren't you?" said Annie.

"Yes."

"I've got something for you then." She put her hand in the pocket of her apron and took out a bar of chocolate. She moved to the bed and put the chocolate by Jordan's hand and moved away again.

"But that's your ration."

"It doesn't matter. I get a bit extra usually. Emerald doesn't like sweet things, so I sometimes get some of her ration."

"Thank you very much," said Jordan. He picked up the bar and held it. He smiled at her.

Annie blushed.

"Who's Emerald? Is that the girl who sits in the back of the post office?"

"Yes, she's my sister.'

"She's a bit . . . funny, isn't she?"

"She's a mongoloid," Annie said seriously.

"Oh," said Jordan. He was sure she'd got it wrong.

"Well, I better really be going now."

"Alright. And thanks for the chocolate. It's super of you."

"Would you like me to come and see you tomorrow?" Annie asked shyly.

"Yes," said Jordan.

And after that Annie came every day until he got up and was allowed downstairs. In exchange for the chocolate he gave her several of the apples Uncle Colin had sent.

He also ate one of the apples every day himself, not because he particularly liked apples but because it was decent of Uncle Colin to send them and rather nasty of Aunt Mary to look down her nose at them. Just because they didn't come out of the rectory orchard didn't mean they were no good. In fact, they were rather better than the crabby little things which appeared on the dining-room table at the end of every meal. Besides, they were *his* apples.

Uncle John approved of them. "Sensible man, Colin." Sitting on the end of the bed, he took one bite of an apple and put it down on the blanket. He ate no more of it. "Much better than all these flowers." He waved his hand at the narrow vase of daffodils. "Can't stand flowers in the bedroom," he said with a momentary vehemence which seemed immediately to exhaust him. His shoulders fell inward and he stared out of the window. His hands rested open, palms up, on his thighs.

It was hard to talk to Uncle John now. He would catch a stray phrase, like a quick glimpse of a kite behind the trees, and hold it and repeat it, then lose it and go back to silence and staring.

Suddenly his hands were active. He took out his pipe and blew it and tapped it and put it in his mouth. Then he opened his tobacco pouch, felt in it, shook it and, energy gone, let it lie empty on the bed.

Uncle John puffed at his empty pipe. In the last year the faint blond stain of nicotine had completely vanished from his moustache, leaving the clipped hairs silvery white. "Supposed to go down to the village with Mary and get some tobacco. Yesterday. Yesterday. Slipped my mind. Just an excuse, of course. Mary needs an escort— don't want to get her alarmed though. That would never do. Dangerous place, the village, these days." He laughed abruptly, then took the pipe from his mouth and rubbed the bowl with the heel of his palm. A gentle massaging. "When I was C.O., used to have a car—a Humber, with a flag on it. A pennon. Beige seats and a carpet on the floor. Need a carpet in a car, you know." He laughed once more.

He looked at Jordan and away again. "Sorry I haven't popped in to see you before. Busy, you know. These days."

"Are you working on a puzzle?"

John frowned. "Staff work. Lot of planning. Command's not easy. What d'you do with an O.C. who takes his boots off and lets his dog lick his bare feet during company office, eh? Good man, though. And these damn forms, yards of 'em." He sighed. "Oh, I'm busy alright."

Jordan had not entered the attic workroom since that terrible first day of the summer holidays last year. He refused to think about that. He had been up many times since and had stood outside and listened to Uncle John's military step going backwards and forwards and the occasional mutter and the quick, barking cough and then silence until the marching began again. And every time he had gone away without knocking on the workroom door, as he had promised himself, this time, surely he would, this time.

Sometimes Uncle John would make a hurried sortie downstairs or even into the garden. If Jordan saw him on these ventures, the old man would usually turn away or rush past muttering, "Busy, busy, sorry," or "There's a war on, you know," and run upstairs as though his life depended on it. He was not allowed outside the rectory grounds unless accompanied by Aunt Mary or Uncle Trevor. But often he would stand guard at the rectory gates in the morning, waiting for the postman or, most recently, for Annie. He would salute her, Annie said, as she came into the drive and then walk her to the kitchen door. He never said a word, except at the end, when he'd salute and say, "Think you'll be alright now." And then he would march away humming.

"Given up smoking for Lent," said John abruptly. But he had not smoked for longer than that. He'd taken to leaving his burning pipe anywhere that came to hand and tapping out a loaded and lighted bowl onto the floor. Eventually tobacco had been taken away and the old soldier had been forbidden fire.

"Magnificent campaign, you know, Jordan." He hit his palm smartly with the bowl of the pipe. "A stroke of genius—living off the wilderness like that. No logistical problem, you see."

"Tell me a battle, Uncle John," Jordan said impulsively.

"A battle, Jordan?" John brightened and turned his head to look steadily at his nephew. "Haven't done that for a long time, have we?" He was suddenly his old self. "What would you like?"

"Waterloo."

"Ah, Waterloo." He beamed. "Know what the Duke called it? 'A pounding match.' Everyone made mistakes. Remarkable. Wellington had almost a quarter of his troops fifteen miles up the road. Napoleon did the same with Grouchy." He paused. "Eighteenth of June. Miserable day. Sun didn't come out till the last hour of daylight. Everything dark with smoke—confused. Lot of the ground was nothing but a quagmire from the rain the night before. Troops tired, hungry. Muddy. No gleaming brasses or pipe clay that day." He was gazing out of the window again. "Nine days of it. Pinned out there in the open. Down to ten per cent battalion strength. War is not a pretty business, Waidlaw, but this . . . When will it end?" He stopped.

"What happened, Uncle John?" asked Jordan after a few moments.

"Eh? Happened?" He blinked his eyes furiously. "Aha! Yes. A pounding match!" He thumped his pipe into his fist. "A damned pounding match. Where the Grenadiers got their name. Waterloo . . ." He shook his head slowly. "Waterloo," he murmured again. He couldn't manage it though.

"Uncle?"

"Ummm?"

"Don't you want to finish your apple?"

"My apple. Yes." He picked it up and put it in his pocket. Hastily, as if they might be taken from him, he tucked away his pipe and tobacco pouch. "Got to get back now. HQ needs me." He stood up.

"Can't you stay a bit longer?"

"Afraid not." He strode to the door and turned. For a moment he smiled. Then, "There's a war on, you know." And he was gone.

Jordan got up and went to the window. It was a sunny, windy April day. Not like Waterloo.

He wanted to get out—go for a long ride, by himself. He could ride all the way to Istoke Park and climb the Domesday Oak. He was tired of being ill. If only he were back at school—the thought startled him and he turned from the window. He hated school.

He went slowly back to his bed and climbed in. Perhaps when he was better Uncle Colin would ask him up to London for a few days. "Fat chance," he said.

He closed his eyes and thought of Sir Lionel Bassington-Bassington-de Lancey. But he was bored.

He wished Annie would come.

He jumped out of bed and put his head out of the door to see if she was in the passage.

"Hello, my boy. Just off to the—ah?" Uncle Trevor always called the lavatory the ah.

"No thank you," said Jordan. "I just came back." Nowadays he treated Uncle Trevor with the same careful civility that was given to Mr. Prideaux, his housemaster at school.

"Well, can I come in then?"

Jordan got back into bed and Uncle Trevor perched himself on the end.

"How are you feeling?"

"Alright, thank you."

"That's splendid. So glad you're feeling better." He glanced at the plate of apples and said, as he had every day, "Apple a day keeps the doctor away."

As things had stood since last summer, silence could be rebuked as "sulking." So Jordan said conversationally, "I expect it won't be long before you'll be getting the figs."

"Oh, dear me, no. Not until August, my boy. You should remember that. But I suppose you have so much to fill your head at school, uh, it's difficult to remember our little concerns at Sibley." He smiled. "But that's quite natural. We're going to have a splendid crop this year—if the blackbirds don't get there first. We'll have to bring the airgun out soon, won't we?"

Jordan nodded. All summer the airgun reposed on the dining-room window sill, to be periodically fired at the fig tree to scare away any bird that might have got in under the netting. Firing at random into the tree, Jordan had once accidentally killed a blackbird, which had fallen in a great flurry of rustling leaves. Uncle John, whose bedroom was directly above the tree and who waged a summerlong battle with the fig leaves which grew to cut out his light, had leaned out of his window and shouted, "Good shot!" Uncle Trevor had delivered a short lecture on the birds of the air being creatures of Jesus too. Even defence of the beloved fig tree did not require killing. Jordan had told no one that it was a fluke.

The rector cleared his throat. "Your report came this morning. You seem to be getting along quite well. But I think the Latin could do with a little improving, couldn't it?"

"Could it?"

"You were only twelfth, you know, my boy. I think perhaps if you and I sat down together for an hour every day, we might advance the cause a little, eh?"

"Oh, Uncle Trevor, not in the hols!" The protest was expected of him, but he made it mildly. He would never again tempt that horrible animal fury which had mottled Trevor's flaccid cheeks and shaken his short body. Not, at least, until he was old enough to . . . to get away from Sibley forever.

"Well, a little extra coaching never did anyone any harm. You may find me a bit rusty, I'm afraid." He smiled. "An hour directly after breakfast, when we're both fresh, shouldn't take too much out of your day, should it? No—well, that's settled then."

Jordan knew that his uncle would look forward to that hour of Latin as much as he, Jordan, would hate it. It was almost an excuse for Uncle Trevor to enjoy himself. Jordan sighed.

"Come, come, it won't be as bad as all that. We'll have some good fun." He looked embarrassed. "And I'm afraid we old folks aren't much fun for you, my boy. I worry sometimes that you will find Sibley a little on the dull side in the holidays."

"Oh no. Not really," he said dutifully. It wasn't exactly dull. It was empty. He had taken long walks, covered every inch of the hundred-acre field, down to the river, over to Istoke Park. But the campaigns he invented and the military engagements were laborious and without joy. He told himself he was growing out of those games, but he knew that really it was the absence of Uncle John.

"I just wish that you had some companions your own age." Uncle Trevor spoke with sudden emphasis. "Youth should be the really happy time. Of course, when I was your age, there were four of us Freemans: Mary and John and Lily—your mother—and myself. I believe we even had the reputation of being a rather gay lot. I expect you'll find that difficult to credit. We played a great deal of tennis, I remember, in the summer; and in the winter we used to go skating on the canals. I remember . . ." He smiled a little sheepishly. "Dear me, I must be boring you."

"Not a bit. I don't mind at all."

"Alas, those days are gone forever. The war came, and suddenly . . . I'm afraid we haven't got as much time to give you as we should like. The war is responsible for that too, unhappily. Now that we have no maids, Aunt Mary has a great deal of extra work. And John isn't—isn't what he used to be."

Jordan looked out of the window at the tiny patch of sky he could see from his bed.

"I'll tell you what," said Trevor hurriedly, "I've got to go into Istoke next week to see the archdeacon. I expect you'll be up and about then. Would you like to come in with me? We could have lunch at the Grange and perhaps spend some of the afternoon at the secondhand bookshops in the market."

"Yes, I'd like to. That would be very nice."

Jordan decided he would take the opportunity of going into the bicycle shop. He still had Uncle Colin's Christmas money, and secondhand bikes couldn't be all that expensive.

"It won't be very exciting, I'm afraid, but it'll be a change, my boy, eh? You and I haven't had lunch together for a long time."

"No." Wearily Jordan gathered himself to his social duty. "Did you have bikes when you were young, Uncle Trevor?"

"Bikes? Oh, yes indeed. They had solid tyres in those days. We used to have some jolly bike rides. . . ."

15

They were silent for a while. The visitor's box they occupied was the one nearest the door. Apart from the two prison officers, one on each side of the barrier, there was no one else in the room. The steam pipes thumped in a sudden tattoo. The prison officers studiously avoided looking at prisoner and visitor.

"Can't smoke in here, I suppose," said Colin. He had taken out his morocco cigar case. He picked a cigar and put it under his nose and sniffed. It was odd, thought Jordan, to see the same old ritual at work, and, in a way he could not define, disheartening.

"Havanas cost the earth now," Colin said. He slipped the cigar back into its case. "My cigar man tells me they often have to ship them halfway round the world before they get 'em in. That damned American embargo. Indian ships, Spanish ships. They're not used to handling cigars. Entire shipments are ruined. Oil leaked into one lot recently, he was telling me. They had to destroy the whole consignment—burnt 'em. What an aroma that must have been." He gave Jordan a quick smile and then looked down again.

Colin had something serious to say. Jordan knew all the signs, but he hoped vaguely that if he proffered no help, Colin would let it go, whatever it was.

"Get the papers in here, do you?"

"No. I could take them if I wanted, but . . ."

"Don't blame you. Rags," he said vehemently. He hesitated. "There's been an awful lot of tripe about the case."

"Oh?"

"Yes. At the magistrate's court, when you were committed. I expect it'll all blossom forth again at the trial. Weeds from a midden. They can't say much about the case, of course, so they're reduced to dredging up a lot of refuse they call 'background.' I had a couple of reporters barge in on me at the office."

"What did they want?"

"Gossip, a lot of gossip. I turned them over to Miss Lawley. 'Thou shalt keep thyself to thyself' is the eleventh commandment to her. They didn't come back after that." He cleared his throat.

"There isn't much food for gossip in my life."

"No—o," Colin said cautiously.

"Pretty dull stuff."

"Well . . ."

Immediately he thought of John. But they couldn't, not possibly, have . . . "Not John?"

"John? Good lord, no. But—there's your father, of course."

"My father? But he's been dead for thirty years."

"Yes. But he was a well-known name. Charles Maddox. Rather spectacular in his way. Not just any old run-of-the-mill R.A." Colin paused, and Jordan was aware of being closely watched. "I see Willy hasn't told you anything about it."

"About what?" Jordan asked unwillingly.

"The press have dug up one or two rather—well, unpleasant things about Charles."

Jordan refused to be drawn.

But Colin went on anyway. "I think you know what I mean. After Lily, after your mother died, Charles went off the rails a bit. Before he committed himself he got himself into a few scrapes that all of us hoped were dead and buried long ago. The worst was when he beat up the father of an eighteen-year-old girl he was having an affair with. The man was quite severely injured and—"

"I know all that. You told me all that years ago."

"Yes. But the press have dug it up again. Jordan, when you get out of here, there are going to be one or two things which you'll have to face."

"What has it got to do with me? What has my father got to do with me? I hardly knew him. I can't even remember him."

"Yes. I know that. But the press don't—nor the public, thirsty for warmed-over scandal. It's unfair. But the inference is there. Like father, like son."

"Why are you doing this? What are you trying to say?" Jordan asked wearily.

"Just this. It's a roughish time for you, I know. But when it's all over, I don't want some of the things that have been raked over to come as a shock to you. I think you ought to know now, so you'll be prepared."

He stared at his godfather. They insinuated themselves into this prison just to attack him. The police at least had the honesty to warn him, but . . . It was too damn much. "And you were deputed to tell me all this, I suppose?"

"Deputed? What do you mean?"

"I suppose Willy and Short and the Freeman clan put you up to this, didn't they?"

"Good lord, Jordan, surely . . . I'm only trying to help. We're all only trying to help."

"Like the last time."

"The last time?"

"When you warned me off Annie. So trivial you've forgotten it, no doubt. Something else you hoped was dead and buried long ago."

"Jordan, my dear good chap, you can't possibly—"

"Can't I? Why not?" But even as he spoke, he didn't understand his own challenge. Almost visibly his words seemed to rise up like smoke to the ceiling and disperse.

Colin said slowly, "I've never been very proud of that, Jordan. At the time, I thought it was for the best. I still think it was for the best. You've been happy, haven't you? But . . . all the same, I don't . . ." He was silent, tensely concentrated, as a man in unaccustomed territory, aware of mines.

"Oh, why don't you leave me alone!"

Colin stared at him, then nodded. "We must be a bother." He patted the pocket where the cigar case made a smooth bulge. "I was wrong to mention it," he said. "I know how you feel. But this mess isn't going to last forever. It's not easy for any of us. Willy particularly."

"Willy particularly," said Jordan without expression. He just wanted Colin to go now.

"These damn journalists had the cheek to ask her to write some articles about it, you know. For publication after the trial, of course."

"I didn't know." The thought of Willy's strained epistolary formalisms transformed into Pictorialese was suddenly funny. "Publisher's Popsy Not Pretty, Says Loyal Spouse." If he'd had the energy, he would have laughed. "Look," he said, "I'm sorry, Colin. I shouldn't have burst out that way."

"I understand." Colin managed to smile.

They both stood up.

"How's the firm?"

"We're managing. We'll be putting the Ballard manuscript into production next week."

Jordan had to strain his mind to remember who Ballard was. "The village idiot," he said.

"Yes. I lunched him at Blain's, as you suggested," Colin gave his tentative old maid's smile.

"Have you got a new secretary yet?"

Colin shook his head.

"You ought to look around right away," said Jordan. "Better not leave it to me."

16

"I couldn't, Jordan. Really. You know I've got to study in the afternoons."

"Oh, come on, Annie. Forget the books. Let's have a bit of fun."

"No, Jordan, really. What with Christmas and everything, I'm already behind."

He smiled. "Then an hour or two more won't make that much difference—it'll freshen you up. Besides, don't you want to help me celebrate?"

"You make it so hard to refuse you anything, but—"

"Anything? I can think of one thing you're pretty adamant about."

"Jordan!" She blushed. "Alright then, just this once."

At lunchtime she went home to change. They met, with their bicycles, at the corner of the lane out of sight of the village. Today Jordan succeeded in forgetting the furtiveness they were forced always to observe. Usually it irked him and, in some peculiar way, frightened him.

"I say, you look snazzy," he said.

"Snazzy! What a dreadful word." But she was pleased. Underneath her old black raincoat she wore dark-green slacks and a big polo-neck pink sweater. "It's awkward riding a bike in a frock."

"I know, all those dirty old men crouching behind the hedges, leering."

They laughed together. He felt exultant and tender.

They rode fast, for the shallow wind was with them to Istoke. The clouds were low and deep and moved sluggishly but, although it was warm and humid, it didn't feel like rain.

They chained the bicycles to the railings by the gates and went into the park. He took her hand, hot and rubbery from the handle of the bike, and she let him take it without hesitation.

"You'd never think we've just had Christmas. It feels like spring," she said.

"Thank heavens Christmas is over."

She glanced at him. "I thought you liked Christmas. Don't you?"

"I used to. But I don't any more. It's a bore." He didn't think about what he was saying. She had let her hair free from the scraped-back style of domestic servitude. With her small face rising out of the baggy pink sweater she looked enchanting.

"I don't know. I still like it."

"It's really nothing more than another date in the calendar."

"Oh Jordan."

"Today is a much better day than Christmas."

She smiled at him and freed her hand. "Where are we going?"

"Let's go up to the plantation."

They walked up the low hill, through the brown dead bracken to the iron fence which guarded the New Plantation.

"It's not really new at all," said Annie. "It's a hundred and twelve years old."

Jordan laughed. "Those poor little children still in their cradles, they don't know what's coming to them. By the time you've finished teaching them, it'll be coming out of their ears."

"Facts are important."

"Oh, yes. And the fact is . . . Let's go inside."

114

She looked round, but there was no one about. "Okay."

They climbed the fence and dropped onto the dead leaves on the other side.

"Where shall we go?" Annie asked.

"Into the middle. There's a clearing there and a vista, so you can see Istoke."

The path was mossy and cut at the edges with old cart tracks. Yet sometimes the rhododendrons from either side would almost meet in the middle, so that Annie and Jordan had to rustle their way through the musty, cobwebbed leaves.

There was a peeling green seat in the clearing, but it was surrounded by a huge puddle.

"Come on," Jordan said, "it's not so bad here. It's higher and won't be so damp." He took off his raincoat and spread it on the small hillock.

They sat, knees up, on the raincoat and looked down the open avenue between the trees to Istoke. The cross in the marketplace was clearly visible, but the prospect as a whole was spoiled by the massive red Victorian barracks of the Hampshire Light Infantry which stood on the top of the hill.

"Aren't you glad you came?" he asked.

"Yes, I am." Hunched forward, she stared down the avenue. "It's so wonderful about your exhibition."

"It'll help," he said.

"Is it a lot of money then?"

"Only forty quid a year—that's if I manage to keep it." Jordan raised his hand to her neck and began to rub gently. "It means I can save a bit more for when we get married."

Annie turned her head on her knees to look at him. "I wish you'd not talk about it, Jordan," she said softly.

"Why not?"

"It's so far away, it doesn't seem real somehow."

"Of course it's real. And it's not so far away, either. We could get married while I'm still up at Cambridge."

"Jordan, don't say it. How could we?"

"Listen, in two years you'll have your teacher's certificate. Right? You don't have to teach in Istoke. Why not Cambridge?"

"You'll have to be studying and—"

115

"Do you think you'll stop me working?" He smiled.

"Besides, a teacher doesn't earn much, Jordan. And I can't see the rector supporting a married couple."

"He won't have to support us."

"Forty pounds a year won't go very far." Puzzled, anxious at his lack of realism, she stared at him.

"I've got more than forty pounds," he said, looking away suddenly. "I've got about five or six hundred pounds a year. John's money. Uncle John left me everything he had."

"Oh, Jordan, he didn't!" But she was not contradicting him. When he turned to her, she was crying.

"I wouldn't have anything if it hadn't been for Uncle John. Without him," he said slowly, "well, I wouldn't be anything either. I wouldn't be free. I think that's why he left me the money. He understood that."

Annie's neck was warm and the little tufts of hair at the nape were soft and slippery. Lulled by his rubbing, she closed her eyes. "That's nice," she murmured.

"So you see, we don't have to worry about Uncle Trevor or Aunt Mary or any of them."

They stayed silent for a while. Then Annie said, "But Jordan, I'm scared of what'll happen when they find out that we—we want to . . ."

"Get married. Say it, Annie."

"Get married."

"There isn't anything they can do. They may not like it, but there's nothing they can do."

"I'm scared though. It seems so . . . distant. Not impossible—I know you don't like me to say impossible—but so far away."

He leaned forward and kissed her.

They lay down on the raincoat and, heads back, looked up at the low, grey sky.

Above, the young trees rose loftily around an occasional ancient oak or beech which had been there long before the plantation. A heron's nest rested untidily in the higher branches. But the herons were dying out; the gradual pollution of the River Is was destroying their feeding ground.

"It makes you dizzy, doesn't it?"

116

"Yes," she said. "If you were a bird—a heron—you'd see everything so different. The ground wouldn't matter. You'd be so sort of . . . removed."

"Detached."

"Yes."

"And lonely."

"Yes, I hadn't thought of that."

"Detached and lonely—I don't think I'd care for it much." He propped himself on one elbow and bent down and kissed her. She didn't turn away as she so often did after a moment or two. She kissed him as though the kiss would resolve all doubts and send away her fears.

He rested a hand on her stomach and then slipped it under the pink sweater. Her flesh was marvellously warm.

He moved his hands upwards. She pulled her head away then and whispered, "No, Jordan darling." But he kissed her again, and her body did not shy away.

She just quivered a little when he touched her breast. He was startled that she was wearing no bra, nothing. He had never tried to touch her there before. Gently he caressed her, moving his fingers against the firm obstruction of her nipple.

As he pushed her sweater up and bent his face to her flesh and kissed her breast, he was filled with awe and joy. She pressed his head against her with both hands.

"Jordan, we shouldn't," she said, but she might have been speaking to the herons. He kissed her lips and she his, with eager anxiety, and their bodies touched at every point. And when, awkwardly managing the zipper, he thrust his hand downwards, she shook her head but did not relinquish his kiss. Her negatives were phantasms which neither attended to. As he pulled at her slacks and short cotton pants, she even raised her buttocks so the clothes would slide more easily to her knees, and only momentarily did her thighs grip tight before opening for his hand—and for his body.

She interrupted once, quickly, despairfully that some one was coming. But no one was, and, come the whole populace of Istoke, nothing could prevent the final cure of their flesh.

For a long time they lay together, until the greyness of the day began to be the greyness of evening.

117

She was shivering as he dressed her and kissed her and held her. And then suddenly she laughed and ran away down the avenue. And he ran after her.

She stopped at the other side of the plantation and leaned back against the fence and watched him come running up to her.

"The gate's open!" she called.

He stopped in front of her, so that they could feel each other's breath on their faces.

"Probably is where we came in, too." He smiled.

"And we never even tried!"

"I thought they always locked the gates in winter."

"Yes." She swung the iron gate on its hinges. "So did I. To stop the kids larking about—like us!"

They went through the gate and came out on the stretch of grass which led up to the bandstand.

"It looks so different now, doesn't it?" said Annie.

"Yes." He did not quite know what to make of her.

"Dad used to bring me here before the war. This bit was all cut short and covered with daisies. I remember that. I used to be afraid of treading on them and crushing them."

Jordan said, "I remember you when you were little. You used to sit up there at the counter by your mother in the post office, sorting the letters and looking very important. I envied you."

"They weren't real letters," Annie said. "Just some old envelopes Mum gave me to play with. Did you ever come here?"

"Yes. Once before the war. A long time ago. Uncle John brought me on my birthday."

You'd hardly know it now, he thought, as the same place. The grass, where the bracken had not already taken over, was long and forlorn. The bandstand was paintless and rusty, the balustrades broken where the children had swung on them. Before the war it had been bright with colour and gilding, and there had been chairs set in rows and ice-cream men and children and the band in scarlet and brass. But now it was a ruin.

"It was the best birthday I ever had," Jordan said. "It was the best day I ever had—almost." He turned to her. "Except this one."

They had not touched since coming out of the plantation, but now she took his arm and lifted her face so the hair fell back and revealed her small, faintly pointed ears. "Jordan. It's going to be alright, isn't it? It really is. I'm sorry I . . ."

"I'm not." He kissed her nose. "Come on, I'm hungry. We ought to be able to get some dinner at the Grange by now."

"Oh, not the Grange. Look at me." She turned, showing herself leafy and dishevelled.

He laughed. "Okay, we'll make it the local fish and chippery."

17

"What are they playing now?"

"Regimental march medley." Uncle John had scorned a programme. "Let's see." He hummed for a moment with the band. "Ah—'Fare Ye Well, Inniskilling.' The march of the Royal Inniskilling Fusiliers. Now this—ah, hear that, Jordan? They've speeded up. That's 'Lutzow's Wild Hunt'—60th Rifles. Splendid, eh? Jaunty, eh? They march fast, those little fellows. Never slope arms, you know. Used to be the Royal Americans."

"They're light infantry, aren't they?"

"Rifles, Jordan, Rifles. The King's Royal Rifle Corps. They wouldn't thank you to call them light infantry. Though, in fact—now listen to this. . . ."

The flat-capped Kiddies sat superb in scarlet. The brass instruments winked with sun as the French horns bent to turn a page. The bandmaster's elbows went up and down with precise military jerks and, as he turned to bow, the medals silver and bronze swung away from his chest. A lady in the front row held a bouquet of roses wrapped in green paper.

"Like it, Jordan?"

Jordan turned his head for a moment and nodded.

"Good, eh? You should hear the Guards going up the line, though." His shoulders stiffened. "Going up the line . . ."

"What does 'going up the line' mean, Uncle?"

"Going to fight!" he answered fiercely. He stood up abruptly. "Like an ice?"

"It isn't over, is it?"

"Just an interval."

The Scots Guardsmen were being served glasses of lemonade. One or two of them were standing up and moving their legs in an odd knees-bend.

"Yes, please. I would like an ice," said Jordan.

The two of them walked down the grass gully between the green seats. Uncle John stared above the flouncing summer audience as though they were so many blown pieces of litter. At the edge of the crowd he stopped and gave Jordan two pennies.

"Run over and get us each an ice. I'm going to stand under that tree."

"What kind would you like?"

"A strawberry one," Uncle John said, moving away towards the tree where two girls were sitting eating cornets.

The queue by the Walls man was long but patient. There was something exciting to Jordan about the chattering strangers standing close to him. It was different from the Rectory Fête, where everyone would know him and smile and call him Master Jordan. Here they didn't know him but smiled all the same as if he were one of them.

As he received the two strawberry fruit ices in their cold triangular sleeves from the Walls man, it was a great temptation to begin on his right away. But he resisted it. Upright, one in each hand, like an acolyte he carried the ices to the tree.

He handed one to Uncle John, who had been talking to the two girls.

"Thank you, Jordan." He turned to the mouse-brown girl, who was nudging her friend. "This is my nephew."

"Pleased to meet you."

"Jordan, these, er, young ladies are employed at Ackerman's. It's their half day."

Jordan nodded. He began to eat his ice, staring at the girls.

Uncle John cleared his throat. "Er—wouldn't you like an ice?" he asked the mouse-brown girl.

"I've just had one, thanks."

"Well, have another. Here, have mine. I don't really need an ice." He half turned to Jordan and smiled.

The girl hesitated. "Well," she said, "well, I don't mind if I do." She bit into it. "Want a bite, Molly?"

120

Molly took a large bite and handed back the ice.

"Thanks ever so," said the girl to Uncle John.

"Pleasure, my dear." He beamed. But Jordan's stare seemed to make the two girls uncomfortable.

They stood in silence eating their ices, Uncle John sometimes clearing his throat with a fierce rasp.

Jordan finished. "We'd better get back to our seats, hadn't we?"

"Yes, yes. I suppose we had." Uncle John tipped his hat to the girls. "Goodbye," he said. As soon as he and Jordan had gone two yards, the girls began to chatter.

"Charming little things, charming," murmured Uncle John as they took their places.

The second half of the programme was orchestral, and the woodwinds did a lot of twittering. At first Uncle John's attention didn't seem to be fully concentrated on the music, but after a while he began to hum, and Jordan felt better.

"Let's get away from these crowds," said Uncle John when the concert was done. Hand in hand, they skirted the plantation and went to the heart of the park—too far in the heat for all but lovers to penetrate.

"Just suppose, Jordan," Uncle John said, stopping on the brow of a ridge, "just suppose you had to give battle here, now."

Jordan grinned with delight. "What date, Uncle?"

"Napoleonic wars. You've got fifteen thousand infantry, but only four battalions you know you can rely on. The rest are raw. Three thousand cavalry. Three batteries of horse artillery. Now the details. One of your infantry battalions is Rifles." Frowning into the sunlight, Uncle John slowly ticked off on his fingers the precise regimental make-up of Jordan's force. They had done this so often, there was no need of pencil and paper. "The enemy outnumbers you. Twenty thousand infantry, five cavalry. But only a single squadron of horse artillery. One third well-seasoned troops—the rest the dregs of Bonaparte's latest conscription. You have definite intelligence that . . ." Uncle John glanced at his watch. "Right now, you have an hour to make your dispositions before the enemy arrive on the field."

Jordan surveyed the ground carefully. On the right the ridge on which they stood sloped down to a large pond surrounded with marsh grass. On the left the ridge curled in a walking-stick crook towards what would be the French line. The front bulged very slightly outward in the centre, and on the bulge was a group of birch trees and gorse.

"I think," Jordan said, "it will have to be a defensive battle."

Uncle John nodded. "Right. Let them come to you. Right you are."

Slowly Jordan outlined his plans. His right was well protected, but because of the nature of the ground his left was vulnerable. He would therefore hold the right lightly, putting most of his cavalry and his seasoned infantry on the left. The main body of artillery in the centre, and . . .

"You ought to make use of that cover, Jordan," said John, pointing to the birch trees and gorse. "Put a detachment of your Rifles up there and let them fire at will into the enemy centre. Rifles are always good sharpshooters and skirmishers."

"Why, Uncle?"

"Your rifle has twice the accurate range of your musket—two, even two hundred and fifty yards. On the other hand a rifle takes longer to load—because of the rifled barrel. So for accurate fire use your rifles. For steady volume of fire power, close range, rely on your musket."

Uncle and nephew stood on the ridge, thrashing out the detailed dispositions and, eventually, with John taking the French part, fighting the battle. They had fought on every scrap of ground for two miles around Sibley and knew each nook and cranny, hedge and stream, the soft ground and the sudden hollow. But Istoke Park was new and exciting territory.

The battle was long and one of the best. Really, thought Jordan as finally they walked to the park gates, the best.

"A draw, I'd say, Jordan," said Uncle John. And then, magnanimously, "but slightly in your favour. I mauled you pretty badly, but you did the same for me and I didn't get through. I can't advance, so I'll have to retire—find another way round. You blocked me. Good work."

They had late tea at the Mill House, which was the best teashop in Istoke.

"Uncle John, would an airgun be any good in battle?"

"An airgun!" John turned a shocked face to his nephew. "That popgun Trevor keeps to guard his wretched fig tree? Useless, absolutely useless. Couldn't stop a crippled sparrow at ten yards."

Looking covertly round the other tables in the teashop, Jordan decided that no one could compare with Uncle John, who sat stiff and determined, every inch a fighter.

18

"You wanted to see me, sir?"

"Yes, come in, Maddox." Mr. Prideaux got up from behind his desk and sat down in the leather arm chair by the comfortably poppling gas fire. "Sit."

The housemaster was tall and languid. He was reputed to have a large private income, for he offered even parents an excellent Spanish amontillado.

"I'm afraid I have some rather bad news for you, Maddox." Mr. Prideaux fitted a cigarette into a platinum holder.

Jordan thought quickly of his crimes, but there were none whose discovery could warrant such ceremony.

"Your uncle has met with an accident."

Uncle Trevor, his old Wolseley swaying about on the road, his mind on the selection of next Sunday's hymns. It had happened before, but . . . "A bad accident, sir?"

"I'm afraid so." Mr. Prideaux moved his unlit cigarette from one hand to the other. "You must brace yourself. Yesterday evening. He suffered fatal injuries—he, er, fell out of a window. He died this morning."

"Uncle Trevor fell out of a window?" It was absolutely impossible.

"Yes." Mr. Prideaux took a scribbled note from his pocket and glanced at it. "Er—wait a minute. Oh no no, not your guardian. It was Colonel John Freeman."

Jordan was on his feet. "No!"

"Now sit down, my boy."

"No!" He stepped forward, as if to—as if to what? "Somebody pushed him!"

"Pull yourself together, Maddox," snapped Mr. Prideaux. "Sit down."

Jordan sat. He looked at the gas fire. It became a hot gold blur. "Which window?" he asked. His voice trembled.

"Which window? I don't know. Does it matter?" The housemaster paused, and then infused his tones with stern sympathy. "Look, er, Jordan, you mustn't let yourself go, you know. I understand you were fond of your uncle. These things hit hard. I know."

Jordan said nothing.

Mr. Prideaux stood up and lit his cigarette. "John Freeman. I remember now, of course. He was in the house, wasn't he?" The housemaster's words came from somewhere far above Jordan's bent head. "Before my time, of course. But I've seen his name up on the shields. A fine athlete. Had a splendid war record too, didn't he? Don't I recall? M.C.?—D.S.O.? You must have admired him very much, Maddox. He—"

"D.S.O. and bar," said Jordan almost inaudibly.

"Did he, by Jove?" Mr. Prideaux enthusiastically jangled the change in his trouser pocket. "A brave man. That's what you must think of, Maddox. Courage. There's all too little of that about nowadays—I mean of course, er, before the war, that is. We're all pulling together now, aren't we? Pulling together. Courage. Now your uncle wouldn't have wanted to see you like this, would he?"

"He wouldn't have cared."

"Oh, come now, Maddox, I'm sure—"

"He cried himself."

Mr. Prideaux laughed gently. "Now, Maddox, I'm sure—"

"He cried. He couldn't help it." In the attic workroom that terrible day . . . Jordan's mind darted to Uncle John, stoop-shouldered and tears pouring unhampered, yes, pouring. . . .

"Maddox."

"What?"

"I said, would you like a glass of sherry?"

"Oh yes."

Mr. Prideaux talked over his shoulder as he poured. "Don't usually dispense sherry to the boys. But after all, you're a senior man now, aren't you? Not playing a match tomorrow, are you?"

"No, sir."

"Well, that's alright then. Here. Steadies you, doesn't it? Steadiness is a great quality, Maddox—stamina. Not something people notice much, you know, but in a crisis it's steadiness that counts. Waterloo. Dunkirk. Cicero said—not that I'm a wholehearted admirer of his, but the old boy had some points—Cicero said—"

The phone rang.

124

"Blast," said Mr. Prideaux. "Yes. Prideaux speaking. Yes. I have him here now. Very well. Maddox, your godfather wants to speak to you. Hold on a minute, Mr. Sutlif." He handed the receiver to Jordan somewhat reluctantly.

"Jordan, that you?"

"Hello, Uncle Colin."

"Prideaux tells me you've been told about John. Well now, the funeral's the day after tomorrow. You don't have to come, of course—in fact Mary thinks you might prefer not to. But I thought—"

"Yes, I want to come."

"Right. Thought you might. I'm having a car take me down tomorrow evening. I can pick you up on the way. I'll be at the school at about six. Can you be ready then?"

"Yes."

"Good. Tell Prideaux, will you? I'll deliver you back on Thursday. Alright, got it?"

"Yes." Jordan paused as the three-minute beeps sounded. "Uncle Colin, what happened?"

"He fell out of his bedroom window. I'm not too clear about it myself, to tell you the truth. But we can talk about it on the way down to Sibley tomorrow. And Jordan—don't let it get you down too much. Jordan?"

"Yes?"

"I'm not very good at this sort of thing, I'm afraid. But—well, don't let it get you down."

"No."

"Goodbye, old chap."

"Goodbye."

The car was a prewar Humber with a glass partition between driver and passengers and handles covered with tight netting to hang onto when the car cornered.

Colin and Jordan sat in the back. They didn't say much.

Halfway down they stopped for dinner at a pub with a small restaurant attached.

"I told Mary not to expect us till after dinner," Colin said. "I don't suppose she feels very much like cooking at the moment."

Colin enjoyed eating. And, although she had been cooking all the meals now since the maids left in 1940, Aunt Mary managed to make all food tasteless. Jordan was not hungry.

"It's almost always unwise to give advice, you know," Colin said. He was drinking gin, which he disliked, but it was the only kind of spirits the pub had. "But I know—well, dammit, you were more attached to John, and he to you, than anyone else, I think."

Jordan said nothing.

"None of us—well, least of all me, I'm only a proxy member of the family—but Trevor and Mary, they never understood him, I feel, in quite the way you did. I'm not a very perceptive person myself—and I may tell you I've never wanted to be—but I don't see things in quite such a black-and-white fashion as Trevor and Mary, particularly perhaps Mary." He drank half of his gin.

In the back of his mind Jordan was aware of Colin's awkwardness, but he was not really thinking about Colin at all.

"We're all liable to go off the rails once in a while, you know." He paused; the expression on his face was one of complete absorption, as though what he were saying was surprising and profound.

"When John had his mishap and that's the way I think of it, a mishap, not a deliberate, er, immoral act. After all, John was never quite normal. Not since the war of course, before that . . . I remember John when he was the last person on God's earth you would think of as simpleminded. He was—well, what he was is neither here nor there. But he was never malicious. I'm wandering a bit, I'm afraid." He finished his gin. "Well, you couldn't expect Mary to understand really, could you? A sexual offence, that's all Mary saw—and she's never in her life wanted to see much beyond the flowers and the bees. But even then, even if she and Trevor had not been so— straightlaced, it's difficult to know what else they could have done. Obviously John couldn't be let out on his own again, could he? And they weren't unkind, you know." He turned towards the room and raised his hand slowly. "A large gin and orange."

He waited until the drink was brought and then went on. "What I'm really trying to say is, no one is to blame for what has happened. No one. You understand that, Jordan?"

Jordan smiled mechanically.

"No one," Colin said, "except the Jerry shell in 1917 that hit John's battalion HQ. It might have been better if there'd been no survivors from that. Perhaps it might have been better."

The food arrived. Colin looked speculatively at his plate. "I've never told you much about your father, have I?"

Jordan said, "He was a drunk."

Colin's head jerked up. "He was the dearest friend I ever had in the world."

Jordan sighed. "I'm sorry, Uncle Colin."

"Let's forget the 'Uncle' from now on, shall we, old chap? I've never been very good at this *in loco parentis* business." He smiled.

Colin began to eat, slowly at first, but gradually getting into the rhythm. Once or twice he frowned. Once or twice he started to say something. Jordan could not eat.

When Colin had finished and had ordered a Van der Hum, Jordan said, "It wasn't an accident, was it?"

Colin took a cigar from his case and dipped the end carefully into his black coffee. "I don't know. Mary—I don't blame her—was a bit cagey on the phone."

"Aunt Mary phoned you?"

"I gather, reading between the lines, that Trevor was in rather a state. When John fell, he apparently tried to save himself by grabbing the fig tree. Well, the whole thing came with him."

"The fig tree came down?"

"Yes. The whole thing was rather a mess." He began to light his cigar.

"That must have broken Uncle Trevor's heart."

Colin looked at Jordan over the end of the cigar he was gently drawing on. When it was fully alight, he said, "Another odd thing. John wasn't wearing any clothes. Nothing. Stark naked."

"Aunt Mary told you that?"

"No. No, she didn't. But I phoned the curate—Mansard—and had a word with him."

"Then you do think there's something funny about it?"

Colin stirred his sugarless coffee. "This bloody war," he murmured. He laid the spoon down and looked at Jordan. "I don't know." He seemed to make a great effort. "It may—and I only say may—have been suicide."

Jordan sat stone still. Ever since he'd heard, nothing else had been in his mind.

"You've got to face the possibility, Jordan. Face it and dismiss it. We'll never know." Colin was firm. "For all practical purposes, it was an accident. I don't know if there'll be an inquest. But if there is, that's what it'll be—an accident. We all know how John used to lean far out to clip the leaves of the fig tree away from his window and—"

"Only in summer."

"Well, that's not . . ." Colin frowned.

"Why did he do it?"

"God knows," Colin said. "If he did do it. We can only surmise. Perhaps it all proved too much for him at last. He had been, well, going downhill. He was not—happy."

Jordan laughed.

"We had better be off, I think," Colin said at last.

Outside in the dark they stood for a few moments before getting into the car.

The night in some way concealed their embarrassment. The end of Colin's cigar brightened and dulled, brightened and dulled.

"Look, old chap," he said, "it's all over and done with now. And that's the way you should try to think of it. It will take time, of course. But time passes quickly. Too quickly. Remember that."

The driver was waiting in the car.

With his hand on the door, Colin said, "I'm afraid I sound awfully sententious at times like these."

They got in and the car started.

"We'll be there in an hour."

19

They were standing, waiting for him in the solicitors' room.

Jordan sensed at once that something was up. "Hello, Bartlett. Tom. This is unexpected." He tried to shut off his automatic smile.

"Sit down, Maddox, will you?" Bartlett said.

The three chairs scraped the unpolished linoleum.

Tom was flushed and breathing audibly. But it was Bartlett Jordan looked at. All the others in their familiar aspect could be ignored: landmarks along a road he travelled every day and therefore did not have to attend to. The hedges, the ditches, the red new council houses, the stretch of high glass-topped wall, the clock on the post office, the green barrows in the station yard. But Bartlett bore watching, a sign on the verge just where your eye must fall. STEEP HILL. BENDS FOR ONE MILE.

"Shall I . . . ?" Tom began.

"Just one moment, Short, if you would." The barrister touched the base of his ear. The lobe was very small and white. "You'll recollect our talk last week, Maddox, when I suggested that one of the weaker aspects of the prosecution's case was a lack of evidence of motive?"

"Yes."

"The Director of Public Prosecutions' office has now produced some evidence, or what purports to be evidence, of somewhat closer ties between yourself and June Singer than has hitherto been suggested. This was communicated to us this morning. I suggest Short run through this quickly for you, and then we can take it up point by point and let you cast any light you can upon it." He paused. "Short?"

Tom had taken some papers from a black attaché case. He glanced down at them. "There are really six points." He cleared his throat. "I'll deal with them as they come. First of all there's a letter you wrote to a publisher in New York called Timberley. You remember that?"

"I must have written a hundred letters to Jack Timberley over the years."

"Short," Bartlett interrupted, "let's just give Maddox the full picture, shall we? We can go into the details later."

Tom flushed. He looked as though he had drunk a great deal for lunch. "Right. This letter was written on February the eighteenth. Essentially you're asking Timberley about the prospects of a job for June Singer. There's his reply, actually offering her a job—through you, that is. And then June's letter—a photostat—to Timberley, refusing the job. The point of all this being, of course, that—"

A tiny gesture from Bartlett stopped Tom in midrack.

"To get on. The next item is a photograph of June Singer which was found in the drawer of your desk at your office."

"A photo of June in my desk?"

"Yes. She's wearing a summer frock and—" he looked down at his notes—"the photo appears to have been taken in the country."

"Can I see it?" Jordan held out his hand.

"The D.P.P.'s office hasn't seen fit as yet to provide us with a copy," Tom said angrily, as though it was Jordan's fault. "Bartlett and I have seen it, though."

"What in God's name would I want with a photo of June? Why, I saw her every day. . . ."

Tom's effort of restraint was evident from the rigidness of his body. And suddenly Jordan felt he'd been through all this before.

"And to tie in with that," Tom went on, "there was found in June's handbag a photograph of yourself. You're wearing—"

Jordan laughed. "That is ludicrous."

"Shall we continue?" said Tom tightly. "The letters and the photographs will be exhibits. In addition to this, we are served notice of three additional witnesses the Crown will call. First is a fellow called Lambert. He's a chemist's assistant—assistant dispenser. He'll give evidence that Singer purchased several bottles of a laxative preparation over a period of two or three weeks in February and March."

"What—?"

"Laxatives are commonly held to be an abortive agent if taken in sufficiently large quantities."

And Jordan remembered: *All that stuff she was taking. All that time you were urging her to get rid of it.* He shook his head.

"You don't agree?" said Tom.

"Agree with what?"

"I was telling you," Tom said very carefully, "about the testimony that will be given by Mrs. Payne. Mrs. Payne is the woman who lived below June Singer and her mother in Putney. She used to give Mrs. Singer lunch and generally looked after her if June went out. She's a widow. We are informed she'll testify that you wrote a number of letters to June, that you frequently gave June flowers and that she, June, talked of you with great affection."

Jordan stared at the solicitor. "Tom, you must be making this up."

"*I'm* not making it up, old man."

"But—"

"Let's just get to the end of it, Maddox," said Bartlett.

"Finally," said Tom, "there is a Mr. Harold Grand, waiter at Blain's Restaurant, who will testify that he saw you having dinner alone with June Singer on the night of January the tenth—indeed, that he served you—and that you appeared to be on intimate terms with her." Tom blew out a long breath. "That's the lot, in a nutshell."

"It's absolute, utter nonsense. I've never heard such an extraordinary tangle of lies and half-truths." But he had, of course. He remembered it—the hot dry smell of the suffocating little room at Sarah Street.

"I'm interested in this evidence of Grand's," Bartlett said. "Did you in fact dine with Singer on the night of January the tenth?"

"I'm not sure whether it was the tenth," said Jordan slowly. "But I did have dinner with her one night at the beginning of January, I remember now."

"Why so late?" Bartlett asked.

"Late?"

"Grand is going to say that you were there between ten forty-five and midnight."

"Oh well, after the theatre, you know—"

"You took her to the theatre?"

"I didn't exactly take her to the theatre," Jordan said petulantly. "It was—well, I had given her a couple of theatre tickets, you see. And she told me, after a bit of pressing, that she didn't have anyone to go with. Well, I felt sorry for her. Her mother had died not long before, you know. And there was no reason why I shouldn't go with her. Willy—my wife and daughter were spending a week down at Sibley with my aunt and uncle. That's why I gave her—June—the tickets, as a matter of fact. And then . . ."

"And then?"

"What? Oh well, nothing really."

"Nothing?" The barrister made the word sound unlikely. "What was the play?"

"I don't recall."

"Any idea which theatre?"

"I really don't, no."

"And after the theatre, you took her to dine at Blain's?"

"We had dinner, yes."

"Drinks?"

"I suppose so."

"And then—did you take her home?"

"I rather believe I did, in a taxi."

"To Panton Place?"

"Yes."

"Did you go up?"

"Of course not."

"Did you kiss her good night?"

"Certainly not. Now look—"

"Maddox, please understand I'm only trying to elicit what happened, and—"

"Nothing happened."

"Ummm." He paused. "That week your wife was away, did you take Singer out again?"

"No, I did not. It was the purest accident that I took her out in the first place."

"Did you tell your wife you'd taken your secretary out?"

Jordan was aware of Tom looking at him. "I didn't think it was necessary," he said, trying to match Bartlett's detachment.

"You didn't think it was necessary," said the barrister coldly. "I'm very glad, Maddox, that no jury is going to hear those words."

Bartlett sat quite still. He was very angry, it came to Jordan.

"Maddox—is there any reason why you should not have informed Short or myself of this earlier?"

"No, I don't think so—I . . .." There was a tremor in his voice, in his body. And he had again that strange sweet sensation. . . .

"Well?"

"I—I had forgotten all about it, I suppose. It didn't seem important."

"Good God, man," Tom said loudly, "this isn't some kind of a game. Bartlett's absolutely right—" He was brought up abruptly by a light tapping of the barrister's fingernail on the table.

"You had forgotten. Or you remembered, but it didn't seem important," said Bartlett. "Which?"

"Well, I suppose it was at the back of my mind. But I didn't consciously think about it."

Bartlett took a few moments to light a cigarette. He didn't offer one to Jordan or to Tom Short.

Jordan said, "I'm sorry if I messed things up."

"Messed things up?" Tom laughed. "You could hardly of done a better job if you had actually murdered the blasted girl."

"You think I murdered June Singer?" He spoke to Tom, but the question was for Bartlett.

"Oh, for Christ's sake, Jordan," Tom burst out, ignoring the barrister's movement of restraint, "of course you bloody well didn't do it. You wouldn't have enough backbone. And that's just the point. Every time—"

"Short!"

"—every time we get onto firm ground, you just casually come up with something that knocks the whole bottom out of our strategy. Anyone would think you bloody well wanted to—"

"I must ask you to be silent." Bartlett's slicing courtroom voice cut Tom off.

Tom's big footballer's body was still as in the second before kickoff, head up, heavy red cheeks rigid, throat strained for the yell of attack. But there was no yell, only a faint grunt.

Bartlett brushed some smoke away from his face. He smoked the cigarette rapidly, as though anxious to get to the end of it. When he did, he stubbed it out briskly.

"Maddox," he said, "as counsel for your defence, I am of course completely in your hands. I form the impression, however, that you are not entirely aware of the seriousness of the case against you."

Jordan felt something slipping away, a sharpness within him becoming blurred by reasonableness. He shut his eyes for a moment and could almost imagine himself back at Sarah Street. He looked up at the bare bulb with its fringe of dust, and the light seemed to sway.

". . . very serious. In law we are not obliged to prove that you did not murder June Singer. That is fortunate, for we cannot prove it. What we have to rely on is establishing real and reasonable doubt of your guilt. Our chief hope of instilling such doubt into the minds of the jurors lies in the fact that, if you had killed Singer, it would have been a motiveless murder. Thus we must establish, or see to it that the Crown fails to establish, two things. First, that you are not mentally unbalanced, in other words, that you would not be likely to commit a pointless and profitless crime. Second, that you were not in love with the girl, did not have an affair with her, et cetera. In sum, we must establish that you are a reasonable man without the slightest motive for murder. That is our assumption. Do I make myself clear?"

Jordan looked down from the light. The image of the bulb hovered about the lawyer's face. "Yes."

"In the light of that assumption, anything—anything whatever—in your relationship to Singer outside the usual and normal intercourse between employer and employee automatically becomes evidence for the prosecution. Anything whatever, no matter how small. Evidently, Maddox, you had not fully grasped that point. Do you now?"

"Yes."

"And so that means that we must produce and substantiate, insofar as possible, a reasonable explanation for every point which the prosecution produces to suggest a guilty association with the girl. You must, for instance, reasonably be able to explain why you took Singer to the theatre."

"Yes."

"You must be able to explain in reasonable terms why you wrote that letter to Mr. Timberley in New York."

"Yes."

"You must reasonably explain . . ."

"Yes. . . ." If he could just go on effortlessly saying yes, everything would be alright. They would be happy and he would be happy. He would be able to go back to his private ward and drift away. He became aware that Bartlett had stopped talking.

The image of the light had gone now, and he saw that the barrister was looking at him with a slight smile.

"Yes," said Jordan, not knowing to what he was assenting.

"Good. Then, first of all, I think we'd better go back to that Monday morning, the morning of the murder. Let's go over it again and make quite certain there is not a single point we have missed. Please tell us everything that happened, everything that you can remember."

Jordan was silent for a moment. He was more tired than he had ever been in his life. Now he was going to have to walk up a long steep hill with a great weight upon his shoulders. Perhaps when he got to the top they would allow him to collapse.

20

"Why, it's you, Mr. Maddox."

"Hello, June. I'm afraid I got you out of bed."

"Oh no, that's quite alright." She stood holding the front door ajar, as if uncertain what to do next.

"I'd better come in, hadn't I?"

"Oh yes. I am sorry. I hope you don't mind." She looked down at her flowered dressing gown.

He smiled. "As long as the neighbours don't see."

She tilted her head to one side, which was her way, rather than any blush or fussing, of showing embarrassment.

"It's only one flight up," she said. He followed her up the stairs. She wore slippered boots, blue suede outside, fur bulging over the edge. Somehow they did not seem very like June.

"Watch out for the stair carpet here," she said. "The runner's loose and always slipping out. You could have ever such a nasty fall, if you weren't careful."

She let him into the flat. Just a large room with a couple of gas burners. Yet it was not in the least austere.

"You really shouldn't have bothered," she said. "I could just as easy have come up this morning."

"I wouldn't dream of it. On your holidays. Bad enough me routing you out like this. When are you off?"

June shut the door behind him. "I'm lucky I get the morning sun," she said.

"It's a nice room."

"I'm glad you like it. Oh, the bed." She quickly pulled a velveteen coverlet over the unmade bed. Jordan caught the smell of warm sheets.

"When are you off?" he asked.

"Well, I'm not going abroad like I planned. I'm going to the country instead. It looks as though I've got the good weather, doesn't it?"

"It'll be summer before we know it."

"Well, you brought it with you. Wouldn't you like to take off your coat?"

He looked at his watch.

"I finished the typing up," she said, "but there are one or two things I want to show you. They don't seem to make much sense."

"That's par for the course."

"I could make you a cup of coffee. If you don't mind Nescafé. It'll only take a second."

"Well, alright," he said. Then, "I'd love it. Much better than tea."

"Don't you like tea?" She was astonished.

"Well . . ."

"An' I brought you tea all these mornings and you never said anything."

"Thank you. I did say thank you." He smiled. He put the tulips on the table. "These are for you, if you'd like them."

She touched the closed yellow buds with the tip of her finger. "They're lovely. They even *feel* fresh. But I oughtn't to, really. I'll be leaving tomorrow. It would be a waste."

"Well, you can give them to your Mrs. Ardley. That should send up your stock."

June made a face and Jordan laughed. She reminded him for an instant of Georgia.

June went to the washbasin in the corner of the room and filled a small enamel saucepan with water.

He took off his coat and scarf and gloves and sat down. There were three neat piles of manuscript on the table. But he didn't look at the manuscript. The room was almost familiar, so much did it remind him of Cambridge, the early days of Cambridge. The two Van Gogh prints framed in plain wood, the sideboard filled with crockery and with books on top—an even bet they'd include *A History of Western Philosophy*, a Pelican edition of *Outline of History*, and perhaps even *The Bible Designed to Be Read as Literature*—the gas fire, the ashtray that looked as though it had been taken from some foreign hotel. But no, June had not been abroad.

"You changed your mind about going to Switzerland?"

"Well yes. I didn't fancy somehow being in a strange place. I am a bit silly, I suppose, after making all those plans." She lit the burner and put the saucepan over the flame.

"Oh, I don't know." She had been eager to have her holidays early this year. Her mother had left her a few hundred pounds apparently, and she had wanted, he thought, to blow it—or some of it. "It's more fun in a way not making up your mind in advance where you want to go." It was a point he had never been able to get across to Willy.

"Yes, isn't it? You never really see the spring in England, not in an office, not in London."

He wondered what she did with her weekends. A drab London Sunday with nowhere to go but this little room.

"I'm glad I didn't go to New York," she said.

"Are you?"

"I couldn't bear to leave England. Although it was very nice of Mr.

Timberley to offer me the job. New York would be a very lonely place, I think."

"It can be a very exciting place, too, I'm told."

"I don't care for excitement much. I'd rather be stodgy and English."

"And type manuscripts for dull old Sutlif and Maddox."

"But it's not dull! I love working for Sutlif and Maddox."

And he believed she did. He didn't pretend to know why. There were no people her own age. And there was no position to which she could be promoted.

June put two cups of coffee on the table. "Would you like a piece of Swiss roll?" she said.

He grimaced.

"You don't mind if I do then, do you?" she asked apologetically. "I've got ever such a sweet tooth."

He shook his head and watched her. She placed the knife consideringly on the chocolate roll, then moved it an inch to give herself a larger piece. As she pressed the blade down, white cream oozed fatly and a few dark-brown crumbs fell to the plate.

"There," she said, withdrawing the knife.

He said, "You do that as if—"

"As if what?"

With a kind of slow, contemplative greed that disturbed him. He said, "As if you thought it was pretty important."

She said seriously, "Mum would never let me have cake for breakfast. When I was a little girl, I thought it would be the most wonderful thing in the world." She smiled. "I still do."

"I couldn't imagine anything more horrible," he said.

"Most people seem to feel like that." She looked at him mischievously. "It makes me quite guilty." She picked up the cake and took a bite. For a moment there was cream on her lips, and then her tongue shot out and gathered it up.

Jordan could not prevent himself from watching her. "Well," he said, "I think we'd better get down to it."

She nodded. "I've put paper clips on the problem pages. Now this paragraph here, I'm sure that's supposed to go at the bottom of the page. It doesn't make sense otherwise. . . ."

They weren't difficult problems. And her solutions were sensible. They always were. Jordan only had to give the appearance of attention. For he had realised some time ago that she was actually a rather better editor than he was.

While she explained, he watched her rather than the manuscript. There was still an aura of sleepiness about her. Perhaps it was the lack of lipstick, but she seemed smoother than the office June, whom sometimes, when he was feeling businesslike, he called "Miss Singer." She was certainly not Miss Singer now. She was a girl in a dressing gown with sunlight on her face—a distant relation of the precise secretary at the office. When she smiled at him, he could see brown stains on her teeth from the chocolate Swiss roll. It fascinated him.

"Well, that's everything, I think, Mr. Maddox."

"Good," he said. Mr. Maddox! How ridiculous. There ought to be something in between Mr. Maddox and Jordan. Initials? J. J. M. No, the anonymity of initials was even worse than the surname.

"Would you like some more coffee?"

"Yes, I think I would." He got up and went to the window. He looked down on what must have been a bomb site, but the rubble of bricks had been crushed and smoothed pancake flat.

"They're going to build a block of flats there soon," she said from beside him. "Next year I won't have any more sunlight."

He turned to her. It was a pity she didn't get married and settle down and have children. Of course he'd never get such a good secretary again, but it would be worth the sacrifice. It was on the tip of his tongue to tell her. . . .

"I like it here," she said, and smiled. Again the trace of chocolate roll on her teeth.

He said quickly, "It's very comfortable. But there's such a thing as too much comfort." Why on earth had he said that?

"Oh I know, Mr. Maddox." She frowned.

"I'm sorry," he said. "I've no right to make that sort of remark."

"No, you are right. It's just that, just that . . ." She looked, almost sadly, he thought, out of the window.

"I'm afraid I've depressed you, just with your holidays starting too." He touched her arm with his hand but withdrew it quickly. He felt an odd sense of strain.

"Oh no. You've cheered me up. I'm much happier about going away now we've cleared up all this." She indicated the manuscript on the table.

"You'll have a wonderful time," he said.

"Yes I shall." But she didn't sound completely confident.

Jordan wondered why not, as he sat talking to her and drinking his second cup of coffee. They talked mostly about the office, and he had the impression that she would have liked not to be going away, not just then. He glanced at the old-fashioned alarm clock by her bed.

"I think I'd better be off." He stood up and she helped him on with his coat. "Have a good time," he said, "and don't think about the office. I'll manage without you, I expect."

She opened the door for him.

"I can manage," he said.

"I'll see you to the stairs."

He turned clumsily at the top of the stairs and stepped down. The carpet came away and he knew he was going to fall backwards. Hand outstretched to shake his, June grabbed quickly. He hardly felt the sharpness of her nails on his wrist as he crashed heavily backwards against the banister, slid down, and ended up kneeling, but still clutching manuscript and typewriter.

"Oh, dear. Are you alright, Jordan? That carpet. Are you hurt? Oh, I'm ever so sorry." She was kneeling beside him.

He was dazed, trembling a little at the shock. "That was a narrow escape." He laughed.

She took his hand and held it palm up. "Oh, look what I done to your wrist. My wretched nails."

He looked down. The fat globules of blood from the torn skin were already beginning to join up in a scarlet streak. "Just a graze."

"Oh I'm ever so sorry."

Her mouth open, her eyes—oh lord, surely she wasn't going to cry.

"It's nothing," he said.

"We must put iodine on it. I got some in my room."

He tried to move his hand, but for a moment she held it fast, and suddenly he was abnormally aware of the contact. He pulled away. "It's nothing. I think it's upset you more than me."

"I am so sorry. I wouldn't hurt—"

"Come come. It's not as bad as all that." He stood up. For a moment she remained crouched, then slowly she raised herself.

"I really ought to put some iodine on it."

139

"No no," he said cheerfully. "I'm going to be late as it is. You go on back to your room. Have another piece of Swiss roll—that'll cheer you up."

He wished she wouldn't look so forlorn. "Come on." He held out his hand, and she shook it. "Forget about it," he said. "Have a good time."

"Thank you, Mr. Maddox."

"Goodbye." He was eager to get away.

"Goodbye."

He went down the stairs and opened the front door. He glanced back. She was standing in the same position on the stairs. "Goodbye," he called. He didn't hear what she murmured in reply.

He shut the door behind him and stood for a moment on the front step. He blew a frosty breath into the air. The sun shone. The day was a perfect one—and he'd missed the rush hour by now.

He ran down the steps and into the street. Despite the heavy package of manuscript and the typewriter, he decided to walk a little way before taking the bus. June was quite right, one never did really see the spring in London, cooped up in an office.

He put his head back and straightened his shoulders. As he walked briskly along the pavement, he began to hum a military march.

THE TENDER DEAD

21

"Put up the prisoner!"

The cell door was pulled open.

"Right. Come on." Denver, amiability gone, stern, suit pressed, squared-off cap. Jordan went first, then Denver was beside him; they wheeled; an unfamiliar warder fell in on Jordan's left.

"Get a move on," said a voice behind them. Jordan had to half run to keep up.

Halt, one-two. The strange warder stamped his boot.

"Five seconds."

"Right."

"Snap to it."

Denver ran quickly up the stairs ahead of him.

"Up you go then!" The warder gripped Jordan's elbow and pushed him up the stone steps.

He stumbled, grazing the toe of his shoe, and then he was in the dock, a warder on each side of him.

He faced the judge. There seemed to be no one else in the court. Jordan risked a glance to his left. Yes, that would be the jury—nine men and three women. Below him, to his right, like strange insects with their brains exposed, were the moving, wigged heads of counsel.

Jordan stood at attention. Eyes front. The judge—a face straight out of the National Portrait Gallery. A face carved and detached by time. The judge opened his mouth and shut it. He did this every few seconds. False teeth? Jordan started to smile but managed to stop himself. It wouldn't do to smile. They'd think—if they saw—they'd think his nonchalance monstrous. A nonchalant monster.

He looked down at his shoes. The left toecap had a deep scratch.

Otherwise he was well-dressed—blue-striped shirt, stiff collar, his best grey suit—as though he were going to a party later on. Willy had brought the suit up the day before, specially pressed. *The accused was modishly attired in a charcoal-grey worsted suit by Ticklers of Bond Street.*

He stiffened as he heard his name: "Jordan John Maddox." The voice was far away, as though it came from a faulty wireless. The unknown warder nudged him.

"What?"

The volume was turned up sharply.

"Do you plead guilty or not guilty?"

They were waiting for him. He trembled. He had not used his voice for years. He didn't know if he could. He tried to think. Why hadn't someone told him the answer? How could he be expected to think with the clerk of the court bobbing up and down like that, dancing, weaving? It was ridiculous—an absurd programme. Turn it off—turn it off!

The judge was saying something now, champing. It must be false teeth. And then the voice boomed again with the rundown hollow sound of a tired gramophone.

Jordan put his hands on the bar before him. There were two judges, two clerks—dancing Siamese twins. He had to try. If his voice didn't work, he must mouth the words. Guilty—not guilty. Not guilty—guilty. Guilty not—guilty. His mind caught the rhythm and timed it to the frivolous, shimmering image of the wigged clown in front of him. *Click, click-click*—alternate flashes of a lighthouse whose warning he did not understand. And then the courtroom tipped, slowly to the left. Ponderously it steadied, stopped, and began a slow arc to the right. At the centre of the seesaw, Jordan clutched at the rail, bracing his arms, his legs till the knee joint trembled. A thousand tiny points of blackness enveloped his brain, cleared, then came again, tempting his carcass to slack oblivion. He fought it off and held to the rising nausea which promised the bitter, clean relief of vomit. Like salvation, he tasted it upon his tongue. All their courts and counsel and briefs meant nothing now. He shut his eyes and bowed his head to summon strength. Then, eyes open, head suddenly back, limbs rigid, he opened his mouth and spoke.

What words they were, where they went, he did not know. It did not matter. He was free, a patient purged. Yet not quite—there was something missing, something undone. Some word unspoken. Trivial, vital. Good night? Farewell? Sweet dreams? No—no. It was . . .

"My Lord."

The images shivered and became one. The motion ceased. He could see and hear, but remotely—with the detachment of a convalescent.

The clerk was now asking him if he wanted to object to any member of the jury. Jordan turned and stared at the twelve bodies. He observed their faces, the women's hats. They were dressed in their unobjectionable best, except for one man who was wearing a light-green shirt. Was that grounds? A green shirt might be a good sign—a man of outward and visible, and thus mild, nonconformity. Or was it an ostentation denoting deep disturbance? But then one would have to know if Green Shirt wore it especially for the occasion, or as a regular thing, or because his wife liked it—if he had a wife. . . . But the others—what sickness might be skulking beneath the pinstripe and the check? How could he tell if one of them was a drunk or psychotic? It took years to discover that sort of thing, and already he was tired, ready for a cup of beef broth and a water biscuit.

The moment passed, and the jurors were being sworn.

He was allowed to sit down.

A goose walked over his grave. He felt the quiver of goose flesh at the back of his neck. A silly goose. Who used to say that? He looked at his hands. The palms were wet. He wiped them carefully on his trousers. His forehead was damp too. His throat painful. He was a weak vessel.

He must listen, though. Yesterday, the day before—a procession of shaky days—he had done a lot of talking, with Bartlett. Now it was his turn to listen. He must ready himself for appreciation.

"May it please your Lordship . . ."

That, he knew, was Mr. Pollen. The case for the Crown had begun. He heard the voice clearly—a thin thread of ancient music—but the sense of it was hard to follow.

It was his trial. His very own trial. Yet it was meaningless—fortuitous as an attack of chicken pox. There was no reason, no point, no purpose in it. The hand of God perhaps? But who would look for the hand of God in an attack of chicken pox or whooping cough or German measles? It was merely something else to be endured—no benefit, no harm, nothing accrued. Unless he were a woman pregnant—damage to the child within, some weird distortion.

Then, suddenly, as if he had walked into a room where naked strangers were making love, blood and embarrassment filled his face. June was pregnant. June, the naked stranger, her belly filled with child. Under the dressing gown so close to him her white skin was taut and bulged—and he had known nothing, cared nothing, patronized her about America. He had not even tried. . . .

". . . the degree of moral turpitude in such a relationship is not for you to consider. Whatever the nature of that relationship, and you will hear . . ."

The nature of the relationship! Jordan smiled, and, as in a glass held up before him, he saw his own smile bitterly reflected back. He did not care what they thought. Let them imagine him a nonchalant monster. They wouldn't be so far wrong. Nonchalant, blithe, blind. Relationship! What idiocy was that? There had never been a relationship. He had been in another country from June—a country of complacency, of wry jokes and boredom and stale custom, of . . .

". . . What are we to make of this girl whose life was bounded on the one side by her job and on the other side by constant companionship with an invalid mother? An ordinary girl, you might say, except in her extraordinary sense of duty and devotion. A shy girl, perhaps—she had no friends or companions of her own age. And, therefore, a lonely girl. A sheltered girl—innocent perhaps of the ways of the world." The monotonous voice took on a shade of emphasis. "Too innocent. There is not a particle of evidence to suggest that June Singer had or had ever had a boy friend. . . ."

. . . of innocence? No. He forced his mind back, as he had with Bartlett, but this time to search for a grain of nourishment, a single grain for himself. Surely in all those years there had been something, some one thing.

Then he heard his own voice, speaking into the telephone: "Are you all right? . . . Is there anything wrong? . . . Oh, I see. Dear, dear, I am sorry. . . . Yes of course. Good lord, no. Well, on Monday then, if you feel up to it. . . . Uh, I'm sorry. . . . If there's anything I can do to help, Miss Singer, just . . . Well. Goodbye." And then, as he had put the phone down on the news of her mother's death, he had said aloud, "What a nuisance." *Miss Singer—the cool*

146

retreat into formality. No—no retreat; he had not moved, he was exactly where he had always been. *What a nuisance, Miss Singer, that your mother has died. Too bad. Tut-tut.*

". . . Now why did Maddox not admit, in his first interview with the police, that he had visited Panton Place on the morning of the murder? Because, in his own words, 'I clean forgot.' That is how Maddox explained it. Yet it would take a rather singular lapse of memory, you may think, to forget—only two days after her death—the last time he had seen his secretary alive. An outstanding lapse of memory. Or a deliberate intention to deceive? For it was only after he had been positively identified by Mrs. Ardley, as you will hear, that Maddox miraculously recovered his memory. . . ."

Not innocence. He had never wanted to know. But now he did. He must search and scrape. If only they would stop talking; the continuous thin drone, like a strand of electrified wire, prevented him from getting in, getting back. All those days with June, day after day, and the other times . . .

". . . moment to adjourn. . . . Resume at two o'clock."

"On your feet. Go on."

The judge was rising and immediately the place filled with talk and stirring.

"Get a move on."

Down the steep steps, along the same corridor, into the same cell.

". . . or you can send out," said the warder. Denver had disappeared. "Do a nice steak-and-kidney for seven and six."

Jordan sat down. "Yes. Thank you."

"Pay in advance if you don't mind."

"No, of course, really." He gave the warder a ten-shilling note.

Now he would be left in peace.

But he wasn't. As the warder went out, Samson, the hospital orderly, came in and sat down.

"Hello, Maddox."

"Are you going to stay here?"

"That's right, Maddox."

"Why?"

"It's regulations, Maddox. Don't want you to get any funny ideas like stringing yourself up with your braces. You'd be surprised how many of them try it. Mind if I smoke?"

"No. Go ahead," said Jordan irritably.

147

"Not that you're the suicidal type, mind, but . . ."

Coming up in the police van this morning, Samson, unlike Denver, had not been affected by the sternness of the occasion. He had talked on and on, sprightly with lugubrious tales and sententious moralism.

Jordan turned his head away. He had to think. But he needed time and solitude and green fields to think. June Emily Singer. June. The details of her life as the law presented them fell into no particular place. Like a bad portrait, where every point of dress and feature was exact, yet each remained separate, all you could conclude was, "She was an ordinary girl."

An ordinary girl. And he himself knew no more than this.

Once he had asked Colin what his mother had been like. Colin had said, "You've seen your father's portrait of her often enough. What do you think?" Well, Lily Maddox had been beautiful. "Yes, she was beautiful." But Jordan had wanted more than the generalized ideal. He wanted to detect a trace of life. "She was very like John, as a matter of fact. You could always tell they were brother and sister. Strong attraction for the opposite sex, both of them."

And from Aunt Mary he had got even less. "Lily was the baby of the family." After a time he had given up asking, for, although his mother was not exactly a taboo subject, Mary talked of her in a grief-hushed but aggressive tone, as if Jordan might be expected to nourish some grievance over his lack or might accuse Aunt Mary of the loss. So every Sunday when he was a child he had stood silently with Mary by his mother's grave, obediently attempting to mourn a woman he knew nothing of. He had felt uneasy then, as though caught out in a lie.

He shook his head. This was beside the point. It was June he must think of. What was June really like? The law, marching purblind and unbeautiful through a green forest, could enumerate the trees of each variety, measure the acreage to the square inch, note with instruments the amount of rain, but it had no eye for life. "Extraordinary only in her sense of devotion." Surely there was another type of examination possible?

His lunch came. He was without appetite. Steak and kidney pudding. Stewed plums and custard. Two slabs of buttered white bread. Medicine.

"I expect you'd agree with me there, wouldn't you, Maddox?" Samson looked at the food and pursed his lips.

"Yes," said Jordan. He began to eat, deliberately, angrily, as though at gun point.

Everywhere he was prevented.

2 2

Each minute was a slow drop of water, forming lethargically at the end of a tap, swelling gradually and then, after infinite waiting, pulled loose by its own heaviness to fall. And then another, and another. And he couldn't turn his eyes away or refuse to watch. Like a man tortured with urgent business, yet forced to linger politely on some old fool's tale of triviality, his attention was helplessly focussed on the court. Each word, each wart, each motion were vivid and irrepressible as fantasy. For he could not believe in the reality of this paraphernalia —the white pillars and arches, the royal coat of arms gaudy with red and blue and gold, the sword of justice, the judge high in his red dressing gown, the neckless lawyers low in whispers and black robes, the precise, endless voice of prosecution.

It seemed to Jordan that the first witness—the Home Office pathologist—was deliberately unhurried. The weightiness of the irrelevance made Jordan want to cry out "Get on with it, man, get on with it." Mr. Pollen was, thought Jordan, curiously inept. Out of the long slow pedantry of question and answer emerged facts so simple they could have been put in a single paragraph. The time of death could be fixed "with some certainty" as having occurred between 9.30 and 10 A.M. on March 9. Death by strangulation. Small pieces of brown wool had been found adhering to the victim's neck, and they did indeed match the cashmere scarf, Exhibit Number One. Vestiges of tissue under the fingernail matched tissue taken from the prisoner. The girl was in an early stage of pregnancy; the pathologist would put it at about nine weeks. Yes, it was possible—a reluctant, cheek-pulling admission—that the consumption of large quantities of laxative, Gleason's Palliative, might have an adverse effect on the course of pregnancy—a remote possibility. Only a fool would try it. Certainly it would not by itself cause the foetus to be aborted.

Heavy-faced and heavy-handed, Pollen sat down with obvious satisfaction at the job he had done. He was the type of man who did himself well and, in the process, ruthlessly bullied waiters, or anyone else if he could. He would be better with a hostile witness.

Bartlett to Pollen, an eaglet to a dodo. His plumpness concealed by his gown, Bartlett gave the immediate impression of modest but confident intelligence. His voice was pitched on a level of easy and pleasant politeness.

"Doctor, you have stated that only an ignorant woman would resort to taking laxatives in order to procure an abortion. 'An ignorant woman'—those were your words. Ignorant of what?"

"An uneducated woman."

"In what respect uneducated?"

"No woman in her right mind would try to procure an abortion."

"No no, Doctor, my question was not directed at the moral principles or emotional stability of a woman who wishes to abort. Did not your use of the term 'ignorant' mean 'ignorant of medical matters'?"

"Of course she'd be ignorant of medicine. Even if a woman was successful in procuring a miscarriage by this method, it might have quite disastrous consequences."

"In what way disastrous?"

"There would be the possibility of internal bleeding, infection. Only a woman quite ignorant of the dangers would incur such a risk."

"Doctor, is it not a commonly held opinion that violent exercise, scalding baths, gin, cod-liver oil, various poisonous or noxious substances may assist in procuring a miscarriage?"

"It may be a commonly held opinion, sir. But it is not a commonly held medical opinion. Any understanding of the dangers inherent in such an undertaking—"

"Doctor—a woman knowledgeable in medical matters, would she not submit herself to a surgical operation under proper medical supervision?"

"That happens to be illegal, except in very specialized circumstances."

"Illegal, yes. Being illegal, it is very difficult to find a qualified medical man to undertake such an operation?"

"Very difficult."

"Difficult and expensive?"

"Doubtless a criminal abortionist would charge heavily."

"Doctor, insofar as the procurement of a criminal abortion under proper medical supervision is both difficult and expensive, might not even a knowledgeable woman resort to other means for bringing on a miscarriage? Means such as hot baths, exercise, the taking of laxatives?"

"My Lord—" Pollen was standing—"I really must object to that question. It is calling for an opinion on the putative state of mind of an entirely hypothetical female."

The judge champed his jaws. "Mr. Bartlett?"

"My Lord, the Crown has obtained expert testimony from this witness to the effect that the consumption of large quantities of laxatives may be held to have an abortive effect, but it has not, as yet, adduced any evidence to show that June Singer in fact consumed large quantities of laxatives. While I am quite prepared to concede that she did so, until it is proved we are still somewhat in the realm of hypothesis."

"Well taken, Mr. Bartlett. I shall allow the question," the judge said. "But try to be as specific as you can."

"Very well, my Lord," said Bartlett. Pollen sat down, and the question was repeated.

"Well," said the doctor, tugging at a fold of flesh in his cheek, "I suppose it's possible."

"Now, Doctor, let me read you something." Bartlett picked up a fat book and flipped quickly through it. "Ah. I quote, Doctor. 'Massive doses of nonprescriptive laxative preparations are sometimes taken in the early months of pregnancy by women desiring to induce a miscarriage. For obvious reasons there are few authenticated cases of an abortion being effected by this means alone, although it may undoubtedly be a contributory factor, particularly where predisposition to miscarriage already exists.' Would you accept that as a fair statement, Doctor?"

"I should have to know from what authority it was taken."

"Why? Are you not yourself an authority?"

"I'm not an obstetrician," snapped the doctor, "nor a gynecologist."

"You're not an obstetrician." Bartlett paused, marking the page with one finger. "Nor you are. How long since you were in general practice, Doctor?"

"Twenty-two years."

"In that twenty-two years, how many pregnant women have you had as patients?"

"I am not in general practice, I don't—"

"How many pregnant women as patients, Doctor?"

"None."

"In the last twenty-two years, how many babies have you delivered?"

"None."

"None. Not overburdened with practical experience, eh, Doctor? Well, in that case, I'll be glad to tell you the source of the quotation. It comes from what I believe is generally regarded as one of the leading authorities in the field. A work entitled *Pregnancy* by Professor W. H. Jardin. I was quoting from the fourth edition, quite up to date, published three years ago by the firm of, ah, Sutlif and Maddox. Are you familiar with it?"

Smythe sewn, strawboard, grade B London Linen plum, matching topstain, no headbands, twelve square inches rolled imitation gold. The specifications leapt into Jordan's head. June had wanted damson cloth, but all previous editions had been plum. *Pregnancy*— "preggers four" they'd called it affectionately. Affectionately because it was almost the oldest book on the list, a quiet, steady money-maker. Damson—it wouldn't have mattered.

"I am familiar with Jardin, yes. I know the third edition better."

"It is, you would say, a standard work on the subject?"

"Yes. I used the second edition when I was a medical student."

"Now that you know the authority, Doctor, would you accept the statement I read to you as a fair one?"

"I would accept what Jardin said on the matter, yes."

"Anyone who had read, with even ordinary care and attention, the whole of Jardin, could hardly be described as ignorant, could she, Doctor?"

"It is impossible to say. Someone without medical training could not be relied upon to interpret correctly a medical text."

"It is impossible to say she was ignorant?"

"Well, a reading of Jardin is not going to make anyone automatically knowledgeable."

"It is impossible to say she was ignorant?"

"An intelligent woman—it would be unlikely, I suppose."

152

"Impossible, Doctor? Impossible was the word you used."

"Impossible, then. One simply does not—"

"Thank you, Doctor." Bartlett snapped the book shut, but he did not put it down. "Now, Doctor. You stated earlier that in your opinion Singer was at the time of her death in the ninth or tenth week of pregnancy. Is that correct?"

"Eight or nine weeks pregnant. Yes."

"That is the same thing, is it not?"

"Well, yes."

"And your opinion that she was in her ninth or tenth week of pregnancy was based upon the development of the foetus?"

"It was."

"The determination of the duration of the pregnancy by examination of the foetus is a comparatively easy matter, would you not say?"

"It is not as easy as all that. There is the foetus itself, its position in the womb. But there are a number of other factors which must be taken into consideration, such as the metabolism of the mother, her general state of health, et cetera."

"The diet of the mother during the early weeks of pregnancy, that could be an influential factor, too?"

"It might."

"In this case, it was a factor unknown to you, wasn't it?"

"It was. But all these things must be taken—"

"Quite. A history of complication in the early weeks of pregnancy, this would also have bearing upon the development of the foetus, would it not?"

"If there was a history of complication, that would have to be taken into consideration, yes. But in a normal—"

"And in this case—the case of June Singer—nothing was known about the history of the pregnancy, was it?"

"We know that she tried to abort the baby."

"And what effect would that have?"

"Difficult to say. It's not a matter upon which a great deal of work has been done."

"But it would have some effect upon the development of the baby?"

"It might, yes. As I say, it's—"

"An adverse effect?"

"It would hardly be likely to be beneficial."

"The effect, if there was an effect, would be adverse in the sense that it might retard the normal growth of the foetus?"

"It's conceivable. But we are in a large measure in unknown territory here. It's impossible to be positive on—"

"Unknown territory. Unknown to whom?"

"Medical research has not—"

"Unknown to you, Doctor?"

"Obviously it would be unknown to me if—"

"And what steps did you take to remedy this lack of knowledge?"

"My duties require me to keep abreast of the current medical literature."

"Abreast of the literature—I see." Slight touch of sarcasm. "Doctor, what were the qualifications of the physician upon whom you called to make a second examination of the foetus?"

"Qualifications? I am afraid I do not understand. There was no second examination called for, or needed, in this case."

"None at all?"

"None."

"You are not an obstetrician?"

"I have already stated that."

"Nor a gynecologist?"

"No."

"And for over more than twenty years you have had no experience with pregnant women?"

"I have said that, Mr. Bartlett."

"And yet you did not consider getting a second opinion?"

"It was not necessary."

"Despite all these unknown factors?"

"They would have been equally unknown to any other physician."

"Oh, I see, your opinion was just as good as any of the experts. What happened to the foetus after you had examined it?"

"It was destroyed. That is perfectly normal procedure."

"It was destroyed. Well, then, I suppose we shall just have to place our reliance upon you. At the time of her death on March the ninth, Singer was, in your opinion, in her ninth or tenth week of pregnancy. That would mean that conception occurred some time between December the twenty-ninth and January the twelfth, would it not?"

"I don't have a calendar. But I'll take your word for it."

154

"Thank you, Doctor. So in your opinion there is a two-week margin of doubt. In that margin, what weight did you give to the unknown factor of the effect of large quantities of laxative upon the development of the foetus?"

"I am afraid I do not understand the question."

"You have acknowledged that large doses of laxative might retard the growth of the foetus. What allowance did you make for such possible retardation?"

"Possible retardation is based upon a hypothesis which can neither be proved nor disproved."

"In other words, you made no allowance?"

"One cannot allow for a factor which in all probability does not exist and, even if it did exist, could not be measured."

"You made no allowance?"

"No, sir. I did not." The pathologist had long ago ceased to pull at his cheek, the sign of judgement deeply considered. He gave his answers now with the lofty contempt of a philosopher ignoring the sallies of an impertinent wasp.

"This factor, which you did not take into account, how long might it have retarded the normal process of development?"

"Quite impossible to say."

"A month?"

"Out of the question."

"A week?"

"It is quite impossible to give an opinion upon this matter."

"Doctor, can you conceive that this factor might have retarded the growth of the foetus by as long as one week?"

"I can conceive of it. I can conceive of a lot—"

"It's conceivable?"

"It's conceivable, but totally unverifiable."

"Yes, the foetus was destroyed, was it not?"

"That is not what I meant, and I strongly resent your imputation." Compelled now to slap at the wasp. "Your whole hypothesis is unlikely, improbable, highly dubious and—"

"But possible?"

"I have never denied that it is possible."

"Very well. Then it follows that June Singer may have been in the eleventh week of pregnancy, that she may have conceived as far back as December the twenty-second. Is that not correct?"

"It's not actually impossible."

"It is possible, Doctor, is it not?"

"If you must have it—possible."

"It is not a question of what *I* must have!" Very sharp. Then hard and emphatic: "Doctor, I surely do not need to remind you that a man here is on trial for murder. These are not debating points, but matters upon which the guilt or innocence of this man may hinge, matters which must, therefore, be tested to the utmost for accuracy, and on which every possibility must be closely examined." Pause. "We have established that it was possible for conception to have occurred as early as December the twenty-second. Now let us consider the matter of diet—another unknown factor. I take it, Doctor, that an inadequate diet would be likely to have an adverse effect upon the normal rate of foetal development?"

"You'll have to define what you mean by 'inadequate.'"

"Let us refer once again to Jardin." Bartlett opened the book. "I read you the following passage, Doctor. . . ."

As Bartlett read the dreary statement about calories and carbohydrates, vitamins and protein, Jordan began to feel sick. If he closed his eyes, he felt his head would fly away, like a kite snapping loose in a strong breeze. But the taut string held his attention to the courtroom.

"That is quite true," said the pathologist. "But if the baby were suffering from the effects of the mother's undernourishment, one would expect to find signs in the mother of such undernourishment."

"I'm not talking about prolonged undernourishment, Doctor. Six or seven weeks of inadequate diet—the physical symptoms of such malnutrition would not be immediately evident, would they?"

"Again, you must define more closely the nature of the inadequacy."

"Let us say then a largely unrelieved diet of, for instance, chocolate cake and coffee. . . ."

Jordan tasted on his tongue the nausea of plums and custard. As he gripped his hands tightly together, his mind was stirred to a sudden memory of Georgia. Himself and Georgia in the back of the car coming away from the afternoon at Cheppingden Castle, Willy driving in her straight-backed, old-fashioned way, as though the car were a temperamental steed. And Georgia turning to him: "Daddy, I'm going to be sick." Leaning across, trying to hold her and open the window at the same time, and then the quick rush of vomit over her frock, the floor, the leather seat, his jacket. Something within him had become frantic as he tried to clean her up with rapid, clumsy dabs of the car rug. His meaningless jabbered soothing had only made louder her howls of horror at the desecration.

"Oh, Jordan, you are an ass." And as Willy dragged the little girl out of the car and stripped off the sodden summer frock, Jordan had stood by, sticky fingers wiping idiotically at his jacket, thinking that something terrible had happened and yet not knowing what it was.

"Now don't make a fuss, Georgia. We'll soon be back at the hotel. It's probably that ice and a touch of the sun."

But it wasn't the ice or the sun, he was sure. It was the row they'd had below the tower.

Georgia was stripped swiftly, wiped clean with a handkerchief, wrapped in Willy's cardigan, and sat in the front seat. Finger in mouth, she turned, solemn, to look at him where he sat among the odour of sick and the muddled rug in the back. He had endeavoured to smile. "I like sitting in front best of all." she'd said as she looked away.

". . . unlikely. But it is just barely possible. And I must emphasize that the combination of factors you—"

"Thank you, Doctor." In his long whittling at the calendar, Bartlett had gained an extra two weeks. She might have conceived as early as December 15th. Highly unlikely. Wildly improbable. Fantastic. But possible. Ridiculous, absurd, outrageous.

Jordan swallowed.

"As a result of your post-mortem examination you have placed the probable time of death at between seven o'clock and eleven o'clock of the morning of March ninth. These are fairly narrow limits. Would it not have been possible for death to have occurred as late as twelve noon of the same day?"

"Oh, yes, I thought I made that clear. It was my determination that death probably occurred between seven and eleven A.M. Once we get outside those time limits I regard it as progressively less likely, but by no means out of the question."

"I see." Bartlett paused. "Your examination of the contents of the stomach led you to conclude Singer died some ten to twenty minutes after eating a piece of chocolate cake?"

"Yes. The state of the digestive process is an accurate guide."

"But only if one knew the exact time at which the chocolate cake had been eaten?"

"Yes, quite."

"It has been suggested to you that if a piece of cake had been eaten by Singer at nine-thirty A.M., then death would have supervened at between nine-forty and nine-fifty. It would follow, would it not, that if a piece of chocolate cake had been eaten at, say, eleven-forty, then the time of death could accurately be placed at between eleven-fifty and twelve noon?"

"Up to a point that's true."

"Up to a point?"

The pathologist pulled hard at his cheek. A warning signal. "Well, if the cake had been ingested at eleven-forty, then no cake could have been ingested at nine-thirty."

"Is it not possible she might have eaten two pieces of cake?"

"No. If she had eaten a piece of cake two hours before eating the piece just before she died, then there would be evidence of it in the digestive system. There is no such evidence."

"You are stating that after two hours the cake would still be identifiable as cake?"

"No, sir, I am not stating that. But there would be evidence of *something*. In fact, Singer had eaten nothing for at least twelve hours prior to her death—except the cake—and probably for even longer."

"That was not in your report."

"It was in my notes."

"Why was it not in your report?"

"I did not consider it in any respect significant. It is quite usual, you know, for a twelve-hour period to elapse without food—particularly at night."

It was a dangerous cul-de-sac, a dead end—even Jordan could see that. And Bartlett turned quickly. "Now, Doctor, you have said that the process of digestion . . ."

And he remembered the smudge of chocolate on her tooth. He could have said, "You've got chocolate on your teeth." But he wouldn't have done that—it was too like Willy who, just when he'd got to something important, was always apt to say, "There's a piece of spinach on your lip, darling." Besides, there was something fascinating about that dab of brown on her even, white teeth. For somebody who liked sweets so much . . .

Something had happened. The loud tones of Pollen jerked Jordan back to attention. Pollen and the pathologist restoring the ponderous harmony between them.

And then there was the cry for "Henry Lambert!"

"You are an assistant at Marben's Chemists in Panton Gardens, Mr. Lambert?"

"Yes, sir." Small, hair neatly brushed with water, he looked about seventeen, but must be more.

"How long have you been employed there?"

"Two years and seven months."

"Would you describe the nature of your duties?"

"Well, I serve behind the counter mostly, when it's busy. And then I help Mr. Latch, that's in the dispensary."

"Were you acquainted with the deceased, June Singer?"

"Not exactly acquainted. I knew her, so to speak. By sight, that is. She often came into Marben's. But I didn't know who she was till I saw her picture in the paper."

"You saw her picture in the paper after the murder?"

"That's it."

"And what did you do then, Mr. Lambert?"

"I thought about it a lot. I knew it was her. And, well, then I went to the police."

"Why did you go to the police?"

"That's a bit hard to explain exactly. But, you see, well . . ." Lambert looked away unhappily.

"Perhaps you thought—" gentle Mr. Pollen, cloying with condescension—"you had some information that would be of assistance in their investigations?"

"That's right. That's it. It didn't seem much, really, but . . ."

"When do you first recall seeing June Singer?"

"Christmas Eve. That was the first time I served her."

"And what did she purchase from you, Mr. Lambert?"

"Well, er—" Mr. Lambert blushed. "Well—" his voice was low—"it was a box of Tampax."

"A box of Tampax," came Pollen's stentorian echo. "Was that all?"

"Yes. She didn't buy nothing else." A sudden burst of confidence.

159

"That's why I remembered her particular at first. She seemed sort of—lonely, I suppose you'd say. I mean, just the one purchase. You know, at Christmas—most people are getting, well, bath salts and things."

"So you paid her particular attention?"

"That's it. I could see she was shy."

"And in the succeeding weeks, did you serve her again?"

"She came in quite often. I always served her myself if I could."

"And on these other occasions, what did she purchase?"

"Oh, well, you know, lipstick and cold cream and a flannel—I remember she bought a flannel once."

"And Tampax, I suppose?"

"No—" almost a whisper—"she never bought no more Tampax."

"In all the weeks after Christmas, she bought no more Tampax?"

"No, sir. Not off of me."

"Do you recall anything else she purchased?"

"Gleason's."

"She bought a bottle of Gleason's Palliative, did she?"

"Not a bottle. Lots of bottles."

"What size bottles?"

"The big ones."

"The big ones. How many bottles is 'lots,' Mr. Lambert?"

"I couldn't say exactly. But a lot."

"Ten?"

"Not as many as that."

"Five?"

"Five or six, maybe."

"Five or six. And when did she make her first purchase of Gleason's Palliative?"

"February the fourteenth."

"Do you have any particular cause to remember that date?"

"Oh, yes. Valentine's, see? I mean, I was thinking, if only I'd known her name and where she lived, I'd 'ave sent her a valentine, and then in she pops and asks for Gleason's. A Saturday, it was."

"And when did she make her last purchase of Gleason's from you?"

"Right about the beginning of March."

"You mean that she bought five or six bottles, large bottles, of Gleason's Palliative between February fourteenth and the beginning of March—a period of two weeks?"

"Yes."

"And then what? She ceased to buy it?"

"Yes. From me, that is. But I don't think she came into Marben's again. That was the last time I saw her—till her picture was in the paper."

"The last time you saw her was at the beginning of March when she purchased a bottle of Gleason's. Is that correct?"

"Yes. See—well, I think I scared her off. When I handed her the bottle, done up, I said, joking like, 'You want to watch out, you'll get hooked on that stuff.' The moment I said it, I could have bit my tongue out. She went all white and then . . ."

"And then?"

"Well, she just ran out of the shop and I never saw her again."

"Yes. Now, Mr. Lambert, has it been a common occurrence within your experience for a customer to purchase as many as five or six bottles of Gleason's in a period of two weeks?"

"No, sir."

"Or any other laxative preparation?"

"No, sir."

"Has it ever happened—within your experience—that a customer bought so large a quantity in so short a time?"

"Once, yes. In my experience. And she was pregnant too."

"You knew that Singer was pregnant?"

"I didn't know. But I guessed. Why else did she buy all that Gleason's? And she stopped buying the Tampax, didn't she? If only I'd 'ave known her name before, maybe I could have helped her. Poor kid."

"Thank you, Mr. Lambert."

"It was obvious she'd got herself in trouble and was trying to get rid of it. She was desperate. I could see what she was up—"

"Thank you, Mr. Lambert," Pollen roared. Then, with a massive smile, "No further questions."

Bartlett rose. "Mr. Lambert, you have said that, if only you had known Singer's name, you could perhaps have helped her. How could you have helped her?"

"Well, you know. I mean I could have done my best." He was blushing.

"How would you have proposed to help her?"

"Well, I might have been able to . . . talk her out of it."

161

"Talk her out of attempting to procure her own miscarriage?"

"Yes, that's it."

"Did Singer ever ask you for the name of a doctor?"

He was bright red now. "I—I don't know what you mean."

"I mean, did she ask you for the name of a doctor?"

"Of course not!"

"Why the 'of course', Mr. Lambert? It would be quite a normal request, would it not?"

"Normal?" Lambert was lost. "I don't . . . It depends what you mean by normal."

"Don't new residents in your district sometimes ask you for a recommendation to a local physician?"

"Oh!" Lambert smiled. "Oh, yes. Sometimes. Yes, they do. But June didn't."

"June?"

"I mean Miss Singer."

Bartlett stood quite still for a moment, staring at Lambert. Then slowly the barrister nodded his head. "I have no further questions to put to this witness, my Lord."

Lambert left the witness box quickly. He did not look, somehow, so young and fresh as when he had entered it.

Jordan sat rigid, each bone in his body a fixed metal bar.

She was desperate!

He heard and saw with unbearable accuracy—the departing squeak of Lambert's shoes, the judge shuffling his notes, the old man's grunt, the gold of the police sergeant's chevrons, the clear call for the next witness—"Superintendent George!"—and the whisper of swing doors. Unbearable.

Poor kid!

He closed his eyes. And then the kite string snapped, and he could fly away.

23

"Well, no disasters after all," said Jordan, tucking the ends of the scarf under the shoulders of his overcoat.

"Disasters?" June looked up at him seriously.

"Friday the thirteenth." He nodded at the wall calendar and smiled. He was reluctant to leave the office tonight. The idea of the jaunty music in the grey cave of Waterloo Station, the stale urine-and-tobacco smell of the Southern Railway, and the fish pie that he would eat alone because it was one of Willy's meeting nights—did not tickle his fancy. He had once, he thought irrelevantly, seen Sir Adrian Boult having dinner by himself in the Railway Hotel at Waterloo. He had looked like a prosperous but melancholy family solicitor, eating sausages and mash in the half-empty dining room. There had been something indescribably gloomy about the sight which still haunted Jordan.

"I'm not superstitious, really."

"Well, just to be on the safe side." Jordan tore the date from the calendar, revealing the fourteenth and fifteenth, Saturday and Sunday, bunched economically together on the next sheet. The days of leisure, he thought, were lucky to be included at all. "Now you'll have to pack up and go home."

"I thought I'd just finish off these galleys."

"What is it, Pembroke and Rose?"

"Yes. I've just got the last chapter."

"That's pretty dull stuff for a Friday night. Friday night is Amarmi night."

"What's that—Amarmi night?"

"It's a shampoo. You stay home on Fridays and wash your hair for the big do on Saturday."

"Oh." June smiled brightly.

He knew he'd put his foot in it somehow. "Of course," he said, "if there isn't a do on Saturday, then you have Friday night off. In which case you could forget Pembroke and Rose and come and have a drink with me."

"Well, I don't think—"

"Come on, June." It was the ideal solution. "I need something to fortify me for the ordeal of Waterloo, anyway."

"Thank you very much then. I'd love to." She frowned a little. "You don't think . . ."

"Don't worry, the Law always leaves early on Friday nights."

"Miss Lawley's really very nice in her own way." June fetched her coat and put it on. It had a grey fur collar.

"Which could be said of practically anyone, you know."

"Well, people are nice—really underneath, don't you think, Mr. Maddox?"

Jordan raised the ring on his umbrella and freed the spokes. "I don't know. Perhaps. I hadn't thought about it."

June faithfully carried the galleys of Pembroke and Rose in a brown envelope. "I'll just finish it up over the weekend."

In the neon-lit Strand they turned off from the crowd intent on Charing Cross and went down the slope of John Adam Street into Buckingham Street.

It was raining a dim February drizzle. As Jordan held the umbrella over June, their elbows touched for a moment. They stopped at the top of the steps leading to Watergate Walk and looked down.

"It's a beautiful thing, isn't it?"

"Yes, it is. The Watergate—did the river really come up to here?"

"Yes. This part of the Embankment wasn't built until the eighteen sixties. Before that, everything along here was right on the river. The Savoy, Somerset House—at one time they were all accessible by water. Useful for slipping away unseen in the night and that sort of thing."

"It must have been ever so wide then."

"It was. You notice it in the old prints. At first you think there's something wrong with the perspective. But of course it was only at high tide, you know. Most of the time there must have been great mud flats on either bank."

"What fun for the children."

"I'd never thought of that." Jordan smiled. He could hardly imagine Georgia—whose greatest grubbiness was jam on her face—romping in the mud. Yet she'd probably love it. Willy kept her too clean and proper; she'd grow up just like Willy, with a horror of dirt and a "thing" about baths. As they descended the steps and went along the stone-flagged alley, there leapt into his mind a blasphemous picture of Willy, immaculate in garden-party get-up, slipping and staggering in the grey-coated mire, smiling with brave horror. . . .

"What would you like to drink?"

"A sherry?"

"It's their specialty. They have thirteen varieties. Here's the card. Manzanilla, Amontillado, Tio Pepe, Oloroso, Amoroso . . ."

"Gracious. Something sweet?"

"Amoroso. And I'll have Manzanilla. Large ones, please."

"I've never been here before. It's a real cellar, isn't it?"

"Barrels and all. It's a favourite haunt of Colin's—Mr. Sutlif. I like coming here on Friday night. It's payday. I believe a lot of these people come here and have their weekly glass or two on Friday. Look at that old fellow over there. He's always in the same spot on a Friday evening."

The elderly man in a bowler hat was sitting impassively before a large port. He wore a dark overcoat, a wing collar, a black tie, and gold-rimmed glasses—and he looked as though he never removed any of them.

"I wouldn't . . ." June stopped.

"You wouldn't what?"

June moved her head in embarrassment. "I was going to say I wouldn't like to work for him."

Jordan laughed. "Watch now."

The old man took a biscuit and consumed it without visible motion of his jaws. He held the glass carefully in his hand and put it to his lips. The old throat swallowed once, and when he put the glass down it was half empty.

"I wonder if he really enjoys it."

"Pleasure so decorous is totally undetectable, probably even to himself."

The waiter brought their sherry. They were quiet for a while.

"How's Mrs. Maddox?"

"She's very well."

"And Georgia?"

"She's always in fine fettle."

"She's four now, isn't she?"

"Yes." Damn, he'd forgotten all about Georgia. He wondered if Willy would be able to get Mrs. Hillman in to sit. Friday was a bad night.

"I remember when she was born, you coming into the office . . ."

"Yes. I was exhausted." Of course there was always Mrs. Oates, but Mrs. Oates had a tendency to nip at the whiskey.

"Oh, no, you were on top of the world."

"Was I?" Then there was the problem of food. Mrs. Oates insisted on being fed. And the fish pie probably wouldn't stretch to two. Perhaps he should give Willy a ring.

"I often wonder what it'd be like."

165

"What, sorry?"

"Having a baby, I mean."

If he hurried he could still get the six forty-five. "Miserable business."

"Do you think so?"

"Absolutely."

"But afterwards, when you've had . . ."

"What? I'm so sorry, I was thinking of something else."

June sipped her sherry uncomfortably. "I've got a friend who—"

"That's good news."

"No, I mean a girl friend."

"I'm sorry, that sounded awful."

"Oh, no. But, I mean, this girl had a baby and the father—well, he died."

"What dreadfully bad luck."

"Yes. It must be awful not having a father—I mean a baby with no father."

"Yes, it's hard on the child. Unless . . ." Ten minutes across Hungerford Bridge to Waterloo. It was now six twenty-five. Which left him ten minutes—five, to be on the safe side.

"Unless what, Mr. Maddox?"

"Oh, unless there are relatives or something. You know, who'll look after the child." Five minutes. That was settled. "That's what happened to me, you know. My mother died when I was born—well, a few days after, actually—and I hardly ever saw my father."

"That must have been awful."

"Not really. It didn't do me any harm. I was taken in, you see, by my aunt and uncle—my mother's brother and sister. It worked very well."

"I see."

"This is rather a morbid conversation, isn't it? Come on, drink up. Would you like another?"

"Oh no thank you. That was lovely."

"Well, let's be off then, shall we?" He stood up, and as June reached down to gather her handbag and gloves and the brown envelope, he thought the drink had not had quite the desired effect. She looked wilted rather than cheered.

They went up the steps into Villiers Street.

"You can get a bus all right from Charing Cross, can't you?"

166

"Yes."

Jordan smiled. "Cheer up. You've got two whole days to yourself. Don't work too hard on Pembroke and Rose."

"I won't, I promise. Good night, Mr. Maddox."

"See you on Monday then, June."

"Yes. And—and thanks ever so much."

As he took the footpath over the river, he glanced to his left. Waterloo Bridge was at its most slim and elegant. High tide. At ebb, when the supports were visible, the bridge had an undressed, ungainly appearance. He wondered if he'd been a bit abrupt with June.

The Shell-Mex clock gave him eight minutes. He'd have to hurry or he wouldn't have time to get an evening paper.

He put June and her hypothetical problems out of his mind.

It had stopped raining, thank God.

24

He held the piece of paper in his fingers. It was a blasted irritant. For the last hour—hour and a half?—he had listened to Chief Superintendent George's answers, unfaltering and fair, to Pollen's questions. He had noticed for the first time a pleasant, distant burr to the policeman's voice. Sensibly and easily Mr. George had given his evidence, and it had soothed Jordan, healing the nausea and the pain. And now here was Bartlett wanting to rock the boat. Jordan looked at the scribbled words:

MADDOX—

In accordance with your instructions I shall not c-examine George re your treatment at Sarah St. I assume, however, that this instruction does not apply to various remarks George made to you at S. St. and which you quoted to me. If my assumption is incorrect, return this note to me so indicating.

G.B.

From Bartlett down the line to Tom to Denver to Jordan the note had come. He'd had it three minutes now. Remarks that George had made? What did it mean? Half his attention was with Pollen's final

167

questions to George; the other half could not decipher the message. All he noticed was the strong dash of Bartlett's handwriting: *t*'s crossed with great vigorous slashes, the *l*'s and *b*'s and *h*'s spikily upright—a strange contrast with Bartlett's plump exterior. Only the loops below the line, the *f*'s and *g*'s and *y*'s, were weak and indeterminate.

He scrunched the note in his hand and shoved it into his pocket. But just as he looked up, Pollen was taking his seat. From behind Jordan came a shuffling and sighing of the spectators. And then Bartlett rose.

Jordan found himself wishing that Bartlett would not attack George, as he had attacked the pathologist. The pathologist had been a pompous ass, perhaps, but George was—well, decent.

"Chief Superintendent George—how long have you served in the force?"

"The metropolitan police force, sir? Thirty-two years, come August. Before that I served for three years in the Cornish constabulary."

"Almost thirty-five years' service? And how long have you been in the C.I.D., Superintendent?"

"Nineteen years. First with Scotland Yard, and then the last twelve years with S District C.I.D."

"And of those twelve years, you have been Chief Superintendent of S District C.I.D. for eleven, have you not?"

"I have."

"And as such, all murder cases in S District are your responsibility and investigations are directed by you?"

"That's correct."

"And in the last eleven years, Superintendent, how many persons have you arrested or caused to be arrested for the crime of homicide?"

"Forty-nine."

"And in how many of those forty-nine cases did you secure a conviction?"

"A quite improper question, my Lord." Pollen up, indignant.

The judge clamped his jaw tight, then released it like a spring. "Mr. Bartlett, surely you know better than to put a question like that. The police, as you are well aware, play no part in the judicial process—in 'securing a conviction,' as you see fit to put it."

"I apologise, my Lord. I shall rephrase the question."

"No dramatics, please, Mr. Bartlett." The judge clacked his teeth.

"Superintendent, how many of those forty-nine cases resulted in the conviction of the person or persons whom you caused to be arrested?"

"Forty-seven. One case is yet to come to trial. And the other one concerns these present proceedings."

"So out of forty-seven murder cases that came to trial as a result of your investigations, all resulted in conviction?"

"Yes."

"A remarkable record, Superintendent." Bartlett put his head on one side, as though turning such spotless brilliance over in his mind. "Very remarkable indeed. You must be very proud of that record, Superintendent?"

"I do my best to do my duty."

"Pity it is not given to all of us to be so infallible. Well, well." Picture of Bartlett shaking himself free from the clutches of hero-worship. And Jordan thought how easy and how cheap it was to make subtle fun of a witness—and a witness was, of all people in the court, defenceless.

"Now I'd like to turn to Exhibit Number Seven—the alarm clock which you found in Singer's room. It was on the floor and the glass face was badly splintered. The clock had stopped as a result of the shock of falling, and the hands stood at nine thirty-nine. Is that an accurate summary?

"Yes. We were able to ascertain that the clock had stopped, rather than run down naturally, because upon examination it was found to be almost fully wound."

"It was an eight-day clock?"

"That's correct."

"So that it must have been wound rather recently?"

"Yes. It hadn't been running much more than a day or so."

"Which would be consistent with it having been wound on Saturday night or Sunday?"

"Yes."

"And yet there were no fingerprints found on the winder?"

"No."

"Nor on the handle that adjusts the time?"

"No."

169

"Nor anywhere else on the clock?"

"Just on the alarm button at the top of the clock. There was a clear print of Singer's forefinger there."

"Right forefinger or left forefinger?"

"Right forefinger, I assume. Singer was right-handed."

"You assume? Don't you know?"

"I'm not positive about it, no."

"Superintendent, might one not deduce from the absence of prints —except on the alarm button—that the clock had deliberately been wiped clean of fingerprints?"

"I'm not sure I follow you there. A neat and tidy person would be likely to dust or polish a clock, incidentally, of course, removing any fingerprints."

"The neat and tidy person would in that case have to wear gloves, would she—or he—not?"

"Not necessarily. The clock could be held steady with a finger on the alarm button."

"Yes. And if that neat and tidy person were right-handed—and we know Singer was right-handed—she would be likely to steady the clock with her left forefinger, while she 'polished or dusted' it with her right hand, would she not?"

"It's possible."

"Well, it would be far more natural and likely for her to use her right hand to polish, would it not?"

"Yes, it would be more likely."

"And in that case we would expect to find the print on the alarm button to be of Singer's left forefinger rather than her right forefinger, would we not?"

"That would follow, yes."

"And yet you 'assumed' the print was that of her right forefinger. Why?"

"I had not considered the point you have just raised."

"Not considered it? Not considered it important enough to investigate?"

"I'm quite sure the fingerprint department will have recorded which finger the print came from."

"Doubtless, doubtless—and it will certainly be interesting to find the answer. But you did not deem it necessary to inform yourself?"

"As I've said, it did not occur to me."

"But you see now that it is a very important point, don't you?"

"Frankly, it seems to me a rather obscure point."

"Then let me enlighten your obscurity, Chief Superintendent." An almost imperceptible emphasis upon the word *Chief.* "We have to ask ourselves who wiped the alarm clock clean of prints and why that person did so. If we assume that this was done by June Singer in the ordinary course of her houshold cleaning—an excessively thorough household cleaning, it may be thought—then we would expect the print to be of the left forefinger. But—yes, Superintendent, what is it?"

"Excuse me, sir." A bustling at the back of the court had advanced to the witness box, beside which the City police sergeant was now proffering a piece of paper to Superintendent George. "This is the answer to your question," George said.

"What question?"

"My assistant just phoned through to the fingerprint department to ascertain whether the print was from the left or right forefinger. This is the reply."

"Very well, tell us."

George unfolded the note and looked at it. He raised his head and said impassively to Bartlett, "The left forefinger."

Jordan felt like cheering—or laughing.

But Bartlett was unmoved. "Very thorough, at length. Were you, Superintendent, equally thorough over the matter of the hands?"

"The hands? The hands of the clock?"

"Yes—the hands of the clock. They stand as we have seen—and can see now—at nine thirty-nine. Were they moved, Superintendent?"

"Certainly not. They are in exactly the same position as when the clock was found."

"Can they be moved, Superintendent? Or were they pinned in their present position by the fall of the clock?"

"No attempt has been made to alter the placing of the hands. They are in the precise position they—"

"You don't know whether the hands can be freely moved, in other words?"

"I do not."

"We can very easily find out." Bartlett moved swiftly forward, picked up the red alarm clock from the table in front of the clerk, carried it to the witness box and handed it to George.

171

"Now. Using the handle at the back of the clock, try moving the hands forward to ten o'clock."

"Yes, that's easy enough."

"Now forward again, to eleven o'clock."

"Yes. I have done that."

"Now move the hands back to nine thirty-nine."

"Nine thirty-nine it is."

"Now, gently, Superintendent—very gently, move the hands back to nine o'clock."

There was a pause. "I'm afraid I can't, without forcing it. There appears to be an obstruction. A piece of glass—must be very small—in the face."

"Obstructing the hour hand?"

"That must be it. The hour hand's set lower."

"The minute hand clears the obstruction?"

"That's right. The minute hand moves clear. The hour hand can be moved clear forward, but moved backward it hits this obstruction."

"And what time is shown on the clock when the hour hand is turned back to hit the obstruction?"

"Nine thirty-nine."

Almost mincingly, Bartlett stepped across the well of the court and took the clock and replaced it on the table.

"Now, just supposing that when that clock had struck the floor and stopped, the hands had shown ten-fifteen. And further supposing that it had been in someone's interest to indicate that the clock had fallen —and that whatever had caused it to fall had occurred—at an earlier time. Short of turning the hands almost a full twelve-hour circle, that person could not have altered the hands to show an earlier time than nine thirty-nine—the very time that was in fact shown by the clock. Could he?"

"No, sir, he could not."

"And did not this thought at any time occur to you, that in fact the hands might have been deliberately set back?"

"No, it did not."

"Then presumably it would also not have occurred to you that anyone so doing might very well be anxious and careful to wipe the clock clean of prints?"

"No, it did not."

"And although, if the hands were set back, we do not know in

172

whose interest it might have been to move them, we can say, confidently, that the one person in whose interests it would not have been was Maddox. Can't we?"

"If the hands were set back—"

"If the hands were set back?"

"If the hands were set back, it would not have been in the interests of Maddox. That's quite correct."

"If. That if marks a possibility that you didn't even for a moment consider in the course of your 'thorough' investigation?"

"The possibility did not occur to me, no. And if it had, I am afraid I would have considered it rather farfetched."

"Yes, I bet you would!" Savage for a second. "Because you had made up your mind very quickly that Maddox was your murderer, hadn't you, Superintendent?"

"No."

"And you were not interested in possibilities or lines of investigation that might complicate your personal certainty that Maddox had committed the crime—were you?"

"That's quite untrue. And if I may say so, you know it."

"Your confidence would be laudable, Superintendent, if it were equalled by your intelligence."

This was all wrong. Jordan forced his hands on his knees to stop the trembling anger in his legs. This wasn't any judiciously framed enquiry into the thoroughness of George's investigations. Nothing to be gained by an attack upon the police! Jordan's ears were so full of the pounding of blood that for a few moments he heard nothing.

". . . statement of March the sixteenth, of course, you immediately went round to Panton Place and checked the state of the stair carpet?"

"Inspector Symington did, yes."

"You did not see fit to go yourself?"

"Mr. Symington is a competent and experienced officer."

"And this was done on the sixteenth?"

"No. On the following day—March the seventeenth."

"After you had already arrested Maddox?"

"That is quite correct."

"Another unimportant matter—hardly worth checking?"

"That's quite untrue. Immediately Maddox left Sarah Street police station on March the sixteenth, I telephoned Mrs. Ardley, the landlady at Number Twenty-seven Panton Place, and enquired into the matter."

"You *telephoned* Mrs. Ardley?"

"I did. She reported that the stair carpet was in good order and that no complaints as to its condition had been received by her."

"So you felt quite safe in postponing investigation until the next day?"

"There were a good many other matters of greater urgency that needed attending to at the time."

"Such as arresting Maddox before verifying the accuracy of his statement? Very well, Superintendent. Now, when you telephoned Mrs. Ardley on the afternoon of the sixteenth, did you tell her why you were enquiring about the stair carpet?"

"No, I did not."

"So she might well have thought of it as a matter of not much importance?"

"I can't answer for Mrs. Ardley."

"Did you tell her that Inspector Symington would be round the next morning to take a look at the stair?"

A pause. Outside it was growing dark, so that the lights in the court began to throw sharper shadows and alter the relationship of shapes. George seemed bigger now and the lines on his expressionless face more deeply scored. Jordan could see the gleam of silver in the hairs of his clipped moustache. "I fancy I may have informed her of Mr. Symington's impending visit, yes."

"Superintendent, has it ever occurred to you that there are a number of rather houseproud women in the world who are not invariably overeager to admit to trivial domestic shortcomings?"

"I had not the slightest grounds for doubting Mrs. Ardley's veracity."

"I put it to you once again, has it ever occurred to you that there may be women, houseproud women, who may have some hesitation— a perfectly natural hesitation—in freely admitting small domestic shortcomings?"

"It may have occurred to me, although I'm afraid I don't have much time to spend in thinking about the mysterious ways of a woman's mind."

A slight stir, very faint—the noise of smiles, thought Jordan. He relaxed a little—Mr. George could hold his own. And yet, Jordan felt a pang of bitterness at the viciousness of it all: this subtle, or unsubtle, tearing down—it recalled years, centuries, it seemed, of commonplace observations concealing the cold desire to destroy. Surely there was a place where words could be gently said and gently meant. But that place, those people, were dead. And he had buried them.

"So no shadow of a doubt sullied your acceptance of Mrs. Ardley's words?"

"There was no cause of any kind to doubt Mrs. Ardley's truthfulness."

"How long would it take to repair a loose runner on a stair carpet, do you think, Superintendent? An hour? Two hours? Half an hour?"

"I am not a carpenter."

"Indeed, no. Every man to his trade. Well, I cannot conceive a comparatively simple repair taking much longer than an hour. An hour. And you telephoned Mrs. Ardley on the afternoon of the sixteenth and Mr. Symington went round to Panton Place—on the *morning* of the seventeenth?"

"Late morning."

"Late morning of the seventeenth—well, let's see, that would be round about eighteen hours. *Eighteen* hours. Am I correct?"

"Approximately eighteen hours sounds right."

"Eighteen hours until Inspector Symington arrived on the spot. Inspector Symington did, I imagine, give you a written report of his investigation of the matter of the stair carpet?"

"He did."

"Give us the gist of that report, Mr. George. The gist of it."

"As I recall, Mr. Symington reported that he had examined the whole stairway from the ground floor to the first floor. He found no marks of any kind indicating a fall having taken place. He tested each runner holding the carpet against the stairs, and he found all of them to be firmly in place, requiring some physical exertion to move them or slip them from their sockets. This applied to the runners on the three top stairs, as to all the others. Mr. Symington made further enquiries of Mrs. Ardley, who confirmed her previous statement that the stair carpet had never been loose and no complaints had been received by tenants in regard to it. Mr. Symington then interviewed several of the tenants, and they had no knowledge of a loose stair carpet, nor had they heard of anyone complaining of such."

"Several of the tenants. How many?"

"Two, I believe."

"Do you recall the names of these several tenants?"

"If I remember correctly, there was a Mr. Furling and a Mrs. Masterman. I have the report here, I can easily verify."

"No, no. Don't bother. It was not Masterman, but Masterson, in fact. Mrs. Masterson. But I take it that Inspector Symington's report fully satisfied you as to the point at issue?"

"I was quite satisfied that the stair carpet had at no time been in a loosened or dangerous condition."

"The report satisfied you of that—the report of a—ah—competent and experienced officer?"

"It did."

"And did the report of Inspector Symington's tell you on what floor Mrs. Masterson lived?"

"I don't believe it did. No, I'm sure not."

"So of course you could not know that Mrs. Masterson lives, and has lived for the last twenty years, in the basement flat, could you?"

George remained as motionless as ever. "Is that true?"

"Yes, it's true, Superintendent. It is true, too, that Mrs. Masterson's flat has a direct entrance to the street, via some area steps, so that Mrs. Masterson has no cause whatsoever to visit the ground floor, let alone the first floor. And in view of this, Mrs. Masterson's opinion as to the state of the carpet at the top of the stairs to the first floor is likely to be of little weight, is it not?"

"In the normal course of events, she may—"

"Come come, Superintendent, Mrs. Masterson's opinion has about as much value as a native of Timbuctoo's, hasn't it?"

"Excuse me." The policeman took the large notebook that had been resting on the edge of the witness box. "Here we are. From Mr. Symington's report: 'Mrs. Masterson stated that she had no knowledge of a loose stair carpet, and further, that she had heard no complaints from other tenants to that effect.' I think that's quite clear. Mrs. Masterson is stating her ignorance. I don't think that carries any implication that she would have been bound to know of a loose stair carpet—if there had been one."

"Superintendent, surely you can do better than that. Patently Mrs. Masterson was ignorant—she was in no position to have any knowledge of the state of the stairs. So why did a competent and experi-

176

enced officer bother to ask? Or, conversely, why didn't he ask any man on the street? He would have been just as ignorant. Or the man on the moon? No, Superintendent, it is not what Inspector Symington wrote down in his report, it is what he did not write down in his report—that is what is misleading. Your competent and experienced officer deliberately misled you, but, what is far more important, he might easily seriously have misled this court and, withal, the very course of justice itself. This is a very serious matter, Mr. George, very serious."

The judge's teeth clacked. "Mr. Bartlett—you are absolutely sure of your ground? You are quite certain that this Mrs., ha, Masterson lives in the basement flat?"

"I'm quite prepared to call proof, my Lord."

"Very well. Very well. Um, Superintendent, I am inclined to take a rather grave view of this. Mr. Pollen?" The old head turned slowly. "Mr. Pollen, we are going to have the opportunity of hearing Inspector Symington, are we?"

"He is the Crown's next witness, my Lord."

"Well. Well." Back again the old face moved. "Superintendent, this is an experienced officer, you say?"

"He is, my Lord." The chief superintendent gravely faced the judge. "Might I be permitted to say a word, my Lord?"

"By all means."

"I'm extremely sorry that the slightest aspersion has been cast upon Detective-Inspector Symington's reputation, because he happens to be one of the most capable and efficient officers I have ever had the good fortune to come across. He has one of the finest records in the Metropolitan Police, in which he has served for thirteen years. He holds the Queen's Police Medal for Gallantry. He is a very thorough and conscientious officer, my Lord, and as an example of that, on this very case, I can tell you that he came on duty at nine o'clock on the morning of the Monday in question, and did not come off duty until three A.M. the following day, Tuesday, on which he again reported for duty at nine o'clock."

"The Queen's Medal for Gallantry, eh?" The judge was avidly attentive.

"Yes, my Lord. It was awarded to him for his action in singlehandedly tackling four men engaged in armed robbery in the West End.

He received three gunshot wounds, but, despite that, he rendered one of the men unconscious and disarmed and arrested two of the others."

"Ah, yes. Penny, Farmer, Wensley and Todd. The case came up before me. Very vicious men."

"Yes, my Lord."

"An admirable effort on Symington's part. Yes, yes, I commended him. What did he do in the war?"

"In the latter part of the war he served in the Commandos, my Lord."

"Did he see active service?" Mouth slightly open, the judge leaned forward.

"Yes, my Lord. He was mentioned in dispatches on two separate occasions, I believe I'm right in saying."

"Mentioned in dispatches? Hmmm." The judge slowly savoured the good news.

"My Lord—" Bartlett, calmly impatient—"if we are done with the eulogies, perhaps I may—"

"Just a moment, Mr. Bartlett. Just a moment." An impatient snap of the teeth. "Superintendent, this business about the stair carpet. How many people were in the house at the time Inspector Symington conducted his investigation? Refer to your notes if you wish."

"Yes, my Lord. There were three people in the house."

"And they would be this Mrs. Masterson, Mr. Furling and, of course, Mrs. Ardley?"

"That's quite correct, my Lord."

"Then Inspector Symington interviewed everyone he could get hold of?"

"Yes, my Lord."

"Umm, yes. Well, I see nothing irregular about that. It was perhaps unfortunate that there were not more tenants available for questioning, but one cannot blame Inspector Symington for that. Yes. Thank you, Superintendent. Well, Mr. Bartlett, let's get on, let's get on."

Bartlett stood poised for a second, and then he said, "Very well, Superintendent, we will take this matter up again with Inspector Symington. I shall merely ask you now whether it was you who directed Inspector Symington to investigate this matter on the morning of the seventeenth of March?"

"I instructed Inspector Symington to proceed to Panton Place at the earliest possible moment to make his enquiries."

"And the earliest possible moment was the late morning?"

"It was."

"And were you aware, Superintendent, that in the normal course of events all the tenants at Twenty-seven Panton Place, with the exception of Mrs. Masterson, go out to work and would therefore not be available for questioning?"

"All the tenants had been interviewed and statements taken from several of them."

"But not on this matter?"

"All persons on the premises were questioned."

"Superintendent, were you or were you not aware that there were likely to be, at that time in the morning, very few persons on the premises?"

"I knew several of the tenants went out to work."

"Then, knowing it, why did you choose a time when most of your potential sources of information would be absent?"

"I would not have felt justified in postponing the investigation any longer."

"You were quite happy about postponing your investigation by eighteen hours, but you drew the line at twenty-four, is that it?"

"I was satisfied that Inspector Symington's investigations had shown that there was nothing further to be gained in pursuing this particular line of enquiry."

"Indeed, all through this case you have been very easily satisfied by somewhat less than indefatigable enquiries into matters which might tend to support the truth of Maddox's statements, have you not?"

"There is not the slightest truth in that allegation."

"We shall see. I now want to ask you about the photograph of June Singer that you found in Maddox's office. Where, precisely, did you find it?"

"In Maddox's desk."

"Where in Maddox's desk?"

"It was in the bottom left-hand drawer of the desk, secreted behind a batch of papers and books."

"It was what?" Ringing.

"It was behind several books and papers in the bottom left-hand drawer."

179

"'That is not what you said. You used another word. What was that word?"

"I said it was found—"

"You did *not* say it was found. What was the word you used?"

"Secreted—is that what you mean?"

"Secreted! Do you know the meaning of the word, Superintendent?"

"It means hidden."

"Hidden. Deliberately concealed. Why should you assume that Maddox had deliberately concealed the snapshot?"

"I did not use the term in that sense. It was certainly not openly displayed."

"I find the word 'secrete' very significant. You assumed that Maddox placed the photograph in the drawer to conceal it, and you are trying to get the court to accept that as a fact. Why?"

"The photograph was concealed, that's the plain fact of the matter."

"And why should Maddox conceal the photograph of his secretary?"

"Because he didn't want anyone to see it. That's the usual purpose of concealment."

"And why should he not have wanted anyone to see it?"

"An exchange of personal photographs suggests a certain intimacy which he may have wished to conceal."

"Who said anything about an exchange of personal photographs?"

"A photograph of Maddox was found in Singer's handbag."

"But who said anything about an *exchange* of photographs?"

"It would be natural to assume—"

"Assume!" Contemptuous. "No, it would not be natural to assume any such thing—except to a police officer already convinced of a man's guilt and out to get him willy-nilly."

"You've no right—"

"I didn't ask you a question! Where did you find this photograph of Maddox?"

"In Singer's handbag."

"Secreted, no doubt?"

"It was inside the lining of the bag."

"Sewn in?"

"No. Not sewn in."

180

"Did it carry Maddox's fingerprints?"

"No."

"Do you have the slightest evidence that Maddox gave the girl the photograph?"

"I should have thought—"

"I'm not asking you what you *think*, Superintendent. I'm asking you whether you found any evidence that Maddox gave Singer the photograph."

"In that sense, then, no."

"So this 'exchange' of photographs is entirely your own idea?"

"I don't find it unwarranted by the facts."

"Answer the question!"

"It is what I thought, yes."

"Without the slightest evidence?"

"Strictly speaking— "

"Yes—strictly speaking, Superintendent."

"In the strict sense, there is no actual evidence of an exchange, no."

"No evidence whatsoever, in any sense. And yet you gaily come into this court and bandy about your own idea of an 'exchange' as though it were a fact, which, if it were, would be highly prejudicial to the accused. And you call yourself a responsible police officer?"

"A policeman is not usually a wide-eyed innocent, you know."

"Are you implying that your obvious prejudice against the prisoner in this case stems from some kind of superior sophistication not available to ordinary mortals?"

"I am not prejudiced against Maddox or anyone else."

"Do you deny that right from the beginning you were certain of Maddox's guilt?"

"It is not my job to pass opinions as to guilt or innocence, it is to collect evidence."

"If it is not your job—and indeed it is not your job—to pass opinions on guilt or innocence, why did you say to Maddox, 'We know you did it'?"

"I never made any such statement."

"You deny saying, 'We know you did it'?"

"I do."

"And do you deny that you also said, 'We can prove you did it'?"

"That is quite untrue."

"You did not make such a remark?"

"No."

This was absolutely monstrous. Trembling, Jordan pulled Bartlett's note from his pocket. He unclipped his pen and began to write on the back of the paper. *It was Symington who said that*, he wrote, *not George*. Not George. He underlined the words fiercely and the nib tore the paper and stabbed through into his thigh. *There is nothing to be gained. You will please stop attacking George in this manner. This is an instruction!*

He watched the note being passed down until it reached Tom Short. Tom peered at it far more than long enough to read it, and then Jordan saw him crush it in his hand and let it drop to the floor. He made no signal to Bartlett, and instantly Jordan knew that he wasn't going to.

He felt a great and futile rage within him, such a rage he had not had since he was a child when . . . blinded with screams and kicking madly, wild, frenzied, prevented. Years later, so it seemed, slackening with sobs, dwindled, drained, emptied. Deadly weak. What did it matter?

He had bowed his head. He raised it now. For a little while he did not try to understand the sense of what was being said. He absorbed the comfort of something going on, George steady and unperturbed. He realised that, after all this time, he still did not know the superintendent's Christian name. Just George. Old George. St. George. He smiled faintly. Farmer George. Gradually he began to listen again. They were onto his letter to Jack Timberley now. How futile, in a sense, futile because nothing sounded as it was, or was as it seemed. "The fact is . . ." "It is true, is it not? . . ." "The fact was . . ."

". . . the fact was that you and Inspector Symington had gone to the offices of Sutlif and Maddox on the morning of Saturday, March the fourteenth, and it was at that time that you discovered this letter from Mr. Jackson Timberley to Maddox?"

"That's quite correct."

"And on Monday, March the sixteenth, you questioned Maddox for several hours, did you not?"

"Yes."

"And the letter was in your possession at the time?"

"Yes."

"And did you ask Maddox about it in the course of your questioning?"

"No. We had not at the time obtained Maddox's letter to Mr. Timberley, nor Singer's letter."

"You did not consider that Maddox might be able to elucidate the letter for you? That he might, in a word, have been quite easily able to explain why Mr. Timberley should be offering Singer a job in America on February the twenty-sixth?"

"The matter was still at a preliminary stage of investigation."

"You did not think it might be fair to ask Maddox to explain—in his own interests, perhaps?"

"It was not until we had obtained a copy of Maddox's letter to Mr. Timberley and Singer's letter, that there appeared to be anything significant to explain."

"And when you did obtain those letters—Maddox to Timberley on February the eighteenth and Singer's letter to Timberley on March the first—what was so significant about them, to your mind, that required explanation?"

"The quite clear contradiction implied in the fact that Maddox was stating that Singer had made up her mind to go to America, and, less than a fortnight later, Singer was refusing the offer of a job there. That, and the wording of Maddox's letter."

"Ah, yes, I thought we'd get to that. What significance did you see in the wording of Maddox's letter?"

"The last sentence, I believe."

"The last sentence? Let me read it to you, then. Yes, after Maddox has recommended her, he then says: 'She has recently had some bad luck personally, but I'm sure all that will soon be forgotten, and a change of scene will be a good tonic.' That is the sentence?"

"Yes."

"And what is so significant about it?"

"I only say it could be significant. There are other interpretations possible."

"That's very liberal of you. But what was your interpretation? I am interested in your processes of thought; you display a quite remarkable ingenuity in throwing a most unsavoury light on the simplest matters. What dirt did you dig up in this?"

"It is not for me to state an opinion."

"But I want to have this out in the open. I want to have this clear. I want the jury to understand these innuendos that appear to have been the guiding lights of your investigation. I am sick of these dark and noxious hints. So I put it to you, Superintendent, that what you chose that final sentence to mean was that Singer was pregnant, but would soon manage to procure an abortion and that it would be a good thing to get her away and out of sight where she couldn't cause any more trouble for Maddox. That's how you read the sentence, is it not?"

"It's a possible interpretation."

"And is it not also a possible interpretation that Maddox was referring to the death of Singer's mother and expressing a genuine concern for her welfare?"

"That might be possible."

"But you didn't see fit to ask Maddox which was the true explanation?"

"You are twisting this. The letters from Maddox and Singer only came into our possession after the preliminary examination."

"I am twisting it? You had the letter from Timberley before Maddox was even charged—there was a mystery there already. Yet you did not ask him. I put it to you that you have never been disposed in the entire case to obtain or accept a reasonable explanation from Maddox."

"I am not conscious of having in any way been derelict in my duty in the conduct of this case. And I'm rather tired of your attempts to bully me into admitting a prejudice against Maddox."

"You do not strike me, Superintendent, as the kind of person who is going to be persuaded into admitting that he might have ever possibly have made the slightest mistake. You are obviously a man who will continue to call a spade a spade even when the prongs are entering your flesh to prove it a fork. It is to your spade work that we will now turn. Once you had fixed on your suspect, Maddox, you really did remarkably little to follow other lines of enquiry that might have suggested the possibility of other suspects. You have stated, for instance, that you were able to find no evidence that Singer had any very close friends or, indeed, that she had any friends at all, of either sex. Now this is a very curious state of affairs, but, I suggest to you, it is due not so much to an absence of evidence as to an absence of effort in obtaining evidence. We know that you questioned Mrs. Payne, who lived below the Singers in Putney, but whom else did you question who might have been expected to throw light upon Singer's personal life?"

"There were two potential sources of information about Singer's personal life and possible friendships. One was the Delmar Secretarial School, which Singer attended for a year and a half, and the other was the Lamont High School at Putney, which she had also attended for some years. On the morning of Friday, March the thirteenth, accompanied by Detective Sergeant Rice, I visited the offices of the Delmar Secretarial College and there interviewed Miss Johnson. She was able to give me no information relating to Singer, as she, Miss Johnson, had not been on the staff of the school when Singer attended."

"Was there no one else there who had taught June Singer?"

"No, sir. Miss Delmar, who had run the school singlehandedly for many years, had died some two months prior to the date of my visit. Miss Johnson was temporarily in charge."

"There must have been records of students contemporary with Singer?"

"I enquired very particularly about that point. Apparently Miss Delmar's policy was to destroy all records dating back more than three years."

"And the Lamont High School? What information were you able to obtain there?"

"I visited the Lamont High School on the morning of March the seventeenth, accompanied by Inspector Symington, and interviewed Miss Cochrane, the headmistress. Miss Cochrane had no direct knowledge of Singer, as she had not at the time been in her present post, but—"

"Who had been headmistress when Singer attended the school?"

"I was coming to that. A Miss Appleby. She resigned about five years ago and went out to teach in Africa. In Ghana, I believe it was."

"And what attempts did you make to contact Miss Appleby?"

"I did not contact Miss Appleby."

"Why not?"

"Because Miss Cochrane suggested that I talk to Mrs. Fremantle. Mrs. Fremantle, who was still teaching at the school, had been Singer's form mistress in her last year and had also taught Singer at prior periods. I interviewed Mrs. Fremantle. She told me that Singer was an intelligent and quiet girl who rather 'kept herself to herself.' Those were her words. I think Mrs. Fremantle's deposition has been made available to you."

"And did either Miss Cochrane or Mrs. Fremantle show you the records of Singer's attendance and the listing of her contemporaries?"

"Yes."

"And what use did you make of those records?"

"I made a note of the names and addresses of the pupils who had been in Singer's form in her last year."

"And you saw these people and questioned them?"

"I did not. Mrs. Fremantle had specifically stated, as you will have read, that she did not recall anyone who might be described as friendly with Singer."

"So you just didn't bother?"

"I secured the cooperation of the local police, and every person still remaining in the locality was seen and questioned by them."

"With what results?"

"Most of them remembered June Singer, but none of them had maintained contact with her after leaving school."

"And what about those who had left the locality?"

"We were not able to locate them."

"And by this time, I suppose, you had arrested Maddox, so that it didn't seem worth going to much trouble?"

"Twenty-one persons who had been in Singer's form were questioned."

"And what about other pupils in the school at that time?"

"The Lamont High School had an attendance of over four hundred when Singer was there. It was not deemed feasible to interview each and every one."

"So, in addition to anyone who had moved away from Putney, anyone a year or so older or younger than Singer, and who might have been particularly friendly with her, would have escaped your attention entirely?"

"As I say, it was not deemed feasible to interview every former pupil at the establishment."

"Please answer my question."

"If there had been any such persons friendly with Singer, we would not have known of them. On the other hand, the case received con-

186

siderable attention in the press, and it might be thought that if there had been any such persons, they would have come forward."

"And do you honestly think that a murderer or someone implicated in a murder would just conveniently come forward?"

"I was not talking about that."

"Yes. Indeed, I have had the feeling progressively all along in this examination that you and I are not talking about the same thing, or even the same case." Bartlett paused.

Jordan was aware of an immense and gentle boredom, and perhaps Bartlett was aware of it too. For the final onslaught did not come. Instead the barrister lowered his tone to the humdrum.

"There is just one final matter I want to ask you about, Superintendent. When you asked Maddox on March the thirteenth whether he would submit to a skin test, did he immediately agree to do so?"

"Not immediately. He asked me what was the function of such a test."

"And you told him?"

"I did."

"Can you recall approximately the words that you used in informing him of the nature of this test?"

"I can't recall the exact wording. But I informed him that if the tissue taken from him failed to match that found under Singer's fingernails, it would go a long way to establishing his innocence. And, conversely, if the tissue matched, that this would certainly not count in his favour."

"You apprised him of this danger—this risk?"

"I did."

"And what else?"

"I don't think there was anything else."

"You did not indicate, perhaps, that, insofar as the results of this test might go a long way towards establishing the likelihood of guilt, or the certainty of innocence, an innocent man would have nothing to fear?"

For a moment George was quite still, and the court was still, with him. "I believe I might have said something to that effect."

"In other words, you were very careful to point out everything that was involved in the matter of this skin test?"

Again the silence. And then, for the first time, Superintendent

George glanced at the prisoner. And Jordan felt a sudden flood of humanity—for a moment he was no longer a cold supernumerary; he was connected, he was part of it.

"Yes, I think I was careful to do that."

"And when you had explained this to him, he agreed to the test?"

"Yes."

"Quite freely? You were not urging him, against his will, to submit to it?"

"There was no pressure of any kind put upon him."

"He assented freely and easily?"

"Yes, he did."

"And what was his demeanour at this moment?"

"I don't think there was anything remarkable about his demeanour."

"Well, did he seem fearful?"

"No. Quite normal."

"Not fearful. Yes. You had pointed out to him, had you not, that an innocent man would have nothing to fear?"

"I couldn't be certain I used those words."

"But," very gentle, "words to that effect?"

"Something to that effect, yes."

"Would it be fair then, Superintendent—" the ringing voice of justice triumphant—"Would it be fair to say that his demeanour was that of an *innocent man?*"

Well? Well? What was this? Answer him, man! Jordan sat up straight. Rigid—and yet he leaned, moved, yearned. Answer!

"Ever since I knew Maddox," slowly, consideringly, "it was always very difficult to judge his state of mind. I don't think, in my experience, I have ever come across any suspect whose truthfulness or honesty was more difficult to evaluate." For the last time the policeman looked at him. "So I really don't think I can answer that question, Mr. Bartlett."

"But his manner was not that of a guilty man?"

"No. No—he did not have a guilty *manner.*"

And as the cross-examination closed, and Pollen stood up and the judge murmured about adjournment—"Just a few points, my Lord." "Time is already getting on. . . ." "Not more than ten minutes . . ." ". . . not got all night. All right, very well." "And it is not true to say, is it, that . . ." "No, sir." "And it was perfectly normal procedure, was it not, to . . ." "Yes, sir." ". . . pertinent facts exhaustively investigated . . ." "Yes, sir." ". . . duty of a police officer . . . no place for prejudice . . . not a question of prejudgment . . . painstaking . . . no reason for . . . fair . . . warning . . . as prescribed . . . the Judges' Rules . . . no question . . . integrity . . . unanswerable . . . openminded, thorough, conscientious . . ." "Yes, sir. Yes sir. Yessir."

The incomprehensible murmur of the close—the chapel evensong, the chaplain congratulating God, God congratulating the chaplain, the pauses, the praises, the whispers, the stirring, the slow shuffling out . . .

But Jordan's mind was already upon the peace of his prison room where he could attempt in all privacy to penetrate to the truth of the matter. . . .

25

"Sorry to disturb you so late, old man. I'd have seen you in the cells, but I wanted to have a word with Geoffrey first." Tom walked up and down the small room, not looking directly at Jordan. "Did they give you dinner?"

"Yes. What's up—a crisis?"

"Not exactly."

"I'm not surprised after today's exhibition."

Tom halted. "What do you mean by that? I thought it all went rather well, except for that old bastard Robbins."

"Robbins?"

"Mr. Justice Robbins. The judge, lost his teeth twenty years ago and his wits with them. The way he whitewashed Symington. You've got to admit that bloody great oaf of a superintendent knows his judges though. Robbins has always been a sucker for war heroes. The story goes he was turned down for military service in the first war because of knock knees. George played that one up to the hilt—makes you want to puke. Mentioned in dispatches! I wonder if he really was." Tom rubbed his chin. "I'd better check up on that first thing tomorrow."

"Why did you destroy my note?" He was too tired to be really angry any more, but he had to go through with it.

"Your note? Oh that! I could hardly decipher it. Besides, I could scarcely interrupt Geoffrey in full flight."

"And that is another thing. I thought we had agreed not to attack the police."

"Attack? That was no more than a gentle prodding."

"It was absolutely monstrous."

"We're not playing croquet, you know."

"I don't think it's funny. Bartlett was deliberately twisting—"

"Twisting?" Tom put his hands on the back of the chair and leaned forward. "Let's get this straight. The whole of the Crown's evidence is twisted—twisted against you. It has to be. And I don't mean anyone deliberately sat down and said, 'Let's nail this bugger.' But, deliberately or not, that's what it amounts to. And come hell or high water our brave bobbies are not going to admit to any failing. I'm not saying many of them are vicious—although seeing the nature of their work, it would be damned odd if there wasn't a sadist or two here and there—but they're not exactly models of openminded liberalism either. And don't let that show of rocklike integrity fool you—it's true enough up to a point, but only up to a point. And right from the beginning you were beyond the point. George has got his record to think of—and you bet your life he's thinking of it. Not that I blame him, that's what policemen are like. But you're just one item on the list to him."

"I don't like this. The man did his duty. He didn't harm me."

"It beats me why you're so fond of the police. What did they do? Brainwash you or something?"

"If that's all you've got to say, Tom, let's cut this short, shall we?" He made a movement towards the door.

"Oh come off it, Jordan." Tom grinned suddenly. "Let's sit down."

Wearily Jordan sat down.

"There are two things," said Tom. "First, I want to report to you about the investigations. We're not giving up, although I'm afraid we haven't got much to show for it as yet. But since we've had a couple of detectives on it, things are going faster. They've got through everyone in June Singer's year at the Lamont School and the people a year ahead. Tomorrow they start on those a year behind. Meanwhile,

190

Gladding's in the morgue of the local newspaper, going through every issue for the last fifteen years—you know, weddings, dances, christenings, that sort of thing. Girl Guides. Singer must have done something. I don't suppose you have any bright ideas?"

"No."

"I thought not." He lit a cigarette. "It's damnable. At this very moment there's some chap sitting down to a pint of beer and the evening paper with the report of the trial, who *knows*. . . . That chap Lambert, for instance—I've a shrewd suspicion he was a lot better acquainted with Singer than he's letting on to. There's so bloody much we don't know. Look, Jordan, I don't like having to take this line with most of these witnesses, police or not, that they're, well, if not exactly lying, certainly biased and unreliable, et cetera. Geoffrey doesn't like it either. It can easily make us look captious and carping, the pot calling the kettle black, and that kind of thing. But there's so much we don't know, can't explain at all, there's just no other possible line to take. Those photos—how on earth did she get hold of a photo of you? How did she plant a snapshot of herself in your desk? Not how, but why? Why on earth? And this Mrs. Payne's deposition —her evidence ought to come up late tomorrow or early on Monday, by the way—and the letters she'll swear you wrote to Singer. The letters she saw—who did they really come from? And why did Singer let the old lady think they were from you? These things are tricky enough—but at least we can suggest and hint and hypothesize that Singer was in love with you and wanted other people to think you were in love with her. God knows, this kind of thing is the stuff of schoolgirl fantasies. But . . ." Tom stood up restlessly, frowning. "It's a trivial thing in its way—yet it worries me and worries Geoffrey too. It's the letter you wrote to Jackson Timberley—that implicates you, that's an *action* on your part. And yet it's inexplicable. We know, from that little squirt Lambert, that Singer was probably stoking up on Gleason's on February the fourteenth. She'd made her decision to try to get rid of the baby. You wouldn't think she'd have room in her mind, only four days later, for plans about emigrating to America. It doesn't make a damn bit of sense." He hesitated. "When she came to you and asked you, did she—?"

"She didn't come to me, Tom. I suggested it to her."

"You what?" Tom gripped the back of the chair. "You never told me anything. Why? Why on earth did you suggest it to her?"

"Why?" Why had he? Tom's presence blocked Jordan's mind. It must have been after that evening he'd taken her out for a drink to the wine cellar. Jordan stared blankly ahead of him. She had asked him for something—the business about some friend's fatherless baby —for help, for . . .

He looked at Tom. "I don't know why," he said quietly.

"But she took you up on it, or else you wouldn't have written the letter. Are you sure she didn't ask you—indirectly perhaps?"

"No, she didn't ask me for that."

"Well, why did you suggest it? You must have some idea."

Jordan braced himself. "I must have thought she needed a change —the death of her mother, you know. . . ."

"Yes, yes. I know. That's half of it, and, well, as you heard, Geoffrey's plugging that. Although it was three months since her mother kicked the bucket. Still . . . But why did she take you up on it, then? Just to please you? That sounds pretty feeble. If she was in love with you, surely to God she wouldn't have wanted to leave you. She knew she was pregnant, must have done, by the fourteenth, and almost certainly long before that, and yet—"

"She knew before that, all right."

"What?"

"She was certainly aware she was pregnant before the fourteenth."

"How do you know?" Tom was wary.

"She told me."

"She what?"

"She told me. As plain as could be. I was just too—too stupid to understand."

"You mean she just hinted?"

"I suppose you could put it that way."

"Well, look, old man," said Tom, with relief, "nobody can be blamed for not getting a hint. Women are congenitally incapable of saying anything straight out."

"You do not understand."

"Of course I understand. You needn't think that sort of thing hasn't happened to me. I'm not exactly a monk, you know. The things that get told in an office would—"

"It wasn't in the office that she told me."

"That's beside the—what?"

"I took her out for a drink. To the Wine Cellar. On Friday the thirteenth of February."

"Good God almighty." The words were low, as if spoken in private prayer. "Good God almighty." He rubbed his forehead slowly and hard.

"I don't see there's any need to make such a fuss."

Tom lowered his hand and leaned forward towards Jordan. "Were you," he asked softly, "in court today?"

"Don't be damn silly."

"Did you happen to notice what was going on? It was a trial, you know—a murder trial. You are being tried for murder."

"For God's sake, I'm not a mental patient."

"I'm not so bloody sure. This drink you had with the girl—you just remembered it, I suppose? Just popped into your mind out of a clear blue sky, eh?"

"That is exactly what happened."

"By Christ, if I didn't know you, I'd think . . . Think what it looks like, man. You take the damn girl—"

"Tom—June is dead."

"You don't say?"

"I'd rather you didn't talk about her in that way."

Tom Short's face was dark red, except for a white hand mark on his forehead. "What the hell do you mean?"

"Show her some decency at least. No one did while she was alive."

Tom straightened up. He took a long breath that ended in a kind of sob. He muttered something to himself. "Look, I'm sorry. Let's start again, shall we? You say you took the girl out for a drink on Friday. I've little doubt that somebody at the Wine Cellar spotted you. The waiter knows you? Yes—well. Now the next day—the very next day—the girl starts trying to get rid of the baby. The jury, any reasonable man, might well see a connection between those two events. They'd think, at the very least, that you let her down in some way, which doesn't—"

"I did let her down."

"I'm not talking about your conscience or whatever it is. I'm talking about the facts." Suddenly Tom seemed very tired. He pulled the chair out and sat down slowly. "I accept the fact that you acted in all innocence. That's one of the chief troubles—you were so much of the complete innocent, it's almost incredible." He looked at Jordan speculatively. "You and I have never been on the same wave length, of course. Still . . . Well, look—the prosecution isn't going to accept the innocence of your motives. On the contrary, the real gravamen of their case is that you had a guilty relationship with June Singer and that you acted in terms of it. I suppose we ought to thank our stars they don't know about your little drink with her. But all the same—all the same, Pollen is very likely to ask you a question like this: 'Did June Singer at any time tell you that she was pregnant?' How would you answer that question?"

"Well, not in so many words. I think that's what I'd say. It's the truth."

"All right. Next question: 'She implied to you that she was pregnant, is that it?' "

"Yes, she did, but—"

" 'And was this implication given on a specific occasion?' "

"Yes."

" 'When?' "

"I'd have to tell him, Tom."

"Okay—so you tell him. We'll take it from there. Pollen: 'You state that you took June Singer out for a drink on the night of February the thirteenth. Were you in the habit of taking your secretary out for a drink?' If you said Yes, you'd be damned right away. And yet to answer No is almost worse. Because Pollen will say: 'So this was a special occasion?' And you'll have to admit it was unusual. And then he'll ask you why you took this unusual and special step. And what'll you say to that?"

"I don't know. I don't know why I took her out for a drink. Perhaps I thought she seemed a bit down in the mouth."

" 'Now, Maddox, is it not in fact true that you took this unusual step because you had something of the greatest importance to discuss?' "

"No."

" 'I put it to you that you knew very well that the girl was pregnant, that you knew yourself to be the responsible party, and that you sought to persuade her to dispose of the baby in order to conceal your adulterous relationship?' "

"That's absurd."

" 'And do you think it absurd, Maddox—an absurd coincidence,

194

perhaps—that the day after you took her out for a drink, June Singer was taking steps to procure a miscarriage?' "

"Tom—I . . ."

" 'Was it a coincidence, Maddox?' "

"No. Tom, you see—I don't think it was a coincidence."

Tom grunted. "Alright, Jordan. You're putting nails in your own coffin, you know."

"Coffin? I thought it carried a sentence of life impris—"

"Listen, will you?" A moment of savagery. "I want you to see quite clearly the picture that the jury is going to see, if you persist in this. Pollen's next question ought to go something like this." Tom paused, squinting his eyes. "Right. 'And as a means of persuading her to undertake this dreadful thing, you held out to her the promise of a job in America, did you not?' "

"No, certainly not, I—"

" 'And you thought, did you not, that it would be highly convenient, once this was all over, to have the girl safely out of the way in a distant place?' "

"Not at all."

" 'And when she refused the job, refused to go away, that was a great blow to you, was it not?' "

"Nothing of the kind. I thought it might have been best for her, but—"

" 'It was on March the first that she wrote that letter refusing to go to America. It was about that very time, too, that she ceased her purchases of laxatives at Marben's Chemists. I put it to you, Maddox, that these two actions of Singer's rose from her decision to give up her efforts to procure a miscarriage, to stop this wicked thing.' "

"I know nothing about that. It has nothing to do with me."

" 'On the contrary, I suggest you knew full well of her decision, that you urged her to reconsider, because, if she did not, the whole thing would come out with consequences you could not bear to face. And I further suggest that, having failed in your pleadings, you went to Number Twenty-seven Panton Place on the morning of Monday, March the ninth, to make one final effort of persuasion, and that, having failed once more to shake her decision to have the baby, in an access of rage you murdered her. Is that not what happened?' "

"Tom, I'll tell the truth. And the answers are No."

"This is one of those times when the answers are not anything like as important as the questions. I warn you, Jordan, once you start to fiddle about with fancy notions of spiritual responsibility, you're done. At least in the courtroom—the law isn't one whit concerned with the state of your soul. If you stand up there and say that June Singer told you she was pregnant . . ."

"I don't think I have any alternative."

"But it's not true, man. You've told me it's not true. No—June Singer did not tell you that she was pregnant at any time."

Jordan shook his head. "You want everything to be simple, don't you? And tidy. It just isn't, Tom. I'm sorry to disappoint you."

"Me? I don't matter a damn. But there are others who do. Jordan, I'm a lawyer, not a moral philosopher. Perhaps I'm out of my depth. But aren't you being rather selfish?"

"Selfish?"

"You're wallowing in it a bit, aren't you? Don't you have a duty—not just to yourself, but to your family, to Willy, to Georgia?"

Jordan smiled faintly. "I've listened to that sort of simplemindedness for years, Tom. I'm not sure it convinces me any longer. If I'd been able to see outside it a little, perhaps I wouldn't have failed June."

"You think you can make up for that failure—if failure it was—by sacrificing those who depend on you?"

"You're arguing like a lawyer. Let's drop it, shall we?"

"Very well," said Tom heavily. "I'll talk to Geoffrey. He'll want to see you. If you feel like this, we'll have to think again about calling you. And that—that knocks the bottom out of our whole strategy."

"I don't care a damn about the strategy," Jordan said irritably. "You lawyers can sort that out."

Tom Short stood up. He was a big man. "You don't care a damn. I wish . . ."

Jordan rose. "You wish what? That you could take yourself off this case?"

Tom picked up his briefcase. He hesitated and then said, "If it wasn't for Willy . . ."

Jordan's forehead pulsed with anger. "Well, Tom, you never did like to be associated with failure, did you?"

He thought then that the lawyer would hit him. But after a moment in which his bloodshot face lost all its colour, Tom merely nodded, as if some deeply held conviction had been confirmed at last.

26

He enjoyed going up to Frank's office. He liked the wide automatic lift, each wall a different colour, sliding smoothly upward, and the doors parting with a small *ping* from a hidden bell; the perfumed secretaries; the quick glimpses through glass-panelled doors of men in shirtsleeves; the pattering of electric typewriters; the pastel-coloured filing cabinets; the sudden vividness of a poster. No invisible layers of dust. A bright casual carefree fantasy.

"Can I help you?"

"Is Mr. Wade in?"

"Are you Mr. Maddox?"

"Yes."

The dark girl smiled. "He said for you to go right in." She rose smoothly and opened the door for him to the inner office.

"Hello, Frank."

"Jordan, come in! Oh, Sheila," Frank called out as the door was closing, "I shan't be back till four. If anybody calls, tell them I'm designing St. Paul's. Look at this, Jordan, look here—I just got it this morning."

Jordan looked at the fat white telephone. "What does it do—shave you while you talk?"

"It lights up. Never rings, no vulgar noise. Just lights. Look here." He took Jordan's arm and dragged him round the desk. "Twelve of 'em, see? Three whites for outside lines. The green chappie's a direct line to Clotard's. The others are interoffice—different colour for each. The red light's for the chairman of course—Sward, the old whore himself." He burst out laughing.

"And can you tell which light is for who?"

"Not really, but it doesn't matter. I just pick up the phone and say 'Quite' three or four times in a pensive voice, then hang up. I'm thought to be rather profound."

Suddenly the pink light flashed, and Frank grabbed the receiver.

"What? No. I'm not Mr. Fillmore. You are Mr. Fillmore. Well, you're a pink light, aren't you? Fillmore's pink, you're on pink. Ergo, you are Fillmore. If you don't know who you are, what's the point in my talking to you?" He dropped the receiver back into its cradle, and smiled sheepishly at Jordan. "Well, it works for Sheila," he said.

"You're in good form today."

"Ellen's away. That always helps. Father had another stroke or something." He grimaced. "Come on, let's have lunch. The club?"

"Yes." Jordan stared out of the broad window onto the park. "I like it here."

"Ah, but if you worked here, you wouldn't have the time to watch them snogging in the park, you know."

Jordan half-closed his eyes till the sunlight shimmered. "I never get any sun in my place."

Frank pulled on his overcoat clumsily, as he always did. "You don't come up here for the sun, we all know that."

"Why do I then?"

"To pinch the secretaries' bottoms, what else?"

He reached over and straightened Frank's grotesquely twisted collar. As he did so, he thought vaguely, guiltily, of the little dark box June Singer shared with Miss Lawley.

"By the way," Frank said, as they walked through the outer office, "what do you think of my latest?"

"Your latest what?"

"Christ. Secretary."

"Is she new?"

"I've only had her a couple of weeks. Bit long in the tooth for me—all of thirty. But toothsome all the same, don't you think?"

"Is she American or something?"

"That's shrewd of you. No, but she worked in the States for three years."

The club was within easy walking distance, but they took a cab. Frank had long ago lost the use of his legs.

Jordan ordered a Manzanilla. Frank drank neat whiskey with three cubes of ice. "The difficult thing in advertising, you know, is to get the right mixture of integrity and—bezazz. You know what I mean, Geordie?"

"Aye—I do that," Jordan said broadly—an ancient jest—and smiled.

"Seriously. You've got to take it seriously—no good thinking it's a hell of a lark. Integrity, principle—you've always got to bear the principle of the thing in mind."

"Sell more soap."

"Don't be naive. Advertising is *informative*. That's its nature, its function. Informing—it's got to be accurate information, but never stuffy. Part of informing, what I call essential public enlightenment, is to attract. You can convey all the info you want, but if nobody's going to listen, you're a dead duck. That's where the attraction element comes into it. After all, who'd ever have got the message of the Gospels if it hadn't been for all that rich full-blooded stuff in the O.T. first? Bait."

"Balls."

"Aha! There you are. That's it! You protest—you want to register disagreement. Now you could easily say 'Nonsense,' but you don't. Why? Because it won't get attention. So what do you do? You introduce an attraction element—in this case a genital one—to get notice. Your message is the same, but now it's got through. But that's method. What I'm talking about is principle. There's a tendency for admen to be faintly shy about their profession. Oh, not on the surface, but in their heart of hearts. As if they were doing something the head wouldn't quite approve of, instead of, well, instead of seeing themselves as the spearhead of free enterprise." He finished his whiskey, set the glass down hard, and said, "Small," without looking at William. The glass came back refilled at once. Frank lifted the glass and examined the contents thoughtfully.

"That's a hell of a large small," Jordan said.

"Haha! You're very observant today. It's a neat little trick. Whatever I may say, William's got standing orders to disregard it and give me triples." He laughed. "I got that one from old Sward. I used to notice at these client get-togethers old Sward got remarkably well oiled in a very short time. Yet he's got a head of teak and he kept exactly level with the rest of us, drink for drink. And he'd always be very insistent about having a small one. He let me in on it eventually —triples, he was knocking back three to our one. Damn useful with clients—they think you're a pretty sound, sober chap, but it doesn't interfere with your drinking."

"You don't surely bring clients here though?"

"Oh no—it's just a habit. But to get back to the point. It's fatally easy to compensate for this feeling that one's engaged in something not quite-quite, a bit frivolous, by being solemn, oversolemn. I catch myself at it sometimes. But if you overdo the solemnity bit, you wind up with solemn advertising. And that's no good at all—unless you've got the Royal Family account, of course."

Jordan laughed. "Sometimes I think you're insane."

"Not a bit of it. I don't think solemnity and integrity are the same thing. I get a lot of fun out of advertising." He smiled into his whiskey, then looked up at Jordan. "I expect it's rather the same sort of thing for you, isn't it? After all, there can't be much joy in reading about lower intestinal tracts and ingrowing toenails all day."

Jordan ordered another Manzanilla. "There's a bit more to it than that. We do publish a nonmedical title here and there."

"What?"

"Well, there's rather an interesting manuscript I've got in on village idiocy in East Anglia since—"

"Jordan, you're priceless. Village idiocy—that's almost as good as the campaign we're doing for Clotard's. Lavatory-paper limericks. I remember at Cambridge when you were all on fire to publish . . . oh well."

Jordan took a sip of his sherry. "It seems a long time ago."

"It is a long time ago. I shouldn't worry. After all, I was going to be a big hit at the bar."

They both looked down at the oak-topped counter and burst out laughing together.

"Let's have some lunch."

He didn't get back to Sutlif & Maddox till after three-thirty. It had begun to rain. As he walked through the office shared by Miss Lawley and June, he didn't allow the Law's statuesque disapproval or June's anxious smile to perish his elastic mood of benevolence. Frank was a stimulant. Whenever he saw Frank he was touched by a world so strange that he did not really believe in its existence. He felt like a boy listening to a tale of the conquistadors—its charm was its distance, its excitement was its improbability. If ever he felt a little guilty, it was because he realised that Frank did actually live in that peculiar macabre place of rationale without reason, philosophising without philosophy. The very word *campaign* suggested an endless war, without distinction of cause or possibility of peace.

A dream related at breakfast—interesting, curious, rich perhaps, but always meaningless. It was only when Frank, eyes down and then suddenly looking at you with great simplicity, tried to probe at something beneath the fantasy that Jordan became uneasy. Soothed with sherry now, Jordan thought about this. It did not happen often, but there would be the hint or, worse, the straight-out statement of aimless lust or agonized emptiness. And Jordan knew instinctively that he was supposed to offer some answering terror of his own. But he had none, and he felt uncomfortably a traitor to the placidity of his own life even in listening to Frank.

Yet Frank was good for him. Perhaps that was why Willy disliked Frank. No, he had phrased it wrong—it was the foreignness in Frank, beneath the right noises, which she sensed and feared. And of course there was the Lymbridge business—but her adamant outrage at that had been almost an excuse to dismiss Frank once and for all. Not because he had made a pass at her, but because he was subversive of the whole structure of decency and normality.

She had not forgotten. He knew the cold "Oh?" with which she would greet the news that he had lunched with Frank Wade. And she would accurately estimate how much he'd had to drink and treat him with just that touch of disdain which she always managed to convey to erring children and the lower classes.

He didn't really mind; his benevolence could encompass that all right.

He took a pencil from his desk and began to write. "The Panther," he began. It was always at these times that he could compose the best animal verse for Georgia. It was going to be a good one.

He had just finished when June came in with his afternoon tea.

"There we are, Mr. Maddox."

"Thanks." He smiled up at her.

"I brought you some biscuits. I thought you might like . . ."

"Ladyfingers. My favourite. You shouldn't spoil me, June."

"But I thought Nice biscuits were your favourite."

"Oh yes. These too, though." She didn't look well, he thought. Or was it just that she was ill at ease? That would be unlike June.

"Do you want to do those letters now, Mr. Maddox?"

"Hang the letters. They can wait till the morning. There's nothing urgent, is there?"

"No," she said. "Well, I'll do a bit of filing then."

He didn't want her to go. He suddenly had a sharp impulse of generosity. She was pathetic somehow, poor thing. . . . "Why don't you sit down for a moment, June."

"Shall I get my tea?"

"Yes, you get your tea. We'll have a party."

Obviously she was depressed. It was a depressing time of year. And then, of course, her mother. That's not something you get over quickly. Perhaps it was a good thing she was taking her holidays early this year. She ought to get away for a bit. That was the thing. Or . . . The idea came to him. It would do her the world of good, change her outlook, and, well, if it meant he'd have to make a bit of a sacrifice, what did it matter?

She came back and sat down. "Is it sweet enough for you, Mr. Maddox?"

"Oh yes. Just right." He smiled. "Depressing weather, isn't it?"

"It is a bit. Not that I mind really."

Jordan stirred his tea. "It doesn't help much though, does it? Particularly when you're not feeling up to much."

"No, it doesn't."

He was surprised by her agreement. She really was upset. "I know you're going through a rather trying time just now. I don't want to intrude, but I know what this sort of, er, trouble—"

"You do?"

"Well, let's put it this way. I can guess. It's not easy, I know, and sometimes you think—well, you begin to think rather lugubrious thoughts. Not that they aren't real enough at the time, I don't mean to say that."

"Oh Mr. Maddox."

For a horrible moment he thought she was going to cry. But he resisted his impulse to shy away. "Yes. You see—" he drew a breath— "I've been through something of the same thing myself."

She looked at him so intently that he felt stupidly inarticulate.

"Yes," he said. "Yes. Of course it wasn't so bad, I'm sure. I had other people—someone to share, you know. And then . . . it was my uncle." He turned to the window. He hadn't expected that to come out. He hadn't meant to raise . . . ghosts. The light drizzle had formed three or four drops of water which moved jerkily in little darts and sallies down the window pane. "But it isn't the end of the world. The best thing to do—" he was pulling himself back to the lunchtime benignity—"the best thing to do is to get away. Oh, I don't mean for good. But a change of atmosphere. A new place, new people—so that you have to, well, respond to them. A new job even. Take America . . ." He turned back to June. The anxious expression was still on her face—anxious and puzzled. Perhaps he wasn't making himself very clear. "Have you ever thought of taking a job in America? For a year or two, I mean."

She opened her mouth. "America?" she whispered.

"New York, say. A tremendously stimulating place. Quite different, exciting. It wakes us English up. Gets you out of yourself—despite yourself, so to speak."

"You mean me go to America?"

Jordan felt a touch of impatience. "Well, why not? There's nothing like living in a foreign country for a year or two to broaden your horizons." He had a quick, guilty thought of Willy's two years in Bordeaux.

June shook her head. "No, I never had thought of it," she said, but as though she were thinking of something else.

"Why don't you then? It would be easy for someone with your qualifications to—"

"You mean leave Sutlif and Maddox?"

"You could hardly get a job in New York and stay here too, could you? Why don't you think about it? A year, say. And if you wanted to come back, well there'd always be a job here."

June took a sip of tea. "I will think about it. Thank you, Mr. Maddox."

"It'd get you out of yourself. Now I have a practical suggestion. Why don't I write to Jack Timberley—you remember Mr. Timberley —and see whether he has anything to suggest?"

"Thank you. It would be exciting, I suppose," she said tentatively.

"There you are, you see. You're already beginning to catch on to it."

June smiled. "Perhaps I am."

"Of course you are. I'll drop a line to Jack Timberley, then. It can't do any harm."

June nodded.

"Good. Even if it comes to nothing, the great thing is to feel you're doing something—prospecting, as it were. Well."

June got up. "Thank you, Mr. Maddox. You're very thoughtful."

Jordan watched her as she left the room. She was a sensible girl. He noticed she'd forgotten to take her cup out. He was about to call her back but thought better of it.

He'd do the letter to Jack right away. He fetched the portable from the cupboard.

Yet, as he started to type, he could not quite recapture the warmth he'd felt earlier. He stopped. He disapproved of drinking in the middle of the afternoon, but this time . . .

He got out the authors' sherry and poured himself a glass. A distinct improvement. He began to type again, smiling now—as he always did when he caught himself doing a good deed for the day.

27

He had denied himself dreams. All night long he had sat on the bed, his back against its black iron bars. He had dozed; dozed and woken, and dozed again. The head sagging and then snapping up, wide awake in the dimness of the little room. Punishment: a small boy slowly painting iodine on a cut finger; pressing a hand hard onto the hot pipe, the elation of pain, the secret pride of the blistered stigmata.

But it was far more than those simple penances for unknown crimes. Lying down, he would have been overwhelmed. If he had let go the helm and allowed the ship to broach and wallow broadside, the waves would have sunk her. It would be so easy to founder and drown. But he could not permit that, for he had to reach a destination, wherever it was. Then, perhaps, surrender.

Now, sitting hard and upright in the dock, he could maintain himself. He was not in the least tired. He had never been so alive. His mind moved at a great speed, so that all that went on in the court was in slow motion. Bartlett was having a difficult time cross-examining Symington. The inspector gave a remarkable performance of earnestness and touching modesty, so that Bartlett was forced to abandon outright assault and attempt, instead, to swamp the policeman with monotony. The juror in the green shirt had discarded it today in favour of a greyish-white one. His colourlessness reflected the obvious boredom of the jury.

Jordan felt a momentary sympathy for the barrister, who would know by now of the prisoner's recalcitrance.

Willy knew. When he had seen her this morning, she had been white-faced and calm, her secret anxiety drawing the blood from her lips. There had been very little to say. Their marriage policy of avoidance unblinkingly revealed now, when the only thing that mattered could not be mentioned, the poverty of their intercourse. Jordan was at once grateful and impatient.

Shortly before she'd left she'd said, "We're longing to have you home and safe."

"Are you?"

A faint moment of colour touched her cheeks. "Of course we are. Georgia . . ."

"How are you getting on with the animal stories?"

"I've—I've given them up. I'm so absolutely useless at it and—"

"I bet she misses them."

"Oh yes. Yes she does. Very much."

He knew she was lying.

"Jordan, I hope you don't mind, but I've asked Frank Wade to come and see you tomorrow."

"You what?"

"I've asked Frank Wade—"

He interrupted her with laughter. "Frank Wade. My God!"

"Just because I don't happen to care for Frank Wade doesn't mean that I don't realise his—his value to you as a friend."

"To cheer me up, that's it, isn't it? To stiffen the Maddox spine?" His mirth wounded her blanched stoicism.

"Jordan, I . . ."

"Yes?"

"Nothing." She gave a quick bird shake of her head.

He felt a stab of vindictiveness. "Nothing," he repeated. "Well, I expect Frank will have plenty to tell me about his latest. It's his secretary, you know." He laughed again. "Sheila something or other." And then it was no longer funny. "Frank's the last person on God's earth I want to see. Just tell him not to bother, will you?"

She nodded tightly. He was glad to see her go. Glad to get rid of her and return to the pain of his private surgery. For each memory now was a sharp tool, his only care the selection, the cutting away, the exposure of dead tissue. He did not have much time.

"Your name is Harold Grand?" asked Pollen portentously.

"Yes." The new witness was a little man, perky.

"What is your occupation?"

"Waiter." And the sort of waiter to whom Mr. Pollen would certainly give a very small tip.

"Where are you employed?"

"Blain's—in the Strand."

"And how long have you been employed there?"

"Two years plus."

"Plus?"

"Plus a coupla months." The edge of Mr. Grand's lips moved into a grin.

Jordan watched closely, but he could not place the waiter.

"Were you, er, on duty at Blain's on the night of January the fifth?"

"I was."

"And do you recall that night?"

"Definitely."

"Do you recall it very clearly?"

"Definitely."

"How is it that you recall this night so clearly?"

"I remember every night, see? I got a memory like a razor." Mr. Grand smiled.

"But was there a particular reason why you should recall this night of January the fifth?"

Mr. Grand was puzzled for a moment. "Well," he said uncertainly. Then he brightened. "Oh yes. There was. It was a Monday, see? It was right after my holidays. My first day on. Me and my old— my wife just come back from a fortnight in Switzerland. I always like to take a winter holiday, it's—"

"Yes. Thank you. Now, Mr. Grand, would you describe that night as a busy one?"

"Quiet, dead quiet. I only 'ad nine."

"Nine people?"

"Nine parties."

"And do you recall all those parties?"

"Definitely."

"Could you describe them?"

The judge clicked his teeth. "Mr. Pollen, is it really necessary for the witness to itemize his entire evening?"

"My Lord, I wish to establish this witness's quite phenomenal memory."

"Very well. Very well."

"Mr. Grand, will you briefly describe to the court the nine people—parties on whom you waited that evening?"

"Well, five of them was regulars. There was old—I mean Mr. Turner and his wife; the Thrussels—they always take the beef; Mr. Vaughan, he was by himself, his daughter'd gone off abroad; Mr. Bann and a lady, he always has a different one; and Mrs. Cockshot—Mondays is her night out, you know. Then there was a bald party in a brown suit, on his own; two old girls—I mean two middle-aged ladies who come in early, and three Krauts—"

"Krauts?" Pollen reproved.

"German gentlemen. They had pork chops. Swine flesh." Mr. Grand was pleased with the murmurs this piece of information caused.

Jordan remembered the Germans. He remembered mentioning them to June. Something amusing. Something about the way they ate? Napkins tucked under their chins. Concentration.

". . . a man and a girl," Mr. Grand was saying.

Jordan tried unsuccessfully to picture Mr. Grand's face above a black tie.

"And did you know the man?"

"Oh yes. Mr. Maddox. Him there." He raised his finger to point and said impressively, "The prisoner in the dock!"

"Did you know Maddox from previous occasions?"

"Yes. He used to come in for lunch sometimes. Not regular, but I'd served him six or seven times myself. He'd make a reservation, see?"

Six or seven times, and he'd never even noticed the waiter, whom he must have talked to, smiled at, tipped.

"And did you recognise the girl?"

"Never seen her before in my life."

There was a shuffling, and then a photograph was handed to the witness.

"Do you recognise that photograph?"

"That's her alright."

"You are quite positive that this is the woman you saw dining with Maddox?"

"Definitely. Buck teeth."

"You recall her buck teeth?"

"Well, not buck exactly. But they stuck out a bit in front. Like this, see?" He drew back his lower jaw and grinned. "Kinda sexy."

A tittering murmur stirred the court, and the judge looked over his glasses at the witness.

"Now, Mr. Grand, was there anything unusual about the behaviour of Maddox and the young woman?"

"Well, not unusual exactly. They was kind of lovey-dovey."

"My Lord—" Bartlett was on his feet—"I must object to these expressions of purely personal opinion, which seem to be the only object of my learned friend's questions."

"Yes. Mr. Pollen, you must frame your questions more carefully." The judge stared at the witness for a moment. "And Mr. Grand, please curb your witticisms. This is not a music hall."

"Yessir." Grand bobbed his head. He served up contrition as easily as lamb chops.

"But, my Lord," Mr. Pollen said, "I am going to ask this witness to substantiate his observation. As a matter of fact."

"Very well, Mr. Pollen, if you can do so. Proceed, proceed. But please use caution, Mr. Pollen, and—ah—celerity."

"Thank you, my Lord. Now, Mr. Grand, will you please tell us what you saw or heard that led you to conclude that the accused and the young woman were—er—"

"Oh go on, Mr. Pollen," said the judge. "Lovey-dovey."

"Thank you, my Lord."

"She drops her napkin, see?"

"Yes?"

"And then he picks it up for her."

"She dropped her napkin and he picked it up for her. Is that all?"

"No—of course it isn't. Before he picks it up he says—" Mr. Grand frowned and looked up at the arched skylight—"he says, 'I'll pick it up, love.' "

"Let's be absolutely sure of this, Mr. Grand. Maddox said, 'I'll pick it up, love.' Is that correct?"

"That's right."

"Very well. That concludes my examination, my Lord."

Bartlett stood up. He looked down at the papers on his desk and stroked them gently with the fingers of one hand.

Poor Bartlett, thought Jordan; he wouldn't know what to make of it. It had been "luv," not "love." His Geordie accent—the feeble hilarity hung over from a long-dead programme on the B.B.C. He couldn't even recall the name of the show.

"Mr. Grand," Bartlett began, dragging his words, "you have stated that, in your opinion, the accused and Singer were 'lovey-dovey.' As evidence of this, you relate, over a distance of several months, the words, 'I'll pick it up, love.' What else do you remember of that conversation?"

"Well—not much."

"Nothing?"

"I remember what they ordered, like."

"But nothing more than that?"

"No. Not really."

"And how much of the conversation that went on between your other patrons that night do you remember?"

"I remember Mr. Vaughan telling me 'is daughter had gone off to Austria and—"

"That's not my question. I am not referring to any conversation conducted by you or directed to you. I am asking you what, if anything, you overheard going on between your patrons."

"Well, I . . ."

"Come, Mr. Grand, surely you overheard something?"

"I'm not an eavesdropper, if that's what you mean."

"Answer the question. Do you recall any portion of any conversation conducted by your patrons on that night—apart from the alleged words of the accused?"

"No—I can't say I do."

"And yet you expect us to believe that you are able to recall exactly the words supposedly spoken by Maddox to Singer?"

"Oh yes. See, Mr. Maddox there didn't look the type to come out with that sort of thing. So naturally it stuck in my—"

"Quite. Please confine yourself to answering the questions. Did you see the accused and Singer hold hands?"

"I can't see under the table, can I?"

"Yes or no, Mr. Grand?"

"No."

"Or kiss?"

"What—in Blain's?"

"Yes or no?"

"That'll be the day."

"Yes or no?"

"No."

"Did you observe anything else which might merit the description 'lovey-dovey'?"

"Not exactly."

"Yes or no?"

"It's hard to explain."

"Yes or no?"

And there came upon Mr. Grand's face that age-old look of servile obstinacy, that inch of integrity asserted in the glass of water requested, promised, but never produced.

"It's hard to explain."

Bartlett paused. "Well, try to explain then. Do your best."

Mr. Grand frowned. "Well, most of the couples in Blain's—they're not exactly young. And they—well, a lot of them, the old parties, that is—they sort of carp at each other. You know what I mean?"

"They argue?"

"Not argue, no. Carp—not in a real nasty way or anything, but there it is. I mean like, she'll ask him what he recommends, not nasty, exactly, but as if she knows it's not going to be no good whatever it is."

"And what bearing does this have upon the behaviour of Maddox and Singer?"

"They weren't like that."

"They were not like that." Bartlett, slow, sarcastic.

"Oh no," said Mr. Grand, unperturbed. "They was happy. You could tell."

Geoffrey Bartlett hoisted his gown to settle it more firmly. "Now, Mr. Grand," he began.

But although Jordan remained aware of what was going on—of the barrister's patient dissection of the waiter—the voices and the movements, like the streamlined rush of images seen from a railway carriage, filled him with a gentle, mesmeric calm. *They was happy*—the words had the comfort of wheels and the promise of destination. He smiled.

28

"That was lovely, Mr. Maddox."

"It was fun, wasn't it?" He meant it. He took a gulp of his martini. He hadn't drunk a martini since . . . Cambridge? It was warm and good inside after the chill and the rain. His socks were damp, but the thought that he could not, even if he had wanted, rush to change into dry ones added to his pleasure. Socks and scarves and gloves and umbrellas—the paraphernalia of dread.

"I do like historical things," June said.

"Yes. I do too. Of course, it wasn't strictly accurate, you know. Take Henry, for example: it's extremely doubtful if he ever . . . " As he talked, he thought back to the last time he had taken anyone to the theatre. Not ballet—he had sat unstirred and stoic through innumberable vapid hours of ballet for Willy's sake—theatre. It must have been that vacation when Annie came up and they had gone together to the Old Vic. Othello? No. Hadn't Annie, too, said something about history? It would have been like her.

"Do go on," she said.

"Oh no, I'm being a bore. How's your drink?"

"It's very nice. But please, you're not being boring."

He smiled at her. "You're very good company, June. I haven't chattered so much for ages."

She was embarrassed, but it pleased him to see it. "Look at those chaps over there," he said.

"They're enjoying themselves, aren't they?"

"I suppose they are, but they don't look very happy, do they? That air of concentration—I think they must be Germans."

"They are a bit piggish."

"Piggish?" He was surprised. "Why do you say that?"

"They are pigs, really, aren't they, Mr. Maddox? I mean they don't, don't . . ."

Jordan was silent. And then he remembered. "Your father was killed in a raid, wasn't he?"

June nodded. "I don't even remember him. But I can't help hating them, all the same."

"I don't know. It seems to me that if one hates the Germans for what they did—well, we caused some pretty wanton destruction, too. Dresden, Hamburg. On the other hand, if you hate them for what they are—what led them perhaps to do what they did—then you have to begin with an historical examination. How did this or that character trait come into being, what were the causes and motives, et cetera. And, well, I don't think one can work off one's prejudices and passions on history. I mean, I don't think one *should* do that."

"I hadn't thought of it in quite that way. I'm sure you're right. But I just can't be calm about it like you."

"I'm probably calm because it never happened to me." He smiled. "But I do believe that you have to step away from these things a bit, if you're going to keep your judgement intact. In a way, that's what civilization is all about."

June frowned. "But isn't that—not running away, exactly. I mean, if something happens, you've got to face up to it, haven't you?"

"Yes, of course. Yet when you think what man was, say, ten thousand years ago, things don't seem quite such a matter of life or death. And I tend to think that history, and a vast acreage of our private life too—much more so than most people will credit—is very closely predetermined."

"Do you really think that?"

"Yes."

"But that's—frightening."

"Oh no, on the contrary, I think it's comforting."

"But surely . . . "

It reminded him of high and mighty conversations long ago. Like an old lesson, the soaring generalities would come glibly out from an attic which he had forgotten all about. He could repeat them by rote, like *The Death of Sir John Moore*. He was quite fond of them. Moore at Corunna had been Uncle John's last puzzle.

"I don't know, June," he said. "One gets rather tangled up in these things. It's like a game. Whatever we think—predestination, say—doesn't really make any difference to what we do. There was a time when an idea, a faith, could move men to action. But today we just hobble along, trying to avoid the grossest errors—keep our heads above water, as it were. All things grandiose are in the past, almost by definition."

"Yes, but it does make a difference to how you *feel*, doesn't it? And that's important. If you really thought life was predetermined, then you wouldn't feel such a sense of responsibility."

"Responsibility?" Jordan saw her eagerness. She was waiting for a word from him of some sort. He shuffled quickly round the old attic, but the worn phrase books contained nothing suitable. All for each, each for all. Members together in the body of Christ. Involved in mankind. "Responsibility," he repeated. "Well, one tries to do one's best. There's no use flagellating oneself."

"But that's just it. If you are responsible, then if you fail, you can't help feeling . . . well, guilty—it's your fault."

He smiled at her. "Now what have you got to feel guilty about, June?"

She was silent, and he realised how stupid the question was. He was aware of the sticky dampness of his socks. Damn.

"My mother," she said, not looking at him.

"Now, June, my dear, you can't, I mean, you mustn't—"

"She committed suicide, you know."

"Yes, I know. I—I'm sorry. But you mustn't blame yourself. I remember you telling me that your mother, well, suffered. And . . . " The inanities bubbled from his mouth, and his shame at them only made him talk the more.

"Do you mind if I tell you about it?"

Under the table he clutched his knee, pressing the damp cloth against the flesh. "No, no of course not. It'll make you feel better."

"I don't want to embarrass you, Mr. Maddox."

"No no. No. These things—" five hard points dug into his leg— "are better once you get them off your chest."

"Well, she—I don't know how to begin, really. She—she was always in pain. I don't remember a time when she wasn't. But it got worse all the time. And she couldn't hardly do anything for herself towards the end. I mean, that got worse too. The arthritis just stiffened her until. . . . She could just put her hand to her mouth. I had to cut up all her food. But she never said anything even when it was at its worst. The doctor gave her some pills for the pain, pain-killers, but I don't think they did much good really. And when she came home from the hospital last time, last summer that was, he gave her some sleeping pills too. One for every night. Like small orange lozenges they were. I used to keep them right at the top of the kitchen cupboard. I knew she couldn't reach there and . . . well, you see even then I thought perhaps—it did cross my mind I suppose that she might not be able to stand it one day. The doctor, he must have thought the same because he said, joking like, 'You want to keep those locked up safe, June; don't want some kid thinking they're sweets, do we?' Of course he knew there weren't any kids in the flat. I didn't have any place to lock them—but I did put them out of reach. And every night I'd give Mum one of the pills and a glass of water and help her to swallow it down. But sometimes she did it on her own; she could just manage that. And I'd see the pill was gone and some water and I thought, well, she's taken it. If she didn't take one, she'd never sleep, I knew that.

"I didn't think, I never dreamt she'd save them up. But she did. The doctor said she must have taken fifteen or twenty pills when she . . . I worked it out afterwards how she did it. Some nights before she went to sleep she'd ask me to bring her jewelry box. She liked to look at it, because it reminded her of when Dad was alive and they used to go out dancing. She knew I'd never look in that box unless she let me, and that's where she must have kept the sleeping pills because that evening when I came back and found her I noticed the box open on the table beside her.

"And all the time that's what she was planning, Mr. Maddox. And I never dreamt. I never thought to watch Mum that close. But she knew. And she must have laid there all those nights, not sleeping, not being able to sleep with the pain. And never a whisper. She never complained. And every morning I'd ask her how she slept and she'd always say the same thing, 'Oh I had a lovely night, Junie.' And every day she'd say, 'And what's on the menu for today?' As if it wasn't always going to be the same. And the last day, the day she did it, she didn't say anything different. She didn't want to let me know. She never asked for any pity. She never asked for anything."

June sat and looked at Jordan. She didn't cry. He was hell's own grateful she didn't cry.

He said, "She must have been a very courageous woman. You can't blame yourself."

"I do blame myself. For what she did. But I blame myself even

214

more for not knowing what was going on in her mind. Don't you see, I should have known that? You see, she couldn't trust me. She couldn't tell me what it was like, that she couldn't bear it any longer. Because I would have stopped her and she was helpless. But I keep thinking if I'd been a real daughter to her, she would have told me and . . . and I'd have helped her. That's what I'm sorriest for, Mr. Maddox. She couldn't trust me to understand. And she was right. I wouldn't have understood. Not then. I had to keep pretending that everything was alright, when it wasn't alright. I had to pretend that she wasn't just going to get more and more helpless, have more and more pain. . . ."

"It's alright now, June. We can't all have that sort of courage. Like your mother. We can't blame ourselves for all the ifs. We can just try again next time. That's all."

"I keep telling myself that, Mr. Maddox, but it doesn't seem to help much somehow."

"Yes, I know. I'm afraid I'm not very good at this sort of thing."

"Oh, I didn't upset you, did I, Mr. Maddox? I am sorry, I didn't—"

"Good lord no. I was thinking of you. There ought to be a sort of magic password that would—would help to put everything in perspective. But of course one can never find the password, that's the trouble."

"You've cheered me up a lot, Mr. Maddox. Just talking, as you said, helps. Doesn't it?"

"Yes. It's a good way of getting it out of the system." He took a deep breath, hoping that she would not notice. It was nearly over now. "I think we could do with another drink." He felt the thinness of his joviality—an Uncle Colin manqué. "One needs something to cling to."

He took a large swallow of his new martini and shivered.

"Are you cold?"

"Just a goose over my . . . grave." He laughed feebly.

June sipped her drink and smiled. And Jordan felt the earth tremors recede. Poor kid, she'd had a rotten time.

"There are compensations for this beastly weather, I suppose. Being comfortably inside—with a drink and the prospect of food and, er, charming company."

June put her head a little to one side. "I think that too. I always love it when it rains cats and dogs."

"The nesting instinct, I imagine. We ought to be thinking about food."

"I'm not really very hungry."

"I'll bet you will be when you begin. All that exercise running from the taxi."

And she was hungry. It pleased Jordan to see her tucking into pâté and roast spring lamb and a horrible pineapple confection. He had ordered a bottle of Moselle, and he drank most of it himself. He suddenly found it easy to talk to June—he had struck the right vein. He started telling her about the history of Woodley Hall, and from that to royal palaces, Hampton Court, Sheen, Nonsuch.

"A damned shame they pulled it down. Surrey isn't very distinguished architecturally. Nonsuch was a magnificent curiosity. Charles II gave it to one of his mistresses, Duchess of Portsmouth, I think. No, I'm wrong—Cleveland, Duchess of Cleveland, and she didn't have much use for it. Built by one womaniser, destroyed by another. . . ."

He sketched Nonsuch on June's napkin. She was a good listener. He could never talk like this to Willy. She would be bored to death. For someone who worshipped tradition and convention and never wanted to see anything change, she was oddly immune to history. But that was probably the reason—it was vaguely blasphemous to investigate one's deities.

The alcohol expanded him. He ordered a brandy. He could afford that tonight. There would be no disapproving frown awaiting him at home. The empty house and the empty bed. He wouldn't even have to bother to clean his teeth. And tomorrow there would be a faint and enjoyable haze between him and the world. And that other pleasure of the mild hangover—the constant desire, so easily satisfied, to stretch the limbs and yawn.

He took June home in a taxi and, as he let her out and she thanked him, he thought how really very odd it was that she didn't have a boy friend. Perhaps she did have one but there was something peculiar about him—in prison or married or something.

216

29

"Your evidence has been a model of clarity, Mrs. Ardley. There is in fact very little left for me to ask you." Bartlett spoke with unsmiling respect. Respect the landlady had already revealed as the touchstone of her existence.

And yet was this not verging on flattery—something which Mrs. Ardley would uncompromisingly reject? Jordan listened with great attention, for there was a quality about Mrs. Ardley that he had heard in no other witness. A quality or an attitude? He wasn't sure.

She was exactly the same as she had been that day at Sarah Street—the same dull clothes, the same hat, the same flourish of tiny orange feathers, the righteous face, the same unfaltering precision: "This is the man." She was indeed clear—her quiet description of June's room, of the placing of June's possessions, of June's body, had carried the conviction of a scholar's lovingly accurate footnotes. Jordan's attentiveness was mingled with a curious excitement.

"But there are just one or two questions." Bartlett frowned, as though the very idea of interrogating such a witness was distasteful. "I should like you to cast your mind back to the day on which you first met June Singer. When was that?"

"December the fifteenth."

"She came in answer to your advertisement of a vacant room?"

"Yes."

"And she took the room. Now, what impression did you form of her at that time?"

Mrs. Ardley was obviously vexed at the generality of the question. "She seemed respectable." Unwillingly. Large opinions and sweeping judgements were not carelessly bandied about in Mrs. Ardley's world. "But she did not take the room at that date."

"Why not?"

"I do not rent rooms without investigating references."

"What references did Singer give to you?"

"Miss Delmar of the Delmar Secretarial School and Mr. Maddox of Sutlif and Maddox, her employer."

"And these references proved to be satisfactory?"

"Yes."

"And that is why you gave her the room?"

"Not just for that reason. There were other applicants with equally good references." Mrs. Ardley was not permitting simplifications. No matter what, thought Jordan, she would be accurate—accurate even in her lies. She reminded him of someone.

"Ah, she was a preferred candidate. Why?"

"Her references were excellent. I did not know at the time that Mr. Maddox—"

"No no, Mrs. Ardley, that was not quite my question. Why did you give the room to Singer rather than to another applicant with equally good references?"

Jordan was certain that she had not misunderstood the question. She was being obstinate.

"She told me about her mother."

"I see. You felt sorry for her?"

"I—I appreciated her position." It was the landlady's first hint of hesitancy.

"Oh come now, Mrs. Ardley, compassion is nothing to be ashamed of. You were sorry for her, were you not?"

"Yes," said Mrs. Ardley, as though she were admitting to adultery.

"And you considered that Singer would be a good tenant?"

"I saw no reason to believe that she would not be."

"Did you later have any occasion to alter that opinion?"

The court was still. And although the landlady remained quite silent, it was as if some disdainfully crystalline voice had answered: A respectable person would not permit herself to be murdered in my house.

"Mrs. Ardley—did you later have any cause to alter your opinion that Singer would prove a good tenant?"

And then Jordan remembered. Implacable in the rectitude of a mind filled with unspoken, perhaps unspeakable, thoughts, the landlady was cousin to Miss Lawley. The Law did not suffer frailty kindly, and least of all her own. And Mrs. Ardley was now being asked to admit that she was frail, that she had made a mistake, that her judgement had erred.

"You must answer the question!"

218

Then Mrs. Ardley muttered. It was a shocking act, coming from those precise lips.

"What did you say? Speak up, Mrs. Ardley."

"I said—" she braced herself—"that I did not know at the time what was going on."

"You did not know what was going on? What *was* going on?"

"She was having her fancy man in, right under my nose. Mr. Maddox there—"

"Mrs. Ardley—"

"Just a moment, Mr. Bartlett, just a moment if you please." The judge touched his teeth with the end of his pencil, as if to steady them. "Mrs. Ardley, are you suggesting that Maddox was in the habit of frequenting Singer's flat?"

"Yes."

"Do you know that this was so?"

"Yes."

"How do you know?"

"He must have done so."

"There is no *must* about it, Mrs. Ardley. Apart from the day of the murder, did you ever on any occasion see Maddox entering or leaving your house?"

"No."

"Or inside your house?"

"No."

"Did Singer ever speak to you of Maddox visiting her?"

"Of course she wouldn't."

"Did she or did she not?"

"No."

"And did any of your other tenants ever speak to you of Singer receiving a male visitor?"

"No."

"Then your reply to Mr. Bartlett was pure supposition, was it not?"

"Yes, but—"

"There are no *buts*, Mrs. Ardley. You are under oath. To say that you have knowledge where you have none is a very serious matter. A very serious matter indeed. You know what perjury is?"

"Yes."

"Be careful then, Mrs. Ardley. Members of the jury, I direct you to

219

disregard Mrs. Ardley's reply to counsel. Put it out of your minds. Very well, Mr. Bartlett."

"All the same, I know what I think," Mrs. Ardley said sharply.

"Mrs. Ardley, you must behave yourself," snapped the judge, "or I shall hold you in contempt."

I know what I think—and she had looked at Jordan with savage judgement. And he also knew what she thought. It was no game to her, as to Mr. Grand; no simple duty, not just another item on the list, as it was to Superintendent George. She believed him guilty. He had murdered June Singer, and there was no doubt about it. She was ruthlessly certain.

For the first time since Sarah Street, Jordan felt something resist his touch. All things had yielded, all dissolved, but here was something firm-cast and steady. The suspension of judgement, the reasonable doubts, the tactics, the worried frowns, the soothing tattle, the wise smiles, the not-quite-straight looks—threads in a shielding curtain, yanked now momentarily aside.

"Let us try again, Mrs. Ardley. Leaving aside all suppositions, did you, at the time when Singer rented the flat from you, and later, did you consider her to be a good tenant?"

"I didn't know—"

"Did she pay her rent on time?"

"She was prompt, yes."

"Did she cause any disturbance—too much noise, rowdy behaviour, anything like that?"

"No."

"Did any of your tenants complain in any way about Singer?"

"No. She didn't have much to do with the other tenants."

"Did you, at any time, have any complaints whatsoever about her conduct as a tenant?"

"Not—no."

"It would be fair to say then that you considered her a satisfactory tenant?"

"Yes."

"Not the sort of girl, you would have said, who would be capable of carrying on a secret liaison under your roof?"

"I haven't been a landlady for thirty years without learning human beings are capable of anything. No matter what they may seem to be."

Slowly, as Bartlett probed the habits of the house, it became evident that Mrs. Ardley was the guardian at the gate. From a special frill-curtained living-room window which looked out onto the hall and the front door, she observed the goings out and the comings in. There was not much she missed, and never the doorbell. She went out occasionally in the afternoons—the cinema, a walk in the park, a trip to the shops—but she was always back by half-past five and at her post.

It was not the pleasure of gossip, nor the satisfaction of curiosity, which moved her, but moral vigilance. Appearances were deceitful, she knew, unless stitched firmly to the fabric of conduct. No men visiting women. No women visiting men. No visitors after nine. No parties except by permission. No secret drinkers. No jobless wastrels. No laughing on the stairs. Low rent, clean rooms, plain living. No debts, no duns, no delays granted.

"Mrs. Ardley, you told my learned friend that the front doorbell can be heard from anywhere in your flat."

"It can."

"Good. Now let's refer again to the layout of your flat, just briefly. As you enter the living room, on the wall directly facing you are two doors, one, on the right, to the kitchen, and the other, a little to the left, leading into the bedroom. Is that right?"

"Yes."

"The bedroom is at the back of the house, and leading off it, to the right, is a bathroom and lavatory, one room. Now, Mrs. Ardley, when you are in the bedroom, with the door closed, you can still hear the front doorbell. Correct?"

"I never close the door of the bedroom. It is always open."

"I see. You keep it open so that you can be sure of hearing the doorbell?"

"I could hear the bell with the door closed."

"Then why do you keep it open?"

"To hear it better."

"To be absolutely sure that you do not miss it?"

"Yes."

"Do you also keep the door of the bathroom open when you are in the bathroom?"

The landlady opened her mouth, then shut it grimly. "Of course not," she said.

"And could you hear the bell when you were in the bathroom with the door closed?"

"Yes."

"Mrs. Ardley, you have just testified that there is an element of doubt in your mind as to whether you would always be able to hear the bell from the bedroom, if the bedroom door was shut. But the bathroom is further away from the front door than the bedroom is. So would not the same element, indeed a rather stronger element, of doubt exist about your ability to hear the doorbell from the bathroom, with the door shut?"

"I would be likely to hear it."

"Likely—but not certain, Mrs. Ardley. You would not be certain to hear it, would you?"

"I've never missed it yet."

"Are you stating that, if you hear nothing, there could be nothing to be heard?"

"I would hear the bell."

"Mrs. Ardley, when you run the bath water, that makes a considerable volume of sound, doesn't it?"

"Well, it makes a noise, yes."

"And flushing the lavatory—that makes a noise too, doesn't it?"

"Of course."

"Let us suppose that you are in the bathroom with the door shut. The bath water is running, or the lavatory has just been flushed. At that moment, the front doorbell rings. You would not be likely to hear it, would you?"

"I suppose I might not."

So on that particular morning, the morning of the murder, at about nine-fifteen, what was Mrs. Ardley doing? Drinking a third cup of tea and reading the *Daily Telegraph*, as she did every morning. But was it not possible that she went to the lavatory? Bartlett embarrassed, uneasy, accusing a maiden aunt of prostitution. And Mrs. Ardley hesitated; for only the second time, she was uncertain. But of course, thought Jordan, Mrs. Ardley knew; she would be, of all people, *regular*. A timetable, a schedule—perhaps it was nine-fifteen, perhaps that was the exact time. Whether or not he had rung the bell and, hence, whether or not he had a duplicate key to No. 27 Panton Place—and if he had, the presumption of his guilt must be strong—all this, beyond a reasonable doubt, hung upon Mrs. Ardley's bowel movement.

She was looking straight at him. As he looked back, he smiled faintly. He knew, of course, that she had been in the lavatory. There was no other explanation. And she knew it. For a moment, they exposed their joint knowledge. But she also knew that Jordan had killed June Singer. To be honest, she might be letting justice, his conviction for murder, go by default. To be just, she would have to lie.

But it was more than that. She had taken June in; through pity she had allowed herself the weakness of trust. And June had betrayed the pity, and the trust. Or, not so much June as Jordan Maddox. He had been oblivious of, he had mocked, Mrs. Ardley's pity. Just as, in his stupidity, he had mocked June. He had murdered the vestigial humanity that had lingered in the landlady's heart. Just as he had murdered June.

He nodded—a fractional movement of his head, but Mrs. Ardley caught it. She had every right; and only the weak make the excuse of humanity not to exercise their rights.

Mrs. Ardley looked at Bartlett. "No," she said decisively, "there is no doubt. I did not go to the bathroom. I was in the living room from the time the postman came at half past eight until the milkman rang just after eleven. I could not have missed hearing the bell—had it been rung."

Bartlett would not let go. There could be no expectation now that Mrs. Ardley would relent, confess to temporal error or domestic negligence. From the day it had been put in, the stair carpet had been as fixed and rigid as, from the hour he is born, man is doomed to sin. The object now was to show Mrs. Ardley brutal in her righteousness, callous, wilful, small-minded, foolish—untrustworthy where her pride was touched.

And yet, somehow, it seemed that Mrs. Ardley became the more impressive. Jordan did not follow closely, but now and again he caught her looking at him, and in her eyes he thought he saw, behind the judgement, a melancholy.

30

" . . . don't you agree, Maddox?"

The petrol fume-filled van jolted over a rut, and the links of the handcuff which attached Jordan to Denver clicked metallically.

Samson leaned forward from the opposite seat. "You'd agree with that, wouldn't you, Maddox?"

The other prisoners chattered, a hooter blared in the street outside. "Oh, shut up!" he shouted furiously.

"Well, I must say . . . "

There was silence in the van.

"Now, Maddox," Denver, dignified and kindly, "there's no call to fly off the handle. Sammy means no harm."

They all stared at him, and, when they began to talk again, the malefactors, vicious or mild, they kept their voices low with respect.

Jordan closed his eyes and put his head back so that it pressed against the side of the van, and the vibrations of the journey were conveyed directly to his brain.

Oh God, he thought, oh God. The innocent phrases of the plump, myopic Mrs. Payne stabbed at him randomly. She had meant no harm either. But the damage she had done . . . he had to sort it out. Arrange it somehow. Calm the fever which possessed his head, and look at it. He'd let the sickening, falling motion take over, submit to it.

Mrs. Payne, silly, smiling, artificial lilies pinned upon her shoulder. "Now, Mrs. Payne."

Her lips politely poised as if to accept a cup of tea at a social gathering in the best of Putney circles. She was quite unaware that Bartlett was not going to offer her a lump of sugar or the rich top milk which Pollen had fed her.

"Now, Mrs. Payne. I would like to touch on your statement to my learned friend that Maddox frequently 'bought' flowers for June. How—"

"Oh yes. Every week, at least."

"How do you know, Mrs. Payne, that he *bought* flowers for her?"

"I don't know how else he'd get them really." The lilt of her final word made each answer sound like a question.

"Were these flowers delivered to the house?"

"Oh no, Junie brought them back with her from the office."

"How were they wrapped?"

"In paper, always nicely wrapped."

"As a florist would wrap flowers?"

"Well, I don't know really about florists. They weren't like wreaths, if that's what you mean?"

"Just wrapped in ordinary paper?"

"But nice."

"And you do not know, do you, that the flowers were *bought* at all?"

"Well, I thought they were. But she never said. Why should she? It didn't make much difference, did it?"

"It makes a great deal of difference. You knew June Singer all the time that she was working at Sutlif and Maddox, didn't you?"

"Long before that. Why, Mrs. Singer and Junie moved in the top flat right after the end of the war. Mr. Singer, poor soul, was killed in a raid. When my Mr. Payne passed away, Mrs. Singer was ever such a tower of strength to me, she was. She'd been through it herself, you see, and—"

"And when did June begin bringing home flowers as a regular thing?"

"I don't know about that. I couldn't say exact. I've never had a head for dates, really?"

"A year ago?"

"It might be—a year?"

"Two years?"

"Oh, dear—yes, it might be two years."

"Three?"

"Perhaps. You mustn't muddle me."

"Do you in fact recall a time when June was working at Sutlif and Maddox that she did *not* bring home flowers?"

"Well, if you put it that way—" Mrs. Payne smiled. "No, I couldn't rightly say I do. Why didn't you ask me that at first?"

"So that June's bringing home flowers was just an ordinary, normal, regular thing?"

"Yes. I always thought it was ever so thoughtful of him."

"You attached a particular significance to the flowers?"

"Significance." Mrs. Payne mouthed the word uncertainly. "Well, I—I mean it showed he liked her, didn't it?"

"And into that liking you read the signs of a romantic attachment, didn't you, Mrs. Payne?"

"He liked her, that's all I said. Why not?"

"No. You have been suggesting far more than that in the evidence you have given. You have been suggesting that Maddox was *in love* with Singer. You—"

"Why shouldn't he be? Junie was a lovely girl—a real little lady she was, right from when she was no more than a baby."

"I am not asking you that, Mrs. Payne. Please pay attention to my questions. Did you or did you not think that Maddox was in love with June Singer?"

Mrs. Payne quivered softly. "I've said that. I told the other gentleman that."

"And when did you first begin to think that Maddox was in love with Singer?"

"It sounds so strange when you call poor Junie 'Singer' like that. I told you—I did tell you I'm not good at dates."

"Well, was it when June began to bring home flowers as a regular thing, from the time she first went to work for Maddox?"

"Oh no. She was never one to rush things."

"Then it must have been later. If it was not the matter of the flowers that put the notion of romance into your head, Mrs. Payne, what was it?"

"You talk as though I made it all up."

"You are a very soft-hearted woman, are you not?"

"I'm not *hard*, like some I could mention, if that's what you mean." The soft, powdered skin beneath Mrs. Payne's dim eyes began to pucker.

"Mrs. Payne—" a rare Bartlett smile—"I would be the last to suggest that romance is not a charming thing, even when it exists chiefly in the eye of the beholder."

"If you think I'm making it up—what about those letters?"

"Ah yes, the famous letters. Did you ever see a single one of those letters?"

"I couldn't help but see them. They came near every day."

226

"But you did not see the letters. You saw the envelopes, didn't you?"

"Oh I see. Yes, that's right. But I could tell it was from him—always ever so neatly typed they were. Miss J. Singer."

"How did you know those letters came from Maddox?"

"Well, she told me!"

"What did she say?"

"She said they was from him."

"What were the words she used?"

"I can't remember that. I can't remember the exact words."

"Well, did she say, 'I've got another letter from Mr. Maddox'?"

"Oh no. No, I don't think she'd have said that. Junie was never one to say much, but you could tell. . . ."

"So, in fact, she never said the letters were from Maddox at all?"

"She might not have in so many words. But she'd smile—I always handed her the post, me being in the ground floor flat, you see. And, well, I could tell. She'd brighten up ever so."

"If she never actually said the letters were from Maddox, why did you assume they were from him?"

"Assume? I didn't do no assuming. Why, Mrs. S. and me was always—"

"If you say something to be true which you don't *know* to be true, then you are either lying or you are making an unwarranted assumption."

Mrs. Payne gasped. "Me lying? Why, I . . ." Her lips quivered.

"I have not said you are lying, Mrs. Payne. I don't believe you are lying. I do believe, however, that you have made a number of assumptions and statements for which there is not the slightest evidence, and that you have constructed in your mind a whole fabric of romance between Singer and Maddox, a fabricated romance which did not exist and never existed."

Mrs. Payne blinked her soft eyes and her lips trembled. And then she seemed to master herself. "Well," she said. "Well then, just you tell me why those letters began coming right after Junie spent that Saturday with Mr. Maddox in the country. You just tell me that!"

Bartlett was quite rigid. "*What* Saturday in the country? What are you talking about?"

"The Saturday she spent with him last June at Wooly, that's

227

what I'm talking about. That was the start of it, if you ask me. She was that happy, she was. And the very next week, or near enough, the letters began. I don't call that no coincidence."

"Mrs. Payne, what evidence have you that June Singer spent a day last summer in the country with Maddox?"

"I've got my five senses, that's what I've got. I saw her go and I saw her come back—and a perfect picture she looked, too. And she told me. There! With her own lips she told me. She told me what a lovely house he had at Wooly. She told me how he took her out for a drink at a lovely pub where you could see all the country for miles round. She told me what they 'ad for lunch and what they 'ad for dinner. I never heard Junie talk so much before or since, fair bubbling over with it she was. And if you think I'm making up that, then you can think anything."

"Why was this not in your deposition, Mrs. Payne?"

"Nobody asked me."

"Is this something else you made up?"

"I've never made up anything. I swore I'd tell the truth, and that's what I'm doing."

"But for all you know, June Singer could have made up this tale of a day in the country with Maddox?"

"She could, anyone can do anything. But she didn't—I know she didn't."

"How do you know, Mrs. Payne? A sixth sense?"

"Them photos, that's how I know—as if I needed to know Junie would never tell a lie about something like that."

"What photos?"

"Them photos—the one what was found in his desk and the one of him that Junie kept in her bag. You can't argue with a photo."

"Where did you see those photos?"

"In the paper. I knew at once—she'd showed 'em to me and her Mum. Only the two came out, they did, but they was nice."

"You recognised these photos as having been taken at the time you allege Singer and Maddox spent a day together at Woodley?"

"Yes."

"Why did you not come forward before, Mrs. Payne? Why did you not tell the police of this matter?"

"Nobody asked me. Nobody said anything. I thought they knew. I was waiting for the other gentleman to ask me, but he didn't."

"Mr. Bartlett, a moment." The judge turned to Mr. Pollen. "You knew nothing of this, Mr. Pollen?"

"No, my Lord. It is completely new. The police—"

"Yes yes. Quite." He turned to the witness. "Mrs. Payne, you are quite certain of what you say?"

Mrs. Payne fluttered happily.

"Oh yes, my Lord."

"In this conversation between yourself and Singer, after her return from the day's outing, did she tell you the name of the place to which Maddox had taken her? Or the name of the pub?"

"I expect she did, my Lord. But I'm not one for remembering names—not of places and that."

The Goat at Round Hill—Jordan murmured the words to himself. She had brought a camera—a Brownie—and she'd taken several pictures. She had asked an old man smoking a pipe to take a photo of them together. And he had, without a word or a smile, and gone back to his beer. That must have been one of those which didn't come out.

". . . how is it, Mrs. Payne—" Bartlett now—"that you remember the date of this occurrence so clearly?"

"I know it was the end of June. The last week. I know because every year that's the week Mrs. Singer would go to the hospital for treatment and things."

"And did Mrs. Singer know about this?"

"Why, of course she did. It was a big moment for June."

"Mrs. Singer talked to you about it?"

"Oh yes."

"And did she not express any qualms about the fact that Maddox was a married man?"

"She didn't know he was married. I didn't neither. She never knew."

"But June knew?"

"Yes—yes, she must of." Mrs. Payne a little anxious.

"Then it follows that June must have lied to her mother—and to you—about the fact that Maddox was married?"

"I don't think she said either way, really."

"Just let her mother assume, as she did assume, that Maddox was a single man?"

"Well . . . well, yes."

229

"That is tantamount to lying, is it not, Mrs. Payne?"

"Well, it's not . . . it wasn't very nice of Junie," feebly.

"She deliberately let her mother form a total misapprehension?"

"Well, I don't know about deliberate."

"But June knew that her mother thought Maddox was single. She could have easily, in three words, have cleared up this misapprehension by telling the simple truth. Why did she not do so?"

"Well, I expect the poor thing thought . . . maybe she was shy about it. And then—then she wouldn't want to shock her Mum, I mean, not in the condition she was in?"

"Easier to let the misunderstanding exist?"

"Yes, I expect it was. I don't blame her."

"Has it occurred to you, Mrs. Payne, that if June was willing to let her mother completely misunderstand the situation—Maddox's marital situation—that she might have, in all probability did, let both Mrs. Singer and yourself misunderstand the entire nature of the relationship between Maddox and herself?"

"Oh no. Junie wouldn't do that."

"Yet we have seen, where it suited her interest, she was not a truthful person."

Mrs. Payne shook her head. "If she didn't tell her Mum about that, it was out of kindness. But the way she felt about Mr. Maddox—well, you couldn't make no mistake about that. She was always talking about him. It was always 'Mr. Maddox said' and 'Mr. Maddox did,' and sometimes she'd say 'Jordan.' It would just slip out. She worshipped the very ground he trod on, and you can't disguise that."

"Her attachment to him, romantic as it may have been, in no way proves the fact that he had an attachment to her, does it?"

"What about all them letters?"

"You have no proof that the letters ever came from Maddox."

"Well, the day at Wooly?"

"A single day in the country is hardly evidence of a blooming romance such as you are suggesting. I put it to you, Mrs. Payne, that the whole idea of a romantic attachment between Singer and Maddox was a dream built upon faulty foundations, eagerly seized upon by a suffering old lady anxious to see her daughter married, embellished by you, and passively, if not actively, encouraged by the girl herself. Is that not the true picture, Mrs. Payne?"

230

"No, sir. You're very clever, but that's not like what it was. I don't see so well, and I'm not one for mental things. Perhaps you think I'm a silly old woman, and perhaps I am. But Mrs. Singer, she wasn't silly—she was sharp and bright and clever to her dying day. She'd have known if there was something not right."

"But there was something not *right*—Maddox was married—and Mrs. Singer didn't suspect that, did she?"

"I don't believe she did. I couldn't say for sure. She didn't always say what was in her mind."

"But if she had known there was no chance of her daughter marrying Maddox, she would not have encouraged June's romantic notions, would she?"

"I don't say she'd have been as happy as if he'd been a single man, I'm not saying that. But I don't say she'd have tried to stop it either. She always spoiled Junie a bit—June was all she had. And if that's what Junie wanted—well, him leading her on like that, he couldn't have been that happy with his wife, could he? And it's the lucky ones that have love all easy and uncomplicated."

"You mean to say that Mrs. Singer would have encouraged her daughter's attachment to a married man?"

"I'm trying to answer your questions, sir. I can't say more than I'm not sure. Mrs. Singer was not—a conventual person, if you know what I mean. She didn't judge things by rules. She was strong-minded, she was. And independent. She was a wonderful person, she was." Mrs. Payne's eyes glistened.

"Mrs. Payne—" Bartlett was very gentle—"I am not doubting your word for a moment. But it is a fact that, at the time, Mrs. Singer was not the woman she had been. In the late summer and autumn of last year, Mrs. Singer was in no fit state to make a proper judgement of this matter, was she?"

"Her arthritis never affected her mind. She was just what she had always been in that respect."

"But we know, don't we, Mrs. Payne—" quietly—"and I am sorry to have to raise this matter—that Mrs. Singer committed suicide while the balance of her mind was disturbed? And that she did this in early December, but that she had been planning it—saving the sleeping pills, an overdose of which she died from—for weeks, perhaps months, prior to that?"

"There was nothing wrong with her mind."

"But the verdict at the inquest was that Mrs. Singer died by her own hand while the balance of her mind was disturbed."

"It was wrong. That verdict was all wrong." Mrs. Payne was whispering.

"Mrs. Payne, I have a transcript of the proceedings at that inquest. You yourself gave evidence, clear and unmistakable, that Mrs. Singer was in very great pain, which had affected her judgement and permitted her to do this terrible thing."

Mrs. Payne shook her head slowly from side to side.

"Mrs. Payne, I can read from the transcript the very words you used."

"I know what I said. You don't have to read nothing to me. I was wrong."

"You mean that you have now changed your mind about the matter?"

"No. I haven't changed none. That—what I said then, it wasn't true."

"Mrs. Payne, it is my duty to warn you—it is a very grave admission to make that you lied under oath."

Mrs. Payne opened her mouth, but the judge forestalled her. "Mrs. Payne, you must consider what Mr. Bartlett has said. This would be an admission of perjury. You would be saying that you perjured yourself. Do you fully understand that?"

Mrs. Payne nodded. "Yes, sir. I mean, my Lord. I hoped it wouldn't . . . wouldn't, but there's no help for it. What I said then wasn't true. Mrs. S. wasn't afraid of pain. She believed in living. She'd have never made away with herself because she was in suffering, however terrible it might be. She'd have thought that was cowardly."

Bartlett paused, waiting for her to say more. And then he said, "If this is so, if this is what you truly thought, why did you lie at the coroner's inquest?"

Slowly, a deep breath, "For Junie's sake."

"And how would that have helped June, Mrs. Payne?"

"She thought—Junie thought it was her fault, in a way."

"But it was in no way her fault, was it? She was absolved by everyone, Dr. Yardley, the coroner himself, of the slightest negligence."

"Well, you see—it wasn't exactly her fault. It wasn't her *fault*. But she, well, she was the cause of it."

"In what way?"

"It doesn't matter me telling, now Junie's dead too." A tear trickled down Mrs. Payne's nose, but her voice was steady enough. "Mrs. S. was always worrying, see? Worrying that she was in Junie's way. She said it several times to me, but I never gave it much attention really. Not till later. Without Junie, Mrs. Singer couldn't really do nothing. She was always urging June to go out and that, but she knew she couldn't. And she felt she was spoiling Junie's chances. She said to me once, she said, 'There's nothing worse than a young girl wasting her life on a silly old cripple.' And then when she saw June so happy about Mr. Maddox and all, why, I think she made up her mind there and then. She didn't believe in standing in someone else's way, see?"

There was a long deep silence.

Bartlett roused himself. "I see. Thank you, Mrs. Payne. I have no more questions." He sat down.

"Mrs. Payne," said Pollen, "I will keep you but a moment. It is still your belief, is it not, that June Singer was in love with the accused?"

"Yes."

"And the indications that June gave you of Maddox being in love with her—you still believe in the validity of these, that he was as much in love with her as she with him?"

"Yes. And—"

Pollen was already lowering himself to his seat. He halted. "Yes, Mrs. Payne?"

"Can I say something, sir?"

"Please do."

"He was always a perfect gentleman in the way he treated Junie, and I've never believed he done it. In my opinion it was one of these night prowlers."

Mr. Pollen's mouth opened. The judge leaned over towards the witness. "I'm sure," he said, "that you are quite sincere in what you say, Mrs. Payne. But we cannot allow such unsubstantiated opinions to be expressed in court. Members of the jury, Mrs. Payne's last remarks will be taken from the record, and you must forget them. Dismiss them from your mind."

233

31

He walked up and down the room, four paces forward, four back. He wanted to look out of a window, to the country, hills.

He pushed the chair against the wall and stood on it. Vertical bars, glass, wire mesh. A tall chimney far away. A piece of sky. It was forever raining.

She'd had a better view than this. A bomb site. What was it? A vacant lot. What had she done that evening? Shut the door and turned on the light and gone across to draw the curtains. She must have glanced out of the window. Twilight—no, darkness, then; it was February. Winter. Begun in summer, ended in winter.

Had she lain down on the bed and wept? Deciding, quiet and businesslike and deserted, to still the tremors in her belly. He remembered the smell of the bed, of the sheets, on the morning. The smell of life on the morning of death.

She must have remembered the day at Woodley.

"Wish you were free to lend me a hand on the weekend, June." Jokingly.

"I am."

"What about your mother? I thought you had to look after her."

"Mum's in the hospital this week. It's her annual check-up. They make all sorts of tests and things. So I could come in and help Saturday."

"Come down to Woodley then. A day in the country would do you good."

She had come, fresh and delicate in her white summer frock. And she had sat, demure as Georgia, in the front seat of the car as he drove her to the house.

"I hope it's not too much trouble for Mrs. Maddox, my coming."

"She's not here. She's down on the coast with Georgia. We always go away from the end of June to the end of August. But I couldn't make it this weekend."

They lunched off tomatoes and cold overdone roast beef, which Willy had wrapped in greaseproof paper and marked *Saturday*. And he'd opened a bottle of the better claret. They'd worked hard all day until the phone call, which she had answered automatically.

And Jordan could hear now, tinny in his memory, Tom's voice: "I say, old man, whose are those dulcet tones at your end of the line? What are you up to? Tiddlywinks, old man?"

"My secretary, she came down to clear—"

"Don't have to explain it to me. You can trust me. You know that. See no evil, hear no evil, speak no evil—that's me, except professionally, of course, ha ha. Norah thought you might be lonely and would like to pop over for a drink. But I'll tell her you're all fixed up . . ."

He'd put down the phone and turned to June and they'd called it a day.

She guarded her camera in her lap as they drove over to Round Hill. In the garden of the Goat she insisted on her photographs and Jordan was pleased to please her, although normally he hated those dead grins of the past, the idiocy, which one would prefer to forget, frozenly exposed. Even the elderly mute pipe smoker yielded to her eagerness and gravely snapped them together.

They sat on the crooked bench and drank beer and watched the summer evening light going gently from the Sussex hills. Others came and chattered and laughed, but left them alone on their bench. It grew cool and June put a cardigan over her shoulders. He helped her. It was easy and tender.

He did not know what they talked of. But into his mind slipped a line of Trevor's favourite hymn: "Let all thy converse be sincere . . ." And as he spoke, the quality of unctuousness melted from the sentiment and he smiled with involuntary fondness.

"What are you smiling at?"

"Oh, the light. The beer. You. The ease of evening." His characteristically deprecating gesture didn't diminish the promise of the dusk.

They ate at Cochrane's—ten miles away, due south. But it was Saturday night, and they had to wait an hour in the Jacobean cocktail bar before eating. Willy wouldn't have been caught dead in the place. They drank Americanos among the glowing copper and the bulbous fakes.

"It's a lovely place, isn't it?"

"Pure Jacobean cocktail." Then he smiled. "Yes, it is."

"Are these very strong?"

"They've got a bit more pep in them than a glass of cold water."

"I expect I'll go to sleep on the train."

"Oh, forget the train. I'll drive you home."

"What, all the way to Putney? Oh no, I couldn't—"

"Well, you're going to miss the last train anyway. The alternative would be to spend the night at Woodley."

She put her head on one side. "Thank you then. But it does seem an awful bother."

"It's a lovely drive on a summer's night."

And it was. Fifty minutes to Putney.

"Just drop me on the corner."

"No no, I'll take you to the house."

When he stopped and switched off in the silent street, they sat for a few moments. He looked at her shadowed face. Her flesh dived darkly into the whiteness of her dress. He could smell her. He could touch her.

"It was the loveliest day I've ever had," she murmured.

Then they were standing on the pavement. He shook her hand and mumbled, "We must do it again some time." He watched her go into the house; then he turned to the car. As he drove back to Woodley, he felt a mingling of excitement and relief. He meandered through Kingston and Hampton Court and Esher and Guildford, over the base of the Hog's Back and down into the valley where the mist hung ghostly about the road. It was a calm night and fresh and cool.

He had a whiskey before going to bed. At four o'clock his own shout woke him from a nightmare. For a second he remembered it—a great darkness suddenly and horribly illuminated. And then it was gone. He lay back sweating and soon fell asleep without dreams.

The next several days, as he packed up to go home, it was often on the tip of his tongue to ask June for a drink. But he didn't. An old unrecognised eagerness dwindling over the weeks, lost amidst printers' schedules and proofs and the rained-out seaside summer—which was no more than to be expected. And when she had given him the photo, shyly, he had been clumsy; the black-and-white image of her had frozen him.

Woodley to Waterloo, Waterloo to Woodley, morning and night the regularity of his own thin reflection in the window, and a detached distaste for the passing landscape. The tactical withdrawal over years, become so automatic that he could not even recognise his troops had been committed in the first place.

He got down from the chair.

He stood in the centre of the room and looked round. Bed, chair, table, basin—the simple necessities of shelter, no more.

Poor Annie, he thought.

He spoke aloud, "Annie?" But he was not really surprised.

32

That June—that other June—he came down from Cambridge happy.

He put his bags in the left luggage at Paddington and took a taxi to Sutlif & Maddox. He looked out of the window at old, grey London and everything seemed especially good. He relaxed in the genial knowledge that something better awaited him. For the first time that he could ever remember, he was looking forward to returning to Sibley. And Annie.

"Hello, Jordan, you're looking well. You know Miss Lawley, don't you?"

"Mr. Jordan." Miss Lawley inclined her head with acid grace, bitter perhaps at having to promote him at long last from *Master* to *Mister*.

"She's the law in this office, aren't you, Miss Lawley? Well, let's have lunch. I thought we'd go to the Berkeley."

"A celebration, Colin?"

"Oh, I don't know. A change is always good. You'll have enough of Blain's and the club when you come into the business. Mustn't fill you with publisher's gloom too early."

Jordan smiled. Already he knew of Colin's unspoken worry that Jordan would not join the firm, and the rueful joviality that he used to probe Jordan's intentions.

But a drink soon soothed Colin.

"Have a martini, Jordan? I don't care for them much myself, but I'm told this place makes the best martinis in town. Got the knack from the Americans in the war, I expect."

"Alright, I'll be American."

"Well, what sort of a first year have you had, old chap?"

"Pretty good. Very good."

"How were the prelims? Or shouldn't I ask?"

"They weren't bad. I quite enjoyed them, actually, although there isn't much of any interest at this point."

"I wonder whether you'll turn out to be academically inclined."

"Not a hope. I'm not keen enough on the proper things. I go off on tangents that would give the professional heart failure."

"That's not a bad sort of a mind for a publisher to have, though."

"A medical publisher?"

"How like your father you sound sometimes. He used to call our books the corpses. I was the chief necrophiliac. He was always trying to get us to publish something that was *alive*, as he put it."

"But he didn't succeed, did he?" Jordan jerked back his head as he took a harsh mouthful of martini.

"He once got me to put out a book of verse. He told me it was just the thing for us. *Death Sentences* it was called; by a fellow named Oliver Beaney. Unreadable muck. Charles got me absolutely tight one night and then told me the next morning that I'd agreed to do it. He had my illegible signature to prove it."

"How did it do?"

"I printed five hundred—you could get away with that in those days—and twenty years later I still had four hundred and sixty-odd in inventory. I never remaindered them. I didn't have the heart to, perhaps. They always reminded me of Charles, you see, breezing into the office, slapping everything in sight till the dust flew, giving Miss Lawley a great kiss. She seemed to like it. So I let *Death Sentences* gather dust. Then just before the war a curious thing happened. I'm damned if there wasn't a run on the book. In two years I didn't have a single copy left."

"Did you reprint it?"

"No. No, I didn't. The war came, and the paper shortgage. But I don't think I'd have done a reprint in any event. I came across a copy only the other day when I was in York. Priced at four guineas, believe it or not—it was far from a mint copy, too."

"Perhaps there's money in poetry after all—or at any rate a diversified list. Have I got that right?"

Colin laughed. "You have. Have another martini."

"I will."

"Another odd thing about that book. Lately I've had several requests from anthologists for permission to use some of Beaney's poems. It's put me in rather a quandary. I can't find Beaney."

"Maybe he's dead. What was he like?"

"Never saw him. Never had an address for him either. Charles got the contract signed. We still owe Beaney about sixty quid in royalties, but I doubt if he'll ever collect it. To tell you the truth, I always had an idea that *Death Sentences* was one of Charles's spoofs."

"You mean he wrote it and . . . "

"It would have been like him. That's really why I don't make much effort to find Mr. Beaney. I think it would amuse Charles. I could almost feel him grinning over my shoulder the other day in the club. I found myself sitting next to Stewart. By mistake of course—he's a pompous ass to my mind, but he's supposed to know about these things. So I asked about Beaney."

"What did he say?"

"Guff—his usual unadulterated guff, but I enjoyed it. Something about it being, let's see, 'an agonized gem.' I asked him how a gem could feel anything, let along agony. 'That's exactly the point, my dear Sutlif, *exactly*. It's the hard and lacerating experience of non-feeling, of glitter without heart, the predicament of the non-sensory in a sensory world. The brilliant perfection of sterility.' I may have got that mixed up, but the general tone's right. I may say, telling Stewart that I'd published it completely made my lunch. He wouldn't believe me at first. He's as tight as an oyster, you know, but I got him to stand me a brandy, so impressed he was." Colin emptied his glass. "Shall we order? Or do you think another round first?"

"Let's have another," Jordan said buoyantly. "Colin, I'd like to see a copy of *Death Sentences*."

"I thought you might. I've got a copy for you put aside. You come back to the office after lunch and collect it."

Colin's shy, almost sly, fondness for him filled Jordan with gratitude. He felt a fleeting, tear-filled moment of benignity. Perhaps it was the gin, or the prospect of Sibley, or the hearsay evidence of his father. But really, of course, it was Annie. After dinner he would go down to the post office and knock on the post-office door. And she would come and they would go walking out, formal, a little, at first, until the village was left behind and there were only fields about them. And then . . .

239

"I'm not opposed to a bit of diversification, Jordan. Charles wanted to do it all at once. And of course he wasn't interested in publishing. He was interested in everything. But he wasn't inclined to branch out a little here and a little there. No, he wanted to plant an entire new forest overnight. But I don't say that S. and M. isn't in a rut. It is. It's a paying rut—but, well, I haven't the imagination, or the energy, to change very much, you know. That doesn't mean I'm not alive to the need. But somebody else will have to do it."

Jordan touched his third martini to his lips. "You mean me?"

Colin smiled. "I hope you. I hope you very much, Jordan. It's time we had a Maddox active in the firm again."

They drank in silence for a while. They ordered, carefully, a large meal. And they would drink Montrachet.

"Trevor's expecting you to get a first, you know."

"He's going to be disappointed. I'm not first-class material."

"I wouldn't say that. You may not get a first—and personally I don't think it matters a damn what sort of degree you get—but that's not to say you're not first-class material. Unfortunate phrase. If something interests you. What about that exhibition of yours?"

"Sheer fluke. If it hadn't been for . . . Well, I just scored a lucky hit."

"I see." Colin nodded. He ate with deliberation but rapidly. "Trevor's a bit worried about you."

"Worried about me?"

"Yes." Colin put his knife and fork together. "Yes. About this girl. Annie Brierly, isn't it?"

The elation of gin drained immediately. "Annie?"

"Yes. She's the girl you've been—seeing. Isn't she?"

"Yes."

"Serious?" Colin didn't look at him, merely poured himself some more Montrachet.

"Yes. We're—we're going to get married."

"Ah. Her mother just died. You know that, though?"

"She wrote to me and told me."

"You've kept rather quiet about all this, haven't you, Jordan?"

"Yes. How did Trevor find out, by the way?"

"Nothing much gets past Mary." Colin raised his eyes and stared briefly at Jordan.

"Prying old bitch," said Jordan, suddenly furious.

240

Colin picked up his glass and looked at it. "Well, I dare say. Up to a point. But I think it's only her concern for the welfare of others that leads her to step over the boundaries of other people's privacies."

"Or is it the other way round?"

"I don't think so. Look, Jordan, don't underestimate Mary. I don't want to be pompous, but she's a remarkably fine woman in many ways. A long time ago now she was very much in love, and he with her. But she wouldn't marry him, out of loyalty to her brother. She knew Trevor would be lost without her. And then John. There was considerable pressure towards the end—perhaps you know this—to commit John. Mary wouldn't have it. She fought that tooth and nail. And after your mother's death it was Mary who took you out of the peculiar menage Charles had set up. But she never said a word against your father, you know. She always welcomed him to the rectory. And . . . well, the point I'm making is that you've got to balance Mary's occasional high-handedness against her very real courage and loyalty and, yes, tenderness—for I think under her abrupt common-sensical manner she's a very tender woman. Although you may not believe it."

"I don't."

"Well," said Colin slowly, "that's beside the point, really."

"And the point is that Trevor's in a puritanical tizzy. I suppose he thinks that—that my affair with Annie will ruin my chances of a first."

"That may be part of it. But only a small part. Jordan, you're very young, you're just beginning, and—"

"I know very little of the world and I shouldn't be thinking of burdening myself with a wife at this stage of the game. Is that it?"

Colin opened his hand palm upward and stared at it as though it contained the symbols of wisdom. "In part, perhaps. But there's also rather a considerable difference in background, isn't there?"

"I don't know. We come from the same place. We know the same people."

"I meant social background."

"Not our class? So what?"

"It matters, you know. Differences in upbringing, outlook. Marriage is a long pull, and sometimes the connections between man and wife become, well, strained. Some of these connections are social, matters of upbringing—links of mind and attitude which are possibly

241

the more important for being unspoken. It seems to me to be a handicap to a marriage to have those links missing. I don't say it's an insuperable handicap, but it's there all the same. Have you considered that?"

"No. I mean, yes. There are other things that are more important than that." He heard his voice tremble.

"Love, you mean. Yes, love." Colin shifted in his chair.

"What's wrong with love?"

"Nothing. Only—sometimes it wears out. It's a bit of an unknown quantity until it's tested over time. I'm not advocating free love or anything, but there are lots of women in the world. In Cambridge too, I expect." Colin smiled.

It was not finished, Jordan knew. He was trapped in the Berkeley Grill. He was filled with unspeakable resentment against Colin and the cage of quiet reason that he was constructing.

"How's that girl you introduced me to when I was up in the spring? The one with the farfetched name. Wilhelmina, wasn't it?"

"She's a nincompoop. The only good thing about Willy is her mad mother."

"I thought she seemed rather fond of you."

"Did you?"

"Yes. Coffee? Will you have a brandy with me?"

"No thanks. Oh yes, yes I will." He needed something to make him reckless against the deadly sobriety that walled him in.

They were silent until the brandy arrived, and then Colin said, "Jordan, I don't mean to pry, but you mentioned something about an 'affair' with this girl—Annie. Have you slept with her?"

"I don't think that's any of your business, Colin."

"No, it isn't, you're quite right. I just wondered if you, er, had been taking the proper precautions and that sort of thing."

"Precautions!" Jordan's laugh was tremulous beyond control.

"Jordan, believe me, I'm not saying anything against Annie Brierly—"

"Then what are you saying?"

"I just want to find out how you feel and—"

"So that you can report back to Mary and Trevor."

Colin shook his head quickly. "No. I want to give you another view, that's all. I'm not disinterested, Jordan, and I'd be a fool if I pretended I was. But if you've made up your mind to something, that's your business and I respect it. Perhaps I can be a bit more objective than you, and objectivity never did any harm. I hardly know Annie—of course when I've been down to Sibley at Christmas and . . . well, I knew who she was, but I have no basis of judgement of her as a person. But there are other things that go beyond the immediate consideration of person when you are thinking in terms of marriage. That's what I wanted to say, to make sure you understood. There's the family. You have to be prepared for reactions. When it comes to marriage, you can't conduct the thing in a vacuum. And it's not only you, but it's her, too. If everything isn't plain sailing—and it won't be—how do you think she'll take it? Have you asked yourself that?"

"Do you think that it's been plain sailing, as you call it, up to now?"

"I simply don't know."

Jordan finished his brandy. He put the glass down on the smooth white tablecloth. "What makes you such an expert on marriage, Colin?"

"You've got a point there." Colin laughed. "Your immediate family circle is a bit short on experience of wedlock, I'm afraid. Firsthand, that is—I suppose old Trevor's married hundreds in his time."

"Why didn't you ever marry?"

"I was in love with your mother. I was always in love with Lily. But she always loved Charles, and he her." He smiled at Jordan. "He was much the better man, and he made her completely happy. That was the comfort I had. Still have, as a matter of fact."

Jordan could think of nothing to say.

"Well," said Colin, "shall we be getting back? You're coming with me to collect your copy of *Death Sentences*, aren't you?"

Jordan stood up. "Alright," he said. He felt the alcohol then, fumbling his mind, wearying him.

He was met at Sibley station by Trevor with the old Wolseley. Trevor stood on the platform, book in hand and one finger marking his place, and regarded the train with a hesitant smile as though, by stopping, the engine would do him an honour of which he was both uncertain and unworthy. The station was at the parish limits, and there Trevor's assurance terminated. He would be excessively polite and vague with the ticket collector, as though the man were the representative of another world, touched by a foreign majesty.

"Ah, well well. A good term, my boy?"

"Not bad, thanks." Jordan avoided looking at his uncle. He put his bags in the boot and sat in the front seat.

There was no vestige of joy left in his return. They passed the war memorial with a few of last year's derelict poppies at its base. The walled pound filled with nettles and tall grass. The school with its drab patch of fenced-in playground.

He hated the dead familiarity of it all. He knew every aspect of this desert to the inch: Trevor's tentative cough as he worked himself up to ask about the prelims, Aunt Mary's cheek quickly presented and withdrawn, the smell of his room, the celebratory chicken for dinner, junket with nutmeg and stewed plums, the glass of cheap port, the deadly seriousness of the trivial. . . .

The post office was already shut. Behind the metal grille on the door, in the back room, would be Annie and her father and Emerald. As the Wolseley drove slowly by, Jordan wanted to fling open the door and run into the post office and hear Annie tell him that nothing had changed. He had had no letter from her since the brief note when her mother died—two weeks ago. She was busy, of course, and the natural grief—he had told himself that it was understandable.

"Well, my boy."

"Hello, my dear."

"A glass of sherry, eh?"

"The tomatoes are doing quite well this year."

"No great events at Sibley, you know. Poor old Mansard's having trouble with his kidneys again."

"Malingering."

"Oh no, my dear. He is getting more forgetful than ever though, I'm afraid. Only last Sunday he . . ."

It was exactly as he had known it would be.

After dinner he told them he was going for a walk.

He went slowly down to the village. He had written to Annie that he would come at nine. She must be expecting him, yet he was reluctant. He walked as though to an ordeal, nerving himself.

There was no one about as he knocked at the post office. The pub was at the other end of the village and the men would be there. But Sibley had always been a silent place as long as he could remember.

The bolt was pulled back and the door opened. It was hard to see her in the dusk.

"Hello, Annie."

"Hello, Jordan."

He tried to smile at the dim figure in the doorway. "Would you like to come for a walk?"

"I'm sorry, I can't, Jordan."

"Didn't you get my letter?"

"Dad's out, and I can't leave Emerald."

"Well then, may I come in?"

"I don't think . . . Alright. Not for long though. Dad'll be back soon." She held open the door.

He followed her across the worn boards of the post office and into the back room. A tiny room—he had never been in it before. He didn't even know what they called it. The living room? The parlour? Three huge chairs, two by the empty grate and one in the corner filled with the mongoloid hulk of Emerald. Annie went to her sister and wiped the thick wet lips carefully. Emerald bubbled and nodded and tried to peer round at Jordan.

Annie turned.

"I was—was sorry to hear about your mother."

"Yes."

He moved towards her, hoping that if he touched her . . .

"Annie—what's wrong?"

She looked at him then. "Wrong? There's nothing wrong."

"Annie, you can tell me. Don't keep it pent up. I know your mother's death . . . well, I remember what it was like when Uncle John—"

"That was different. I was never that fond of Mum."

He could hardly believe her stoniness which yet so closely fulfilled his cold dozing terrors in the train coming down. "What is it then? What is it?" The urgency of his voice attracted the attention of Emerald and she smiled delightedly.

"There is no it."

He glanced round the miserable dark-brown room decorated with cheap prints of jolly red huntsmen blowing horns and drinking jolly English ale from huge tankards. "Annie . . ." The flavour of roast chicken and port rose to his mouth, and with it a spurt of hatred against the desolation of it all. "Annie, I've decided. When I'm twenty-one—it's only nine months away—let's get married at once. There'll be the money John left me and—"

245

"I'm not going to marry you, Jordan."

He stared at her. "You're doing your hair in a different way."

"I'm not marrying you."

"Why?"

"Now Mum's gone, someone's got to look after Dad and Emerald."

Emerald chortled at the sound of her name.

"But that's no reason. I mean, we always knew that—that things might be difficult. But that doesn't make any difference."

"We were just kids then."

"But Annie! You can't. We're in love. Don't you love me any more?"

"That's neither here nor there, Jordan. I've got my duty and that's that."

"Then you do love me still?"

"I said, we were kids then. That was all a lovely dream. But it's over now."

"Over? For Christ's sake, Annie. We're just beginning."

"I've got other things to think of now. I can't leave Emerald or Dad. And I wouldn't. Our marrying would never have worked. I always knew that in my heart of hearts."

"I don't care a damn about Emerald and your father. Hang them. I want you." He tried to beat at her with his vehemence, but somewhere within he was hopeless. He knew this frozen waste too well to believe there was any hope of nourishing green fields and human life.

They stood in silence. Each cold moment made him more incapable of speech.

"You better go. Dad'll be home any minute now." She walked to the door and into the post office. He followed her. He gave one glance back at Emerald. She was grinning, her face shining, her lips wet once more with saliva. She raised a hand and motioned at him in a broken-wristed way. "Bah-bah, bah-bah."

"Annie." He was close to her in the doorway. "Annie, it's not over. It can't be, not like this." But his words were feeble as those of a child protesting against the inevitable bedtime.

"Annie, can I kiss you?"

It was her first moment of hesitation. "Alright," she said then. But as he bent forward, she turned her head, so that his lips only touched her cheek in the brief and dutiful gesture he knew so well.

"Goodbye," she said.

246

"Goodbye, Annie. I'll . . ." But he didn't know what he would do, and, as he stood there on the scrubbed step, she closed the door, quietly and firmly, and he heard her footsteps retreating through the shop into the back room.

He went back to the rectory and up to his room. He sat on his bed with the white-and-blue coverlet, and he didn't turn on the light. He sat there a long time. Then he got up and unpacked his cases and repacked one. In the morning he told Trevor and Mary that he had to do some work at the British Museum. He stayed in a boardinghouse in Bloomsbury. He wrote many long letters to Annie but he didn't post any of them.

He went up to Cambridge for the long vac term and drank a lot of beer and saw a good deal of Wilhelmina Benton.

He returned to Sibley for one night to fetch his things for the Michaelmas term. He didn't see Annie.

33

He and Willy went back regularly for Christmas at Sibley. He would see Annie then, after church on Sunday among the tombstones. Mrs. Brierly had been buried not far from Lily Maddox.

Sometimes he and Annie would speak a few stiff winter words about the weather. Each time it seemed to him her clothes were a little dowdier, her hair drawn tighter to the bun at the back.

He was glad to break away and walk at Colin's slow pace down the long lime avenue that led from church to the rectory. Ahead of them Mary and Willy sped briskly to attend to the roasting beef and the trappings of Sunday lunch. Mary and Willy seldom talked together; they were so beautifully attuned, they did not need to use the awkward tool of words. They met in the ordering of garden and house, of solid meals and men's foibles, discipline and fresh air. Willy arranged a vase of flowers exactly, to the very petal, as Mary would have done. It was a long time since their first visits when he and Willy would sit in the bedroom sipping forbidden whiskey.

Colin took out a cigar and clipped the end. He held it unlit in his hand and said to Jordan, "Can't light up till we're off consecrated ground." He put the cigar under his nose and sniffed. "Matins always give me the itch to smoke."

The even sound of their feet on the gravel walk reminded Jordan of the slow tread of pallbearers. He looked away to the fields and down to the pond covered with duckweed and half hidden by the still lingering morning mist. On the other side a short hill rose abruptly—a fine defensive position against cavalry.

"Damn bad sermon. Poor old Trevor. Still, you can't expect a clergyman to make religion interesting. Years ago I remember when the church was brimming every Sunday. But now when that posse of faithful old women die off, Trevor's going to be without a congregation."

"There'll always be Annie Brierly, I'm sure. And old Goff the organist."

"Ah yes." They came to the wicket gate which opened into the rectory garden. Colin paused and lit his cigar, rolling it tenderly between thumb and forefinger to make sure it was evenly caught. "Sensible girl, that." He drew gently. "Great help to Mary with all these church things, I hear. Surprised they get on so well."

"Surprised—why?"

Colin blew at the tip of the cigar until it glowed. "That business about you and her being engaged. Water under the bridge now, thank God. Great tribute to the girl that she doesn't bear any grudge, you know. I always thought Mary may have been a bit hard on her."

Jordan turned and looked back down the avenue. There were rooks among the high branches of the lime trees. In the churchyard a few villagers were still grouped, talking, waiting for the rector.

Jordan took his hand from the gate and put it in his pocket. "Mary spoke to Annie?"

"You knew that, didn't you?"

"Only vaguely."

"I don't know what she said exactly. I imagine she pointed out the general unsuitability of Annie's marrying you. But I rather fancy there must have been a bit of a row. Mary isn't the most tactful person in the world sometimes."

Jordan squinted at the pale yellow sun. "That must have been about the end of my first year up."

Colin nodded and let a mouthful of cigar smoke drift from his lips. "In my opinion it was all a bit high-handed, but Mary was determined to have it cleared up before you came home for the long vac. And in the event, I suppose she was right. I must say, I was relieved when you broke up with the girl."

So that's what had happened. So very simple, yet he'd never guessed. He remembered the little back room and the idiot Emerald burbling. A child ought to have been able to see in Annie's rigid stance the implacable iron of Mary. How odd that he hadn't. He said, "Mary never thinks anyone is capable of ordering their own affairs without her help."

"My dear old chap, she thinks we're children. But then, what woman doesn't think that about any man?" Colin gave a shade of a chuckle. He pushed through the gate and Jordan followed him. They stood side by side within the garden. The light was kind to the huge ugly rectory, erected in the middle of Victoria's reign to replace a smaller, rose-bricked early Georgian house, of which the only remains were a small print in Trevor's study. The scars of lighter brick on the wall where the fig tree had been were almost invisible now.

Inside, the fire would be refreshed with new coals, the roast beef almost done, and the women would be waiting for Jordan to pour the sherry. As he moved in step with Colin across the lawn, he wondered at his own lack of anger at Mary, wondered at his calm acceptance of the news. But of course, like the coming of the Redeemer which Trevor would declaim from the lectern on Tuesday, it was news staled by centuries. The child was born, and the child had died. And that was that.

"Hungry," said Colin, "damned hungry."

"So am I," he said.

34

The first day of the holidays was usually much better than this. Even Uncle Trevor's giving him a glass of sherry before lunch—"My dear Mary, it won't do him any harm. He's nearly fourteen and had a term, a good term, at public school—one of the men now, eh, my boy?"— had not restored the proper magic to the day.

It was because Uncle John was missing, a stupid prospective new curate sitting in his place at lunch.

"Where's Uncle John?"

"He's in his room. He's not feeling up to much."

"Isn't he having any lunch?"

"Don't be inquisitive, my dear."

"Well, can't I go and see him?"

"No. He's probably sleeping now. He'll be down tomorrow."

"Jordan, my boy—" Uncle Trevor cleared his throat—"I think you and I should have a little talk later on this afternoon. Perhaps after tea, hum?"

"Okay."

"Jordan, we are not Americans—yet."

"Sorry, Aunt Mary. I meant alright."

"One word or two?" Trevor smiled.

"One," said Jordan.

"I was glad to hear you've decided to give up boxing this term," said Aunt Mary loudly, actually directing the remark at the curate. "A wise decision—wouldn't you say so, Mr. Mansard?"

The clergyman raised his head abruptly, and a forkful of cabbage fell onto his plate, splashing gravy on his cassock. "Ah, dear me yes, yes indeed, Miss Freeman. The danger of permanent injury from brain concussion I have always felt does not warrant—"

"Danger? Fiddlesticks. A boy has to stand up for himself. Boxing is not a team sport, that's what's wrong with it. It doesn't develop any team spirit."

"Ah—yes." Mr. Mansard looked down and tentatively stabbed the errant cabbage. "I do agree indeed."

He'd better, thought Jordan. Table manners were a consideration to Aunt Mary—this and the major test of being taken round the garden had important bearing on whether or not the curate would be accepted. Mr. Mansard was failing badly on the table test, and he didn't look, either, as though he knew much about gardening. But clumsiness and ignorance were not fatal bars and might actually prove assets if allied with sufficient docility. Mary could never stand the chatterers and the know-alls. Which was one reason why Jordan did not tell her that his renunciation of boxing was due, not to his liking for team sports, but to his prep school headmaster's refusal, in his last term, to award him the silver medal for having won his weight, which all the other winners had been given. "Maddox will not receive a medal. He did not box. He fought."

By the end of lunch, Jordan had already decided to go to see Uncle John, whatever Aunt Mary said. He would knock very softly and peep in. If Uncle John was really asleep, he wouldn't wake him, and no harm would be done. But Jordan was pretty sure John wouldn't be asleep.

In order to throw Aunt Mary off the scent, he accompanied her and Mr. Mansard round the garden for a while.

"These are the tulip beds. We're particularly proud of our tulips. The soil is very suitable. These will be chrysanthemums; we transplanted them this year. They need more sun. We had a very disappointing show at the Harvest Festival last year."

"Ah, yes indeed, we must pray for improvement, then."

"There are more important matters for prayer, Mr. Mansard. However, we may hope for the best."

In deprecatory panic, Mr. Mansard pointed at random. "And what grows here, Miss Freeman?"

"Nothing. The roots of the fig tree are beneath that bed, and the soil would not give proper nourishment to anything else. You are aware, I suppose, that the fig tree is the finest specimen in the county. It is the rector's only relaxation. These are lilies of the valley. I regard them as a weed."

Mansard was easy meat. If he were asked to tea, he would be in. His urgent submissiveness gave him a good chance, thought Jordan as he wandered off idly, as though to inspect the orchard.

He entered the rectory by the kitchen door and went up the back stairs to Uncle John's bedroom. There was a tray of food in the corridor on the floor. Jordan lifted a metal lid from a dish. Nothing had been eaten.

He tapped softly at the door and then turned the handle and looked in.

The room smelled faintly of leather and tweed and pipe smoke, although Uncle John was strictly forbidden to smoke upstairs. The bed was unmade, but there was no sign of Uncle John.

Jordan went back into the corridor and closed the door. There was only one place his uncle could be. He retraced his steps and took the second flight of stairs that led up to the attic.

He stood in the middle of the attic and listened. Amidst the mustiness of old luggage and discarded furniture waiting its turn for the next bazaar, he stayed still and uneasy. The workroom door was shut, but he was almost certain Uncle John was there. Where else could he be? But why this silence? Perhaps he really was ill. Perhaps he wanted to be left alone. Jordan was suddenly dazed by questions, filled with a dread he could not formulate. He walked forward quickly, loudly, so that his coming could not be missed.

The door was not latched, and he pushed it open.

John sat in the chair in front of the table, his face lifted to the sun which streamed in through the dormer window. He wore pyjamas and his old dressing gown and leather bedroom slippers. He moved his head a little as Jordan entered, but said nothing.

Jordan took his usual chair. There was no sound, for that was the rule. But now there was nothing to watch, for John's hands lay idle on the table, a half-painted puzzle beside them.

Jordan tried the old ritual examination of the workroom. It was all surely the same as before. The neatly stacked sections of plywood, the jars of tempera, the tools aligned in size order.

A fly buzzed on the windowpane.

Jordan could not help looking at his uncle.

There was a deceptive air of concentration to John's unwavering gaze. But the hands, so dexterous and delicate in movement, were still, except that now and again a tiny tremor would curl the fingers.

The old man muttered something inaudible.

Jordan was afraid. He wanted to run from this. Where was John, slapping his hands, sniff-sniffing with military imperiousness, greeting him with a rough handshake, and smiling that smile of hidden knowledge and delight which suddenly would be shared with Jordan as together they fought a battle?

"Uncle John?" He hesitated. "Are you making a puzzle?"

John blinked at the sun. "Puzzle . . . puzzle," he murmured. Beneath the weathered flesh of his neck, the open collar of the pyjamas exposed a V of clear white skin.

"Are you ill, Uncle?" Jordan asked desperately.

"Ah, ah," John's mouth snapped twice. Then slowly he turned his head and looked with sun-blinded eyes to where Jordan sat. "Home," he said, "home, eh?" He seemed to be making a great effort. "Sent home," he muttered. Two tears started in his eyes and trickled uncertainly down his cheeks. "In disgrace."

"What did they do to you, Uncle John?"

John gave his old sharp chuckle. "Sent me to bed. That's it." His voice trembled into apology, "Old wounds. Old wounds, they reopen. Hospital, you see. Wake up and . . . the nurses, dear little things, all smiles and white starch." He became vehement. "The spoils of war. Everywhere roses and laughter, wine and kisses—after all that mud. Shouldn't have made a fuss. How could I know she'd make a fuss?" He pulled the neck of his pyjamas together and straightened his shoulders for a moment. "Eh, eh, eh?" he cried loudly.

"Uncle . . ." What was wrong? He reached out to touch John. But the old man started back.

"You an officer, sir?" he barked. He blinked quickly and leaned forward to where Jordan sat in shadow. "Rank? Regiment?" Then gradually he relaxed, his hand falling from his throat, his face turning back to the window.

Jordan stood up. "What's happened, Uncle John? Has something happened?"

After a few moments of silence, the old man began to murmur as though he were talking to himself. "Disgraced the regiment. An officer and a gentleman. Have to send in my papers. If they let me. No, you see, Henlet will back me up, and Waidlaw. Good boy, Waidlaw. But it won't make any difference. Disgraced the regiment. The verdict any day now. Where there's life there's hope. Waiting, waiting. Confined to quarters." He began to weep again.

Jordan lightly touched his uncle's forearm. Immediately the old man's hand returned the grip, clutching at Jordan's arm. Very gradually he turned his head and looked up at his nephew, and for a moment there was sense again in his blue eyes. "A losing battle, Jordan," he said. "A losing battle." His grasp weakened and his hand slid down to the table and his head moved back to the dusty window and the cross-hatched oblong of cloudless sky.

Although Jordan touched him again and spoke to him most gently, the old man did not respond or shift his position.

At last Jordan left. He closed the door with precision. Something had opened within him, a glacier mouth upon the edge of which he stood and stared. He did not move, but after a while he raised his eyes. Although he did not look, it seemed to him the hole was filled with furious struggling. Anger poured into him and spilled out in a few brief tears.

He walked quickly across the attic and down the stairs and into the kitchen and along the dark passage to Trevor's study. He knocked and pushed open the door at the same time.

Pen in hand, Uncle Trevor looked up with a smile, which turned to a frown as he saw the clock. "I thought we had agreed to have our little chat after tea. Or is my memory failing me?"

"I want to talk to you now."

"It's not a very convenient moment, my boy. Why—?"

"I want to talk to you now."

"Oh well. Well, come in and sit down." He put his pen down and touched the tips of his fingers together. "What is it?"

"What have you done to Uncle John?"

Trevor looked annoyed. "Have you seen your uncle?"

"Yes. And I've talked to him too."

"Didn't your Aunt Mary specifically tell you not to go up to John's bedroom?"

"He wasn't in his bedroom."

Trevor half rose in alarm. "Not in his bedroom? Where was he? Tell me at once."

"He's alright. He's in the workroom."

"The workroom? What was he doing?"

"He wasn't doing anything."

Trevor looked at his watch, then sat down again. "Mary will have to be informed about this. Dear dear. I'd better go and tell her."

"Can't you talk to me first?"

"Well, perhaps. He can't come to much harm in the workroom. But we'll have to cut it short, my boy."

"What have you done to him?"

"Jordan, I'm not at all happy that you saw fit to deliberately disobey your aunt. Rules are rules, whether at home or at school. We mustn't start off the holidays on the wrong foot, must we? Perhaps we can overlook this; after all, it is the first day of—"

"Uncle Trevor! What have you done to Uncle John?"

Trevor opened his mouth angrily, then shut it tight. For a moment he was not the gently dithering clergyman. But almost at once he had control of himself. "I wanted to talk to you about that, my boy. That and your term's work." He gave a mechanical little laugh. "There's something very, er, unpleasant, I'm afraid, I have to tell you. Frankly, I'm not sure you're old enough to understand, but you are bound to be hearing certain rumours in the village, so I, er . . . Well, it's to do with your Uncle John, I'm afraid."

"What's to do with Uncle John?"

"A very unpleasant incident, I'm afraid." With sudden vehemence—"A shocking thing. Shocking. Your uncle has been, well, involved—and involved all of us, I may say—in very serious trouble. Very serious indeed. You may understand when I tell you that it also involves a certain young female. From the village. Most distress—"

"Who?"

"Please do not interrupt me, Jordan. This is not easy for me, for any of us. I'm not at liberty to tell you the name of the girl."

"Was it Greta Candle?"

"What? John must have told you, dear oh dear me."

"Uncle John didn't tell me anything. But I know Greta. Everyone knows Greta. Greta's always in some mess or other. She'll let anybody do anything. I should have thought you'd know that."

"If you think I have time to spare to investigate the sordid side of Sibley life, you are quite mistaken. I must say I am surprised at you, Jordan; it seems to me that you should be devoting your energies to more elevating things than common tittle-tattle. No wonder you're still falling behind in your Latin." Trevor took a deep breath and looked for a moment at the Bible stand under the window. "I am not concerned with this female's reputation. I . . ." He stopped. He seemed to have lost the thread—it often happened in his sermons.

"Did he get her pregnant?"

"Jordan!" Trevor's rather plump face went completely white.

"Well, did he?"

"Jordan, I do not care for your language or your attitude. I understand you are distressed. We all are. But impudence is neither called for nor wanted in this house. What your uncle did was, I'm sorry to say, far more serious than what you mentioned. You may find that difficult to believe. I found it difficult to believe myself, until I heard it from the lips of Inspector Pender. Your aunt has received a wound that I seriously doubt she will ever recover from."

"Is it rape?"

Trevor took out a handkerchief and wiped his lips. He deliberately looked away from Jordan. "The charge—if it is brought, and I may say we are moving heaven and earth to avoid that happening—the charge will be one of attempted rape. So the police inform me."

"Attempted rape? It's impossible! I don't believe it." A terrible, contemptuous fury pulsed in his ears. "Everyone knows Greta Candle's a little tart. She's been shagged by—"

"Jordan Maddox!" Trevor was on his feet, shouting, "Shut up! Filth! Where did you learn that filth? How dare you? Like your father —*vulgar*. Vulgarity! Is that what they teach you at school? Is it? Is it? You dare speak to me like that, you dare import your filth into this house?" Trevor brandished a black ruler. His face was white and wet with sweat, and his lips trembled like speared worms.

Jordan was terrified at this man, black and yelling at him. But the terror was indistinguishable in his blood from his own rage. "Is that what you said to Uncle John? Is that why he's like he is? Because you shouted at him?"

"Sit down! Be silent!"

"Didn't you even give him a chance?"

"Be silent!" Trevor thumped the ruler on his blotter. "Sit down!"

Slowly Jordan sat. He watched Trevor striving to control himself, his arms shaking as though he were operating a road drill. The rector dropped the ruler. "Wait here," he mumbled, and he hurried out of the study.

Jordan heard the door of the small chapel open and close. He was shivering, too. As he waited, he felt his anger dribbling away, leaving his body cold.

When Trevor returned and sat down at his desk and cleared his throat, Jordan looked at him with distaste. As though aware of it, Trevor smiled defensively. "I must ask you to forgive me, my boy. I am afraid I said things I shouldn't have done. It is not always easy. Jesus is a hard taskmaster. A hard taskmaster." He sighed. "This is a trying time. A difficult time. But we must remember Job, eh, my boy?"

"What's going to happen?"

"It is out of my hands. We can only hope and pray. Our position at Sibley is seriously jeopardized. The archdeacon is most upset. Indeed."

"But Uncle John?"

"Yes. He is, of course, not fully responsible for his actions. We've never tried to disguise that from you, have we, my boy? No, no. But I sometimes think we have disguised it a little from ourselves. And this is the result. A foolish charity. John would always have been happier,

I think, with, well, those of his own kind. But your Aunt Mary would not hear of it. Won't hear of it, even now. Even if the police—well, even if nothing more serious happens, we will have to take the most stringent steps. Your aunt has explained this to John, but I'm afraid he is in no condition to grasp, er, the enormity of what he has done, let alone the consequences. We will have to keep a close watch." He paused and brushed imaginary crumbs from his lapel. "I'm counting on you, my boy. To help."

"To spy on Uncle John, you mean?"

"Please. I don't want to lose my temper again. I'm sure you don't want me to either. I can see that I'm going to have to inform Mr. Prideaux of your negative attitude. You are behaving like a child. Obviously I overestimated your sense of responsibility." Uncle Trevor wiped his cheeks, his forehead, the palms of his hands. "You must listen to me. Are you listening?"

"Yes."

"Very well. We shall have to lay down some rules for the holidays. First, you are not to go upstairs at any time during the day without my permission. Is that clear?"

"Yes." He hardly listened. He had already decided not to talk to Trevor ever again, except when absolutely necessary.

"Secondly, when and if your uncle is allowed downstairs, you are not to be in the same room with him—or outside with him—unless either your aunt or myself is also present. Clear?"

"Yes."

"Thirdly, you are not to talk about this matter to anyone. Do you understand?"

"Yes."

"Very well. Now, I intend to enforce these rules. Any infringement will lead to the most severe consequences. I hoped I would be able to trust you, but since I obviously can't, I have no alternative but to treat you as the child you so clearly still are. Do I make myself understood?"

"Yes. Can I go now?"

"You may."

As he reached the door, Trevor said, "Er, Jordan, my boy. We can forget about the little chat we were due to have after tea."

"Alright."

Trevor smiled. "Still friends, eh?"

Jordan gave him a bare nod. He shut the door and stood in the passage. Then he went into the chapel. It had frosted glass in the windows like a lavatory. The floor was never polished. It smelled damply of religion. Jordan walked up to the altar table covered by a heavy brown-and-green embroidered cloth done by the women of the parish. He gathered the saliva in his mouth and let it fall in a blob on the cloth. He watched for a long time, until all the small bubbles of spittle had burst.

As he went into the passage, the gong rang for tea.

He was right; Mr. Mansard had been invited to stay.

35

He came to himself slowly in the half-darkness. For a moment he was a child sick within the soft comfort of a night light. But there was nothing soft about the unwinking eye of the peephole in the door.

He sat wrapped in a blanket. The pipes had long since gone cold, and he was chilly and grubby and stiff in the aftermath of a doze which had not rested his bones. It was after three in the morning. He put his head between his hands and massaged the bristles on his chin.

Outside on the landing the footsteps of a prison officer echoed flatly, as if in an old castle deserted for centuries.

Jordan closed his eyes. He was exhausted, but he could not give up. He was almost there now.

The prison officer halted, then continued. Jordan was stirred by the lonely footsteps marking with melancholy the suspension of all the life that lay there, imprisoned and dormant. The thorn-crowned Light of the World, tiptoeing sadly to his death.

He heard his own steps, tiptoeing too, across the attic floor and stopping at the door and waiting. A hundred times he must have stood there, listening for a movement, a word, a cough, a cry. But though often his hand had been raised to the doorknob, he had never gone in. He could never bring himself to do that simple thing. And inside, he knew, the old man sat, hands motionless upon the table, staring out of the window at the sun, the clouds, the rain, not even fighting old battles any more. But gradually the poignancy had faded, and his attempts at entrance had become less frequent, until at last it was altogether too late.

And then, as the sound of leather and steel upon the stone faded, Jordan remembered Cheppingden Castle.

He had left Willy in the great gardens, among the clipped hedges and stone nymphs and ordered beds, and taken Georgia into the castle.

"Where are the dungeons, Daddy?"

He laughed and, glancing through the sixpenny guide, told her there were none. He shared her disappointment, for the castle's fortifications were purely decorative, and the rooms, though bleak and unfurnished, held no history of bloody murder or mediaeval anguish. In compensation, he related the only story of any interest connected with Cheppingden, about the queen, whose king had died, and who had secretly married her lover and come to live at the castle. The secret had been discovered, the lover disgraced, and she herself had died giving birth to a stillborn child.

"But they had a year," he said, "almost a year to the day, I believe, of happiness. They must have strolled in the gardens and walked these rooms and felt safe from the world. So it wasn't as sad as all that."

Everywhere they went, their feet sounding on the flagstones, Georgia asked, "Did the queen die in this room, Daddy?"

"I don't think anyone is sure where she died exactly."

Georgia pulled him quickly to the next room. "Here then?"

"I shouldn't think so. This was, let's see, the small hall."

Georgia was not convinced. "I expect she probably died here." She ran over to the fireplace and walked in. He watched her looking up the chimney.

"I can see sky. Come and look."

He went over and knelt by her side and stared up.

"We can't see sky in our chimney at home, can we?"

He put one arm round her and held her tight. "See those pieces of iron all the way up inside the chimney, Georgia? They were for chimney sweeps. Children not much bigger than you, very often. They'd climb up those spikes and sweep the soot away."

She looked up for a long time without saying anything. Jordan felt

259

her soft flesh under his hand and smelled her hair, and a great wash of tenderness came over him so that he kissed her. She paid no attention except to lower her head and frown.

"Didn't the children ever fall down, Daddy?"

"Yes, I expect they did."

"They'd hurt themselves then, wouldn't they?"

"Yes, they would."

Georgia paused and glanced up quickly and then back to her father. "The children might even be killed, mightn't they, Daddy?"

"Yes. If they were far up enough and fell, they might have been killed."

Georgia nodded with slow satisfaction. She went into the middle of the hall and regarded the fireplace. "Does it smoke like ours, do you think, Daddy?"

"It probably did when the wind was in the wrong direction. But in those days people didn't worry much about that kind of thing. When this castle was built there were still a lot of houses that didn't have a chimney at all. They just had a hole in the roof, with a louver arrangement, and the fire underneath it. If there was a strong wind, the hall would have been filled with smoke. But they were used to it, you see, not like us."

Georgia was pensive and wouldn't hold his hand for a while as they went through the rooms.

At last she said, "Why doesn't Mummy come with us?"

"She prefers the fresh air."

"I don't like the fresh air. Daddy, if you died, would Mummy marry a lover?"

"I'm not going to die."

"But if?"

"I don't know." They came out into the courtyard, at one corner of which was a squat tower, the only part of the castle to predate the Tudors. "She might, I suppose." The sky was clouding over what had started out as one of the few fine days of the summer. As the sunlight faded, Jordan felt mildly depressed. The castle had not lived up to expectations of excitement.

"Let's go up the tower."

"Well—" Jordan looked doubtfully at his watch. They had used up the half hour which he'd told Willy was all they'd need. "Well, I don't see why not. If it's open."

260

They walked across the cobblestones and pushed at the heavy nail-studded door. It opened grudgingly and the light fell on a floor scattered with bird droppings.

"It's lovely and dark," Georgia said gleefully, "just like a dungeon, Daddy."

Jordan stood on the step, resisting her pulls on his hand. "I'm not sure your mother would approve."

"But you said, Daddy, you said!"

He smiled. "Alright, I don't suppose it'll do any—"

"Jordan!"

He turned as Willy entered the courtyard from the garden side. "Jordan, where on earth have you been?"

Georgia tried to pull him inside the tower and whispered fiercely, "Don't let her spoil it, Daddy, please."

"You mustn't talk about your mother like—"

"Oh Jordan, you haven't taken her up that filthy tower, have you?" She advanced briskly across the yard, voice raised and touched with impatience. Her tendency to shout in unfamiliar surroundings had always annoyed Jordan. "Come along now, or we'll be late for tea."

Jordan waited until she was closer and said, "I thought we might stop somewhere for tea on the way back."

"There's nothing wrong with the teas at the hotel. You know how whiny Georgia gets if we keep her out too long."

"But, Mummy, we haven't been up the tower yet."

"And you're not going to, my little poppet."

"But Daddy promised—"

"Yes, I did say I would, Willy. It'll only take a minute or two."

Willy peered into the doorway. "Jordan, you are simply not taking Georgia into that filthy, smelly place. It's probably dangerous too."

"Oh don't be ridiculous. It's perfectly alright. Why don't you start the car?"

Willy raised an eyebrow. "Darling, you are being unreasonable, aren't you? If you can't be polite to me, you might at least consider my daughter's safety."

"I'm not asking you to come. Just because you're terrified of heights—"

"That's absolutely beside the point." The flesh over her cheekbones was white with anger.

"I'm not sure it's beside the point at all." He regretted having said it, but there was no help for it now. "You're pushing your own fear onto Georgia and—"

"I will not listen to that—*psychology*. You'll be saying I'm mad next. If anyone's mad in this family it's—"

"You're damn well paranoiac at times, and you know it—"

"—on your side. Your uncle was round the bend for years," she enunciated with precision, "and your—"

"That was a war wound!" he shouted at her.

"—your father was a dipso. So please don't let's have any of this vulgar name-calling."

He let go of Georgia's hand and stepped towards his wife. His arm seemed to move involuntarily.

"Don't you dare hit me!"

He never knew whether or not he struck out, for the next thing he remembered was leaning against the doorpost with a dizziness in his head like a top wobbling to the end of its spin and seeing the figures of his wife and daughter tilting away from him across the courtyard.

Jordan raised his head from his hands. He was surprised to find that he'd been crying. He stood up, and the blanket fell away from his shoulders. He was not cold any more.

He went to the door and put his eye to the peephole. In reversed magnification, the deserted landing was endlessly far away and yet quite clear and sharp. He watched for some time, but no one came. He turned and leaned with his back against the door.

Then he moved to the corner of the room and wet his hands with cold water in the washbasin. He dried them carefully on the thin prison towel. He looked up at the window and had a curious fancy that perhaps outside there was indeed a broad spread of countryside, trees, meadows, grass, birds flying, bees humming. He put his hand on the chair to pull it beneath the window and look out and verify. He resisted the impulse—he was finished with the pursuit of dreams.

He looked down at his hand, a shapeless white on the back of the chair. He held the hand up, but it was too dim to see closely. He sat down at the table and lit a match. By its light he examined his right hand. There was no mark or scar on it, nothing strange or special. As the wood curled and the flame shivered and went out, he thought that if he were taken to a field of severed hands, he would never be able to pick out his own and match it to the stump. The lines and figures on the palm meant nothing to him, and the back of his hand was indistinguishable from ten thousand others.

And yet it was this hand that had clasped June's to save himself from falling, this hand poised at the attic door but never turning, this hand seizing innocence but not held out to help, this hand wrenched from Georgia's, raised to Willy, but always withdrawn unused, unscathed. Except for that one slim, sharp scratch, now healed and gone. And yet not gone—for it had been noted, tested, photographed. A murderer's hand.

Fitting and just. He remembered George: "Come on, son, why not make it easy on yourself?"

Not easy, though, to stretch out a hand and lay it, veins up, on the blood-smoothed wood. The ancient penalty for traitors.

But he would do it. He could do it now.

He was filled with quiet contentment. He lay down on the bed and pulled the blanket over him.

Tomorrow—no, on Monday—he would change his plea to guilty; tomorrow he would instruct Tom Short. He smiled faintly, and immediately he was asleep, smiling.

THE LIVING

36

He shaved with great care, going over the rough parts of his flesh again and again until they were entirely smooth. He washed the razor and dried the blade.

He dressed slowly, attentive to every detail, lingering over the buttoning of his clean white shirt, the insertion of the cufflinks, the attachment of the collar to studs, as though it were some kind of final parting. His shoes, the socks, suit, blue tie knotted perfectly, were of great value. Perhaps because they were tokens of a normality, of the happiness of things used every day, to which he had so long been blind and could see now only when they were gone. He felt a gentle sadness for all that life they stood for, and from which now he was irrevocably separated.

He felt, he was, purified. With his handkerchief he patted the razor-fine cut on his left cheek. And he remembered how June had kept a roll of cotton wool in her desk drawer for just this occasion. When a shaving cut opened again and bled, as it often did, she would hand him the cotton wool without a word. A solemn, small ritual which amused them both. There were many such things, he remembered now. Habits and words of daily closeness he had hardly noticed. The warm smell of her hair as she bent over his desk—not sallow, like poor Willy's.

That last morning her sleep-charged softness, her fur slippers—like a child, like Georgia.

He smiled at the memory of all the endearing things that were now quite lost.

He was glad for the bareness of his room; glad that soon these clothes, smooth and fitting, would be taken away. He would wear garments of proper anonymity. And eat the food that the other prisoners ate.

Sadly, the past was bearable now. Even the dreams and visions and imaginings—the urgencies and quietness, the meetings and the partings—had the sweetness of a prior innocence. He could see her go up the stairs before him and into the room. And, as he shut the door and leaned against it, she put her hands on his lapels to help him off with the coat, and he kissed her. He unbuttoned her blue-and-purple-flowered housedress and slipped the pyjama top over her head. Her breasts were big and the nipples upright. He touched her white rounded belly. The bed was open for them. He never had such joy as in her eagerness for him. The sunlight bathed their bodies and she closed her eyes at the brightness as they made love. . . .

This was permitted, as one is permitted a glass of water before communion.

He'd have liked to have stayed the whole day silent and unmoving. But he was quite resigned to the impossibility of this.

He went calmly with Denver, listening to every word the prison officer spoke, to the solicitors' room, and he nodded courteously to Tom.

"I've told Geoffrey." Tom looked grim.

"Oh, yes."

"He's anxious to see you. He's coming in tomorrow afternoon. All the way from Suffolk."

"I don't think he'll need to bother. Not when you've heard what I've got to tell you."

Tom sighed. "What is it this time? Come on, spill the beans."

"I'm going to change my plea to guilty." Jordan was surprised to hear the tremor in his own voice.

Tom looked away with an air of heavy boredom. "You won't need me then either, will you?"

"No, Tom, I shan't. But I'm grateful for all you've done. I shall see the governor this afternoon."

"Oh for Christ's sake!" Tom banged the table with his fist. "This is too bloody much. Maddox, you are without a doubt the most unmitigated fucking bore it's ever been my disastrous luck to deal with legally—or, I may add, in any other way. No one expects someone in your position to be sensible, but you're featherbrained to the point of lunacy. What the hell do you want, man? To be convicted of murder? Let me—"

"It's not a matter of what I want. It's what's got to happen. It's a matter of simple justice."

"What are you trying to do? Get yourself interviewed on the telly? Do your memoirs for the *Sunday Pic.*?"

"I'm sorry, Tom. It is bad luck for you, I—"

"Balls!" He yelled the word. And then, with an enormous effort which left him white-cheeked, Tom spoke calmly. "Alright, Jordan. Tell me about it, then. You owe me that."

"Tell you?" Jordan was nonplussed. There was really nothing at all to tell, nothing to . . . "What do you want me to tell you, Tom?"

"What happened? Did you just wake up one morning and decide it would be rather fun to pop round after breakfast to Number Twenty-seven Panton Place and croak June Singer?"

Jordan smiled. "It goes back a long way, Tom. I don't know that I can begin to explain to you really."

"I don't want your life history. When did you decide to murder June? That's what I want to know. When did it all start?"

"Well, I suppose . . . I suppose you could say, really, on that day June came down to Woodley. The day you rang up to ask me over for a drink."

"Aha! I wondered when we'd get round to that. That was a nasty, unexpected little kick in the teeth from dear old Mrs. Payne, wasn't it? Not unexpected to you, of course. You must have had a good deal of fun these last few days watching Geoffrey make a fool of himself."

"Tom, believe me—"

"Why in hell should I believe you? You've lied from first to last—"

"Tom—"

"—lied and then forgotten, deceived your lawyers with inanities and half-truths, done your best to—"

"Tom. What you say is quite true. But I'm telling you the truth now." It pained him, but he saw now what he had not seen before— that he would have to lie, even if it was only a lie about little matters of legal proof, in order to reveal the whole truth.

"Alright. I'll listen—but don't expect me to believe, chum. The famous day in the country then—are you trying to tell me you had an affair with June? Laid her in the long grasses, is that it?"

Jordan hesitated—he didn't want to do this, so soon after the cleansing. But there was no other way. Slowly, he nodded his head.

Then to his amazement, Tom broke out into a great guffaw.

Jordan stared at the lawyer. What a strange animal he was.

"Sorry, old man." Tom wiped his lips. "Well well well well." He lit a cigarette. "So you're a bad lad after all." He seemed to find the idea irresistibly amusing. "My dear Jordan, please don't think I'm unsympathetic. Quite the contrary. I know only too well what goes on, only too well. What a mess. Hard to keep your hands off 'em though, isn't it?"

He thought of the last moment in the car, the dappled lamplight, the smell of warm tarmac and the motionless summer night. "Yes," he said.

"Well—no need to go into all that," Tom said expansively. "I understand exactly what you feel. My God, old boy, you shouldn't bottle it up, though. Bad thing." He began to look a little less amused. "Particularly in our circumstances. I'm not blaming you, don't think that. It must have been a blow when she was . . . no wonder it knocked all the stuffing out of you. Someone like you. No wonder . . . but all the same, I wish you'd owned up at the beginning. You really shouldn't have lied like that, you know. Really not. Damn it. Damn it." He sucked at his cigarette. "This is going to make things a bit awkward—Geoffrey'll be upset. Still—it clears the air. We know where we are now. And I rather fancy the Crown's shot its bolt. They'll close on Monday. As it stands, we've got a fighting chance. Of course, in the state you're in, there's no question of your going in the witness box. Far too tricky. Awkward. Still . . ." He looked speculatively at Jordan. "Tell me, did you put the bun in her oven?"

"Did I—what?"

"Did you get her pregnant or was it the other chap? Or didn't she tell you about him? No, of course, she wouldn't have."

"Other chap?"

"The fellow that bumped her off. Now think carefully about this, Jordan. Any information we can get about him is vital. Did she give you the slightest hint, eh?"

"Give me one of your cigarettes, would you, Tom?" He hadn't allowed for this—this total misunderstanding, disbelief. It was hateful, hateful that he should have to do this to June in death. It would soon be over though—he reached for the thought and held it. It wasn't Tom's fault, or anyone's fault. The cigarette trembled between his fingers.

"Yes," he answered, "Yes, it was me." And he was filled with an overwhelming pity for the child that had never been born, the dead little boy. His child, his boy. "Yes, Tom . . . I don't want . . . I can't . . ." He knew that in a moment he would weep, and he could not allow that to happen.

"Of course, old man. I'm sorry—tasteless of me, I suppose. But, look, about this other chap—"

Jordan pulled himself together. "There wasn't any other chap. *I* murdered June." That was better, the quaver in his voice had gone, and he felt at once stronger. This is what he had come here to say.

"You can come off it now, Jordan."

Poor Tom, poor fool. "It's true. I can't say more than that."

"Damn!" As though he had missed a place kick, Tom took a deep breath. "Very well. Tell me then. Tell me what happened. Tell me how you murdered her. Every detail. Tell me what happened from the moment you rang the doorbell at Number Twenty-seven Panton Place."

Surely, they were the very words of Superintendent George? Jordan smiled faintly. He had come round to it at last. How much simpler if . . . if . . . but this was different. "I didn't," he said, "ring the bell. I let myself in with the key." Sadly, but without a tremor, he related what had happened. The greeting, the loving, the killing, the flight. And, as he spoke, he felt his whole being eased. For it was, he realised, no real defilement of June. It was what she would have wanted, that they should be close like this, devoutly wished and, now, freely given.

"I don't believe a word of it." Tom sat staring, a fat angry owl. "Not a word."

"I'm sorry," said Jordan.

"Sorry? No, *I'm* sorry—sorry for you. You're welcome to your opinion that you murdered Singer. You can believe you killed Thomas á Becket, for all I care. That's not why I'm sorry for you. I'm sorry for you because you're a pitiable creature who is blandly proposing to ruin the lives of others. Serenely, sanctimoniously sacrificing your wife, your daughter, your parents, Sutlif—"

"My parents have been dead for many years."

"Yes, your father was a dipso—died in a lunatic asylum, didn't he? And you're doing a pretty good job of following in his footsteps."

Jordan was touched by a flicker of curiosity. "How did you know about my father?"

"Common knowledge. I don't know. Let's stick to the point. So far, I've treated you as a supposedly responsible human being, but I think the time has come when we need the help of a head shrinker. There's a chap called Blaydon. Wimpole Street. The quiet type, you'll like him. I'm sure I'll be able to get him in this afternoon. Will you consent to see him?"

"I don't think so, Tom." Jordan shook his head slowly. "No, I don't think I would. This is the end, Tom. Try to understand that. There is nothing you can do."

"Goddammit to hell—"

"Tom. If you'd feel easier, you can leave the case, cease acting for me. There isn't very much to be done now anyway."

"Drop the case? But what . . . what . . . ?"

"Perhaps it would be best all round. I'll discharge you—is that the right word?—discharge you, if you like."

"I believe you're serious. I do believe." Tom sat motionless. "Look, let's talk it over."

"No, no more talking, no." He stood up.

"Well, look." Tom stood too. "Look, at least—I mean wait until you've seen Willy. She's coming in this afternoon anyway. And Bartlett. You can't just let them down, bang, like that. In all fairness. You've got to tell them yourself. You've got to hear Willy's side of it. You see that, don't you?"

"Yes, alright." He wondered if perhaps Tom would not be glad to be rid of the case. He couldn't blame him. "Alright, I'll see the governor tomorrow, then. You'd better tell Bartlett to make it early tomorrow—before lunch."

"That's splendid. Very wise. About this other thing—I won't leave you in the lurch."

"You wouldn't be doing that. It's up to you. Whatever you do, I shan't blame you."

Tom was silent for a moment. "I'll get things moving. Ring Bartlett. We're still investigating, you know. . . ."

272

Jordan smiled. The first part of it, perhaps the worst, was over.

"I'm—" Tom cleared his throat—"I'm still on your side, old man, remember that."

37

She sat opposite him in the neat blue suit she always wore when going up to shop at Harrod's. She was crisp and even and brittle. A tiny gold fillet in each ear, but no other decoration. She never wore the early Victorian pieces her mother gave her from time to time. She was soured on all things that gave pleasure to the eye by her mother's inexhaustible and delighted instinct for the beautiful. Their house at Woodley was so ugly simply because, he had often thought, her mother's small Georgian mansion at Cambridge was so perfect. And the gentle humour which had led Lady Benton, whose husband had briefly been ambassador to The Hague, to name her daughter Wilhelmina, was for Willy a source of unremitting disdain.

Once he had given her a slim silver Scandinavian brooch, thinking the interdict might not apply there. She wore it occasionally so as not to hurt his feelings, but he knew she thought it mere modern rubbish. He saw, sadly, that she was wearing it today.

"Georgia—Georgia sends you her love." Her voice was hushed, as though the visitors' room were a chapel.

She looked so immaculate—and lifeless. Jordan would have liked to reach out and touch her shoulder with reassurance, but the flat, cross-hatched wire between them prevented any contact.

"Did Tom talk to you?" he said gently.

She gave him a small, grim smile. "I didn't really believe him. Poor man, he looked ghastly. But . . ."

"I'm changing my plea to guilty, Willy."

"That's what Tom said, I thought . . ." She hesitated. "It's a sort of joke, isn't it?"

"No joke."

He knew her hands were clasped tight under the counter where he could not see them.

273

"Darling. I know it's been an awful strain for you. Perhaps it's my fault that I haven't—haven't shown you I know that. But, darling, this isn't making it any better for us, is it? I mean, please don't—don't. . . . " She looked down at her lap. "I know I'm not very sensitive, Jordan. And often I haven't understood. Perhaps sometimes I haven't tried hard enough to understand, but—"

"Willy. I'm sorry. This has—well, it has nothing to do with you."

Her head jerked up. "How can you say that? Jordan, you've always been good and kind and gentle. Please don't turn on me now with this—this thing. You don't know how upsetting it is. I don't care if it's a joke or what it is—I don't understand—but, please darling, don't make it worse. It'll all be over soon. Tom says they've got some new evidence and . . ." Her voice began to tremble.

"I'm not turning on you, Willy." God knows, he did not wish to hurt anybody else. "But this is something I have got to do. Nothing in my life has ever been more clear to me than this."

"I don't understand!" she cried, so sharp the pacing prison officer behind her paused. "I don't understand what you want to do. Why do you want to hurt me? What have I done wrong?"

"Nothing—you have done nothing. I'll try. I'll try to make you understand." He was aware of the enormous and fruitless effort—like describing the country to a child who'd never left her city street or seen a tree.

"I want to understand, Jordan. I do. I want everything to be right for you when you come home. I want—"

"Willy—I shan't be coming home."

"Oh Jordan, please! What do you mean?"

He hesitated. It would be utterly incomprehensible to her. The sweet-sharp painful truth—she would not, could not, believe it. She would think it was an excuse—an attack, masked with mumbo jumbo, mounted upon her. And she would be left still crying "Why? why?" —her wound kept open by bewilderment. It would be better to close it, give her a reason she could grasp, a drug she could take. But surely, surely it didn't have to be this way. Again he felt his own clarity marred by necessary, trivial untruths. He looked round the barren savannah within him and, seeing the absolute aridity, knew that he would have to invent green fields and growing things in the distance behind him. There was no other way.

"Willy, I was in love with June Singer."

274

"Jordan really! Lots of men have schoolboy crushes on their secretaries. For heaven's sake, darling, I don't blame you for that."

"I—I had an affair with her."

"It doesn't matter." She leaned forward earnestly. "Lots of men do. Men are like that. I don't blame you a bit. But don't you see it doesn't matter? Don't you see it isn't *real* any more—even if it was once? Oh darling, you can't afford to take your dear old dreamy self seriously now, of all times. Poor Tom and Mr. Bartlett have their work cut out for them as it is, without you taking it into your head to . . ."

He watched her through the wire screen. She was completely remote from him. She had always been remote of course—for all the years he had lived and bedded and boarded with her. The irremediable damage was that he could not touch her or move her except by hurting her.

"Willy," he said with terrible reluctance, "will you listen to me?"

"Yes, darling. Of course. I'm listening. I promise not to interrupt."

"I'll tell you then." He could not swallow properly. "We were in love. For—for a long time I didn't know it, didn't realise it. Then last summer, when you and Georgia were away, I—June came down that day to Woodley. That's when it started." Like a horrible dream, what he was saying took possession of him.

"For months it was difficult—we couldn't see each other except in the office. And then June moved to Panton Place, when her mother died. It wasn't easy even then, but we managed a few afternoons—and three or four nights when you stayed on at Sibley over the New Year. And we . . . Then, later, June discovered she was pregnant." Suddenly he was no longer in control of the dream at all. "I wanted to marry her then. I wanted to leave you and marry her. But June wouldn't have it. She was a good person, you've no idea how good a person she was. I tried to persuade her again and again. But she said she wouldn't break up my marriage. It was Georgia she was thinking of more than anything else. She was an only child herself, you see, and her father died when she was very young. So she knew. . . . She refused, point-blank. She even refused to have the baby." His voice quivered as he thrust back the tears. "She tried to bring on an abortion. And then—then she was going to leave me. It wasn't I who wished her to go—it wasn't like they think at all. I begged her to stay. But she wouldn't. She was going to leave me. Don't you see, I couldn't stand that? What could I do? I had no alternative. I couldn't let her go. I had to kill her. I loved her . . . I couldn't let her leave me. . . ."

"You poor darling."

"What?" He was shaking all over. He blinked quickly. For a few moments he'd forgotten completely about Willy sitting opposite him.

"You *have* been in a state. But you don't have to do this for me. I don't *mind*, darling, don't you see I don't mind? I know how you feel. You've been terribly hurt by all this. Of course you have, you . . ."

"What are you talking about?"

"You dear, funny, tender thing. Don't you think I know you after all these years of looking after you?"

"You . . ." He was bewildered. "You don't believe me?"

"Does it really matter whether I believe you or not? You've never been strong, darling, but I've never minded that. I know it's not you talking, darling."

"Who then . . . who is?"

"It's some terribly hurt, strained person. But you'll be your old self again, darling, after the trial. We'll go away and have a real holiday—together. Aunt Mary would love to look after Georgia, so we can be away as long as we like. We haven't done that for ages, have we?" She smiled at him.

It was all collapsing, all slipping away from him. He tried to struggle back. Poor Willy, she couldn't conceive, couldn't begin . . . He braced himself. "I murdered her, Willy. And I shall say so—I have to."

"Jordan, you're not well. You're nervous and overwrought, you must see—"

He shook his head. He hated this. "No. I may be, yes—all those things. Mad is perhaps what you mean. Like my father, like Uncle John. Perhaps . . ." The mention of John brought him a moment of calm again. "But I've still got to do it. And they'll believe me, you know. They'll accept it because they have thought it all along. That I murdered June."

"But Jordan—even if you did kill her, I don't care. If that's what you want to think, I don't care. But *she's* dead. She's dead! I'm not, I'm alive. Don't I count?"

"It won't be as bad as you think. Willy, I bear you no malice. It's outside all that—it's nothing to do with you. I'm so—"

"Nothing to do with *me?* I'm your wife, aren't I? I'm the mother of your child. You vowed to love me and to cherish me. Doesn't that mean anything to you at all?"

"Yes, it means something." He turned his head away. "But there's something more important than that."

"Oh God, haven't you any loyalty?"

He looked back at her, unyielding. He said slowly, "If you love something, somebody—"

"Love? And *what* do you love? What do you love?"

"I—I don't love you, Willy. I'm sorry. I was fond of you. I am fond of you—but I don't love you."

"What then? What?"

"The truth perhaps. Being true to something I'd forgotten all about, some part of me I deserted years ago. Or perhaps something I never really had."

"Annie. That Annie girl."

"What?"

"That Annie girl with her imbecile sister. I've seen the moon eyes you make at her after church. You think you're in love with her, don't you?"

"It's much more than—"

"A stupid schoolboy crush, and you want to break up our marriage and—and disgrace me and your whole family for a sloppy little—"

"It's more—"

"Let me tell you something, Jordan." Her face was hard. It was as if not flesh, but some unyielding substance, had been stretched across the bare bones and ruthlessly tightened. "You're incapable of love. You don't know what it means. You're weak. Feeble and weak. You always have been and you always will be. I thought once I could make a man out of you. But you're not a man. You're nothing. You're utterly contemptible."

He put his hand up to the grille between them. "Please stop this, Willy. I—"

"No—it's your turn to listen to me now. I hate you. I hate your stupid little schoolboy ways. I've hated you for years. I hated the way you couldn't ever do anything for yourself. I hated the way you touched me as though I was made of bone china. I hated you for what you are—a weak, contemptible, useless *thing!*"

He clung to the wire. He'd thought it was she who needed protec-

277

tion; he'd thought that he was invulnerable, that she could not touch him, that he was beyond wounds. He summoned his last scatterings of strength. "You . . . I didn't know such frustration was—"

"Frustration? Yes, I was frustrated alright." She stopped, and the wings of her nostrils became whitely transparent. "I was frustrated for a long time. But I found a cure."

"A cure . . ."

"A cure. A man. Don't you want to know his name?" There was something vulpine in the way she looked at him.

"No." He closed his eyes. "No, I don't."

"You wouldn't. You always try to avoid anything unpleasant. Well, I'm not going to let you avoid this. It was Tom, Tom Short."

He couldn't breathe. Suddenly there was no breath, only a furious churning where his lungs should have been. "Tom . . ."

"Yes, Tom. Would you like me to tell you how *he* makes love? He's a man, darling. A wonderful lover."

He opened his eyes, but the blood thumping in his head made him dizzy. He tried to push through the grille at her and he heard words which must be coming from his own mouth but which he did not understand.

"Stop it!' she whispered. "You're making an exhibition of yourself!"

He could feel her breath on his face through the wire.

"And don't call me a whore," he heard. "I never let Tom make love to me for money. It was desire, Jordan, sexual desire. Lust. Passion. Something you'll never know anything about."

"I'll . . ."

"What? *What* will you do? Kill him, is that what you were going to say? Kill Tom? My dear Jordan, you couldn't kill a fly except by accident. That's why the thought of you killing that little June is preposterous. You may be able to convince the police. You're quite smooth when you want to be, I'll admit that. But to anyone who knows you . . . I doubt if you even touched her. If you made love, all I can say is it can't have been much fun for her."

"Willy . . ."

"Oh, for heaven's sake, don't *plead* now, Jordan."

"You . . . this isn't going to make me change my mind. What-ever—"

"I don't care what you do with your piffling little mind. You can

278

confess to murdering the Archbishop of Canterbury for all I care."
She reached for her handbag, which rested on the ledge in front of
her.

"Wait a minute." There was something vital he had to know. He
fumbled desperately. "Do you want to marry him?" No, that wasn't
it

"I'll cross my own bridges, no thanks to you."

"How—how long?"

"My affair with Tom? Five or six years." She watched him coolly.

"Georgia?" he managed.

"I'm afraid I really couldn't say."

He was ill, fearfully ill—far worse than the pox, the pleurisy, the
choking lungs. The rampant fever sped like fire across the dry, dead
grass, delving into and burning up every corner of his quiet, certain
calm.

38

Five or six years ago. Six, five, four—four years ago. Four years ago
and six months.

They wouldn't leave him alone.

"I've brought Norah to back me up, old boy." Tom hunched his
shoulders in his overcoat.

"Now, Jordan, you must come over to us. We can't let you mope
here all by yourself."

"Cold as a mortuary in here."

"That's very sweet of you, er, Norah." He always found it hard
to remember her name. "But the hospital might ring any moment."

"I've taken care of all that. I asked them to ring us if they couldn't
get you here. You'll feel much better with one of Tom's whiskeys
inside you."

"Nothing much that isn't the better for a stiff drink, Jordan."

"Tom's right. They say it may be hours yet. They'll ring the minute
anything happens, and Tom will drive you straight over."

"So you can get as plastered as you want."

"And we are nearer to the hospital. Come and doze in front of our fire. You must be exhausted, poor thing, after—"

The phone rang, and Jordan picked it up on the ring. It was Willy's mother.

"No news yet, Celia."

"Poor thing. I expect it's the narrow hips—just like me. I sometimes think that's our only resemblance. Do you think I should come down? I'd like to come down. But she'd hate having Mother hovering around, wouldn't she?"

"You don't hover, Celia, you glide. But they've got everything well under control."

"You're a dear, Jordan. I always said there was more to you than met the eye. She sounded, well, almost brusque when I rang on Thursday. I was afraid she was upset about something. I mean something besides the baby."

"Oh that's just her manner, Celia. She doesn't really mean it."

"Yes yes, I know. Underneath lies a warm and loving heart. But sometimes I ask myself, Jordan, why does it have to lie so very deep? One has to dig and dig—and I can't manage much more than a trowel these days. So cold. Did I ever tell you I used to call Ned and Willy the Hot and the Cold? Yes, of course I did. All mod cons. Poor Ned. My fault, I'm sure—didn't change her nappies often enough, I expect. Well, you will ring me at once, won't you? I do hope it's a little boy."

"Of course, Celia."

"Goodbye then. Goodbye goodbye."

He turned with a smile to Norah. "I'd like to come then," he said. "It is a bit gloomy here. I keep thinking I hear the ghostly patter of little footsteps on the stairs."

"Ha ha. Throw some things into a bag and we'll be off, old man."

"I'm so glad, Jordan."

As he sat drinking a huge whiskey in her drawing room, he concluded, with mild surprise, that she really was glad to have him.

Tom kept disappearing and then coming back again, usually in time to refill Jordan's tumbler. He would sit down for a minute or two and then get up and look out of the window or poke the fire.

"Oh do stop fidgeting, Tom," Norah said at last. "Why don't you go and do some work?"

"Perhaps I will. I do have rather a heavy load. You won't think me rude, old man? Good. I shall be right on top of the phone, you know, so don't worry about it. And help yourself from the decanter, eh?"

When he'd gone, Norah smiled at Jordan. "He's a dreadful fidgety Phil."

"Rather like an expectant father himself."

"Yes, isn't he? It's his Welsh blood really."

"Tom's Welsh?"

"He likes to think he is." She sighed. "He feels it's an excuse for being temperamental. Although why he needs an excuse I don't know. I always think a temperament adds a bit of spice, don't you?"

"I suppose it does."

"We English are so deadly dull. I really get quite bored with myself sometimes." She laughed lightly.

He could not reply with any truth, so he poured himself more whiskey.

"Of course it's more difficult for us women. To be temperamental, I mean. We're so brought up to be retiring, it becomes second nature. and then, of course, something comes along when one's not supposed to be retiring and then one discovers one just doesn't know how to respond any more. If one ever did. Do you know what I mean?"

"The sort of vital spark's missing?" He was becoming hazy with drink.

"That's it. It's all sex, really, isn't it?"

"Sex? Well, sex isn't, er, everything."

"Not everything, but a great deal. I've never been very good at sex. I always imagined, before I married, it would come naturally. But it didn't. It's not so much that one feels one has failed—although of course one has failed—"

"Norah, heavens, you haven't failed." He took a huge swallow of whiskey.

"Oh yes, I have. But I don't mind that so much. After all, if one tries, the only alternative to success is failure. But at least one tried. No, it's not that. It's the feeling of being wasted. You know what I mean? One was meant for something, and somehow that something just never materialized. Am I embarrassing you?"

"No." And suddenly she wasn't.

"I'm so glad. Most men are embarrassed by that sort of thing. I'm a dreadfully silly woman, you know. And that makes it worse. Being

281

silly. If I had brains, maybe I wouldn't mind so much about not having anything else. I don't know why I'm talking to you like this."

"It doesn't matter why. Go on talking."

"I think I will have a whiskey now. It's Willy, I expect. Going to have a baby. Babies always make me talk. Perhaps it makes me realise what I've missed. Life or something like that. I don't usually drink, you know. I think if I started I might just go on and on and become one of those poor sad drunks. But it's alright with you here. I don't suppose I'll ever really talk to you again."

"Oh yes you will, Norah."

"You're a nice man." She sipped the drink he gave her. "No. And you'll forget what I've said. Why not? I once overheard a man at a party describe someone as 'eminently forgettable.' I knew at once he meant me. That's how I feel, so it must be true, mustn't it? Not that I'm complaining. Oh dear, people who say that really always are complaining, aren't they?"

"Yes. In a way I think they are. But there are times when complaints are definitely in order."

"Perhaps. At any moment the phone's going to ring and I'll go back to being forgotten. Do you ever feel forgotten?"

He watched the fire, feeling the heat of it in his cheeks. "No, I don't think I do. In fact, rather the opposite. I wish sometimes that I were forgotten."

"You don't know how lucky you are. But I expect it'll be better when you have a baby."

Jordan frowned at her. In the dark of the late afternoon she was remote.

"You don't know what I'm talking about, do you?"

He stood up and, back to the fire, looked down at her. "No," he said, "I'm not sure I do."

"Oh well, that's frank. Just silly me. Babbling. It's the drink, I expect."

He was too lazy with whiskey and warmth to pursue it. A little later he fell asleep in front of the fire, to be woken by Tom. "It's a daughter, old man. You lucky beggar. Mother and child both blooming. Come on, we'll be there in ten minutes."

Georgia had weighed four pounds, ten and a half ounces, and already could curl her hand around a finger. As he touched the minute, damp flesh, he had been moved to an inexpressible joy which had left him thick-tongued and awkward at Willy's bedside. He had listened to Tom's hearty garrulity, thinking only how curious it was for her to be lying palely abed and for him to be the healthy one.

39

The church bells rang and the sun shone, and he allowed himself to imagine a layer of new snow on the landscape. And for good measure, a robin would sing and the male holly blaze with scarlet as bright as a full-dress tunic.

Halfway down the lime avenue, by now, would be the little party from the rectory—Mary and Colin and Willy Benton. Cassocked and nervous over his Christmas sermon, Trevor had left earlier. Most of the villagers would be already settled, the pews murmurous and rustling with Sunday best. And Mr. Goff had certainly begun his annual off-key medley of Christmas carols.

Jordan was propped high with pillows in the bed. "Got to keep you sitting up, young man," the doctor had said. "You'll find it easier to breathe." He had turned to Miss Flanders: "See he doesn't slide down, Nurse."

"Yes, Doctor," said quiet, deft Miss Flanders, who slipped in and out without fuss or display, taking his temperature, pouring the medicine, changing the covered bowl into which he coughed the matter from his charged lungs, plumping the pillows. As though she were merely a smooth-working extension of his own body, he hardly noticed her.

But then he was too listless to notice anything very much. Drowsy. He would doze the whole time, he thought, if it had not been for the spasmodic bursts of coughing that came out of nowhere and convulsed him with the violence of an intemperate schoolmaster shaking a stupid boy, and left him weak, wet, and obscurely frightened.

Miss Flanders wiped his face with a damp flannel, dried him, removed the bowl, and gave him something tasting of peppermint to drink.

There was a pile of parcels at the bottom of his bed, just within reach of his foot. It was a tremendous and pointless effort to move, though. He would open the bright paper parcels tomorrow, or the next day perhaps. To smile and nod and cluck with pleasure and thanks were far beyond his powers now. But he enjoyed wondering vaguely what he had been given. It was odd how, as one grew larger, presents became smaller. When he was a boy, there had always been one or two big packages. The biggest and best—no, most expensive; the best was always John's puzzle—from Colin. But gifts from Colin were usually small now—tortoise-shell hairbrushes, a silver hip flask, gold dress studs, binoculars in an initialled leather case: the trappings of luxury, but to Colin's mind, essential, "Got to have binoculars, young-feller-me-lad. Always come in useful. Bird watching, race meetings, things like that."

Bird watching was not one of his hobbies. He thought of bird watchers as retarded adolescents at heart, whose libidinous impulses were secretly stirred by the intense study of our feathered friends because their knowledge of carnality had been fixed at the level of their prep school headmaster's final life lecture. The only use he had ever found for the binoculars had also partaken of voyeurism. From his rooms in college he had a view of one of the seedier hotels; and he had once briefly focussed upon the uncurtained chamber of an elderly lady exposing emaciated breasts.

The room became dim as he went into a light doze. It seemed to him that he was then in another room. A large room with a counter down one side and gloomy depths in the back. A shop of some sort. He looked down at his body and saw that he was naked. He didn't feel naked. The shop was filled with an amazing assortment of things: a tricycle hanging from the ceiling, a toy fort manned by broken soldiers, a set of fret saws, a blackbird in a cage—he couldn't make out if it was stuffed or alive. On the counter were displayed his binoculars, his silver hip flask, the leather box that contained his gold studs and, on a special stand of its own, a copy of Death Sentences. He realised with a start that everything in the shop belonged to him—all his suits on a string line, from the green tweed he'd bought last term to a tiny, tattered red soldier coat that he couldn't remember but knew must have been his. Just then, a man appeared behind the counter. The light was poor and it was difficult to see his face, but it seemed to be the doctor. Jordan shifted in trepidation. The doctor put both hands on the counter and leaned forward slowly. "And how long," he said in sombre medical tones, "has this been going on?"

"I don't know," said Jordan uneasily."

"What don't you know, dear?" asked Miss Flanders as she set down a cup of beef broth and a piece of toast cut into slender strips on a plate. "I expect you had a dream. I've brought you a little lunch."

He sipped his soup sleepily and watched Miss Flanders rearrange the fire. The doctor had, in fact, asked him just that question. It was difficult to know. He'd had a cough and a lingering cold all term. In the evening he would get very hot and the headaches would begin. Willy insisted on coming up to his rooms and feeding him with aspirins and hot lemon juice laced with whiskey. She always seemed to be fiddling with the fire or putting the kettle on the gas ring. She could not sit still and, however quiet she might be, her sharp jerky movements distracted him. But he found it more and more difficult to ask her to leave him alone. It had been a relief when term ended and he could come down and away from the clutches of her concern.

Then a couple of days after he had been consigned to bed and Miss Flanders had been installed, Aunt Mary came to tell him he had a visitor: "A friend from Cambridge." The only person he could think of was Frank Wade. But that was impossible because Frank was spending the vacation packing up contraceptives in Harrod's basement to pay off his debts.

"Hello, Jordan."

"What on earth are you doing here?" He felt a lacerating irritation.

"I heard you were ill." She smiled uncomfortably. "I thought I could be of help." He knew she was rather proud of having taken some advanced course with the Red Cross or something.

"I've already got a nurse," he said.

"I know—Miss Flanders. I thought I might be able to give your aunt a helping hand with the house. I mean, having an invalid . . . How are you, poor darling?"

Jordan closed his eyes. "Tired," he said. He wondered who had been so dotty as to summon Willy.

"Well, I'd better leave you to sleep." She had touched his hand. "Is there anything I can bring you?"

"How long are you going to stay?"

"Well, as long as I'm needed. As long as I can help."

"Mary'll make a housemaid of you if you don't watch out."

She laughed eagerly at his crumb of response. There was silence, and then she said, "Jordan, you don't mind me being here, do you?"

He opened his eyes. "Glad to have you aboard," he said, and almost immediately drifted off to sleep.

"A splendid girl, that friend of yours," Trevor had said to him a few days later. "Splendid. I can't think why you've kept her hidden away all this time." He gave his clergyman's chuckle.

"I am a sly boots." He was peevish with all his visitors. He found everyone very trying, even the doctor. The only exception was Miss Flanders.

"Ah yes. Very natural, my boy. A most interesting girl. She knows Menaggio quite well. From her description it has hardly changed at all from our day. Mary and I often used to spend our holidays there before . . ."

"Before I came on the scene?"

"Well, yes. Before the war, you know. And you know another thing we discovered? Colin was at school with Sir Reginald Benton, Willy's father. Amazing, really amazing."

"He must have been knighted young."

"Oh he wasn't a knight then. Ah, yes, ha ha. You seem in better spirits today, my boy. Am I wrong?"

Jordan was mildly disturbed at the family's enthusiastic appreciation of Willy. Only Colin seemed immune. "Remember you introducing us at Cambridge. Nice girl," he'd said and then gone on to tell Jordan not to worry about his degree—"An aegrotat will get you into Sutlif and Maddox alright." He laughed jovially. "This spot of bother will put paid to your military service, of course. I can't say I'm sorry. It'll be good to have you in the firm a bit earlier."

"Do you remember the last time I was ill in bed, with chicken pox, you sent me a case of Cox's Orange Pippins?"

"Apples. Did I? Did I now? That must have been in the war. I wonder how I got 'em."

Jordan's mind was often invaded with memories of that other illness. He put them away when he could, for, although they were dim, they had the peculiar habit of making him want to weep. This, like his bad temper, was, he guessed, the effect of the pleurisy, as everyone had agreed to call it.

He tried to be less ungracious to Willy because in a way he felt grateful to her. And also because, when his wrenching cough had become less violent, he was, to his great surprise, pricked with little pins of lust. She came in to clean his room every day, and she would stand by his bed, removing the objects from his bedside table and carefully dusting them. At such moments he was seized with the impulse of a lecherous old man to put his hand up her neat tweed skirt. Then she would move away and his spasm would pass, leaving him weak. He didn't know whether she had any inkling of his feeling—the extent of their physical contact had never been more than kisses hardly passionate enough to disturb her hairdo.

When in the New Year he was well enough not to need a nurse, Willy took over Miss Flanders' functions. She also inherited Miss Flanders' exemption from Jordan's bad temper. He talked to her quite a lot and, maybe because she made no demands upon him, he became comfortable with her. Comfortable and disturbed. More and more he caught himself imagining her naked. He was glad of the contagion that outlawed their physical connection.

"Jordan," she had said tentatively one day, "Jordan, I've got to go back to Cambridge next week."

"Do you? I am sorry. Why?"

"Well, I think I ought to. Mummy's been creating a bit and—and I don't want to outstay my welcome."

It didn't sound a very pressing engagement. "You've given Mary and Trevor more stimulation than they normally have in a month of Sundays. I'm sure they'd be awfully sorry to see you go.

"Would you?"

"Yes, of course I'd be sorry to see you go."

She came and sat on the bed and held his hand. "Would you really?"

"Yes, of course. What is this all about?"

She counted his fingers. "The doctor says you're going to need looking after for quite a long time."

He smiled at her head bent over his hand.

"Jordan. I'd be willing to look after you. I'd *like* to look after you." She looked up at him.

"I don't know how we could manage that, Willy." But as he said it, he suddenly knew only too well how it could be managed.

"If you'll have me," she said, as though she had not heard him.

"Get married?" His hand began to tremble in hers.

"We could live with Mummy until you get your degree, so I could really take care of you. And then you won't be going in the army now.

287

will you? So you could go straightaway to work for Uncle Colin and we could find a nice house nearby, so that it wouldn't be too tiring for you. Getting to work, I mean."

He was not fully aware of what she was saying, although he heard himself answering that it sounded like a grand idea. He was only conscious that he was gripping her hand very tightly in his and that she was evidently willing to forget all about contagion for the moment—"Just this once," she murmured before he kissed her. And then she was lying beside him. Before very long, the immaculate skirt was above her knees and his lecherous hand deep between her smooth white thighs.

They announced their engagement to the family next day, and in *The Times* two days later.

"Of course, you'll have to take things easy," said Trevor on the first day Jordan was allowed downstairs, for tea before the living-room fire. "And that means there's no possibility of a first now. What a pity, after your close miss in the first part of the tripos. Still, we must remember, my boy, there are many things more worthwhile on this earth than academic distinction."

It was a fantastically magnanimous remark, and Jordan curbed his smile. He felt faintly ridiculous with a rug over his knees and united benevolence mantling him at every turn.

"You mustn't overdo it, darling," said Willy as he took another chicken-and-ham paste sandwich.

"One more won't do him any harm, Willy my dear. Build him up." And Aunt Mary smiled benignly.

It was a weird sensation to be thus cosseted and, if it had not made him inexplicably uneasy, he would have found it diverting. He thought of the line, "The condemned man ate a hearty breakfast," but it didn't amuse him as it should.

They were pleased—even Colin, up for the weekend—to have him safely set for marriage, a good marriage. He was easily tired and still very feeble—were they pleased at that too, pleased to have him at their mercy? The imagination of the sick. Yet as he looked round at them, he was inescapably reminded of another, similar scene in this room. More than four years ago. Mr. Mansard had partaken of that funeral tea, but otherwise it was the same. Except, of course, it had been Annie, not Willy, who had passed round the cups of tea and proffered the sandwiches and lifted the lid from the crumpet plate.

It was on the tip of his tongue to ask, "Do you remember . . . ?" But he didn't need to. From their very cheeriness he could read the answer. They remembered alright.

He shook his head.

"Anything the matter, darling?"

"Just a touch of heartburn."

40

"Hello—tea."

"Hello, Annie."

"Ah, the cup that refreshes."

Outside it was cold and greyly raining. Inside it was dim, but still too early in the afternoon to light the lamps. Aunt Mary treated the onset of darkness as though it were a disease which it would be weakness to admit until the last possible moment. And yet, although it was still October, she had caused a fire to be lit—not usually allowed until November the first. The fire smoked uneasily and threw little warmth into the living room. They sat round it closely.

"The fire could do with a bit of livening up," said Colin, reaching for the poker.

"I'll do it, Colin. Let me." Trevor woke out of his musing stare and picked up the poker and got to his knees. But energy seemed to desert him; he pushed the poker listlessly four or five times into the heart of the fire and then let it drop with a rattle. He had succeeded only in loosening a little slack, which trickled down to extinguish a single preliminary sprout of flame. He reached up to the mantelpiece and pulled himself to his feet.

"Tea, Trevor dear," called Mary. He turned with a vague murmur and took the cup which Annie proffered him with lowered eyes and subdued movement. Her black church clothes were unadorned with the usual apron, Jordan noticed. Her servile status had been temporarily mitigated by the common grief, though not sufficiently for Aunt Mary to ask her to sit down to tea with them.

Common grief. What were they grieving for, thought Jordan as he watched Trevor stir his tea round and round? Not for Uncle John. Perhaps they were grieving for their absence of grief. Or for this sudden, unhappy intrusion into the even tenor of their days.

He still did not know what had really happened. Late last night he had gone to the rectory chapel where John's body lay. But the lid of the coffin had already been screwed down, as though the corpse were something shameful, better unseen. As he watched the coffin jerkily lowered into the grave this afternoon, Jordan knew that he would always wonder what John had looked like in death. Had the jaw been set strong, or slack? Had those always so wide-open light blue eyes really been shut? Had anyone thought to clip and brush the military moustache? And had they arrayed him in his colonel's full-dress regimentals?

He knew the answer to the last. There had been not the faintest touch of fanfare to the funeral. In church they had sung thinly, "Fight the good fight with all thy might," but Jordan could not bring himself to carry the shallow tune. He thought of the way it ought to have been, of the way it might have been. He thought of Moore at Corunna. The solemn steps of upright men, the muffled drum, the lowered flag, the last salute. Instead, they had stood coldly and without ceremony in the drizzle, Trevor muttering over the grave and Mansard twitching slightly, his lonely Defence Medal pinned back to front on his surplice. They hadn't even asked a representative of the regiment, for which Lieutenant-Colonel John Freeman, D.S.O., M.C., had sacrificed the full sunny use of his reason not really so very long ago. It seemed to Jordan, angrily, that they had let John go in bitterness, without any of those things—military honours, they call it—which might have in some sense restored the order of an old dignity.

"Why didn't you get a bugler to play the last post?" he heard himself ask.

There was silence and then the quick motion of spoons in teacups.

"I mean, couldn't you at least have sent over to Istoke barracks for a bugler? He was a battalion commander . . . "

Trevor murmured something about "no fuss."

"We thought things were better left as they were, dear," said Aunt Mary firmly, but in her voice that odd deference which both she and Trevor had shown him since yesterday.

"John," said Trevor, blinking his eyes, "John didn't have much to do with the regiment in his later years, you know."

No. He was warned away. Not allowed out. Cut off from even the small remnants of regimental life and memory.

"What the Lord giveth the Lord taketh away," said Mr. Mansard, and immediately blushed and bowed his head over a piece of crumbled seed cake.

Jordan's anger slipped back into the recess from which it had briefly broken out.

"I think—I think," said Colin, "that I'd like a whiskey and soda, Mary my dear, if you don't mind, instead of this tea."

"Of course, Colin. How thoughtless of me." She rang the bell briskly, startling Mr. Mansard. "Annie, Mr. Sutlif would like a whiskey and soda."

"Very well, ma'am." Annie nodded. Everyone in the room was content to watch her as she deftly mixed the drink. It seemed to give them an excuse for stirring, wiping their lips, putting down their cups —movements which a moment before might have broken the fragility of the normal taken-for-granted tea-and-crumpet calm. Wordless fulfillment of her duty freed Annie from any pretence of community of spirit. And yet, Jordan thought, she seemed more than ordinarily aloof. She was not going one inch beyond the dutiful. She would not look at Jordan.

Annie handed Colin his drink and went over to the fireplace. With a sure, quick hand she attended to the fire, and, a minute after she left the room, it began to catch and then blaze.

"Ah," said Colin, "that's better."

Aunt Mary said, "I'm so glad no one sent a wreath or anything of that kind. Simple garden flowers are so much more suitable. What a pity the best was over."

Colin cleared his throat. "Mary, I think Jordan and I should go back tonight, you know."

"Oh dear, we were looking forward to having you for the night, weren't we, Trevor?" Mary looked at her brother. He nodded slowly. His usually bland countenance was set in a deep frown. Now, as he looked up, the reflected flames of the fire danced in the lenses of his glasses, concealing his pale eyes.

"Is it still raining?" he said. The windowpanes were beaded and glistening.

"Yes, Trevor dear." As though afraid of something her brother might say, Mary turned back to Colin. "I'm afraid you'll have a wet drive back."

"I'm afraid so. Very busy time of year for me. So if you don't mind, Mary . . ."

Mr. Mansard coughed shyly. "Dear dear. What a great pity. I always think slippery roads are such a death trap." He was staring at his empty teacup. "But of course you have a driver." He ventured to glance up. "Your driver . . ."

Mary brought her protuberant eyes silently to bear on the curate. Then she sniffed and turned her head sharply. "Yes, of course, Colin. And I'm sure Jordan is anxious to be back at school too."

"You've got a match tomorrow, haven't you, young-feller-me-lad?"

Jordan looked at Mansard, as though he had asked the question, and smiled. "There is a match tomorrow, but I'm not playing. I'm not really part of the team, only a substitute."

Mr. Mansard nodded tremblingly. "Ah. You're a soccer school, aren't you? I recollect when I—"

"Really, Mr. Mansard, where are your ears?" Aunt Mary snapped. "I should have thought you'd heard us talking about school matches often enough to know rugger—"

Jordan interrupted, "We used to be a soccer school years ago. I expect that's what you're thinking of, isn't it, sir? And we still do play a bit, but not seriously. I don't know which headmaster it was that changed us over to rugger."

"Ah, but I think I do." Mr. Mansard smiled shyly. "What can I have been thinking of? It must have been Winstanley. A great headmaster. One of the great modern headmasters. A quite remarkable appointment at the time. It was considered so. He was very young, you know. As a matter of fact, you wouldn't believe it, but I had once been his fag . . ." Mr. Mansard chattered happily on. Poor old chap. For the first time Jordan saw the clergyman's innocent humility as endearing, as well as pathetic. The end of the war had been the end of the most important job of Mr. Mansard's life, as a sector captain for the local fire watchers. A conscientious and totally inefficient commander, his fire watchers had held him in affectionate contempt and, towards the end of the war, would seldom report for duty. Uncomplainingly Mr. Mansard took over their patrols himself. Danger had only come to Sibley once, when in the early days the low drone of a

292

lost German bomber had been followed by a faint crump. Almost the whole village had turned out at two o'clock in the morning to search for the bomb. But it had been Mr. Mansard who had discovered it. Running excitedly across the hundred-acre field, he had fallen flat into the shallow crater, breaking his glasses and grazing his hands and face rather badly on the gravel. It had been a great hour for the curate as for the first and only time the first-aid kit had been brought out and his wounds dressed and tended. "Our bomb," he still talked of it with deprecatory pride, "our little bit of excitement."

Mr. Mansard's present ramblings were tolerated because he was under Jordan's protection. It was as if they—Mary and Trevor—were afraid of their nephew, fearful of what he might say, of an outburst.

At length the curate's timidity reasserted itself and his rambling monologue faded and died. There was silence.

And suddenly Jordan could not bear it. He stood up. They watched him. For a moment he thought that if he picked them all up and shook them together, like rattled dice they might come out six or three or maybe just one.

"You, er, want to do a little exploring, I expect, my dear?" Aunt Mary said.

"I'm going to get a breath of fresh air."

"Wrap up well, my dear. We don't want to send you back to school with a cold, do we? Dinner is at half past seven. You won't be late, will you?"

Trevor came to life. "Jordan, before you go out, I wonder if you'd spare me a minute?"

"Now?"

"If it would be convenient. As you're leaving tonight."

The study was dark and chilly, but Trevor didn't turn on the lights. He went over to his desk as if to put it between them, for he didn't sit down.

"Well?" said Jordan abruptly.

Trevor turned his head to the window. "Everything's left to you," he said in a muffled voice.

"What are you talking about?"

"I mean the will. The terms of the will. Everything goes to you."

"John left everything to me?"

Trevor seemed to retreat a little at the mention of the name. "The sole beneficiary. Yes. It wasn't the, well, original will. Not the one we drew up some years ago. This is a recent one, very recent. But of course your aunt and I wouldn't dream of, er, disputing it. No."

"How recent? When did John make it?"

"Let's see, it's dated, yes. Last Sunday. There were no witnesses, of course, but . . ."

"The day he died."

"As a matter of fact, yes. Jordan, my boy, this is all very painf—"

"In the previous will, I was not the sole beneficiary?"

"Quite. Er, your aunt and I . . ."

"What did he leave me? What did he have to leave?"

"Not a great deal, my boy. There are the effects of course, the personal effects. I think Mary would like to distribute the clothes in the village, with your permission, naturally."

"Not the regimentals."

"Oh naturally not. If you wish not, of course. And then there is the workroom and, er, these." He slid open a desk drawer and took out, one by one, six small leather-covered boxes. "His medals. I used to keep them here for—safekeeping."

"What else?"

"Well, there was a little money. Let me see, I had a note of the balance in the last statement. Yes, two hundred and forty-three pounds, seventeen shillings and twopence. And the holding in Freeman's Ales. We all were left a holding in Freeman's Ales, you know. One thousand shares. A small but respectable income. Small but respectable."

Jordan picked up the medal cases and held them in his hand. It was odd, but in all these years he had never seen Uncle John's medals. "That's all?"

"Yes, well, indeed I think so. There may be one or two odds and ends."

Jordan went to the door. He stood by it and looked back to the gloom in which his uncle was merely a darker patch. "Two hundred and forty-three pounds, you said?"

"More or less."

"Less?"

"There will be fees, you know." Trevor's voice was hoarse. "Connected with probating."

"And I suppose," Jordan said as he opened the door, "you'll want to deduct something for the loss of your fig tree."

294

Trevor gave forth a queer little sighing gasp. Jordan felt not the slightest pang of pity.

41

He turned up his coat collar and stepped out into the rain. As he walked down the drive, he marked the footprints of the returning funeral party which had formed innumerable small lakes in the soft gravel.

He halted at the iron gates. They had never been closed that he could recall. On either side a high wall, topped with broken glass, encircled the rectory gardens and orchard.

"Take a brigade to defend this position. If you wanted to defend it, that is." Jordan stiffened at John's short bark of a laugh.

They had started here when he was tiny and could hardly keep his feet without John's strong hand grasping his. They moved left, within the rectory grounds, along a little path close to the wall and darkened with tall pine trees. "No field of fire here. Couldn't stop a pack of determined fuzzy-wuzzies. They'd slip over the wall and you'd never spot 'em in all this damn greenery." John's stride lengthened and his step quickened—as it always did when he began to talk of soldiering —until he was almost dragging Jordan along by his side.

"Uncle," he said, "Uncle John."

"Too fast for you, Jordan? Up you come then." With a lithe, easy movement he swung the little boy onto his shoulders. "A sharp look-out, now. Eyes skinned for those fuzzy-wuzzies." They marched through the five-acre grounds like an army. Across the lawn, through the asparagus beds, ducking under the arch which led to the orchard where the dusty apple leaves brushed against his face. Down to the round pond green with duckweed, and back again. Stopping every so often for John to discuss the tactical advantages of holding or abandoning a patch of wall. "Leave this section unmanned, don't you think? Put a platoon behind this hedge, another along the ditch there. Absolutely clear field. Over they come and you rake them with enfilading fire. Splendid, eh, Jordan? Wither 'em. Wither 'em."

High on his perch, clutching John's hair with both hands, Jordan echoed excitedly, "Wither 'em, wither 'em."

"That's the spirit." John gave his sharp laugh. They returned slowly, circling the old stables and the dovecote where the doves purred softly. "Unreliable birds. Can never count on carrier pigeons." Past the curate's house, through the herb garden, then Jordan was lifted down and deposited at the kitchen door. "Fine reconnoitre, Jordan. Thank you."

Jordan opened the door and went into the kitchen.

Annie was getting the plates out and stacking them on the trolley for dinner. She paused. "Hello."

"Hello, Annie."

He turned to the old-fashioned range. Behind the bars the fire gleamed with secret brightness.

"Been for a walk then?"

"A reconnoitre," he said. He turned down the collar of his jacket.

"You're wet."

Jordan pulled out a chair and sat down. He touched his damp hair and then held out his hands to the grate. Behind him the rattle of plates began again, then stopped. He became aware of Annie standing beside him in the semidarkness of the kitchen.

"A reconnoitre?"

"That's what he used to call it."

She drew up a chair and sat down. He looked at her. The redness of the fire was reflected on her cheeks.

"What did happen, Annie?"

"Don't you know?"

"They don't want me to know."

"No wonder. They killed him."

"They killed him?" He observed her in puzzlement.

"Near as no matter." Her lips tightened.

"I'm not defending them, Annie, but Uncle Trevor *is* upset and—"

"Him!" said Annie contemptuously. "You know what's on his mind, don't you?"

"Yes," Jordan said slowly. "He's mourning the loss of his fig tree."

"That. And something else."

"What?"

"Consecrated ground."

"I don't understand."

"He's worried about his stupid consecrated ground. Someone that commits suicide isn't supposed to be buried in a churchyard, you know." Her voice took on the simpering tones of Uncle Trevor. " 'If a man dies by his own hand. Canon law is quite specific on that point. It is most distressing. I must wrestle with my conscience.' I heard him telling her. If Colonel John doesn't deserve to be buried on consecrated ground, no one does. And his own brother!" She looked at Jordan fiercely.

"He's always been like that, Annie. I don't think he means any harm."

"Oh doesn't he? You can do plenty of harm without meaning it. But don't tell me he isn't pleased when he has to tell somebody something cruel for their own good. You can hear it in that rector's voice of his. How often have I heard him say to Mum, 'That Emerald of yours, Mrs. Brierly, is a hopeless case,' he says. 'It would really be more responsible of you to send her to an institution where she could receive proper care.' As if Mum didn't love Emerald especially because she is the way she is, and look after her a sight better than any silly institution could. Mum gets that upset, but of course she just sits there and says, 'Yes, Rector. No, Rector.' And I tell you he enjoys it, being all smug and wise, and upsetting Mum that much, so when he leaves she runs upstairs and cries her eyes out." She got up and poked the fire hard so that sparks flew, and sat down again.

Her voice was quieter when she spoke. "And her—she's worse, Miss Freeman is. What she did to Colonel John. The way she treated him. You know what he wanted Sunday night?"

"No."

"A fire, that's what he wanted. A fire in his room." She laughed and turned her head away abruptly. "He'd had a cold, you see. All week he'd been sniffling round the house. He would sit up there freezing to death in that attic. And of course he wouldn't drink the hot milk I used to bring him."

"You went up there, to his workroom?"

"Of course I did. No one else would. They were just happy he was out of mischief. And then Sunday at supper, as I was handing round the stewed pears, Colonel John says, 'Mary, I want a fire in my room tonight.' You know the way he does—did—sudden, like he was in the army. Miss Freeman didn't say anything, just went on ladling out the syrup onto the plate. Then he says, 'Mary, did you hear what I said?'

She sighs as though she's being tried beyond endurance. And she says, 'John dear, you know perfectly well there are no fires before November. And we never allow fires in the bedroom unless somebody is ill.' Colonel John waits a minute, then says, 'I am ill. I've got a cold. I want a fire.' And the rector just sat there eating his pears and junket without saying a word. And then Colonel John says it doesn't have to be a large fire, a small fire will do. His bones are cold, he says.

"She wouldn't answer him for ever so long. At last she says, 'Please don't force me to repeat myself.' And at that he drops his spoon on his plate and gets up. And he's shaking all over, like he always did when he was angry. And he runs up to his room and you could hear him stamping up and down, up and down. After a bit he quietened down. Then I was just in the middle of washing up when I hear this horrible noise. A kind of wrenching noise—as though some big animal was tearing the house apart. He'd chucked himself out of the window and pulled the fig tree with him. The whole thing came away with him, broke right off clean at the bottom. He must have been terribly strong to do a thing like that. I ran out, and the rector and her. All the doves were fluttering and clucking. The rector had a torch, but we couldn't see much at first. Just a great heap of leaves and branches. You'd never have thought there could be so many leaves. And then the wall—the rector shone his torch up. It was worse the next day in the light—all raw. Suddenly the mistress sees an arm poking out of the leaves. 'It's John,' she screams. 'Get in the house,' the rector tells me. But I wouldn't go. He was dead—he fell straight on his head and broke his neck." She turned her face to Jordan, and she was weeping.

"He knew what smashing that tree would mean to the rector. Like paying them off for all those years. And it served them right, it just served them right. They never understood him. They treated him like a naughty child. Ever since that Greta Candle led him on. As if everyone didn't know it was her fault. They never loved him. They just punished him. And he wasn't a child. Or if he was—well, they should have loved him and been kind to him, shouldn't they? He was the only one in this place with a bit of life to him. I think that's what they hated him for, really."

Jordan gently touched her hand. They sat silent, until slowly her tears dried. "The strangest thing of all was he was naked. That shocked them more than anything. Quite naked he was when we pulled him out. The mistress runs off to telephone and the rector grabs hold of handfuls of leaves and puts them over his body. I felt like laughing somehow. The wind kept blowing the stupid leaves off him. The rector didn't say a word. He just grabs more and more leaves. I could hear him sort of panting. What did he think he was hiding anyway?"

Rain flicked at the kitchen windows. Otherwise the rectory was quiet.

Annie rose. "I've got to get home."

"Aren't you staying to serve dinner?"

"It's cold. They can serve themselves." She shut the stove door with the poker and got her black coat and hat from the pantry.

Jordan helped her on with her coat. "I'll walk home with you," he said.

"You'll get wet."

"It doesn't matter."

She hesitated. "Jordan—you feel like I do about, about him, don't you?"

"Yes."

They didn't speak as they went down the drive and through the gates and along the road past the church.

Annie stopped by the war memorial. She pointed. "They ought to put his name on there."

"Yes."

The rain softened a little and a few leaves blew along the road.

"I'm giving in my notice tomorrow," Annie said.

Jordan faced her. "Why?" The thought of her leaving was unbearable.

"I've had enough. I only stayed because of Colonel John. Besides, we don't need the money."

"Annie, please don't go."

"Why shouldn't I?"

"Because . . ." The rain was wet on his face and the clouds raced high above. "Because I don't want you to." There was a thickness in his throat. "I want you to stay."

"Well, I don't know about that."

"I'd miss you. I'd miss you very much."

"But you're not here most of the time."

"But when I am here. It's not just the rectory being empty and lonely. I miss you even when I'm not here."

"Well, I don't know about that," she said, and her voice quavered. "You never told me about that."

He took her hand and moved close to her. "That's because I didn't know until now. Until this evening."

She gave a little laugh. "You're just saying that because you're sad." Her face was against his and she said into his ear, "You're a funny one."

"You won't leave, will you?"

"Alright. Not if you don't want me to."

"Promise?"

He felt the movement of her cheek as she smiled. "Cross my heart and hope to die."

Hand in hand they walked to the post office.

"Annie, if I write to you, you'll answer, won't you?"

"Yes, Jordan, I will." She bent forward and kissed him. "You better be off before Mum sees us. She'd never get over me holding hands with Master Jordan from the rectory."

He walked back along the mean, grey street, not noticing the puddles he stepped in.

He was soaked through, but he held his head up and let the rain fall on his face. He put his hands in his pockets and touched the leather medal cases.

He entered the rectory by the kitchen door and went quietly up the back stairs to John's bedroom. He shut the door behind him and, as he stood in the centre of the room, it seemed to him that already the typical smell was fading. Tobacco and tweed and bay rum and the faint sweetish scent of John's skin.

There was water still in the willow-pattern jug on the washstand. But the soap was a dry sliver on its dish.

Jordan pulled back the bedspread. The bed was unmade, and the black and white stripes of the mattress stared up at him. He left the spread crumpled. It made up, a little, for the emptiness—the immaculate neatness. As though it had always been like this: spick and span, black and white, neat and decent.

He moved across the room and opened the window. Below, a faint illumination came from the living room. Mary would have drawn the curtains at last. But there was enough light to show the dark grass and the black wounds made by the plunging branches of the fig tree. The tree itself had gone—carted off, chopped up probably, and already stacked for burning.

Jordan turned away from the window, leaving it open. It was proper that the rain and the night should be allowed to drift in. He stared at the empty grate which shone dully with black lead. He saw Aunt Mary on her knees rubbing the ornate iron, polishing away any trace of Uncle John.

He opened the top drawer in the chest. John's handkerchiefs lay in a squared-off pile in the corner. Then, carefully arranged, his pipe and pouch, a tamp to push the tobacco down, a penknife, a yellow pencil with a broken point, a worn notebook, a length of post-office twine, two paper clips, a crocodile wallet, six shillings in silver, and a boiled sweet.

In an instinctive act of preservation, Jordan gathered them together and put them into an old green canvas suitcase he found under the bed. From the wardrobe he took Uncle John's faded regimentals and folded the long red tunic and the blue trousers as John had long ago shown him how: tunic four folds, trousers three. He laid them in the suitcase and added the medal cases and the box of miniatures, gold studs and cufflinks; he filled the remaining space with shirts and socks and John's everyday suit of snuff-brown tweed.

He carried the case up to the attic.

He hadn't been in the workroom for three years. He was surprised —somehow he had expected it to be disordered with dust and aimless despair, as though in his absence all must disintegrate. But it was the same as ever in its military exactness: the ranks of tools, the saws dull with oil, the lengths of wood graded and stacked. The only thing missing was any sign of work in progress.

He put down the case and reached under the work table. Slowly he pulled out the wooden waste bin. He stared at it for a long time without moving. It was full to the top. So John had worked, so the tools had been used. It was filled with the curious shapes of a puzzle —an enormous puzzle. With a swift thrust Jordan tipped the bin, and the jigsaw pieces spilled onto the floor. He bent and picked one up. He turned it over in his palm. It was blank. He knelt down and quickly began to turn them all—the ancient preliminary for all solutions. And all were blank. Smooth-grained, clean-cut, not a rough edge among them. But every one blank.

At last he gathered them in his hands and pushed them back into the bin, pressing down hard against the springiness of the wood.

He looked round the little room slowly, counting and naming. Wood, metal, cloth—and human beings. He would not forget John's years of joyless, pointless labour. He swore it aloud. Not to forget.

As he shut the door and locked it, he was filled with this glad determination. And it would not be him alone. There was Annie now. There had always been Annie, but he hadn't known it. Together they would preserve John's memory. In them, John would continue to live —as he had been, quick and joyful in the old games of war.

Together they would make it up to him.

He put the key in his pocket and went downstairs to supper.

42

Prison Officer Denver edged through the half-open door and dumped the tray on the table. "Ben's best breakfast. Let's see what he put up for you today." He pulled the green-baize covering from the high-sided wooden tray and lifted the lid of the plate. "Sausages, eggs and tommy-artoes. Smells good, don't it?"

Jordan had risen early, long before the lights were turned on. He had smoked continuously, and he could feel the walls of his stomach sticking emptily together. He'd been standing in the corner, halted by a thought which he'd lost when Denver came in.

He went over and looked down at the food.

"Makes you hungry, don't it?"

Jordan shook his head. It did not repel him, this sight of already congealing fried breakfast, but it had absolutely nothing to do with him. He couldn't imagine ever having eaten food. He was not even sure he remembered how to manipulate a knife and fork.

"You want to be like them eggs, Maddox. Keep your sunny side up."

"Sunny side up?"

Denver grinned. "That's what they call 'em in America. Fried eggs —sunny side up."

"You've been to America?"

Denver didn't answer for a moment, then said quietly, "Yes. I was a seaman before the war. Got about a bit. Saw the world, as they say."

"Oh yes. Yes of course. You told me."

Denver put the cover back on the dish. "You ain't half got a fug in here. Like a bit of fresh air?"

Jordan looked up at the window. "I don't know." It was extraordinarily difficult to make a decision. "I don't think so—perhaps. I'm a bit chilly."

Denver frowned. "Are you alright, lad?"

Jordan turned to him. "Yes, I think so. I'm just not hungry today."

"I can get the M.O. up here in two shakes if you feel a bit funny."

"No, I'm okay." Sorry—I mean *alright*. Where did that come from?

"Well, if you say so. He'll be round this afternoon anyway. Governor's inspection today, too. After chapel. You'll be ready for that, won't you?"

"The governor's inspection." He felt baffled—there was something there at the edge of his mind, almost at his fingertips, but . . .

"Every Sunday, remember? Hardly makes it a day of rest, but he's got to do it. All in prison regs."

"I don't mind." Or did he? Yesterday he would have known quite clearly, but he could hardly recall yesterday.

"They don't mean no harm." Denver looked at him anxiously. "The gov's a good bloke. He does try to be human. Look, mate, you'll feel better when it's all over. Try an' eat some of Ben's breakfast, won't you?"

"Will they court-martial me if I don't?"

Denver smiled. "That's better."

"I'll be very quickly convicted." He smiled back.

"Now, now, Maddox, you got no call to talk like that. You take it easy today, forget about it."

Jordan stared at him. "Oh, that!" he said suddenly. He paused. "I will be convicted though, Denver."

"Now you can't know that—why do you want to think like that?"

He remembered now what he had to ask. "I want to see the governor."

"He'll be round after chapel, like I said."

"No—I mean alone." To confess—that's what he'd been reaching for. He was at once impatient.

"A private interview? Oh yes, that's easy. He'll probably be able to give you a few minutes on his rounds."

"Before lunch?"

"Yes, that's right, before lunch."

Jordan quickly lit a cigarette. He offered one to Denver.

"No thanks. Can't smoke on duty." The word seemed to recall him. He tugged at his tunic. "Well, I'll have a look in later on. Exercise this afternoon, alright? If you want anything, give us a yell." He went to the door. "Maddox?"

"Yes, what is it?"

"Do me a favour, will you, and have a go at them eggs?" He nodded and was gone.

Eggs! Suddenly he knew he loathed Denver's anxious kindliness. Food, fresh air, comfort, concern . . . Irish stew!

Do me a favour—he had spent his life doing favours. Doing what they said was best for him, following doctor's orders, wryly taking his medicine for the sake of . . . of what? A cure? Hardly. To confirm his invalid status, someone who needed looking after, needed protection. Like Uncle John.

He sat down abruptly on the bed. A finger of ash fell onto his shirt and he brushed it away, leaving a dark smudge.

Like Uncle John. Good God. He, Jordan, had always accepted their ministrations as though he were a sick man. Always? Not always—his mind spun back to his childhood like a tossed penny. No, not then. Slap, he caught it on the back of his hand and looked.

When John died. That was when. To the very day—to the first moment of Mr. Prideaux's silver-jangling hand-in-pocket sympathy. From a functionless object of neglect, he had become a creature of sympathy. Colin, Trevor—even, in her disdainful fashion, Mary. And, most of all, Annie. Willy. June. He had become pitiable even to Georgia. He attracted pity, like venom, from mankind—womankind—and, like venom, it paralyzed him. A slow death.

But he had accepted it obediently, an obedience only reinforced by humorous protest. He had stretched out his hand, not to take, but for support.

He had been obedient always to what was wanted for him, not to what he wanted. He hadn't failed the world—their world, wrinkled with desiccation and pudgy as an old boxing glove. He'd done what it wanted, saluted its face, done his duty by its commands. The perpetual lamb, shorn and sad-eyed.

He got up and walked quickly up and down the room. He rubbed his face with his hands.

Like John, he had submitted to sacrifice. Uncle John, the very openness of whose innocence had invited destruction—the long sweet cruelty with which humanity revenges itself for its own failure. And Jordan, too, had been a member of that subtle alliance in which each joins to ridicule and crush such faultless life. How often had he stepped up to the attic, stood at the workshop door, waiting—waiting for what? For some lovely trumpet that shall never call retreat—at the sound of which all, without doubt and at once, will join in the universal jubilance? What had he waited for? What had he wanted?

He spoke aloud. "What do I want?"

The rusty machinery of desire shuddered against the encrustation of years of disuse. Love? When had he not moved in a loveless, passionless country? Mary rasping out the thin affection of greetings and farewells. Willy indulgently permitting the invasion of her sex. And Annie—who knew what secret charms abnegation held? Jordan knew. For years he had fondled it.

No longer. That's what he wanted. No longer to placate life with submission. No longer to give up. His change of plea was not a placation of the ghosts of the past. Not compensation. But repudiation—repudiation of his years of mortuary service to them.

There came into his head the doleful chorus of the Armistice Day dirge—"We will remember them." On the contrary, he would forget them. To hell with them. To hell with . . .

He glanced up. The governor stood in the doorway, his retinue behind him.

"Everything alright, Maddox?" Major Forster cocked his head on one side and his mouth crumpled into a tiny, fluted smile, as much as to say that any complaints would be kindly treated as the product of a harmlessly deranged mind.

"Yes."

"You have something of a reputation as a model prisoner, Maddox. Still doing those puzzles of yours, eh?" He wrinkled his lips. "Bit stuffy in here, isn't it? Well, I hear you want to have a word with me."

"Alone."

Major Forster glanced at his watch. "Won't take long, I suppose? No. Right." He turned to the deputy governor behind him. "Perhaps you'd carry on in the ward, Wilton."

Jordan waited until the others had gone. "I wish," he said, "to confess to the murder of June Singer."

The governor's head jerked quickly. "Hold on. Let's be sure I understand, and you understand, what you are saying. You wish to confess to the crime for which you are being tried, is that it?"

"Yes."

Major Forster was no longer jolly. But his hasty assumption of gravity suddenly infuriated Jordan. "Well?" he snapped.

"Yes, quite." The governor glanced sidelong. "You have, I presume, discussed this with your solicitor?"

"Yes."

The governor paused, and then, briskly, "Well, the correct procedure is for you to make a statement, a written statement, which I shall, of course, at once submit to the proper authorities. The police—"

"I'll write it myself."

The governor nodded and stepped back. "You know the form. Got pen and paper? Good. Well, I'll leave you to it then. Date it and sign it. When you've finished, let them know. I'll leave instructions that it is to be brought straight to me. And then . . . You know that you can simply change your plea to guilty?"

"I'll do it this way."

"Right. Yes. Get it down in black and white. I'll leave you to get on with it, Maddox."

He heard the governor talking to the orderly at the end of the corridor. Then a door slammed and there was silence. It was as if the prison—all London—had been deserted. A soft, diffuse sunlight shone through the dusty window, waxed, faded, then grew stronger.

Jordan reached out and turned on the wireless. It hummed for a moment and then, in rising volume: ". . . band of the King's Royal Rifle Corps, under the direction of Captain G. Cutler, will conclude

Sunday Bandstand with their own regimental march: 'Lutzow's Wild Hunt' . . ."

The swift, jerky tune struck into the cell at top volume. Jordan turned his face to the window, holding the beat in his mind, remembering every note. Suddenly the music was split by the high blare of silver bugles. Bugles and fanfares, trumpets and drums—beating out the victories of the past: of Blenheim and Dettingen and Minden and Salamanca and Waterloo. John had heard them, lively and pure, until one day they had all marched past and gone away. But his death had restored that triumphant music over the thin crackle of Sibley, where so few demands were made, so few desires fulfilled. Death for the sake of life, like old Mrs. Singer for June. The last unanswerable victory of an old soldier who chose death on the battlefield over the dim, cruel sadness of just fading away.

And Jordan, having sworn always to remember John, had forgotten him. In that forgetfulness he had himself, as a living being, disappeared. But now he had come to the surface. Now he understood.

And now he knew what he wanted. He wanted to—had to—tear it all down, as John had torn down the fig tree. He would assert what he had forgotten—or perhaps had never known—existed. Assert it over against them, for they, certainly, did not know of its existence.

As he sat down at the table amidst the breakfast dishes and took pen and paper, he thought, If you—all of you—are not guilty, then *I* am guilty.

43

He wrote his signature out in full at the bottom of the page.

The writing of the confession had been filled with the accurate intensity of poetry. He had ascended to an unassailable upland, and his fingers still trembled with the excitement of the climb.

The Governor—Urgent, he wrote on the envelope.

He looked up with a smile as Denver came in. "Just in time," he said, folding the paper.

"You're wanted in the solicitors' room. Your Mr. Bartlett. Feeling better, are you?"

"I am." He thrust the paper into the envelope and stood up. "Give this to the governor for me, will you?"

Denver held out his hand.

Jordan paused. He'd promised Tom he'd see Bartlett first. Very well then, he would wait—he could certainly afford that magnanimity. "On second thoughts, I'll give it to you later."

Denver's hand fell. "Okay. Ready? Don't you want to comb your hair?"

"To hell with my hair."

Denver grinned. "You look like a bleeding fuzzy-wuzzy. So long as you feel chipper. Come on."

He was surprised to find Bartlett in a tweed suit and a bright-green tie.

The barrister smiled faintly. "Excuse the informality. Sunday, you know. God rests but lawyers don't."

They shook hands.

"Short's told me the news. I have some news for you, too," Bartlett said as they sat down.

Jordan took the letter out of his pocket and gave it to Bartlett.

" 'The Governor,' " Bartlett read. "Um—am I to read it?"

"You are."

The barrister opened the flap and unfolded the two sheets of cheap prison paper. He read it very quickly. When he'd finished he said, "Who knows of this?"

"The governor."

"The contents of this? All of it?"

"No. I told him I was going to confess, that's all. He suggested making a written statement."

"Sensible fellow." Bartlett slipped the sheets back into the envelope. "Then you are, I take it, instructing me to alter your plea to one of guilty?"

"Yes."

"As a lawyer, I distrust confessions."

Jordan smiled. "And as a human being?"

"You know the old story—true—of the barrister who addressed the jury with the words: 'I will cast aside the role of advocate, and speak as a man,' to be immediately rebuked by the judge with, 'You will do nothing of the kind'?"

Jordan shook his head. Bartlett, he thought, had put on the aspect of humanity with his Sunday suit. It was as incongruous as the bright-green tie.

"I remember when I was a small boy," Bartlett went on, "being had up by the master for lying over some trivial incident. It so happened that I had not lied, but it was only my word against his. Clearly I was to be beaten, but this particular man had a positive mania that a boy 'make a clean breast of it.' So I had this perplexing choice: to tell the truth and be convicted a liar; or to lie, and be declared honest. As neither course would obviate punishment, there was naturally a strong motive for lying."

"That must be fairly common. What did you do?"

Bartlett smiled. "That's not really the point of the story. But I'll tell you. I set him a little test. I requested him to give me double the number of strokes he had intended if, and only if, he believed what I was telling him to be the truth. I then told him the truth—I had not lied."

"A Solomon." Jordan looked indulgently at the barrister. "And what happened?"

"He dismissed me without punishment. And thereafter he avoided me as much as possible. But to get back to the point I was making. Confessions are unsatisfactory evidence at best, because one seldom knows the circumstances surrounding them. And I don't mean the physical circumstances. A confession may have a compelling motive quite outside that of the actual crime. By its very nature, a confession cannot be regarded as absolutely hard evidence, even when superficially quite convincing—" he tapped the envelope on the table—"as this is."

"But isn't that what trials are for, to determine the truth of the matter?"

"That's too simplistic a view. The law can only deal with facts, and sometimes not very well with those. We're always trying to exclude the nebulous and concentrate on the tangible. Our courts don't care for nebulosity—witness the law's archaic attitude to psychiatry. The law is always trying to be specific. It tries to be precise in matters where precision is not always possible. This limitation, largely embodied in the rules of evidence, this narrowness, one might say, is the source of great potency. There could never be any judgement if one was to attempt to include everything relevant—because patently there is a vast area of experience and motive and attitude which is, in a very positive sense, relevant, and yet cannot be admitted as evidence, cannot be proved, disproved: facts, feelings, conditionings.

"And it is from this large, clouded area that confessions often spring. I hope I'll live to see the day when all voluntary confessions are automatically excluded. To my mind they are only evidence that a man may be persuaded, or persuade himself, of practically anything."

From his upland, Jordan looked down on the barrister. "I think what you mean is that you do not believe what I have written."

"No no," a trifle impatient. "What I am saying is that I am not competent to judge of its veracity."

"You don't want to commit yourself, do you?"

"Lawyers give opinions and take instructions and accept briefs. It's no part of their business to make commitments. Which is perhaps why we're often thought to be cold fish."

"Bartlett, I've told Short he can wash his hands of this case if he wants to. You can too."

"I'd rather *not* wash my hands of your case. You can instruct me to do so, but perhaps you won't want to when you've heard what I have to say."

"Tangible or nebulous?"

"Let's say flimsy. Yet potentially very significant. Your Miss Lawley came to see me on Friday."

"Miss Lawley?"

"Yes. She had an interesting story to tell. Some months ago—in January, she thinks—she had cause to see a letter, or part of a letter, written to June Singer. She cannot recollect the exact wording, but it was something to this effect: 'You are ruining my life'—that particular phrase Miss Lawley is certain of. Then, 'You know we truly belong together. I will forgive you all if only you come back to me.' It was signed, 'Your Bernie Boy.' That, too, Miss Lawley is positive about. It quite struck her, as indeed it might."

"Miss *Lawley* said all this?" Jordan was puzzled.

"Yes. I think the reason she didn't come forward before this was because she thought she had done something despicable in reading someone else's correspondence."

"The Law in its true colours at last."

"Sorry?"

"The Law. We call her the Law—she's renowned for iron rectitude."

"Umm. A fortunate chink in the armour."

Jordan stood up. He felt the need of movement. He walked across the solicitors' room and back again, halting at the table. "She could have made it up, you know."

"The thought occurred to me. She'd have a strong motive, wouldn't she? And yet . . ."

"She has always disliked me."

"Why?"

"It's not too easy to say." He hesitated; he was unwilling to go into it. It was dead and done with. "I believe she felt I was an intruder. And . . ."

"Yes?"

He had never quite seen it this way before. "She was always afraid, I think, that I was going to disrupt the established way of doing things. But it was more than that. This is oddly ambivalent. She also, in some secret way, despised me for not disrupting things. It was as if she was comparing me to . . . to some ideal figure, and finding that I always fell short. Colin Sutlif's father and my grandfather founded the firm, you know. Colin went into it, but my father didn't take much interest. He was a sleeping partner. And yet that's an absurd description. Because he'd have bursts, so I'm told, of frenzied activity. Try to turn the whole place upside down. It never came to anything. I suppose Clara Lawley might just have known my father in his heyday —she'd certainly have heard about him. I have a peculiar feeling that she would have admired him very much. I can't tell you why. But if she did . . . well, then there would be every reason why she wouldn't care for me."

"Because you were not frenziedly active?"

"What?" He'd not been fully aware of the barrister's presence. Suddenly he smiled. "More or less. I'm a relatively dull man."

Bartlett stood up so that they faced one another across the table. "But a plausible one, Maddox. I have been counting on that."

"For what?"

"You'll make a good impression on the jury. One has to be objective about this sort of thing. You're plausible without being smart alec. Juries don't like smart alecs."

"You forget, Bartlett. I'm not going to give evidence. I'm pleading guilty."

"Yes." Bartlett paused. "I am, of course, your servant in this matter,

Maddox. Nevertheless, it is my concern, my duty, to put before you the alternative courses open to you in this case and the probable consequences of those courses. Patently, if you plead guilty, you will be convicted and sentenced to a long term of imprisonment. You will spend a minimum of twelve years in gaol. Few men can survive more than two or three years in prison and emerge as whole human beings."

Jordan made an impatient movement.

"You must consider that, Maddox. You can't dismiss it. This is not a game which can be closed up and forgotten about when it's finished."

"I'm fully aware of that."

"Right. Now, if you continue with your plea of not guilty, if you go into the witness box, and if, additionally, you instruct me to call the new evidence of which I shall tell you, then I will say that there is a good possibility—not probability, but a good possibility—of your being acquitted."

"I'll take your word for it, because I've—"

"You will not take my word for it!" Bartlett said sharply."How can you make a meaningful choice unless you are fully aware of the alternatives? To blind yourself in this manner is absolutely irresponsible."

Jordan stared at those blue eyes, the face perhaps a little whiter than usual, but hardly more different now in anger than in . . . what? Mirth, triumph, love? The Sunday suit did not really disguise the advocate—like the law itself, he would take on the mechanics of responsibility only. He saw him as a little boy, plump in the face, never losing his temper, never weeping, already armoured against the dangerous world.

"Very well." Jordan nodded and slowly sat down. "Let's get on with it. Miss Lawley's letter—where do we go from there?"

"That letter was not a figment of Miss Lawley's imagination, nor a tribute to a misguided sense of nobility. It existed." Bartlett spoke as though he had never left the subject. He resumed his seat. "I'll tell you how we know this. Gladding—Short's clerk—was, with the help of private detectives, eventually able to trace most of Singer's contemporaries. Gladding personally interviewed all the boys and girls that appeared in Singer's school-leavers' photo. With two exceptions: Hetty Smith and Bernard Cole. It is of course Cole whom we're interested in. No one could give Gladding any hint of where Cole might be. Now, most of Cole's contemporaries—he was a year younger than Singer but left at the same time—described him as a quiet one who kept himself to himself. Sounds familiar, doesn't it? To most of them he was, rather obviously, known as 'Bern' Cole. But Gladding recalled an exception—one girl had said that she'd not seen 'Bernie' for some time. Bernie. This girl's name is Regina Copley. You've heard of none of these people before?"

"No."

"No. How one wishes Singer had been a chatterbox. Well, Gladding immediately went out to Putney—this was on Friday evening—to see Regina Copley. He managed to have quite a long talk with her. She didn't tell him very much, and Gladding formed the impression that she knew rather more than she was willing to reveal. But she let fall one thing: Cole had worked for an ironmonger in Clapham by the name of Swail. First thing on Saturday morning, Gladding saw Swail, who told him that Cole had worked in his shop as late as the beginning of January. On January the third he had left, quite abruptly, with no notice and refusing to give any reason.

"Swail also gave Gladding two other important facts. A day or two after Cole left, a girl came into the shop enquiring for him. A girl with a harelip. Regina Copley has a harelip. Swail was unable to help her. He didn't know where Cole had gone—until, and this is the second important fact, a fortnight later, when he received a phone call from an ironmonger's asking for a reference for Cole, whom they were about to employ. The name of that firm is Ramsden and Black —and the shop is located at One Hundred and Twelve Devizes Road." Bartlett paused. "Devizes Road, Maddox—does that suggest anything to you?"

"No."

"Devizes Road is rather less than a quarter of a mile from Panton Place."

Jordan said, "As you would put it, that's a bit tenuous, isn't it?"

"Interesting, nevertheless. Another thing—Gladding checked the home address Swail gave for Cole. Cole left there, also in early January, and no one knew where he had gone. By the way, you might like to have a look at Cole." He reached down beside the table and brought up a small case which he opened. "This is the school-leavers' photograph." He passed it across the table. "Cole's the one ringed in white."

Slowly Jordan looked down. The faces—some smiling, some simpering, some serious with the gravity of the occasion, but nearly all tinged with a kind of eager complacency. *I've left school*—the moment when the accolade of maturity was conferred upon them. Now they were free—what a horrible trick it was to catch them so, what a fraud, what a hypocrisy, what a trap. But Cole—yes, Cole didn't look like the others; he looked uneasy, as if perhaps he suspected as much.

"Not a very prepossessing countenance, is it?" said Bartlett.

Jordan handed back the photo. Poor little bastard.

"I put it to you that we now have the outlines of another candidate for the role of Singer's murderer. A quiet, self-contained man, who knew Singer at school—but not very well, perhaps, not then, for he was junior to her. A man known to his schoolmates as 'Bern'—except to the only girl who showed enough interest in him to enquire where he was, to whom he was 'Bernie.' Was it pure coincidence that Singer was receiving letters—or a letter—from Bernie? Cole, we know, uprooted himself two weeks after Singer moved to Panton Place and planted himself in close proximity to her. Might one not explain that two-week delay as the time in which it took Cole to trace Singer?"

"There's a great deal of supposition there."

Bartlett didn't answer at once. He took out his silver cigarette case and made quite a business of lighting a cigarette. Then he glanced up and said, "Don't you suppose that?"

"I don't . . . Wouldn't it be necessary for your purposes, to show that the thing was reciprocal?"

"No. Reciprocity's not necessary. What is important is opportunity. Did Cole have the *opportunity* of killing Singer? Short's trying to get hold of either Black or Ramsden today. Perhaps one of them can supply the answer. If Cole was late for work that day, then . . . An ironmonger's too, you notice. An ironmonger's would have key-making equipment. Then there's Copley—Gladding is trying her again today. But I don't wish to exaggerate, Maddox. We haven't got much, and we may get nothing more. On what we have, we can't prove Cole was interested in Singer, or vice versa—but we can suggest it, plant a seed in the jury's mind. It's enough to set them thinking: Perhaps it isn't all so simple, perhaps the prosecution's case isn't as cut and dried as all that. Perhaps, perhaps. That's all we need—the reasonable doubt. That would be a great achievement in itself. It could tip the balance."

"And what about Cole?"

"Cole? What about you? It's for you to decide."

"I have already decided." But he felt no warmth now. He was a bit tired after his long climb, and ravenously hungry.

"One moment. Let me tell you what I propose. I want to call Copley, and then Cole himself. It may be necessary also to have confirming evidence from Swail, possibly Black or Ramsden as well. I don't think I need trouble Miss Lawley. Then, then I should want you to give evidence on your own behalf."

He regarded the barrister for quite a long while without speaking. "I'm sorry, Bartlett." He broke into a smile. "It was a good effort. But the answer is no." As he stood up, he knew that he had somehow regained himself. "It's a pleasant dream, but quite idle. For I killed June. I'm guilty, and I shall so plead."

"Very well." Bartlett nodded and got up. He took Jordan's confession from the table and held it in his hand. "Just one thing, Maddox."

"Yes?"

"I wish you'd withold this. Let me simply announce your change of plea in court tomorrow."

"Why?"

Bartlett looked away. "One prefers . . . one would rather not— not have the ground cut from under one's feet in exactly this manner."

Jordan wondered for a moment. "Alright. If you wish it. I see no harm."

"Thank you." Bartlett passed him the envelope. "I'll try to get down to the cells and see you before proceedings begin tomorrow."

"That's kind—but not necessary. Oh, I see, you think I may change my mind?"

"Of course. One doesn't let go easily."

"No . . . no."

44

He walked by himself round the flagged circle in the prison yard. A single prison officer watched him. It drizzled meanly, and in the flower beds the rosebuds were closed tight against the cold. Under the grey prison cape, Jordan's body shivered.

He wondered whether anyone was looking at him from the rows of lifeless windows that stared blankly into the yard. If there were watchers he would surely feel it.

He permitted himself to look forward. He longed now for the ease of company. He wished he had not insisted upon his privacy like this. He craved the chatter and blasphemy of the hospital ward, he would take even the bland banality of the Light Programme. He imagined the ward a haven of triviality, laughter and dominoes. Among the other prisoners he would be with his own kind. What did they call it?—a present dweller.

Soon he would be one of them. He would be numbered. And without the burden of a name, he would be free. He would be simply a body. One of a thousand bodies which ate and slept and exercised and sewed mailbags or picked oakum or whatever they did these days. Each day every day the body, languorous or appetitive, excited or still —pleasure and pain of it the only concern.

"Two more minutes, Maddox," the prison officer called.

"Right." He did an about turn and started the circle clockwise.

Tomorrow. This time tomorrow he would be where he belonged. But today he was neither one thing nor the other. So he was set apart; as a dying man, maybe, will be unable to give full credit to the reality he is leaving. Already they didn't exist, those outside the precincts of the prison. It would be hard even to describe them physically.

Except for Cole. He could see Cole's bleak, small-featured face quite clearly; a face that never expected to be caught and blown up and examined with such intensity. It was the sort of face which couldn't stand much close inspection—alright in the public anonymity of a school group. Jordan wished he hadn't seen the photo. Bernie

316

—the name itself called up the awful coyness of the deprived, the sugar cosiness which the forlorn long for.

But expecting always that impoverished dream of comfort would be taken away. And then—then the little man, for he had to be little, would be capable of any malice, any covert treachery. He would plead his rights, calling upon all in heaven and earth for help—except upon himself alone. He would eat tinned food and keep his change in a flat leather purse. He would . . .

"Okay, Maddox. Time's up."

He let his cape fall onto the pile of others at the door and was escorted without a word to his room.

"Hold it," called Denver, as Jordan was about to enter. "Visitors' room. All the world's after you today, Maddox lad."

Back again. Down the same stairs, along the same passage. "Special permission for a Sunday. What'd you do—bribe the gov?"

The room was only half lit. He was marched along the line of boxes and delivered into one of the open-backed closets.

"Colin."

Colin started, caught unawares. "Oh hello, Jordan. How are you now?" He was not looking well.

"I didn't expect to see you."

"I thought I'd come round and give you a bit of moral support, as they say." Colin managed to smile. "It's hard to believe it'll be all over tomorrow or—"

"Tomorrow? You've heard?"

"Heard what? I gathered it would wind up tomorrow or on Tuesday. Why, is there something new?"

"No, nothing new."

"Pity. I thought Short might come up with something. A very energetic fellow."

They must have forgotten about poor old Colin. "How's the firm?"

"Bumbling along, as usual. Could do with an active partner, of course." He was quiet for a minute, absorbed. Then he pulled himself together. "Something peculiar did happen. Perhaps I shouldn't bother you with it, but . . ."

"What happened?"

"Miss Lawley resigned." He had been looking down at his hands. Now he raised his head and stared at Jordan. "Damn it, Jordan, I don't understand. Blast the woman, she resigned—and wouldn't say why."

"She told you nothing?"

"Not a word. Not a word of sense. No longer able to continue. Long and happy association. All that sort of balls. I'm afraid she's gone round the bend."

"Not the Law."

Colin grimaced. "No. Not the Law. You're right. The rest of the world could go mad, but she'd stay sane." He took out his cigar case, looked at it, and put it back again. "Cap it all, I've got asthma. Haven't had it for twenty years. Now I'm told I can't smoke! God, can you imagine the mess, without Miss L. to dig up the file I want? What a memory—by God, I believe she could repeat by heart every contract we ever signed. Do you know how long she's been with me?"

"A long time," he said.

"Thirty-eight years, Jordan. And she walks out just like that. No notice. No severance. A damn great memorandum on office procedures and a bare apology." He began to cough. The cough turned into the semblance of a chuckle. "I nearly married her once."

"You?"

"She was something in those days. Oh, she wasn't beautiful or anything like that. But she had—how can I put it?—a precision, a precision of spirit about her. But at the same time—sweet, remarkably sweet. Not the arrant old bitch you see nowadays. Never heard her laugh, have you? Amazing—like that sudden great rush of melody in the third movement of Beethoven's First. I used to ask her to laugh for me—and she would, too. I daresay she was amused at my asking. Clara Lawley. Dammit, I wish I could smoke a cigar. Sallow old sultana now. Well, how are you, Jordan? How are you?"

"I'm well, Colin. Tell me about Clara Lawley."

"Lawley? One doesn't watch, you know. Doesn't notice. I went down, after she'd left, went down to the production room. Looked at old Timothy, examined him. He's a senile idiot, Jordan! I should have seen that before. Last year he lost seventeen blocks and a hundred and twenty pounds' worth of art. I knew that. I've always loathed his guts, him and his whining William Morris cant. But I always thought, well, he's a craftsman. He's as much a craftsman as I'm Alice. I decided on the spot that Timothy would have to go. Pension him off. But I couldn't do it. I just couldn't bring myself to sack that silly old sod. It's a job for you, Jordan."

"Colin. Clara Lawley—did . . . ?"

"I wandered. Yes. I proposed to her, you know. It was after Charles died. Lily dead, Charles dead. I suppose I moped. There didn't seem to be much fun around, suddenly. And then I heard that laugh of Clara's one day. When you hear something like that, you don't waste time picking lilies. We had a marvellous time, a marvellous summer. But she turned me down flat. September the twenty-ninth. It was a blow. A great blow. Why do they do it, Jordan? Up stakes and off, just like that. I hate them going off and dying on you, without a word." A blow. And Colin looked as though he had been hit hard in the stomach. He puffed a little and wheezed his asthma.

"I think I can explain why Clara Lawley left you," knowing, as he said it, that today he was raising up, and tomorrow he would strike down. But there was nothing else to do. He could not leave Colin like this.

"You can?"

Briefly Jordan explained.

"I see," murmured Colin. "Clara did that, did she? The poor old soul. Well," with sudden vigour, "we'll get her back. That is, if you think . . ."

"Of course you'll get her back."

Colin considered for a moment. "I couldn't do it, Jordan. She wouldn't come back for me. But you—you could. She's always had a weakness for you . . . What am I thinking of? By Jove, Jordan, it's great news for you! Why, it breaks the case against you wide open! Forgive me, forgive me—this is most excellent news."

"It doesn't matter, Colin. You'll get Clara Lawley back. Just make her laugh."

"Those days are over. No, it's your baby. She respects you. I wouldn't have the savvy these days. Too old. Look how my mind flies to trivialities. I'm getting old. Timothy. Lawley. S. and M. is heavy with the gentle degeneration of years. We need you, Jordan, to put us on the right track. My dotage is approaching. The appalling thing about old age is that one doesn't notice it happening. One day you're ranting against all the bloody old farts who run the show, and then you wake up and you're one of them."

"Colin, you mustn't count on my being there. I—"

"Count on it? I bank on it, Jordan. My dear old chap, I'm lucky, supremely lucky. I see our imprint stamped upon the spine of works of real scholarship, instead of on the products of profitable but plodding hacks." He laughed. "Dear old Clara. God guided her eyes when she broke one of her sacred principles. Even her failings bear fruit. And I am, to tell you the truth, not greatly surprised. Surprised, I mean, at June Singer."

"I thought you liked June."

"I like anyone who works for me until I sack them. Then my accumulated bile wells. As it did with old Timothy—although too sentimental, I suppose you'd call it, to do the actual deed. No, I always thought Singer a bit of a sly puss."

"June sly?"

"Sly. Positively sly. Oh fair enough at her work. But just a wee bit too pleased at always managing to give you the right answer. To my taste. And those nails!"

Jordan smiled despite himself. "That's called job satisfaction these days."

"Job balls!"

They looked at each other and burst out laughing.

Then Colin had an attack of coughing.

They chatted on for a while. At last Colin said he must go.

"You'd better stay where you are, by the way. Trevor's waiting to see you. We came together and I made him toss to see which of us would come in first. Of course he lost. Now I insist I don't hear from you for at least a month. Take Willy away—and rectify this enforced abstinence. Take her abroad. Out of this damned depressing little country."

Jordan stood up.

"Goodbye, Jordan."

"Goodbye, Colin."

The old man's shoulders hunched against a sudden asthmatic assault. Watching him go, Jordan realised that he was not yet inured to the pain of separation.

45

"I didn't know what you might want. Flowers, I thought . . . but you're not keen on flowers, are you?" The clerical collar hung like a white halter about Trevor's grooved and corded throat.

"No. I'm glad you didn't. It's like receiving condolences."

"How you resemble your father. He disliked flowers—fruit too. He had a particular hatred of grapes, I remember—" he gave Jordan a small, withered smile—"except in their fermented form."

"I thought it was whiskey?"

"That was later. No—burgundy, claret, sherry, perhaps. Never anything sweet. He always said, if he wanted to be sick, he'd rather drink cocoa. He couldn't bear what he called 'cheeriness.' His room at the nursing home, you know, was quite bare. No colour at all. I remember once when Mary and I went to visit him. Mary took along some flowers, although she should have known better. I've never seen a man so angry as Charles that day. I remember it vividly. He said, 'Don't you try to pretend this is a living room. Leave it alone. I've come here to die.' I was rather shocked at the time . . ."

"And what did Mary say to that?"

"Ummm? Oh, Mary. She blushed, you know. The only time I've ever seen Mary blush in my entire life. She blushed, yes, and walked out. Never visited Charles again. He died not long after. You were too young to remember all that, though."

"No. I dimly recall the funeral—and Charles, my father, lying in your chapel."

"Do you now? Remarkable. The funeral. I remember the funeral too." He paused for a long while, and then he spoke slowly and sadly. "Mary got her own back, you know, then. The flowers—oh my goodness me, the flowers at his funeral! I should have stopped her." He nodded to himself. "But I didn't . . . didn't understand, perhaps."

"How are things at Sibley?"

"As well as could be expected," said Trevor absent-mindedly, as though listening to some other conversation in another place.

"I heard you were having trouble with a curate."

"Oh yes, a trial—a minor trial, I'm afraid." He made an effort. "But as one gets older these little tribulations don't seem to matter so much, you know. Just as perhaps the intensity of one's satisfactions wanes, so disappointments are less sharp. One should not be sorry for old people. I often think the Lord provides that our ills, as well as our joys, should not be so troublesome to us as we get on. As though he knows we are not so well able to cope . . . perhaps . . . as confident youth, youth in its confidence is . . . can . . ." He gazed down at his lap, as if there he would find the thread of his thought.

"There are compensations, of course," he went on, suddenly summoning the remnants of a pulpit heartiness. "Annie Brierly is one of those. You remember Annie, of course you do. She is a great standby these days. Mary's memory is not as good as it was—an affliction of us Freemans as we get older. I often think your Uncle John . . . Well, of course, it is only small things she is apt to forget—such as tradesmen's bills. The immediate present gets mislaid—the past is as lucid as ever. Tradesmen's bills—well, that causes a little misunderstanding sometimes. Annie is a great help there, with accounts. And now since her sister passed away, she will have more time to . . . Oh dear, that wasn't quite what I meant."

"Emerald died?"

"You didn't know? Perhaps I shouldn't have mentioned it then. Well, yes, the unfortunate girl passed away. In most distressing circumstances. Most. I sometimes have the impression that the, well, tragedies of life—which are indeed a part of life—partake these days of an arbitrariness and a, yes, cruelty which I don't recall. Even during the war. Am I wrong?"

"I'm not certain. But I don't believe it's worse now," he said. "I can't think of anything more arbitrary and cruel than what happened to John."

Trevor moved his head a little. "Yes, it was a terrible death. But—"

"I didn't mean his death. I meant what happened to him in the war and . . ." No, he could not say it. "What happened to him on the Western Front."

Trevor blinked. "Oh. I see."

"How did Emerald die then?" Jordan asked quickly.

"She burned to death. Such a trivial accident too. No one was to blame. You remember Mr. Goff, who used to play the organ? One of the things he liked to do was to sit with Emerald, you know. It re-

322

lieved Annie in the post office from having to pop into the back room
every five minutes to see the poor girl was up to no mischief. Goff
liked to sit there and chat to the girl and smoke his pipe. Of course
she didn't understand a word. But then few people understand what
Goff says, poor fellow—he has no roof to his mouth. But you know.
One day he forgot and left his box of matches on the table by Emerald. When he left, Emerald started to play with them and she . . .
well, she set herself on fire. She didn't cry out and of course she
couldn't move. When Annie looked in . . . The burns were so severe she died within three days. Annie blames herself a little, I'm
afraid. Such a little thing—after all those years of care. Nothing at all
to blame herself for. But that's not how the human mind works, is it,
Jordan? And that poor girl—never harmed anyone, except in the end
herself."

"Perhaps," Jordan said slowly, "she would have been better off in a
home."

"Yes. I always said that. I used to think that," said Trevor with a
sudden spurt of vehemence. "But now . . . I'm not sure. I think of
John a lot these days. I believed—it was my firm conviction—that
he too would have benefitted from being in a place where he could
have had proper care, hospital care. I thought that—but Mary
wouldn't have it. I bowed to her, as sometimes one must bow, Jordan.
But I thought he would be happier, you see, amongst his own kind
there in hospital. For he was not happy, not in those later years. And I
said to myself, this is why—because we were not able to give him the
day-to-day attention, the observation, the security that he would automatically have received in a home, a private institution.

"That terrible thing would not have happened, I told myself, if he
had been where he belonged. I blamed myself for that, Jordan, oh
yes. I blamed myself for not persuading Mary. That was where I had
failed. I thought so.

"But when Emerald died three weeks ago . . . oh, before that
perhaps . . . perhaps when you . . . I don't know. But I asked
myself, 'Where did John belong?' And, do you know, I couldn't answer that? But I think, I feel now, that perhaps he did belong with us,
with his brother and his sister. It seems to me that I was blinding
myself all those years. That my failure was not a failure of—oh, how
can I put it?—of—"

"Organization," Jordan answered.

323

"Yes, precisely. Not a failure of organization, failure to take proper measures. But a failure of a different and deeper kind. A failure of the heart. Yes. I believe Annie and old Mrs. Brierly were right—right to keep Emerald with them. And I believe I was wrong. I failed. *Dearly beloved brethren*—those words have been on my lips for forty years and more now, Jordan. And it doesn't seem to me I had the least understanding . . ." He gazed now steadily through the grille at Jordan.

"How does Mary think?"

"I have not spoken of it. Mary, you know, would not really understand. She is a simple person—that is her strength. But I thought you . . ."

"You thought I'd understand?"

"Yes, Jordan, yes, I do think you understand. Although it is not understanding I need now, I think, so much as forgiveness . . . I am not good at this . . . I failed you. Yes," his voice grew firmer, "I failed you. When Lily died and your father entrusted you to me, I accepted the responsibility in good faith. I determined to bring you up as I would wish any boy to be brought up—wholesome and active in mind and in body. Truth, I was convinced, was open to a clear and willing mind—and the greatest gift of the mind was understanding. I believed that I could teach you to understand. I knew that I was not good with children—I was not as your father was—but I thought that was a secondary thing. No no, Jordan, do not forbid me. I forbade you. I did not understand that simplest of commands—to let a child come to me.

"And when you came here, to this place, accused of this terrible crime . . . I thought, I felt . . ." A little tremor passed through his hands which lay idly curled on the ledge in front of him.

"It's not your fault, Trevor. Good lord, you're not—"

"No no. It is just that I feel somehow—do you understand this?— that it is I who should be in your place."

"Trevor—I'm sorry that—"

"Please do not think I am asking for that. It is I who am sorry. And I wanted you—I wanted to tell you this before tomorrow. For I am in a sense an emissary—I have promised to see what I could do."

"To make me change my mind?"

"I don't suppose it would do any good, would it, my trying to persuade you?"

324

"No. Who sent you, Trevor?"

"Mary wished me to come. She fancied—" he smiled—"that I could, as she puts it, make you see sense. And Willy—"

"Willy?"

"We are staying at Woodley."

"I thought she was at the Shorts'."

"Until this morning she was. But she asked us to come—so we did. She gave me a message—a note—for you. I gave it up to the guard, but he assured me you would get it at once. She told us, of course, what you had said."

"How—how does she seem?"

"She is, I think, in great distress."

"And Mary?"

"Mary will always survive. Your daughter—"

"Yes?"

"—has sent you a note too, I believe, in with Willy's. Willy asks me to tell you that you are not to read her letter until after tomorrow. Unless you feel you must."

"Well."

"Well." Trevor got to his feet. "Well, bless you, my boy."

46

Jordan sat on the bed and held the envelope in his hand. Cream-laid paper. In half an hour the lights would go out and he wouldn't be able to read the letter until dawn.

He was locked in. The window in the door was shut; only the peep-hole was ready to glare at him all night.

He did not want to open the envelope. He wouldn't sleep. They were pressing him too hard now. He had a sudden impulse to burn the letter unread. But he knew he wouldn't. He knew also, as minute to minute he put off the act, that he would read the letter.

He opened it at last, five minutes before lights out. He forced himself to read slowly.

JORDAN,

I know I can't expect you to forgive me for the things I said to you

325

yesterday. It seems so much longer ago than yesterday. It seems years ago—I've been so miserable.

It was not true, all I said. Jordan, please believe that. I *did* go to bed with Tom once. It was after Georgia was born. And I don't know *why* I did it. Perhaps because I thought you wouldn't find me attractive any more. I know that sounds silly really, and I have thought and thought about *why* I did it.

All I know is I've felt guilty for ages. Some people can be unfaithful and not seem to mind at all. Perhaps in a way they are healthier than me. Mummy would think so. But I could never truly think in that way.

Last night Norah said to me—"Oh, I know all about you and Tom, my dear. I don't care about you, but I do hope he enjoyed it." It made me feel so *cheap*.

I couldn't sleep last night. So I went down and made myself cocoa. And as I sat down to drink it, I thought that you couldn't—couldn't get yourself something to drink in the middle of the night however much you wanted it. And I just cried like a perfect fool.

Jordan, please don't do it. I *beg* you not to do it. It's not because I care what people think or anything like that. It's just that I can't think what I'll do without you. Twelve years. I can't bear that. I don't care what you've done. I don't care if you *did* murder her. I don't care if you made love to her. Please please, Jordan, don't leave me!

I'm weak, my darling. That's why I'm going to ask Uncle Trevor to tell you not to open this letter till it's all over. You must do what you think. I know that. But I hope, I *pray* you open it today. I can't ask you to let it influence you. I've forfeited the right to ask you that. But I *do* ask it!

I'm not good at love, Jordan. And I'm not good at anything else. All I know how to do is be *brave*. And I'm not brave at all. I'm the greatest coward there ever was.

Come back to me. Please please come back to me. You are so much more than you think. I will try harder, I promise you that, my darling. And perhaps there is another way. You must teach me—because I don't know anything but trying harder.

I know I've written this as if you'd read it today. But if you don't open it till tomorrow, then remember I love you and wrote it like this because I love you. I'll be faithful. And I'll wait. I *won't* give in. And when you come out of prison, I will be there—if you'll have me.

Your wife,

WILHELMINA

He put the letter on the bed and got up. Something was being taken from him, drawn out of him like a ligature from an amputation.

As the lights went out, he thought, if only she had not said, "But I *do* ask it."

In the darkness he remembered Georgia's note. He turned and fumbled for it on the bed. He struck a match and held it a little way from the scrap of paper:

> DEAR DADDY
> DO YOU LIKE ELEFANTS
> I DO
> LOVE FROM
> GEORGIA PEACH

There was a drawing of a strange fat beast with a curled trunk.

As the tears slipped from his eyes, he strove to recapture the high ground gained in the early part of the day.

Any soldier would have done the same.

A GOOD WAR

47

He held Uncle John's hand tight. John was tall and still as a statue, except for the faint grumbling in his throat which only Jordan could hear.

All the others in the churchyard were listening to Uncle Trevor's "religious" voice intoning the burial of the dead. Jordan was usually excused halfway through a sermon, but he guessed he wouldn't be excused this time. Besides which, he knew the men were soon going to lower his father's coffin into the grave. He didn't want to miss that, even though he was not really quite sure it was his father.

By turning his head slightly, he could see the adjoining grave which was always neatly clipped and crisp with flowers. The headstone read: LILY ALICIA MADDOX. That was his mother. On Sunday mornings very often, while the congregation torpidly suffered the conclusion of Trevor's sermon, Aunt Mary would bring Jordan to this grave. And they would stand together for what seemed like an eternity of silent contemplation. Dimly Jordan grasped that these moments affected Aunt Mary with some deep emotion, and that he too ought to be affected. But he didn't know how—he only gathered it was something to do with being an orphan. But he had not been a real orphan, that was quite clear, because his father was alive.

Now, he thought with satisfaction, I am a real orphan. He had looked at himself for a long time in the mirror this morning, expecting to see a change in himself. There wasn't any. But it didn't really matter. He just wished there was someone who fully appreciated his distinction—and he didn't have any grandparents either. Aunt Mary merely got irritable when he pointed this out. Of course, it would be even better if he had no relatives at all. Aunt Mary and Uncle

331

Trevor, however, were not likely to die just to oblige him. For a moment he imagined a glorious life where the only adult was Uncle John.

But Uncle John was a relative too.

". . . Charles Ardwick Maddox," Uncle Trevor moaned impressively, and the men gripping the ropes began to ease the coffin slowly into the ground. The lid of the coffin was bare—they'd taken all the flowers off. Flowers were too precious to be buried.

It was all over soon after that. The small circle of mourners broke up. Looking back, Jordan saw two of the pallbearers taking off their jackets and then beginning to shovel the dry August earth into the hole.

John took him home, along the sweetly smelling lime avenue.

"My father didn't have many friends, did he?" said Jordan.

"Hundreds."

"Well why weren't they there then?"

"Because it was a hole-in-a-corner affair." John crunched the gravel with steps measured to a slow march he hummed in his high tenor. He stared straight ahead. "Shouldn't have gone out like that," he said suddenly, breaking off his hum. "Should have had a decent funeral—a military burial."

"Was he a soldier then, like you, Uncle John?"

"Not a regular. But for an artist he did well. A military cross. He had a good war."

High away in the sunlight a plane flashed.

"An aeroplane," Jordan said.

"Reconnaissance, I expect," John answered vaguely.

They walked in silence.

"Why didn't my father live at the rectory with us?" He felt a great daring as he said it. It wouldn't have been possible to ask anyone but Uncle John—and even Uncle John . . .

"He wasn't one of us really, Jordan. He was an artist, you know. Always said exactly what he thought. Didn't make him very popular with Mary." Uncle John chuckled. "Come to that, always did exactly what he felt like doing. I liked him. But he wasn't a Freeman. I don't think he liked coming down here and being reminded of Lily."

"My mother."

"Your mother. He missed Lily, you see. We all miss Lily."

332

"Why did she die then?"

"Wasn't her fault. A motor accident. She was bringing you back from the hospital where you were born. You were in her arms, but there wasn't a scratch on you."

Jordan was silent, and Uncle John's humming swelled loud.

"Uncle John?"

"Yes?"

"I'm not a Freeman either, am I?"

"No. You're a Maddox."

"A Maddox." It sounded interesting, but . . .

He heard the drone of the plane now, but he couldn't see it anymore. It was lost behind the holly bushes which linked the trunks of the lime trees.

"Uncle John? Do you think the fuzzy-wuzzies could get through here?"

They reached the wicket gate into the rectory garden.

Uncle John paused and looked down at his nephew. "No fuzzy-wuzzies today, Jordan."

48

He woke up so smoothly he wasn't sure he'd been asleep.

He lay looking at the ceiling. Then he swung himself off the bed. He was fully clothed.

It was already light, though early still. He pulled the chair across the room and stood on it and looked out of the window. The yard below was grey and shadowed, but clearcut, and the piece of sky he could see was without a cloud. A sunny May morning.

He jumped down and swiftly stripped away his clothes. His body was grimy and unused. He filled the basin with cold water and washed himself all over, rinsing himself with cupped hands and scattering drops on the linoleum.

As he was shaving, the door was unlocked and opened. Denver stepped into the room.

"Early bird, again, I see. Have a good kip, did you?"

"Fair enough." Jordan scraped under his chin.

"Breakfast'll be up in ten minutes. Peckish then, are you, after yesterday?"

Jordan doused his razor in the water and wiped the tufts of shaving soap from crevice and lobe. "I'll eat it. Why so early?"

"Schedule's shifted up today. We got to leave at eight. Sammy Samson's doing his nut about it; afraid it'll ruin *his* schedule. Regular as clockwork, our Sammy."

"Eight? Why?"

"Couldn't say. Governor's orders."

Naked, Jordan crossed to the bed and shook out his clothes.

"Looks like you slept in 'em," said Denver.

"I did."

"Got a clean shirt, have you?"

"One left." He pulled on yesterday's socks.

Denver walked over and picked up the jacket of his suit. "Blimey, the bloody army must have marched over it. They're going to think we been knocking you about."

"I shouldn't worry."

"It don't worry me, mate. But we can't have you looking like you spent the night in a phone box at Waterloo. I can just see what the scribblers would say: 'The prisoner slouched in his crumpled suit, etc.'"

"I'll sit straight then."

"Don't make no difference. According to them blokes, if you got a crumpled suit, you slouch. Impresses the jury, that sort of thing, too. Somebody who ain't got a tie comes up, right off they think he's no good." There was an accent of bitterness in Denver's voice that made Jordan look up.

"You don't think much of juries?"

"They're alright. Don't know the odds, that's all. They're so bloody bourgeois, if you'll pardon the expression."

Jordan slowly unfolded his clean shirt. He was puzzled. This was out of character for cheery, kindly, paunchy Jack Denver.

"They never been up against it, that's their trouble."

"Some of them may have been. Some of them may be," Jordan said. "You can't know."

"Alright. I'll give you that. They might have been. But it's all sewed up and forgotten. They never learned nothing. They're just the same

334

way they always was. They're not vicious—listen, they may think the man in the dock is a poor unfortunate alright. But I'll tell you, it's them who's the poor unfortunates. Only they don't see it. And never will see it neither."

Jordan put the shirt over his head and pulled it down. "I've never heard you like this before."

Denver smiled, but it wasn't his usual grin. "Acid indigestion, I expect. Swallowed too much of that newspaper gas."

"Oh." He buttoned the shirt. "How is my press today?"

Denver shrugged. "You know."

"Got a paper I could have a look at?"

"You? A paper? You don't want to look at a paper."

"Bad eh?"

"The usual. They've only had one side of it till now. It's your turn today."

Jordan looked closely at the prison officer. "I see," he said. "Well, perhaps we'll give them a surprise."

"I bloody well hope so." Denver grinned and at once became his old self. "I can't stand here nattering. Let's have these," he said, picking up the trousers too. "I'll see if I can't get hold of an 'ot iron and give 'em a bit of a press."

"Don't bother."

"It's a pleasure, lad. We got to give 'em a run for their money. Do you want to empty these pockets then?"

Jordan did so and handed the suit back to Denver.

"I won't be long. Can't have your breakfast with your legs all bare, can you now? Wouldn't be decent." He gave a laugh as he went out.

At eight Jordan was ready and waiting—filled with kippers and a pint of tea, a crease in his trousers like the edge of a guillotine. Corridors and stairs and more corridors and out into the open air—he was marched the familiar route between Denver and Samson.

The outer yard was still in shadow, but he could almost smell the sunlight.

"Hello, a car?"

"Doing it in style today." They moved in step towards the spotless black police car. "Even got a police escort."

As Denver spoke, Jordan recognised Inspector Symington.

"You were supposed to be here at eight, Prison Officer," Symington said sharply. "It's now three minutes past."

335

"Sorry, sir."

"Morning, Symington," Jordan said.

The inspector gave him a nod. "Alright, get in. Where are your handcuffs, Prison Officer?"

"Here we are, sir."

Jordan was put in the back, between Denver and Samson. Denver snapped the cuffs on his own wrist and Jordan's. Symington got in the front beside the driver and as soon as he slammed the door, the car began to move.

As they left the prison gates, Jordan could see his surroundings for the first time. Street on street of small, ugly houses, neat figures in the ledger of a bankrupt firm. But the morning sun made everything bright, and it wasn't warm enough for there to be any haze. They turned into a street where the houses had front gardens, and Jordan saw lilac and laburnum growing.

"Can we have a window open?" he asked.

Symington turned and looked at him. "Alright. But don't try anything, Maddox."

"What would you do—render me unconscious?"

Symington stared at him silently for a moment, then turned his head to the front.

Jordan's glitter of anger vanished as he smelled the summer fresh air. The usual depression of the south side of the Thames—viaducts and slate roofs and Victorian pubs—was lifted and forgotten.

"Westminster Bridge?" the driver asked.

"No. Waterloo," said Symington.

"Right. Not much traffic in Fleet Street at this time of the morning."

As they crossed the bridge, Jordan looked at Somerset House and the dome of St. Paul's and the blind clock on Shell-Mex House. It was the way he had come every day for years, but not in a sleek black car with four grim guards. An ordinary man, who didn't know the odds, on an ordinary bus.

Within three minutes they were at the Old Bailey. He was hurried into the building—the momentary awkwardness of handcuffs making Symington twitch with impatience. Down in the cells, the inspector's job was ended. "Right, Prison Officer," he said, and then paused.

He moved close to Jordan. He smiled and put out his hand and brushed imaginary dust from Jordan's lapel and shoulder. It was a loving gesture. "Got to keep you looking smart, Maddox," he said. "It's a bloody shame we can't top your sort any more. But don't worry, we're going to put you away for a nice long time." His grin widened.

Jordan said quietly, "In a rational society, Inspector, you would be under psychiatric care."

Symington's hovering hand clenched instantly. "Why, you—by God, if I had you alone, I'd—"

"Come on now, we don't want no trouble," Denver pulled him away, wrenching his wrist on the steel cuff.

In the cell, Denver unlocked them. Each rubbed at his chafed wrist.

"I wouldn't pay no attention to that sod if I were you."

"No," said Jordan. But he wasn't thinking about Symington. He was thinking about Bernard Cole.

All morning he had kept his mind clear, free as the sunny streets of the outside world through which they'd driven. Symington had merely given the order for the inevitable about turn. And now Jordan was looking at them, and they were regarding him, each with their own hope. But dominating them all was the circled face of Cole.

"Sammy, see'f you can't win us a couple of mugs of tea," called Denver through the barred opening in the door. "You'd like a cuppa, Maddox, wouldn't you?"

"Thanks."

"Oh-ah, 'ere's your chap to see you."

The heavy cell door was swung open and, as Denver went out, Tom Short entered.

"Where's Bartlett?"

"Geoffrey's trying to catch forty winks," Tom smiled. "We've been up all night. Old boy, I think we're set fair." But his buoyancy was tinged with anxiety.

"Tell me," Jordan said.

Tom took a deep breath. "It's hard to know where to start. Good to be able to say that. Well, let's begin with Copley. Gladding had a long talk with Regina Copley yesterday, and it's quite obvious she knew Cole much better than she said at first. In fact, we rather think she was, or is, after Cole. Wedding bells. Gladding didn't press her too hard, of course. She also knew Singer—again, probably rather well. In fact the three of them—Copley, Cole and Singer—went out

337

together on several occasions. But she indicated—hinted would be a better word—that Cole was more interested in Singer than in her.

"So we begin to get a picture. Copley running after Cole, Cole running after Singer, and Singer—running away from Cole.

"Now what was Cole doing on the morning of the murder? Could he have got away—did he get away—from Ramsden and Black long enough to visit Panton Place and murder June Singer? Well, the answer is no—because he did not go to work on Monday at all. He was off sick. A sore throat. Tuesday too. Ramsden took me round to the shop and showed me the record, which, incidentally, is now in Geoffrey's safekeeping. Another thing from Ramsden—Cole lives in Rumbold Street. Now, one of the routes from Rumbold Street to Devizes Road—that's where Ramsden and Black is—leads straight through Panton Place. In fact, laddie boy, *that* route is a half a minute quicker than any other way. Thirty-five seconds, to be exact. I spent three hours yesterday checking it—took eight different routes, both ways, twice each. Damn near killed me, not used to walking."

"Did you see Cole?"

"And risk scaring him off? Not on your nelly." He hesitated. "So this is the position. We can prove Cole had opportunity. We can almost certainly prove Cole knew Singer. We can suggest a motive for Cole."

"Do you think Cole murdered June?"

"I think if the police had known what we know now, they wouldn't have been in such a hurry to arrest you. Beyond that," he waved his hand, "it's vague. Part of the vagueness comes from June Singer. She isn't quite the shy, competent little thing she was when we started out, is she? She had one boy friend—Cole. Maybe she had another. Maybe that's why she didn't want Cole hanging around. Or perhaps she *did* want Cole—we may be reading too much into the Bernie-boy letter Miss Lawley saw. But these are the points we hope will be clarified when we call Cole—and Copley, we might get more out of Regina Copley, I fancy."

"Yes," said Jordan. Ever since he'd woken up it had been at the back of his mind that he'd have to see Cole. Hear him. He already knew him in some curious way, knew how he'd waited there outside No. 27 Panton Place, watching for June, knew how he spoke, knew the very tone of his plaint, his letters, his phone calls. For of course he would have phoned. And suddenly Jordan remembered June sitting at

338

her desk, head bowed, murmuring into the mouth piece. An idiosyncrasy, he'd thought, of her modesty.

He had the feeling that he himself had *invented* Cole.

"Can I take it then that you've changed your mind?"

"Yes," he said slowly, "yes, you can. We'll let it stand." He'd not thought about it until this moment, but it did not surprise him.

"My dear man, my dear man," Tom sighed his relief. "Of course," tentative again, "you'll consent to be called?"

It wasn't important. It was Bernard Cole who mattered, not Jordan. And yet he would be quite glad to be his own witness; if someone else were to formulate the questions, perhaps he could find the answers. "Alright," he said.

"Good. Splendid." Tom took a notebook out of his pocket, scribbled something in it, tore off the sheet and went to the door. "Warder," he handed the note through the bars, "see this gets to Mr. Cloke at once. That's the man who came in with me. Immediately. It's extremely urgent."

He turned to Jordan with a smile.

"What was all that about?"

"Just letting Geoffrey know."

Jordan hesitated. "What would you have done if I hadn't agreed?"

"There's no point in going into that now."

"I want to know."

"Well, alright. We'd have tried to persuade Pollen to ask for a recess—that's why I had to get word to Geoffrey. The case for the Crown isn't closed yet, you see. Then we'd have taken what we've got on Cole—not much—to the D.P.P. and tried to get him to reopen investigations."

"You mean I didn't really have any choice?"

"Choice? Look—I'm not even sure Pollen would have agreed to a recess. We've had to let him know we're calling Cole and Copley, and a bit of what we hope for—but he's distinctly unimpressed. Frankly, the D.P.P. is likely to be even less impressed. You'd probably have been convicted and sentenced. Of course—we'd have pressed, gone on pressing for a reinvestigation. But, let's suppose we'd succeeded, there would have been no guarantee that anything would have turned up to cast sufficient doubt on the evidence against you."

"Sufficient for what?"

"Sufficient to cause a recommendation to be made to the Home

Secretary to commute your sentence, or perhaps to grant a free pardon."

"Why didn't you do that anyway—go to the Director of Public Prosecutions?"

"It's a forlorn hope, as it stands. Besides," with sudden energy, "that's not the way we want it. We want a verdict. We don't want the whole thing to fall inconclusively into the murk. You'd be a tagged man for the rest of your life. We don't want Cole in some little room in Sarah Street, lying his head off. We want him out in the open. There's very little risk. Even if we get virtually nothing out of him— or Copley—we'll still have introduced an element of complication. And every complication adds to the possibility of doubt. We've just got to keep our fingers crossed. But Geoffrey's our man. Does that answer your question?"

"Yes, it answers it alright."

"Good. Now let me tell you the procedure. The Crown will close this morning. Unless Pollen wants to re-examine Mrs. Ardley, which I don't expect, they'll close at once. Bartlett will make a brief opening, and then he'll straightaway call Copley. We've warned Pollen about this incidentally, and I don't think he'll make things too difficult, which he easily could. Then Cole. Depending how we get on, we may or may not call Swail and Ramsden, either before or after Cole. And, conceivably, Miss Lawley. And then it'll be your turn. Now, here . . ."

He listened to Tom with only half his mind; he needed no forewarning of what was to come. He was conscious of how airless the cell was without a window, and how drab without daylight. The walls bare of prisoners' scrawls or etched initials. They would always be in a hurry here, waiting to move on to somewhere else. It smelled of urine and sweat and the damp laundry smell of weakish tea. A stopping place, a railway station—but the squalid melancholy of these cells denied the possibility of a happy journey; the only promise was the triumphant chuckle of train wheels on the permanent way to prison. Handcuffs and keys and stone floors and damp—the dungeon carried the contemptuous assumption of guilt. For it was not just that prison shut you up—that is not the deadliness of it—but that it denied you, if it could, even a glimpse of the outside world, as though from the sight you might take heart.

"I understand, Tom."

"Don't let Pollen fluster you. There's absolutely no need to be worried."

"I won't be."

Tom smiled. "No, I know you won't. Your calm is positively unearthly at times. Up to now, it made us all feel rather helpless. Let's hope it has the same effect on Pollen."

"Up to now?"

"Oh well, you're out of it now, aren't you?"

"Out of what?"

"The pre-trial trance you were in. Not that I'm blaming you. It's not uncommon, you know. When a man is accused of an appalling crime—whether justly or unjustly—and banged into a totally different world with totally different procedures and values. Like a recruit, you know—doesn't understand what's happened to him. Hard to believe the whole thing's real. The numbing effect of a nightmare. It would frighten the life out of me."

"You speak as though it were all over."

"As a lawyer, I'd have to refute that. But that's one of the troubles, when one is both solicitor and friend." He paused. "I'm afraid I haven't always drawn the distinction too cleanly over the past few weeks." He glanced away and blew out his cheeks. "In fact, I've probably behaved rather badly. It was because I was involved, maybe too involved. So if I adopted tactics that were a bit brutal, it was because . . ."

"Because you wanted to get me out of the trance, bring me to my senses?"

"Yes, exactly," said Tom eagerly.

"And yet it wasn't quite so simple, was it?"

"What . . . ?"

"It wasn't so much that you were the prisoner's friend as the friend of the prisoner's wife?"

"My God, thank God! She told you." Tom looked behind him and then lowered himself weakly onto the chair. "What can I say? It's been . . . been troubling me for weeks."

"How did it come about?"

Tom took out a handkerchief and wiped his throat. "I don't know. I mean why she . . . I don't know why. I thought I did, but—"

"What did you think?"

"I thought she was in love with me. But God knows the mind of woman, I don't. I always had a thing about Willy. Naturally I didn't do anything about it. I knew there wasn't a hope. I thought that. I didn't just want an affair with her."

"But that's what you got."

"I didn't really get anything at all. Bleak hotel rooms. She wasn't remotely in love with me—perhaps I got that out of it, that piece of knowledge."

"She wasn't in love with you?"

"I shouldn't be here if she had been, would I?"

"Why?"

"We'd be over the hills and far away."

"You would have run off with her?"

"If that's the only way we could have done it, yes."

"And left Norah?"

"Like a shot." He got up and staggered a little. "There's nothing between Norah and me."

"Nothing?"

"Oh company—company. But who the devil wants company? Norah and I are living on what might have been, what could have been—what *isn't*, and never will be. By God, if I saw the chance to have something *now*—" he opened his hand and clenched it hard— "something *alive*—do you think I'd hesitate?"

There was something not quite right about it—but he couldn't just put his finger on it. Something . . . "You mean—amongst it all, you can't find anything?"

Tom grunted. "Not much. Not a bloody thing, to tell you the truth." He thrust the handkerchief back into his pocket. "Well, have to get booted and spurred for the fray." He laughed. "Glad that's over. Got a cigarette on you? Left mine in Geoffrey's chambers."

Jordan gave him one and lit it.

"Thanks. What I really need, of course, is a drink."

49

"May it please you, my Lord. Members of the jury, you have heard the case for the prosecution. You have listened, I am certain, with the greatest attention to the evidence which the prosecution has put before you. And yet, in this case so far, I have the feeling that our position resembles that of a savage who for the first time sees a motor car in motion. The savage must seek to explain the moving vehicle by analogy with what he knows: the running of wild animals, the flowing of a stream, the movement of the wind. But, of course, it is what he does not know which is vital. Without an understanding of the internal combustion engine, he will never be able to explain what he has seen, except perhaps by a resort to magic. And magic is not an alternative open to us." A faint smile. Standing motionless in the well of the court, without a note in his hand, Bartlett was the very model of the quiet, careful man who kept close personal accounts and occasionally wrote a short, impersonal letter to the newspaper correcting some small error of fact.

"I mean simply this: the missing facts may well be the vital ones. Now there are a number of facts in this case which are not in dispute. The fact that Singer was murdered with Maddox's scarf. That Maddox saw Singer in her room within a few hours—perhaps a few minutes—of the time of her murder. That Maddox on one occasion took Singer to the theatre and afterwards to dinner, on one occasion took her out for a drink—simple, social actions which you may consider do not warrant the sinister implications the prosecution suggests.

"In short, Maddox had both the means and the opportunity to murder Singer. And no one else did. That is what is alleged.

"Maddox, we have been told by the prosecution, had a motive for murdering Singer. And no one else did. So, at least, it is alleged.

"Members of the jury, the thought may have crossed your mind—it may be crossing your mind at this very moment—that if Maddox did not commit this crime, then who did? Now I want to emphasize to you most strongly that it is in no way—in no way—incumbent upon the defence to answer this question. For the question before you is not: Who murdered June Singer? The question before you is: Did Jordan John Maddox murder June Singer?

"And yet the probability of the accused's guilt is, must be, psychologically strengthened by the absence of alternative explanations of what happened on that fatal Monday in March. It would be foolish to deny this. Nature, we are told, abhors a vacuum. So does the human mind.

"And there are a lot of vacuums in this case. Consider what we have

343

been told of the murdered girl, June Singer. No father, mother recently dead, no relatives, no friends, hardly even an acquaintance, no special interest . . . no boy friend. There is a vacuum there, is there not? A vacuum which, the prosecution tells us, was filled by Maddox. You may come to the conclusion that it was the prosecution's abhorrence of vacuums, rather than the actual fact of the matter, which led Maddox to be chosen to fill this vacancy.

"For the defence will call evidence which will prove that June Singer was not friendless. She had a friend, one Regina Copley. From her you will hear a side of June Singer's life which has not come to our notice and which, you may think, has great bearing upon this case.

"Singer also had another friend. One Bernard Cole. We shall hear from him too.

"And finally, the accused will go into the witness box, quite voluntarily, on his own behalf. It is, I think, both fitting and proper that, having so long held his peace, this man should at last speak for himself.

"Members of the jury, I beg you to put aside all preconceptions of this case which you may have formed up to now, and listen with the closest attention to the evidence for the defence, which I shall now call."

Bartlett paused, then lifted his head slightly and said, "I call Regina Copley."

Regina Copley—she might, Jordan thought, have been a pretty girl if it were not for the harelip which gave her face a look of disdain. She hardly moved her mouth in taking the oath, and her voice was subdued.

Bartlett took a few paces towards her, but not at all threatening, rather as though he were going to her aid.

His voice was low-pitched and gentle as he asked the first question. "Miss Copley, were you a friend of June Singer's?"

"Well . . ." She was nervous at once.

Bartlett smiled. "You did know her?"

"Oh yes, I knew her." A tiny hint of emphasis on the word knew.

"When did you first come to know June?"

"At school. We was—were—at school together."

"For how long were you at school together?"

"Oh all along."

344

"You were the same age?"

"I was older."

"How much older?"

"Well, not much. Three weeks. I'm Leo and she was Virgo, see."

"You're interested in astrology?"

"Well, a bit."

"Was June interested in astrology?"

"She said she wasn't. She said it was silly. But all the same, she always read the horoscopes in the papers."

Bartlett paused. Then, "Were you in the same form as June at school?"

"Yes, I always was. She was higher up than me though."

"She was usually towards the top of the form?"

"Near there, yes. See, she was one of the favourites."

"She was favoured by the teachers?"

"Well—not exactly favoured. No, I wouldn't say that. But they always liked her. She couldn't ever put a foot wrong with them. Specially Mrs. Fremantle."

"When did you leave school, Miss Copley?"

"When I was sixteen. June too. June and me left together."

"And what did you do then?"

"I went to secretarial college. June and me both went."

"To the same college?"

"Yes."

"So you saw quite a lot of her?"

"Oh yes. We went up and back on the bus together most days."

"After you left the secretarial college, did you continue to see June?"

"Off and on. But not so much. She got a job in the West End and I was working in Putney. But sometimes we'd go to the pictures. Not often. She wasn't a great one for going out."

"Why was that?"

"Her mother. She had to look after her mother. Of course, if she really wanted to go out, she always could."

"What about her mother on those occasions?"

"The old lady downstairs would always look after Mrs. Singer."

"The old lady downstairs?"

"Mrs. Pita." She pronounced it *pitter*.

"Mrs. Peter? That was her name?"

345

"Oh well—no, not really, that was just a nickname like. Her real name was Mrs. Payne."

"Peter was your nickname for Mrs. Payne?"

"It was what June called her. Only it wasn't Peter, it was Pita: p-i-t-a. They was initials."

"Whose initials?"

"Initials of her nickname. They stood for something."

"What did they stand for?"

"Well . . . I don't . . ." She looked nervously at the judge. "It's vulgar, see?"

"You mustn't mind that, Miss Copley. No one will mind that. Just tell us what the nickname was."

"Well . . . it was Mrs. Payne-in-the-arse." She flushed.

"And that is what June Singer called Mrs. Payne?"

"Yes."

"If June could so easily get Mrs. Payne to look after her mother, why did she not go out more often?"

"She didn't like to fling her money about. She had to support her Mum and then she had to give Mrs. Payne something for her trouble."

"When you and June went out together, to the pictures, for instance, who paid?"

"I did."

"Always?"

"Yes. I told you, June couldn't really afford it."

"Would you have said that June was mean?"

"Oh no. Not mean. I wouldn't have said that. She was just careful."

"At that time—while you were at school and then later at the secretarial school and later still when you continued to see something of her—did you *like* June Singer?"

"Yes, I did *then*. I looked up to her ever so. I thought she was the cat's whiskers."

"But later you changed your opinion?"

"Yes."

"What caused you to change your opinion?"

"It's hard to explain."

"Was it because of something that happened?"

"Yes."

346

"Tell us about it."

"Well . . ."

"Take your time, Miss Copley."

"Well—it was over Bernie. He—he was my steady . . ." She trailed off.

"Bernie—Bernard Cole?"

"Yes."

"Tell us what happened then, Miss Copley."

"I'd known Bernie from school, see. He was a year behind June and me. We'd never paid much attention to him. But, well it must have been two years ago now, he began asking me out. And then we began to go steady. He had a good job he did—at Swail's in Clapham . . ."

"Yes?"

"Well then, how it started was one day he said to me, wouldn't it be nice to ask June to come along with us? I didn't think anything of it. So I said yes. He knew her—but not well. But he knew all about her Mum and not having any Dad and he said she must be lonely. He was always worried about people being lonely. He was that good with animals . . ." She stopped. All this time her arms had been rigid by her sides. Now she put a hand on the rail in front of her and gripped it hard. "So the three of us went out together. Then after that, well, the three of us would go out every week. I'm not saying I minded—not then. Bernie and I still went out twice a week by ourselves, without June, I mean. Well then—last year this was—Bernie had to study real hard. He was studying to be an engineer nights. So we couldn't go out, except once a week. And June would be there that time. So it got so I never saw Bernie alone. I'm not saying I minded even then. Bernie had to study, I thought. I knew he liked her but . . . Well then, one night I went to the flicks on my own and . . . I saw them together. At the Gaumont, Kensington it was. I suppose they thought I'd never go there." She quivered a little, then stood there silently, as though nothing more could possibly be said.

Bartlett gave her a few moments. Then, "What did you do?"

"I didn't do nothing. What could I do?"

"You didn't tell Cole that you had seen him with Singer?"

"No. It was too late then. If I'd made him choose—well, he'd have ditched me, not her. That's what I thought."

"But you still continued to go out as a threesome?"

"Yes. For a bit we did. Then Bernie said he had to study even harder, so he couldn't afford the time. I knew he was lying. I knew he was still seeing June but . . ."

"How did you know that?"

"I—I watched them."

"You mean you followed them?"

"Yes. They went out Wednesdays and Saturdays regular."

"And each time you followed them?"

"Yes."

"And yet you never went to Cole and asked him to explain the situation?"

"It didn't need much explaining, did it?"

"And at this time—while Cole and Singer were seeing each other regularly—did you ever go out with June?"

"No. The last time I saw June was when the three of us went to the ice rink together. I never saw her again."

"And when was this—this time you went to the ice rink?"

"It must have been about May last year."

"And thereafter you made no effort to see June Singer?"

"Why should I? She should have come to me. If she had, I wouldn't have minded so much. But I knew she wouldn't. June never could admit she'd done anything wrong."

"And after the time when you went to the ice rink last May, did you see Cole again?"

"Yes. The end of November. Not long before June's Mum died. I went to see Bernie then."

"You went to see *him?*"

"Yes."

"Why—after all this time?"

"Well, see, a long time before, we'd planned, Bernie and me, to take our holidays—a week of our holidays, that is—together just after Christmas. And I wanted to find out like . . ."

"You wanted to find out whether the arrangement still stood?"

"That's right."

"And did it?"

"No. He said he had to study. He gave me a load of excuses. I knew he was lying. I got that angry with him. I told him I knew all about him and June."

"And what did he say to that?"

"Well, he said there wasn't anything between him and June. And I knew it was true by then—I wouldn't have gone if they'd still been carrying on."

"By the end of November there was nothing between Cole and Singer? How did you know that?"

"She'd cooled off. I always knew she'd cool off. That's why I never did anything. June could have done a lot better for herself than Bernie. Bernie was just a passing fancy, I knew that."

"But how did you *know* that she'd cooled off?"

"Because I was watching them. July it must have been they started going out once a week instead of twice. By October she'd stopped seeing him altogether."

"And was it your understanding that this 'cooling off' was mutual?"

"I didn't know for sure. But Bernie promised to take me to the Palais New Year's."

"And did he take you?"

"No."

"What did you do then?"

"Well, I waited a few days. I got a bit of pride. Then I went round to see him—at Elmley Road, where he lived. But he wasn't there. I hadn't been watching him, see, because he made me promise not to. So I didn't know where he was. I enquired at Swail's. But they didn't know either. He'd just vanished."

"Did you continue your attempts to contact him?"

"I couldn't think what to do. Then, after a bit, I went round to see June. I thought perhaps she might . . . Well, she wasn't there either. Mrs. Pi—Mrs. Payne didn't know where she was. Well, that was funny. And I began to put two and two together."

"What did you do then?"

"I thought it over for a bit. Then I rung up June's office. I knew where she worked, of course."

"And you talked to her?"

"Yes."

"When was this?"

"Sometime in February. About then."

"And did you ask her the whereabouts of Cole?"

"Yes. At first she said she didn't know nothing about Bernie. But then when I told her he'd disappeared, she kind of laughed and said she wished he would. She said he was a pest. She said he kept writing

349

her daft letters and ringing her up and whenever she turned round in the street, there he was. She said I was welcome to him. She said she'd be grateful if I took him off her hands. She couldn't stand the sight of him, she said. Then she told me where he lived, and I went round there. A Thursday it was—I just took the day off and went round, I was that upset. He wasn't in, but they told me where he worked. So I went there. I didn't go in. I waited till he came out after they closed . . ."

"And did you speak to him?"

"I asked him what happened to our date New Year's. He said he was sorry but he forgot all about it. I told him he couldn't promise to do something and then just not do it and never a word of explanation. And then I asked him why he left Putney. He didn't answer me at all. So then I asked him if it was all off between us. And he said it was. And I asked him why, and he said because he was in love with June. I told him that was all very well, but she wasn't in love with him. He got very angry and said yes she was and they were going to get married. So I told him he was barmy, June would never marry him. He got furious. He said she would marry him—he said she'd got to. Well, then I knew he was barmy. I said—"

"What did you understand by the phrase 'she'd got to'?"

"That she was going to have a baby. I mean, I really knew he was daft then. I said—"

"A little slower, Miss Copley. Why did the news of June's pregnancy make you assume Cole was daft?"

"Well, I knew it wasn't true. I knew he must be daft if he thought I'd swallow that. I knew June well enough to know she'd never have let him . . . do that."

"But you know now that Cole was right, June Singer was pregnant?"

"Oh yes, but not with Bernie. It was him, wasn't it?" She jerked her hand towards Jordan.

"No—we don't know that at all."

Jordan felt his heart plunge as Regina Copley flicked her thin little hand at him. He could not tell whether in joy or pain—for Cole was the strongest presence in court, and Jordan knew and felt, not his own, but Cole's agony, Cole's rage, Cole's dream of longing.

"But the papers said—" Regina's voice protested.

"The papers have reported the proceedings of this court. The suggestion that Maddox was responsible for Singer's pregnancy has been advanced, but it has not been proved."

"Oh." Deflated, and not really believing.

"Now let's go back to this conversation you had with Cole. What did you do when he told you June was going to have a baby?"

"I gave him a piece of my mind. Spreading rumours like that! Then I just walked off."

"Having gone to considerable efforts to see him, you then just walked off?"

"Well, there was no use talking to him when he was in that state. I knew he'd come round eventually. He'd have to, wouldn't he?"

"You thought that when he finally realised June Singer was not going to marry him, that he would come back to you?"

"I thought he would, likely."

"Has he?"

"Well, no."

"Have you, in fact, seen Cole since June's death?"

"I tried to, once. But he wouldn't speak to me. It's a shock for him, see? I mean, it would be, wouldn't it? But he'll get over it." She said it knowingly.

For a fraction of a second Bartlett seemed to hesitate. Then he said, "Thank you, Miss Copley. I have no more questions."

Pollen rose from his place. He also smiled as he approached Regina —a strained smile which could only just pass muster as benevolent.

"Everything, Miss Copley, that you have told this court is true, is it not?"

"Cross my heart and hope to die."

"Oh, we won't ask you to do that."

Regina decided to answer his smile.

"Now, Miss Copley, I don't have many questions for you. Just one or two points for further elucidation. You knew June Singer very well, did you not?"

"I would say so, yes."

"But after you learned of her assignations with Cole, you had no great cause to like her, did you?"

"No great cause . . . you mean, I didn't like her? No, I didn't like her."

"Up to that point, you liked her very well?"

"Yes."

"Admired her?"

"Yes."

"You were, in fact, her most intimate friend?"

"Yes."

"Shared all her little secrets, no doubt?"

"Well . . ."

"Come, Miss Copley, no secrets?" Genial.

"Well, June never was one to tell you how she really felt underneath."

A momentary frown sullied Pollen's forehead. "But you did know her exceedingly well?"

"Yes. I've said that."

"Quite. But later, when you learned of her friendship with Cole, you became jealous of her?"

"Well, not jealous really. I wouldn't say that."

"You never at any time thought, did you, that there was anything more to Singer's seeing Cole than friendship?"

"Oh no."

"Was it ever your opinion, out of your considerable knowledge of her character, that Singer was or could have been genuinely in love with Cole?"

"No. I knew she wasn't, couldn't be."

"So you did not in fact consider Singer to be a serious or permanent threat to your relationship with Cole?"

"No, I never did."

"So your dislike of her was actuated by the underhand way in which she had treated you?"

"Yes."

"You did not have any malice towards her, did you?"

"No. See, I knew what it was. June always liked things somebody else had. But after she got whatever it was, well, she never really knew what to do with it."

"So you are not here today in spite, are you?"

"In spite of what?"

"You hold no spite against June Singer?"

"Oh no. I'm sorry for her, poor thing."

"Knowing her so well over all those years, knowing so intimately what sort of person she was, are you of the opinion that she would have permitted a man such as Bernard Cole to have sexual intercourse with her?"

"Not in a zillion years."

"Why do you think she would not have?"

"She just never would. She wasn't that sort of person at all. She had respect for herself. She was always saying how wrong it was. If she'd been going to marry Bernie, then it might have been different—even then I don't think she'd have done it. But she'd never even have thought of marrying Bernie."

"And that is still your opinion, despite the fact that she was pregnant at the time of her death and, therefore, did have sexual intercourse?"

"That's different. If she had to have intercourse to get what she wanted, then she'd have had intercourse. But she didn't want Bernie, I know that. But that's not to say there wasn't someone else she wanted."

"But that someone else would have to have been a better catch than Cole?"

"Yes."

"Did you ever hear June talk about the accused?"

"*Did* I!"

"Did you?"

"I should say. Why, all the time, it was Mr. Maddox this, Mr. Maddox that. You'd have thought he was the fairy prince, the way she carried on."

"I see. Just one more point then, Miss Copley. And in asking this question, I am making no suggestion of impropriety in your behaviour. On the contrary, you are clearly a sensible and truthful witness. But I am sure some members of the jury will have it on their mind that you did not, when you heard of this dreadful crime—as you must have heard—why you did not then go to the police and tell them what you knew about June Singer. Why did you not go to the police?"

"Well, see—a policeman come to our house. And—well, I thought that was the end of it."

"What did you tell this policeman?"

"Well, he asked me if I'd been at school with June, and I said yes, I had. Then he asked me when I last saw her, and I said about a year ago. And that's all he asked me."

"You didn't feel that you had anything material to contribute further?"

"Well no, I didn't. I mean—I don't see what all the fuss is about. About Bernie and me, I mean."

"I have no further questions of this witness." Pollen sat down abruptly.

Regina looked in puzzlement at the judge and then at the jury. One of the jurors was whispering hissingly at the foreman, who stood up looking doubtful.

"My Lord—a juryman would like to ask a question. Er, is that alright?"

"A question of this witness?"

"Yes, my Lord."

"Very well."

It was the man in the green shirt who rose. "Well—" his voice was unnaturally loud—"what I think is—"

"No no, juryman." The judge clacked his teeth. "You must not tell us what you think. Just ask your question."

Green shirt flushed angrily. He turned to Regina. "What I want to know, Miss Copley," he said overbearingly, as if to take out on her his humiliation by the judge, "this fellow Cole we've heard so much about. And if you ask me—"

"We are not asking you." The judge's jaw went snap-snap. "You are to ask the witness. What is your question?"

Green shirt sighed. He spoke as if to a child, deliberately emphasizing every word. "If this Cole was to ask you to marry him now, would you?"

As instantaneously as Regina said, "Oh yes," Pollen was on his feet objecting.

"My Lord, this is an absolutely irrelevant question. It is preposterous. It has nothing to do with what has gone before. It—"

"You object to it?"

"I do most strongly, my Lord."

"Mr. Pollen, it seems quite clear to me that this question has been put for the purpose of determining any possible bias on the part of

354

this witness. And that is an issue which you yourself raised in your cross-examination. I may say that I allowed you, and Mr. Bartlett in his examination of this witness, a great deal of latitude in regard to what are strictly matters of opinion. I have done so because, in making the case for the prosecution, you, Mr. Pollen, have made several emphatic suggestions, I may even say declarations, about the character of Singer. The impression of Singer's character which you have been at pains to portray is something that the defence is fully entitled to combat. The reputation of Singer is of great concern in this case, and consequently the truthfulness of any witness who animadverts upon that subject is also of concern to the court. I shall therefore allow both question and answer to stand."

Pollen shrugged and sat down stiffly.

Jordan watched Regina leave the box. She had done him a service. He knew now what June was, had been. It was all so very clear. So very simple. So very pathetic. He thought in some way he had known what she was like all along, yet had not recognised it—just as he had not recognised the lack, the yearning, the pity of them all.

Bernard Malcolm Cole. The word had gone out.

And as Jordan waited for him, his hands trembled on his knees—as if he himself were fulfilling the fear that Cole must feel.

50

Except for his narrow nose and small sharp mouth, Bernard Cole was not recognisable as the schoolboy in the photograph. His cheeks were plump and his hair receding over a suet-white forehead. And he was tall. He had a stoop, and his head was permanently bent to one side, as though used to paying great attention to absent-minded customers. He would be unctuously good with old ladies and properly frocked and toilet-trained children.

"I do," he said in a tone of righteous but muted defiance as though he had already been accused of not agreeing to tell the truth.

Bartlett did not smile at this time.

"Mr. Cole, were you in love with June Singer?"

Cole blinked rapidly, but said nothing.

"I asked you, Mr. Cole, whether you were in love with June Singer."

"Well, I . . ." It was a horribly straight question. Jordan knew instinctively that Bernie Cole was one of those people whose stock answers are, "I don't mind" or "I'll have what you're having."

"You must answer the question, Mr. Cole. Were you in love with June Singer?"

"Well, it depends what you mean by love, doesn't it?" A quick movement of the lips.

"Assume the question refers to what you mean by love, Mr. Cole. Then answer it. Were you in love with June Singer?"

"I may have been."

"You may have been?"

"It's hard to tell, isn't it?"

"Is it?"

"Well, yes. I mean, sometimes you think you . . ." He blinked again as he recognised the danger.

"Yes, go on, Mr. Cole?" Pause. "Were you going to say that sometimes you think you are in love?"

Pollen was up. "My Lord, that is leading too much. This is simply putting words into the mouth of the witness."

The judge nodded. "Quite. Please don't lead the witness in that manner, Mr. Bartlett. However—" he turned to Cole and champed for a moment—"I should like to know what you were about to say, Mr. Cole. Your words were, 'Sometimes you think you . . .' Perhaps you would finish the sentence for us?"

Bartlett held quite still.

"Well," said Cole, "what I was going to say, really, was sometimes you think you never can tell."

"I see," said Bartlett. "To put it in full then, you are saying: 'Sometimes you think you never can tell whether or not you may have been in love with June Singer.' Is that it?"

Cole blinked. "More or less. It's hard to be sure."

"Were you in love with Regina Copley?"

"Oh no."

"You're sure about *that*, aren't you?"

"I never felt that way about Reg."

"But you did sometimes feel 'that way' about June?"

356

"I suppose you might say so."

"Never mind about what I say. What do you say?"

"Well, yes then."

"Yes, you did sometimes think you were in love with June Singer?"

"Yes, I suppose I did—at times."

"What times?"

"What do you mean?"

"When? When were you in love with June Singer?"

"I didn't say I was, did I?"

"You said you thought you were in love with June Singer at times. What times? When?"

"Oh, last year."

"*Last* year—not this year?"

"Oh no."

"Where do you live, Mr. Cole?"

"Rumbold Street." Quick with relief.

"Where do you work?"

"I'm a sales assistant at Ramsden and Black."

"What is the firm's line of business?"

"Ironmongery."

"Where is Ramsden and Black located?"

"Devizes Road."

"At which end of Devizes Road?"

"It's at the north end. One Hundred and Twelve Devizes Road it is."

"How far is that from Panton Place?"

"About a three-minute wa—"

"A three-minute walk?"

"I'm only guessing."

"But that is what you were going to say? A three-minute walk?"

"Well, yes. It was only a guess."

"A very good guess—an absolutely correct guess, as it happens. Did you know that June Singer lived at Panton Place?"

"It was in all the papers, wasn't it?"

"Before it was in the papers. Before the murder. Did you know then that June Singer lived at Panton Place?"

"I may have done."

"Did you or did you not?"

"Well, yes."

"When did she move there?"

"I really couldn't say."

"Guess then. You're good at guessing."

"I really couldn't."

"It's been in all the papers. She moved to Panton Place on December the twentieth last year. You didn't know that?"

"Not exactly. I mean, I may have read it."

"How do you get to work, Mr. Cole?"

"I walk."

"How long a walk is it?"

"Ten minutes."

"A ten-minute walk from Rumbold Street to Devizes Road. By which route is that?"

"Pardon?"

"Which way do you go?"

"I go all different ways. Depends how I feel."

"Do you ever go by way of Panton Place?"

"I expect so."

"Do you or do you not?"

"Once in a while I do."

"How often?"

"I really haven't noticed."

"Well now, you must have some idea. Once a week?"

"Not as often as that."

"Once a fortnight?"

"That would be more like it. It's a bit out of the way."

"What do you mean by that?"

"It's a long way round, see?"

"It's longer via Panton Place than by some other route?"

"Yes."

"You are quite sure of that, aren't you, Mr. Cole? It may be measured."

"Well, I think it is."

"You only *think* it is now?"

"I'm sure it's longer."

Jordan watched Cole intently. And though the only movement of expression upon that face was the sudden stutter of blinks, Jordan knew quite certainly what was going on within the mind. The obstinacy reinforced at every turn with a sense of righteousness which bore only upon itself. The evasions masquerading as pride. The world was on the offensive against Cole—always had been, always would be. But he would never give in. He knew their tricks, he knew their ways to deceive, he knew what they wanted alright.

But he would keep himself to himself, and dispense it sparingly, where and when he pleased. Ask, and you wouldn't receive—not from Cole. Any question was a demand and would be fought off, pronto, as it deserved, unless it was from someone too weak to take anything —infants, the elderly, dumb animals. He knew the injustice of this world, knew it too well to ask for anything that was not rightfully his—and would fight it, bitterly, evenly, carefully.

"If I were to tell you it were so," Bartlett was saying, "would you accept the fact that the shortest route from the south end of Rumbold Street to the north end of Devizes Road is one thousand, one hundred and twenty yards—some forty yards shorter than any other route—and that this shortest route is the way via Panton Place—if I were to tell you that, would you accept it?"

"I know what I think. You're trying to trick me."

"What I say is true, Mr. Cole."

"That's what you say."

"Before you were employed at Ramsden and Black, where did you work, Mr. Cole?"

"Swail's in Clapham."

"An ironmonger's?"

"That's right."

"How long did you work there?"

"Four or five years."

"Four, or five?"

"Well, five then."

"Like the job?"

"It was alright."

"By the time you left, how much were you earning?"

"About eighteen pounds."

"Eighteen pounds a week?"

"Yes."

"Was there ever any suggestion that you might become a partner in the firm?"

"That's what he said."

"Who said?"

359

"Mr. Swail."

"Mr. Swail offered you a partnership?"

"It's easy enough to talk."

"You did not think it was a genuine offer?"

"I didn't say that."

"You *did* think the offer was genuine?"

"I'd have believed it when I'd seen it."

"You got on well in the job?"

"Alright."

"Well now, did you have any rows with Mr. Swail?"

"No."

"Why did you leave Swail's?"

"I wanted to better myself."

"Relations were quite amicable with Mr. Swail?"

"Oh yes."

"When you left Swail's, how much notice did you leave?"

"Well, I . . . I told him I was leaving."

"You told him that you were leaving on the same day that you left, is that what you are saying?"

"I didn't owe him anything."

"Did you give Mr. Swail any advance notice of your departure?"

"There's no law says—"

"Did you or did you not give notice?"

"No, then."

"When did you leave?"

"January some time."

"January of this year?"

"Yes."

"What day in January?"

"I don't remember."

"Was it January the third, by any chance?"

"It might have been."

"Was it?"

"Perhaps it was, yes."

"Why did you leave Swail's without giving notice?"

"I told you, to better myself. A better job."

"You already had a better job?"

"I was looking around."

"But you had not, in fact, got a job to go to, had you?"

"Not exactly—"

"Yes or no?"

"No, then."

"A rather sudden move, wasn't it?"

"I'd been mulling it over."

"At this time, where were you living?"

"Fourteen Elmley Road, Putney."

"How long had you lived there?"

"Five years, I'd say."

"What rent did you pay?"

"Three pounds."

"When did you leave Elmley Road?"

"In January."

"January this year?"

"I told you, yes."

"On the same day that you left Swail's—January the third?"

"No."

"January the fourth?"

"Well, it might have been."

"Was it?"

"Yes."

"Did you give any notice at Elmley Road?"

"No."

"Was it that same day in January that you moved to Rumbold Street?"

"Yes."

"What rent do you pay at Rumbold Street?"

"A bit more."

"How much more?"

"Well, I pay four pound ten. But it's a better room."

"You pay one pound ten more?"

"I told you."

"How much do you earn at Ramsden and Black?"

"About the same."

"Eighteen pounds a week?"

"A bit less."

"How much, Mr. Cole?"

"Well, fifteen pound ten at the moment."

"Two pound ten less than at Swail's?"

"Yes."

"Has anyone offered you a partnership at Ramsden and Black?"

"Not exactly."

"Yes or no?"

"No."

"So. So, without having any new job in prospect, you left a post which you had held for five years and which offered you definite prospects of further advancement, and you left a house where you had lived for five years to take a more expensive room elsewhere. And you did both these things literally at a moment's notice. And you did them in order to *better yourself*. Is that what you are saying?"

"Well—I thought it was time for a change."

"A very sudden change?"

"I'd been mulling it over."

"And during this period when you had been 'mulling it over,' you had also been ringing up June Singer, hadn't you?"

"I never."

"Never?" A whipping echo.

"Well, I may have—given her a ring. I can't be expected to remember everything."

"One ring? Just one telephone call?"

"Well, it might have been one or two. I tell you I can't—"

"Or three?"

"It might have been." The blinks stammered rapidly. "How do I know exact—"

"Four? Five? Six?"

"I don't know, I tell you I don't know. I don't know when you're talking about."

"I'm talking about when you were trying to find out where she had moved."

"It couldn't have been more than . . ."

"You *were* trying to find out where she had moved?"

"Well . . . I may . . . have asked her. Casual like."

"Did she tell you?"

"Well, I don't remember offhand—I—"

"If she'd have told you, you would have known, wouldn't you?"

"Well, yes."

"And you didn't know, did you?"

"I suppose I couldn't have, really."

"You didn't know, did you?"

"Well, not then."

"When?"

"Not at that time."

"What time?"

"Not when I was . . ."

"Yes?"

"I don't recall."

"When *did* you find out her new address?"

"I don't recall."

"January the third?"

"No. I don't remember."

"You knew she had moved?"

"Well, yes. I knew that."

"You knew she left Putney on December the twentieth, didn't you?"

"Well, thereabouts, I suppose."

"Within a day or two?"

"Well, yes."

"How do you account for the fact that earlier in this examination you denied knowing when June Singer had moved?"

"You didn't ask me that. You asked me if I knew when she moved to Panton Place and I said I didn't know. You never said anything about Putney."

"So immediately she moved away from Putney, you began your efforts to find out where she had gone? You telephoned her and wrote her letters and—"

"I never said nothing about letters!"

Bartlett nodded gravely. He moved to his place and picked up a large exercise book stuffed with papers. He opened the book and began to turn the pages and sheets of paper as he slowly returned to the witness. He seemed to find his place, stopped, looked up. "But you did write letters to June Singer between the time she moved to Panton Place and her death, did you not?"

"I don't recall."

"Letters," Bartlett glanced down, "letters which you signed, 'Your Bernie Boy'?"

"How'd you get them lett . . . ers?"

"You *did* sign your letters to June, 'Your Bernie Boy'?"

363

"Well . . . I may have." His voice was hardly audible.

"*Did* you?"

"Once or twice I did, perhaps."

"And you were writing letters to her last December—at her office—were you not?"

"One or two, perhaps, I—"

"And in January of this year?"

"I could have. I . . ."

"And in February of this year?"

"One or two, I could . . ."

"And in *March* of this year?"

"Alright al*right!* I wrote her a few letters. There's no law against it."

"A *few* letters. You were writing her *lots* of letters, weren't you?"

"Not lots."

"Every day?"

"Not every day."

"And you signed all those letters, 'Your Bernie Boy'?"

"Not all of them."

"And do you recall saying in one of those letters you wrote to June Singer this year: 'You are ruining my life'?"

"Well, I . . ."

Bartlett raised the exercise book in his hand. "Did you write that: 'You are ruining my life'?"

"I could have. It's possible."

"Did you *think* she was ruining your life?"

"I didn't like—what she was doing."

"What was she doing that you did not like?"

"She was . . ." He mumbled indistinctly.

"Speak up, Mr. Cole. *What* was she doing?"

"Playing around."

"Playing around—with another man, you mean?"

"That Maddox." Loud, strong, hard.

"You thought she was 'playing around' with Maddox?"

"I knew she was."

"How could you *know* any such thing?"

"She told me!" Yah—clever sticks!

"She told you she was 'playing around' with Maddox? Those were the words she used?"

364

"Not exactly. She said she was going out with him. I knew what that meant. A married man!" He was strong now, vicious against the injustice of it all.

Bartlett put the exercise book under his arm and turned to the judge. "My Lord, in view of that statement, and indeed in the light of this witness's demeanour of reluctance, evasiveness and hostility throughout my examination, I must make application to treat this witness as a hostile one."

The judge nodded impatiently. "Quite right, Mr. Bartlett. I only wonder why you have waited so long. I am very unfavourably impressed with this witness's manner of giving evidence. He is clearly hostile. I have indeed been permitting you to cross-examine him for that very reason. Mr. Pollen!"

"My Lord?"

"You were informed that this witness would be called?"

"This morning, my Lord."

"And as to the nature of his evidence?"

"I do not believe, my Lord, that the full nature of his evidence was known."

"You did not know of the existence of this witness prior to being informed of it this morning?"

"Of course not, my Lord. If I had known, naturally I should—"

"Quite quite. You may sit down, Mr. Pollen. Mr. Bartlett, your application is granted."

There was a kind of heaviness in the barrister as he turned to face Cole once again.

And almost visibly Bernie Cole braced himself, but there was a pleasure in it. A hostile witness—well, they'd admitted it at last, hadn't they, what he knew all along? They hated him, and he'd made them admit it. It was a victory. He'd never been taken in yet.

"Let us, Mr. Cole, go back to last December. Did you see June Singer in December?"

"Yes."

"You had not seen her for some weeks prior to that, had you?"

"No."

"But in December you went round to see her?"

"No. She came round to see me." A touch of pride.

"Was that before or after her mother died?"

"After her mother had passed away, it was."

"Why did she come to see you?"

"She was upset and that."

"Upset over the death of her mother?"

"That's right."

"And she wanted you to comfort her?"

"Well, yes, you could say that. She was lonely, see."

"And did you comfort her?"

"I tried."

"And you saw her on several occasions?"

"Yes."

"Over how long a period?"

"A week it was."

"And did you see her every day?"

"Yes. She was very keen."

"Keen on you?"

"Why not?"

"She was very keen on you?"

"Yes."

"Do you mean by that expression that she was in love with you?"

"I'm not saying she wasn't."

"Did she say she was in love with you?"

"Well, if you want to know, she did, yes."

"And were you keen on her during that week?"

"I'd always liked her. I never said I didn't."

"And did you tell her that you loved her?"

"Well, I . . ."

"Did you?"

"Yes, I—I told her that. She . . ."

"Yes?"

"She was ever so keen I say it."

"So you did?"

"Yes."

"Just to oblige her? Or did you mean it?"

"I wouldn't have said it if I hadn't of meant it."

"And did you ask her to marry you?"

"I . . . she was that keen. She—well, yes, I did ask her that."

"And she said she would?"

"Yes, of course she did. I wouldn't have asked otherwise, would I?"

"She was distraught at this time?"

366

"Well—" Bernie smiled. "I wouldn't have said she was exactly in the pink."

"She was upset?"

"Of course she was upset."

"And she didn't have anyone to turn to, did she?"

"She had me. She turned to me."

"And you were condescending enough to extend your help?"

"Condescending! I wasn't condescending. It's just common decency, besides I—"

"And would you call it common decency to take advantage of a woman in that grievous situation?"

"I don't know what you're talking about."

"I mean, Mr. Cole, did you think it decent—or fair—to have sexual intercourse with June Singer at that time?"

"I never! I never did. That's nothing but a story, that is."

"Very well, Mr. Cole. Now, how did you find out where June lived?"

"I . . . well, I followed her."

"Followed her?"

"I followed her home from her office."

"To Panton Place?"

"Yes."

"And then you yourself moved to Rumbold Street?"

"Well, it was convenient."

"Convenient for what?"

"It was convenient to my job, and—"

"But at that time you didn't have a job, did you?"

"Well, no."

"So I repeat, Mr. Cole, what was your move convenient for?"

Bernie blinked rapidly. "I mean, it was convenient to the shops and that."

"Convenient to the shops!"

"And I had to keep an eye on her, didn't I?"

"Oh! Why did you have to keep an eye on June Singer?"

Slowly Bernie's pudding-white face had grown red, and now his forehead was scarlet. "We was going to be married. I tell you and tell you!"

"Despite the fact she had left you without a word of where she was going, despite the fact she refused to tell you where she lived, despite the fact she never answered your letters—you still thought she was going to marry you?"

"Yes!"

"Why?"

"I . . . I just thought so."

"But you had no reason, not the slightest grounds, for thinking that she would marry you, did you?"

"I . . . She . . ."

"Are you saying that it was a totally irrational expectation on your part?"

"She—she didn't have no alternative."

"Why not?"

"She *had* to get married, didn't she?"

"Why?"

"Well, I mean." Bernie paused, then almost imperceptibly he smiled. "She was pregnant—so I've heard."

"Did *June* tell you that?"

"As a matter of fact she did."

"When?"

"Oh, roundabout the beginning of Feb." Offhandedly. "When she knew for sure, that is."

"You saw her?"

"I wasn't blindfold, if that's what you mean."

"Where did you meet her? In the street, in her flat?"

"We went round to the Kardomah for coffee, if you want to know."

"And it was then she told you that she was pregnant?"

"Yes."

"That was the purpose of the meeting?"

"In a manner of speaking."

"Yes or no?"

"Yes then."

"Why should she come to you with this piece of news, Mr. Cole?"

"She was in trouble, wasn't she?"

"But why should she come to you?"

"Well why not?"

"Answer the question!"

"I suppose it was because she knew I liked her. She knew that. I told you that."

"It wasn't because you were the father of her child?"

"No. No, I keep telling you."

"Then why? What was the purpose of this confidence?"

"I said it once, I said—"

"Oh yes—because she liked you. Well, let's see, did she perhaps want you to marry her, Mr. Cole?"

"I . . . not exactly. I mean . . ."

"But you wanted to marry her—you still wanted that?"

"I . . . I was prepared to forgive and forget." He drew back his shoulders a little.

"Did you want to marry her?"

"I suppose I did really."

"Did you ask her—when you had coffee at the Kardomah then— did you ask her to marry you once again?"

"I had tea—I don't care for coffee. I said I would, yes."

"You said you would marry her. Did she ask you to marry her, Mr. Cole?"

"Not exactly."

"Did you gather that she wanted to marry you?"

"Well, I . . . she'd have come round to it."

"But she did not want to marry you at this time?"

"No."

"Later? Did she want to marry you later?"

"I . . . no."

"What did she want?"

"I . . . She . . . she wanted to get rid of it." Cole shook his head sadly at such human frailty.

"She wanted to procure an abortion? She told you that?"

"She was taking a lot of stuff. They shouldn't be allowed to sell it, in my opinion. And if that didn't work, she said she was going to one of them quacks."

"An abortionist?"

"Yes."

"And she expected you to help?"

"I told her it wasn't right. A person's got to pay for what they've done wrong, haven't they?"

"She expected you to help?"

"I said I'd marry her. In spite of it, I said I'd marry her. You'd of thought a person would be grateful for—"

"What was it that she expected you to do, Mr. Cole?"

369

"She wanted me to give her money."

"For the abortionist?"

"Yes."

"How much did she want?"

"Two hundred quid."

"Did you have the money?"

"I've got a bit in Post Office Savings."

"But you didn't give her the money?"

"I couldn't do that. It wouldn't have been right, would it?"

"Did you meet June again after that one time in early February?"

"Yes. Three or four times."

"And did she also, on these occasions, ask you for the money?"

"She did." He sighed.

"And each time you refused?"

"I told you, it wasn't right."

"And each time she refused to marry you?"

"Yes, but she was in a state. It wouldn't have lasted."

"I see. You fancied you were sitting pretty, didn't you? All you had to do was wait, and eventually she'd have no choice but to marry you? That was your calculation, wasn't it?"

"I didn't *calculate* nothing, I—"

"Mr. Cole, if, as you say, you were not the father of the child, why did June not go to the man who *was* responsible and ask *him* for the money? Did she tell you that?"

"I . . ." He was blinking very quickly now. "She didn't tell me nothing about that."

"Well, it would be the natural thing to do, wouldn't it?"

"I . . . Natural? How can it be natural to want to get rid of a baby?"

"And would you call it natural to want to marry a woman bearing another man's child?"

Cole hesitated, then blurted, "If you ask me, she was lucky to have the offer!"

"Possibly—possibly she was. If what you say is true."

"I'm not a liar."

"Aren't you? I think you are a liar. I think, I put it to you, Cole, that June Singer came to you and tried to extract money from you and counted on your help for one reason and one reason only—because she had a *right* to expect your aid and support. Is that not so?"

"No, it's—"

"And her right consisted in this—that you were the father of the child she carried. Is that not so?"

"Naow!"

"And by refusing her the money for which she asked, you attempted to blackmail her into a marriage she did not want?"

"That's a tale, that is."

"What were you doing on the morning of Monday, March the ninth, Mr. Cole?"

"What?"

"Monday, March the ninth. What were you doing that morning, Mr. Cole?"

"I don't recall offhand. I—I'd have been at work. It depends what time."

"You were at work? At Ramsden & Black's?"

"Yes, I expect I would have been."

"Are you sure?"

"I'm trying to think. I can't say exactly. I might of, then again I might not of."

"Did you or did you not go to work that morning?"

"Well, I think I did. But I was off a couple of days round then, so I can't be sure."

"You did not go to work for two days?"

"I was off sick. A sore throat I had, see."

"You were off sick with a sore throat for two days. Those days were March the ninth and March the tenth, were they not?"

"They could have been, I can't say for sure."

"It's undoubtedly a matter of record, Mr. Cole."

"Well if you know, why do you ask?"

The judge's teeth snapped sharply. "The witness is not here to indulge in repartee. You will confine yourself to answering the questions, Cole."

"I beg pardon, my Lord. Come to think of it, it was those days. Yes, I'm sure now."

"And on that morning, March the ninth, did you leave your lodgings at any time?" Bartlett asked the question softly.

371

"I was sick in bed, wasn't I?" Cole's eyes flickered towards the judge. "I mean, I don't think I did, no."

"You are quite positive you did not go out on that morning for any reason whatsoever?"

"Well I—I might have popped out for milk. But it'd have only been a minute."

"You left your lodgings to purchase milk?"

"It's soothing to a sore throat, milk is. I wouldn't have been gone long."

"I expect we can ask your landlady to verify that. Where did you purchase the milk?"

"There's a machine on the corner of Ludlow Street."

"And you bought milk there?"

"Yes."

"And Ludlow Street is next but one to Panton Place, is it not?"

"Maybe. Yes, I think that's right."

There was a movement on the Treasury bench. Pollen was whispering, flushed with the indignity of it. His junior got up suddenly and hurried out.

"Why didn't you get your milk from the dairy on the corner of Rumbold Street, Mr. Cole?"

"It wasn't . . . I don't care for the management there."

"Were you going to say it wasn't open at that time in the morning?"

"I really couldn't say when it opens. I don't patronise the dairy."

"Are you asking us to believe that, because of your dislike of the dairy's management, you went four streets further on to get your milk —ill as you were on a cold, rainy morning—"

"It wasn't raining, it was . . ."

"Ah, nor it was. Sunny, wasn't it? Yes. I am glad to see your recollection is improving. I wish the same could be said of your truthfulness."

Cole's mouth remained stubbornly shut. In the momentary silence, there was an audible movement at the back of the court. Jordan turned just in time to see the departing figure of Superintendent George.

Bartlett waited until the rustling died. "There is just one more thing that I should like to see whether you can recollect, Mr. Cole."

372

He spoke slowly. "How did you find out that someone else had supplied the money for which June asked you?"

"She . . ."

"She *told* you, Mr. Cole?" Very gently.

"No. I don't know anything about any money."

"But she did tell you, didn't she?"

"No. I was going to say—I was going to say she didn't have no money as far as I know."

"She *didn't* have—but she *got* some."

"No!"

"She didn't get any?"

"I don't know. I don't know what you're talking about."

"What I am talking about is that you knew June's lack of money would prevent her procuring an abortion, and that you counted upon that fact to force her into a marriage which she clearly did not want. Her shortage of cash was your trump card, and—"

"You're twisting it. It wasn't like that!"

"But you thought, indeed you have said in this court, that, failing an abortion, June would have no alternative but to marry you—"

"I was offering her a *home*, and a name for her baby!" And suddenly it was genuine, the furious righteousness with which he spoke.

"The fact that she didn't *want* your home and didn't *want* your name, carried no weight with you at all. You didn't care what *she* wanted, did you? All you cared—"

"I did! I did care!" He leaned forward, as if to leap at Bartlett.

"But only to prevent it!"

"No!"

"You wanted to possess June on your terms, didn't you, regardless of her—"

"Terms? I was prepared to marry her." No blinking now. "What more could she ask?"

"Love?"

"I loved her alright." He nodded.

It was a losing game. For Bartlett now. Jordan knew that, felt it as he felt the dampness of sweat under his shirt.

"And loving her, Mr. Cole, when it became clear to you that she didn't need your support, financial or otherwise, you made up your mind that if you could not have her, no one else should—didn't you?"

"I don't know what you mean."

"I mean—and I want there to be absolutely no misapprehension about this—I mean that when June Singer told you that she had the money and that she did not need you anymore, did not love you and did not need you, you realised finally that she had slipped from your grasp. And rather than live without her, you determined that she should not live without you. I put it to you, Mr. Cole, that rather than lose June Singer, you killed her."

He was silent, as though turning something over very carefully in his mind. Then he said, but quite without anger, "If I loved her, I wouldn't want her dead, would I?"

"Did you kill June Singer?"

Cole sighed slowly. "Certainly not."

"I have no more questions, my Lord." Bartlett smoothed the back of his gown wearily and sat down.

5 1

Jordan closed his eyes. Absolute stillness . . . absolute quiet. Let the poor bastard go, he thought, let him go.

"My Lord?"

"Mr. Pollen?"

"If your Lordship pleases, in view of the, er, circumstances, I should like to request a recess."

"Yes—in any event it is almost time for luncheon. Very well, Mr. Pollen. We will adjourn until two o'clock. Does that suit your purpose?"

"I should like a recess until, er, tomorrow morning, if your Lordship—"

"Tomorrow morning!" The jaws snapped sharply.

"In the circumstances, my Lord, the Crown wishes to consider fully certain matters that have, er, arisen." Pollen's face mottled.

Bartlett rose. "My Lord, I most strongly oppose the Crown's submission. I see no reason for delay. Justice can be done here most swiftly. If the Crown does not wish to cross-examine this witness, I am agreeable. I am ready to dispense with all further evidence. Further, I am prepared to waive my close, if the Crown will do the same. I am ready to let the verdict rest upon the evidence as given."

"Nothing of the kind!" Pollen almost shouted.

"In that case," said Bartlett, "I think we are entitled to know what is in the Crown's mind."

The judge nodded. "Yes, that's fair enough. What are these matters you wish to consider, Mr. Pollen?"

"I . . . It's not a question, my Lord. I am not able to state positively at this, er, juncture. That is to say, I—"

"Perhaps," said Bartlett slicingly, "the Crown's mind is a blank. But I see no reason why we should share my learned friend's suspended animation. If he is planning to nolle prosequi the indictment, he should—"

"My Lord!" Stentorian. "I must insist—"

"Insist? A strange word, Mr. Pollen."

"Crave, my Lord, humbly crave with all the powers at my command, I must . . ."

"Well, you know, Mr. Bartlett, it is the Crown's prerogative."

"As your Lordship pleases."

"I must then accede to the Crown's request. We shall adjourn until tomorrow morning."

Down again to the lower cell, Jordan felt bruised.

"Don't you worry, sir, you'll be alright." Denver cheerful. "We'll have the transportation up in half a mo'. Just you sit tight."

Bruised for Bernard Cole.

"Here's your man."

Still gowned and wigged, Bartlett swept quickly in and sat down. The door shut behind him. With one neat movement he slipped off his wig. He took out his case and lit a cigarette and put the case on the table. All without looking up. And then he did, and smiled. "A hard morning."

"What is going to happen?"

"They'll go for a nolle, I think. Sorry—which means a stop to further proceedings under the indictment. I'll press for a dismissal— that's better, better for you."

"For me?"

375

"An open admission that there's no case against you. Almost as good as a verdict. We won't get that now, not a verdict. But even a *nolle* is not so bad. You don't have to worry. In any event, you'll be your own man tomorrow, Maddox."

"I really meant Cole. What will happen to him?" He saw him standing there, forgotten but patient, while the lawyers debated what was to be done.

"It depends. There'll be a reinvestigation. It depends upon the degree of Cole's loquacity to the police. It will have to be cast-iron before they bring charges. And there is of course a natural aversion to prosecuting the same case twice—whatever the extent of incrimination."

"Did he do it?"

"Cole?" Bartlett poised in surprise—cigarette halfway to his mouth, head a little to one side like a listening bird's.

"Yes," said Jordan. He waited for the lawyer to gather himself, take flight into the abstract blue.

"Of course he did it." Bartlett stubbed out his cigarette.

"There were moments when he was—well, oddly convincing."

"He's quite clever. He knows enough to contrive a half-truth where another man would resort to an outright lie. But he's caught in his own snare now." Bartlett smoothed his hair, rumpled from contact with the wig. He stood up abruptly and held out his hand. "Well, Maddox, we won't meet again, I expect. You'll see me in court tomorrow of course. But it shouldn't take ten minutes. Good luck."

They shook hands. Jordan said, "I have a lot to thank you for. I'm grateful."

Bartlett hesitated, then gave a brief smile. "You know, Maddox, I can't help thinking—if only she'd had enough sense to marry Cole when he asked her, it would have saved us all a great deal of trouble."

Jordan stared at the barrister, holding his wig delicately in his fingers, lips slightly pursed, striped trousers and gown immaculate. "Goodbye, Bartlett."

The lawyer nodded. "Goodbye."

They crawled along the Embankment. There was just the sergeant driver and, in the back, Denver and Jordan. No handcuffs now.

"The last time you'll be going this way, sir," said Denver.

376

"Yes."

"All be over tomorrow. I told you there wasn't anything to worry about, didn't I?"

"Yes." It was high tide. Further down, towards Westminster Bridge, the sun caught the water in a dappled silver gleam. There was the faintest of winds, just enough to lazily curl the fingers of smoke from the stacks on the South Bank.

Where was Cole now? Sarah Street? The cells of the Old Bailey? Home? It was hard now to visualize his features.

Jordan turned his head and looked across the line of traffic to the Embankment Gardens. Wandering in the bright May warmth, the lunchtime crowd was a mixture of loose flapping overcoats and summer dresses bright as fuchsia and forsythia. On the grass, one or two in shirt sleeves, lying as dead from some sweet, benevolent gas. A couple pinioned motionless together.

As the car came to a halt, he saw that yesterday's rain had washed everything clean. The young leaves of the box hedge shone, the needles of yew gleamed softly. The earth was heavy and freshly turned. Tomorrow he would be able to stroll there at his will. He half-closed his eyes and the sun made a haze of the colours—the greens and greys and browns roughly sewn with patches of orange and of pink. The gay frocks of the secretaries, hundreds of them moving their mouths, heads, hands. And, beyond, the flash and twinkle of brass—the band playing on the bandstand. The lunchtime concert. He wound down the window, but he could not hear the music above the traffic—the hooting, the shifting of gears, the deep sigh of airbrakes.

He leaned back again, and something crackled in his pocket. He took out the two envelopes. For a while he sat with them on his lap, then he looked down and turned them over. Willy's letter and his own confession. *J. J. Maddox, Esq.—By Hand; The Governor— Urgent.* He squinted at the crumpled envelopes, and his fingers centred and pulled—a straight, unwavering tear. Across once. He shuffled the four pieces together. Again across. Eight. Sixteen. He held them in his open hands, then slowly closed his fist, crushing the pieces into a tight ball.

There was a prison officer waiting when they got out of the car.

"Visitor for Maddox in the solicitors' room."

Denver smiled. "Well, he made good time, didn't he?"

377

Tom—he hadn't the slightest desire to see Tom. He went with Denver reluctantly.

But it wasn't Tom.

"Willy—how on earth did you get in here?"

She turned jerkily towards him. "Jordan . . . The Governor gave special permission."

He smiled at her.

"Oh darling, it's wonderful, isn't it?" she said. "I—I can't wait."

He still held the crushed shreds of paper. He put them in his pocket. "Willy," he began.

"Yes?" Eager, yet trepid.

He knew that he was right now. Only he hadn't expected to see her today. "Willy, you didn't have to." He frowned. "I wouldn't have minded. No, that's not true. I would—do. But you could have told me. It would have been better."

"I . . . what do you—mean?" She looked at him bleakly.

He moved over to the table. "You didn't have to lie. Tom let it slip this morning. I didn't notice at the time, but it stuck. Bleak hotel rooms, he said. Rooms."

She moved an arm to her waist, but said nothing.

He couldn't wait very long. As if aware of it, she began to speak. "I lost control. I . . . I'm so sorry, Jordan."

She clutched her elbows in that old familiar gesture. He stirred.

He suddenly felt—good God, he wasn't here to try her.

"Not for that," he said. "Don't be sorry for that. The point is . . ." He lost it. She was so clear to him—the Harrods suit, the angularity, the lifeless hairdo.

"Jordan, I know I betrayed you, but can't you—can't you?"

"What was there to betray?"

"Oh Jordan!"

"No no. I don't blame you. Even if it was that stupid oaf—it was at least something. In a way, I've been a cuckold most of my life—a deserving cuckold. But I might have—might have then—hated you."

She took a step forward. "Don't you now?"

"No," he said. "No, I don't."

"Is it too late then?"

"In that way, yes. Far too late."

"But why? Why? Can't we get it back? Can't we at least try?"

"It wasn't much."

"It was it was!" she called out. "It was something!"

"Chitter-chatter, thin meals, chilled house, cotton wool and clean sheets. The fire always smoking."

"Don't! It wasn't like that."

"Yes it was."

They were still. And then she said, "You never told me you didn't like my cooking."

He laughed. "Oh Willy."

"I was weak, I know I was weak."

He shook his head impatiently. "Leave it alone now, let it die."

"But I thought you wanted to discuss . . ."

"Absolutely no."

"I just—I don't understand."

"Well, that's something." He smiled and she smiled back tentatively, as one who knows she will never see the joke, so smiles quickly here and there, hoping to hit the right moment. A blind chance, but not, he thought, more unlikely than hitting an unseen blackbird in a fig tree.

"Jordan—Jordan, can I ask you a question?"

"Yes."

She looked away from him and there was a flush on her cheeks. "Jordan, did you . . . I mean, June—did you, did you?"

"No, Willy, I did not."

"Oh." She opened her handbag and took out a handkerchief. She held it in her hand for a moment, then put it back again. She glanced up at him, as she snapped the catch. "Tomorrow—"

"Tomorrow." He made up his mind. "Tomorrow you and I are going away. We'll take the car and—"

"Oh darling, I'm so sorry. It's out of commission, I'm afraid. It just started making an awful noise. The man said it would be a week at least."

"We'll hire one then."

"But, but what about Georgia?"

"No. You fix that up."

"Perhaps Mrs. Hillman . . ." She watched him. "Where are we going?"

"Brighton."

379

"Brighton?"

"The city of sex murders and illicit love."

"You're joking?"

"Yes."

She laughed tremblingly. "Where shall we really go?"

"Oh I don't know," he said. "We'll just drive and see what happens."